I WANT TO KISS YOU IN PUBLIC

Colette International Book 1

ZELDA FRENCH

EDITION 240721
PROOFREAD BY IWORDYNERDY
COVER BY GABRIELLA REGINA AT GR BOOK COVERS

Meet Zelda and sign-up to her mailing list at:
https://www.zeldafrench.com

BEFORE YOU READ

Read on: a free bonus awaits you at the end of this book.

PARTY BEFORE THE END OF THE WORLD

(AS I KNOW IT)

"You're late again, traitor!"

Wearing a deep scowl, Tony shakes his head but slaps a beer in my hand anyway.

I give a little shrug. "Rockstars never show up on time."

How late can I be? It cannot be that bad. I remove my sunglasses to check my phone. It's 2007, for at least another half-hour or so.

All right. I might have overdone it this time. I take a large swig of beer. It's nice, cold, comforting. I'm already at the limit, just beyond tipsy, not yet trashed, perfect to endure the god-awful music blasting through Sacha's speakers.

Tony groans, but he can't help smiling. He agrees with me. Of course, he agrees. He's the one who taught me that line. Among many others. Once his name was Anthony, but no one calls him that anymore. He's my best friend, my mentor, and in his own words, a prophet.

"I think you may have broken your own record."

My girlfriend Lucie, blonde pigtails, Japanese schoolgirl skirt and Sex Pistols T-shirt, small in stature but as dangerous as a mongoose, is watching me with her arms crossed, her beautiful face flushed with anger.

The booze swirling in my stomach turns even her irritation into a thing of beauty. Laughing, I take another swig of beer. Tonight's gonna be a good night.

"You think it's funny?"

"Yes!" I try to kiss her cheek, but she shoves me away.

Of course it's funny. Ridiculous, in fact.

Have you ever wanted to be special? Really special? To enter the room and your presence stops time? All eyes are on you? Everybody desires to be with you, look at you, touch you, hear the sound of your voice?

I can imitate this effect by entering a party with my favourite songs playing on my iPod and imagine everybody else moving in slow motion, their smiling faces turned to me, their arms stretched out in the hopes of the briefest contact. But when I arrived at this party, time didn't stop, and certainly didn't rewind. My friends are legitimately pissed off, and for all my time slacking and avoiding this moment, I haven't thought about a good excuse to justify myself.

Tony's squinting at me suspiciously. "It's almost midnight, fuckhead. What the hell were you doing?"

"I took my iPod to the store." I tuck a strand of hair behind my ear. "They gave me a new one, you know."

"That explains nothing."

I wasn't always like this. Once I was a scrawny kid, and I had no friends, and a girl like Lucie would have never looked at me. I genuinely wanted to be invisible, but the gods have decided to put Tony and I together. Tony taught me everything, wrapped me in the right clothes, told me to grow my hair long, and soon the scrawny kid turned into something more palatable.

I assume an air of nonchalance. "I was making a playlist for tonight and got carried away."

Lucie's angry flush vanishes from her face. She flings her arms around my neck and swallows half my face in a hungry kiss.

"You taste like booze."

"I may have gotten a head-start at home."

She is too inebriated herself to wonder about that. "Your playlist. Did you put our song on it?"

"Sure did."

Her face brightens up. Of course, I don't have a clue as to which song she's referring to, but no need to panic. I put every good song in the world on it, playing it safe.

"Come," Lucie says, pulling me to her. "Come with me to the bathroom."

Lucie said the first time she saw me, she thought I was so handsome, she decided she wouldn't get through high-school without being mine. This is the sort of thing I'm talking about. She wanted me so much she couldn't think straight.

I chuckle into the crook of her neck. "Isn't it a girl's job to go with you to the bathroom?"

"Not unless a girl can do this..."

Whatever she whispers in my ears is not for the faint of heart, which informs me she's drunker than I thought.

"Sounds great. Maybe later?"

She scrunches up her pretty nose. "No. Now."

"I need to put on the playlist first."

Tony still looks sour. "Yeah, well, don't get your hopes up. The security here's tighter than my butthole." Nodding toward the crowd, he takes the beer from my hands and finishes it.

I twist my neck to locate the source of his worries. Lucie punches him in the shoulder, looking disgusted.

Growing out of my ugly duckling phase has been our ticket to an invitation to every party at school, no exceptions. Tony can complain all he wants. Without me, we would be playing video games together like two virgins instead of muddying Sacha's beautiful parquet floors at the top of a grand Haussmann building in the centre of Paris.

Sacha's legendary parties occur several times per year, so by now, I know the layout of the flat by heart. The sound-system is located under the TV, on the other side of the living room. To get past the dancing crowd would be a feat onto itself. At least the Persian rug is gone this time, but only because her parents had to send it away for restoration. Even if I survive swimming amongst the sharks dancing to Rihanna, I'd still have to step over people sprawled onto the deep leather sofas, and then worse.

François and Yasmine, Sacha's best friends and guard dogs, are flanking the TV. Plastic cup in hand, they're protecting the sanctity of the mediocre sounds of the party with their life. Together with Sacha, our host, they form what Tony calls "The Golden Fork". The three of them are filthy rich, their parents are powerful enough to have ours killed, and despite their lack of academic prowess, everyone knows they will rule us one day.

How will I convince the two sharpest tines of the Fork to replace their bland end-of-year soundtrack with my own very end-of-the-world tune?

François's a classic case of uninteresting people. He's almost ginger but not quite, almost nice but not quite, almost a friend, but who am I kidding? We'll never be friends. He's as arrogant as his father is rich, which means a whole lot.

Yasmine's like a brown Xena, and everybody's terrified of her, for good reason. She's by far the smartest of the lot, but also the fiercest. No one dares to mess with her. An example: she's the one who threw up on the Persian rug a few months ago, everybody saw it, and no one piped a word.

However, though nothing's easy, nothing's impossible.

"I'm going to need a drink before anything else."

I put my sunglasses back on, and I leave Tony, still scowling, with Lucie, and elbow my way to the large modern kitchen, blindingly bright compared to the rest of the flat. It doesn't sit so well with my vodka-filled stomach. Grabbing a beer from the fridge, I pop it open using my lighter. The lighter takes flight and bounces off the head of the brunette in a black dress in front of me.

She turns around, snarling, ready to send me packing, but her face transforms when she sees mine. I've never seen her before, but from the way she smiles at me, her large brown eyes shimmering, I will assume I'm her type.

"You have really cool glasses."

I let out a drunken giggle. "Thanks. It was a gift from my best friend."

She's very pretty. Tony would like her. He should come here, take his chance before anyone else sees her. I glance at him, but he's in great drunken conversation with Lucie. The brunette doesn't follow my gaze.

"How do you know Sacha?" she asks over the music.

"We go to school together."

"Oh, are you going to that English School too?"

Colette International School for Bilingual Students.

CISBS.

Because BS sounds like Bullshit, we usually stick to Colette International.

"I am," I say with a lot of pride, for somebody whose only skill is to be able to lie both in French and English. "But technically it's a French school, it's just that lessons are delivered in English."

I can tell she's not really interested where I go to school, but she wants someone to talk to. I glance around at Tony and Lucie back in the living room. They have their backs turned to me.

Brunette clutches her beer to her chest, her cheeks pink. "I'm Agnes, by the way."

"Lou."

Her cheeks grow darker. "I know who you are."

"You do?"

I hope I haven't made a complete fool of myself in front of her at one point or another like I usually do.

"I mean, I've seen you before. We went to the same college. Everybody knows you there."

"How so?"

"You're the guy that looks like Kurt Cobain."

Ok, let me stop here for those who might have no clue who Kurt Cobain is. Frontman of the band Nirvana, huge in the nineties, still huge today. Kurt committed suicide at the age of twenty-seven and entered the hall of rock-and-roll afterlife fame, drinking kegs for eternity with the likes of Jimi Hendricks, Janis Joplin, and Jim Morrison.

Do I look like Kurt Cobain? Vaguely. We do share the same shoulder-length, unwashed blond hair, bright blue eyes, and grunge style of clothing. On purpose?

Yes, yes, of course, yes.

There might be a time when I might regret this decision. Obviously, tonight's not the time. After all, she just said everybody at my former college knows who I am? I spent four years there and the only times people took notice of me, it wasn't to shower me with compliments, believe it.

"Did you come here alone?" Agnes asks, drawing closer.

I have no intention of cheating on my girlfriend tonight, or ever. But a pretty girl throws you a look and something tugs at your heartstrings. Suddenly I want to give her whatever she wants, be whoever she wants.

Somewhere, though, somehow, Lucie has sniffed out the situation, and before I can answer, she has teleported from the living room to my left flank.

"What's going on here?"

Lucie's got enough booze in her bloodstream to act nasty. Agnes and I better watch out.

Agnes feels the same threat hanging in the air. She even backtracks straight into the kitchen island.

"We were talking about that English school."

"Ah, Colette?" Lucie takes my hand. "I go there too."

Tony, who has followed Lucie to the kitchen, raises his finger. "So do I, by the way."

Tony clearly doesn't think Agnes is the enemy, from the look of it. He would prefer to ask her out. But I know he won't. As brave and bold my best friend is on so many aspects, girls are not one of them.

Lucie pounces on me and flattens me against the fridge while Agnes looks away.

"You look so hot tonight."

"Thanks, baby."

Lucie always tells me I'm hot. It's either flattering or it just means I have literally nothing else of interest to offer. But you don't know Lucie as I do. When a girl of her calibre calls you hot and pins you against an appliance, you thank her and you do what she says.

Rich, super smart, gorgeous and athletic, she could have anyone in the world, but when she arrived at Colette last fall, she gave up her fancy mates in favour of Tony and me. So I let her squeeze and probe me without complaining, even as the amount of booze I have drunk is starting to make me feel completely wasted.

"What's going on?" she asks.

I press my lips together. "Nothing."

"Nothing, really?" Her forehead creases. "You're two hours late, you don't want to go with me to the bathroom, you disappear into the kitchen, and I find you flirting with some bitch minutes after you've arrived."

"Oh, come on, don't call her a bitch. We were just talking."

"Just say it. You're interested in her."

Here's the truth: when you're as anxious as I am, keeping up an air of nonchalance demands a lot of energy, which means I sleep a lot. I either sleep, or run, to make up for all the sleeping. It's as simple as that.

Who has time to have a mistress when one's married to chronic anxiety?

But I say nothing. My silence, which she cherishes on so many occasions, now only serve to antagonise her.

"Forget it." Her tone sounds like the gavel after a death sentence. She whips around and walks off, eyes blazing, toward the dance floor.

"Hey, Agnes?" I turn to her and gently nudge Tony between us two. "Have you met Tony? He's a legend, an absolute rockstar."

Tony puffs up his chest. "Why, thanks, my dear Lou—"

"Do you guys have a band?" Agnes's face lights up.

Tony snorts. "No need for that. It's the attitude that counts, you see."

She seems a little disappointed by his answer, but he doesn't notice.

"It's an act of rebellion, a way of being truly unapologetic about who you are, you know. Fuck the system, the patriarchy, and everything in between. Let me start at the beginning. Have you read Marx?"

Agnes's shoulders sag, but she's stuck with him now. I know this stuff by heart, being his first and best student. I quickly slip out of the kitchen. Now, changing the music is of critical importance, or Lucie's going to stay pissed off, and I've already pushed her too far tonight. Proof: she's dancing to Beyoncé, flailing her arms around and spearing me with her pale glare at the same time. I'm going to have to go in. No looking back.

1

I wish I had more booze.

"Lou, baby, you made it!"

As though she heard my plea, our magnificent hostess Sacha finally makes an appearance, clad in sequins and wearing hoops like Ferris wheels.

She pushes her hips into mine, holds a shot under my nose. She smells of Malibu.

"Why don't you have a little fun?"

Sacha's a horny drunk, and the sequins of her dress are digging into my skin through my clothes, but she's all right, really. She's got a tenacious spirit and can take rejection like no one. Oddly enough, that doesn't apply to women. If a girl hurts her feelings, she'll never be forgiven. I like Sacha, we've been acquainted since we were in diapers.

I take the offered shot, toss it back. I love the way it burns on the way down.

"Thanks, Sacha. Can I change the music?"

She giggles. "If you can get past François. He's made the playlist."

"Yes, I can hear that."

She shakes her head. Her massive earrings catch the light like a disco ball. "Be nice to François, he thinks you're so cool."

The hell with François. I need Lucie to like me again. With a grimace, I toss back a second shot, then slowly wade my way through the flailing limbs, laughing mouths, and glittered hairspray.

Near the sound system, François is trying, and failing, to light a cigarette. The ridiculous hat perched on top of his almost red head says "2008" in gigantic gold letters. He's drinking from a blue cocktail with a paper umbrella in it.

Behind me, Lucie is pretending to have fun dancing to Enrique Iglesias and rubbing her ass against Lars, our only Danish student. He looks both mystified and terrified she might disappear if he makes the wrong move. A side glance informs me Agnes has had enough of Tony. He's hovering on the edge of the crowd, his brow furrowed. The responsibility to save this party is solely mine.

But to get to François, I must first go through Yasmine. I must proceed with caution. She takes shit from no-one, especially not

Tony or myself, whom she's known from before kindergarten. She will flatten me with the back of her hand if I dare make a bad joke. She's also fiercely protective of François, for reasons beyond my understanding.

She sees my sweaty face and arches a perfect eyebrow. "What do you want, Mésange?"

Oh oh, the oldest trick in the book, calling me by my surname. She's all business. My only way out is to feign drunkenness.

"Yas'! I'm so glad to see you!"

I manage to throw her off by flinging my arms around her neck and, in my hasty demonstration of affection, knock over her glass of champagne. The liquid splatters over her navy dress, and she lets out a curse that makes François jump off his perch on the TV stand.

I don't have to fake the apprehension on my face. I'm honestly terrified she might punch me. "I'm sorry, Yasmine. I was just so happy to see you."

"Now I've got to get cleaned up! Don't move, I'll come back for you." Her murderous eyes do not leave me as she stomps out of the crowd toward the main corridor.

That's a problem for future Louis.

Immediately I slither in the tight space between the wide armchair and François and light his cigarette with the flick of my thumb. He watches me with wide eyes. I, too, light a cigarette, accidentally blow smoke in his face, and start giggling nervously.

"I don't get how champagne on a dark dress deserves so much fuss, but I'm not exactly great at understanding fashion."

François gives me look, doesn't smile. He takes a large swig of his cocktail and almost dips his nose in it. He's not having fun at all. I've never even seen him looking so downcast.

This looks serious. I remove my sunglasses and put them in my pocket. "What's up with you?"

"One of these days..." He sniffles. "Everyone's having a good time but I just can't." He looks at my puzzled face and shrugs. "Ignore me. I think I just need to get laid."

I give him an awkward pat on the shoulder. "Then get laid."

"Do you think it's as easy as saying 'get laid'? Unless you have someone for me?"

9

I shake my head, and he lets out a long, terrible sigh. Poor François. He's an absolute dildo but no one should be miserable on NYE, take it from me.

"Hang on, hang on."

After a short while ruffling through my pockets, I fish out a joint, perfectly rolled yesterday by the small and expert hands of Lucie.

"I can't help you get laid, but I can help you get high, so you won't worry about it anymore. How about that?"

François accepts my offer and even returns a smile.

"Thanks, Lou. That's nice of you. Are you sure you want to give it to me?"

"That's all right. I smoke too much anyway."

"You know…"

"What?"

"Since you're nice to me, can I tell you something helpful?"

"Sure. I'm all ears."

François picks up one of my locks and drops it with a grimace. "Your hair, you should, you know... Wash it once in a while."

"It's grunge."

"It's disgusting. And you would be so good-looking if you made an effort."

I'm already good looking, and François commenting about the way I look just feels even more awkward. I have zero ideas what to think about it, even less what to comment about it, so I stick my lighter under his nose to light up the joint.

"So, François. Sacha has asked me to change the music."

Smooth transition. Impeccable. 20/20.

"That's impossible," François says, blowing out smoke. "Sacha hates your music. Everyone does."

Rubbish. But that's not the point. I force a smile. "But Sacha likes me. She said I could change the music."

"It's almost midnight."

"Yes! And do you want to celebrate the new year to this crap, or do you want a hymn that represents youth and hope and ideals and—"

François holds up a hand. "Lou, come on. Stop lying. Tell the truth, for once. And maybe, maybe, I'll let you play your music."

He rolls his eyes and doesn't budge when I try to nudge him away from the sound system. I give up with a frustrated sigh.

"The truth? Really? I need Lucie to like me again."

"Why, what have you done this time?"

I open my mouth to speak, but suddenly don't know what to say.

François clicks his tongue. "I'm sure it's nothing. Your girlfriend is always mad anyway."

François would know. Lucie used to hang out with the Golden Fork before she discovered her inner rockstar and ditched them all to hang out with Tony and me. However, they're still friendly.

"I thought you liked her."

"I do," he says, "but she's always angry, that's true."

"She's only angry at me, not the others."

"Why is that?"

"Because I'm always late, among other things."

"That's true. People call you Ever-Late Lou behind your back."

Wrong! It's not behind my back if I know about it, dumb-dumb. But anyway.

"If you don't do it for her, do it for me. Or I'll spend the first day of the year single and miserable, and it will be your fault."

François puts his head in his hands and groans. "Fine! But only because you gave me weed."

Works for me. François steps away from the sound system, and seconds later, the comforting and feverish sound of Kaiser Chiefs is blaring through the speakers, and Yasmine is glaring at me from the kitchen door, knowing full well what I've done.

Gesturing at François with a grin, I show her I have his permission. There's nothing she can do to me now.

Pushing into the crowd, Tony joins me, shaking his head. "I wish my life was as easy as yours. You always get what you want."

Dancing in place, I pretend I didn't hear that. "What did you say?"

He's drunk, it doesn't matter. What matters is Lucie. She has this baffled look that she reserves for me, the one that says: "I can't believe I'm dating Fake-Kurt Cobain."

She runs into my arms and laughs in my face, all anger forgotten. Tony, bobbing up and down, is shouting more than singing out the lyrics. Midnight is seconds away, and all of our faceless bodies are dancing together, too happy and too drunk, to hurt or to care.

10... 9... 8... 7... 6... 5... 4... 3... 2... 1...

Not yet eighteen but at the top of my world, obsessed with my own madness, sandwiched between the two people I love the most in the world. I don't want it to end.

I think I've got it all figured out.

2

I'M SO HUNGOVER

O k, so it's 2008.
Nothing's changed.

One thing, one thing changed. One number to write at the top right corner of my essays.

I'm still the same.

I even recall having the same nasty hangover last year.

My first attempt to stretch results in me crushing my knuckles against the wall. My bed's usually against the right side of the wall. Not the left... I guess some things did change. Or... I'm not in my bed. Ok. I'm not in my bed. And I'm not alone.

Nudged on my side, her hand dangling from the edge of the bed, Lucie is still asleep, wearing her party clothes and still smelling of booze. We're in Tony's bed and probably passed out right on the spot when we made it back to his place.

On the mattress on the floor, Tony's fast asleep, his face pressed into the mattress and his mouth open, dangerously close to a bunched up pair of dirty socks. Daylight filters through the dark curtains of the only window in the room.

How did we get back here? I don't remember much after the countdown. Alcohol was flowing. I drank in my victory after Lucie jumped back into my arms. I'm hoping I was totally awesome and on top of the world, not some sort of nonsense-slurring brutish thug like poor Lars. Only now I've got to pay for it with a splitting headache.

My mouth is like paper, and there is no water in sight. If I don't go the bathroom before they wake up, Lucie will wake up to find me smelling like a Neanderthal, and fat chance of her ever thinking I'm hot again.

Sliding down the bed inch by inch not to wake Lucie, I quietly stumble out the bedroom and right into Tony's mom, in her nightgown. She's holding Kiki, the family's small and ugly dog, whom Tony pretends to hate.

"Look at you," she says, yawning. "Looks like we both indulged last night."

I force a laugh. Can't exactly tell my mate's mum she looks like I feel, can I? And who wants to stare at someone's mum while she's in her nightclothes? Not that Tony's mum minds me, after all this time. She has seen me practically every weekend since I met her son two-and-a-half years ago.

"Want some coffee?" she asks.

"Maybe later."

"Ok. Happy new year, then."

I bet you I'll be fed up with vows before the day is over.

"Happy new year."

With a small snort of laughter at my bemused expression, she shuffles into her bedroom, and I slink, relieved, toward the bathroom, only to find it occupied.

As I hesitate to retreat to the safety of the bedroom, the lock pops open and Tony's older brother Simon comes out, a large smile on his face. Behind him is a tall blonde with a great mane of hair and an insane amount of jewellery.

"What's up, Lou?" Simon shakes my hand. "Did you have fun last night?"

"Yeah, it was great, thanks for the booze."

Since neither of us is eighteen yet, Simon is usually the one who buys us supplies before our parties. He's cool. And blessed with better looks than Tony's, which would explain the giant standing behind him.

"Remember Gretchen?"

She gives a little wave.

"Sure." A blatant lie. "Are you done in there?"

Simon slaps me on the shoulder. "All yours."

The blonde flashes me a perfect supermodel smile as she clinks back toward his room.

Shaking my head, I lock myself in the bathroom and retrieve my own toothbrush from the depths of their medicine cabinet — like I said, I practically live here in the weekends. One look at my face, and I quickly splash some water on it.

Come to think of it, I haven't been much home since the holidays began. I could drag my sorry ass home right now, do some homework. Start off the year with a bang instead of spending another day between video games, joints, and movies.

The other night weed got to my head, I was starting to feel paranoid, and I was complaining to Tony.

"I don't know what I'm going to do with myself," I said to him, joint in hand. "Every time I think about the future, all I see is fog."

Tony took the joint. "That's just the smoke."

You see what I'm dealing with here.

As I tiptoe back to Tony's room, I can hear him and Lucie laughing. They're awake, then. They turn at the sound of the door being pushed open, and both grin at me.

"Lou!" Lucie crawls over the bed toward me. "I thought you abandoned me."

She pulls me into a rib shattering hug and makes a content sound. Down there, Tony is struggling to get to his feet.

"We need some fresh air."

"Agreed," I say, parting from Lucie to draw the curtains.

A blast of icy cold wind engulfs the room when I open the window, rustling Tony's tired posters on the walls and prompting us to escape into the corridor.

In the kitchen we find Tony's father, already dressed in his usual corduroys and cardigan, a pair of glasses on the tip of his nose, reading newspapers with an actual reputation.

"Happy new year, kids!" He smiles as we enter the room, still blinking at the glaring daylight.

Grunting, Tony goes straight to the coffee machine and pours the life-saving nectar into assorted mugs for all of us.

On the kitchen table, a breakfast for champions is laid out, the type you see in American movies that no one in their right mind would have time to prepare. Not that Tony's parents made this. It clearly came from the bakery down the street.

Lucie stuffs a croissant into her smiling mouth. Sitting opposite Tony's father, I take a long scalding sip of coffee. My favourite.

Tony's father folds his newspaper. "Did you have fun last night?"

Tony grimaces, pretends he doesn't like it. I know better. Tony loves his parents. To be honest, they're okay. They're still young and curious about the world. My parents aren't curious about anything. Including myself.

"We had too much fun, Father," Tony says

"Amen to that."

"Lou looks alright, of course," Lucie says. "It's infuriating."

Tony smirks. "Lou always looks good to compensate the fact that he's an asshole."

"Thanks, Tony."

But of course, he's always right.

He winks at me.

"Enjoy it while it lasts," Tony's father says. "At my age, a hangover lasts for days. And remember to be safe and have each other's backs."

"Yes, Dad, come on." Tony shoves half a pain au chocolat into his hell-hole of a mouth and slams a croissant in front of me. "You, eat."

"I think you eat enough for the both of us."

He slaps his flat stomach. "And look at my amazing body."

"You'll die from cholesterol one day."

He laughs, sprinkling pastry all over the table. "And I'll die happy."

"Lou," his dad says, "I meant to ask you."

My shoulders tense. Tony's parents are strange adults who like to talk, even to other people, like me, who are not even their kids. It always startles me when someone twice my age or more wants to talk to me. It makes me anxious, like I'm about to pass a test and fail it. I much prefer the company of my peers, you know. But Tony's dad is okay, really, so I smile politely and wait.

"Are you still planning to go to London?"

My head jerks back toward Tony, who lifts his shoulder in a half shrug.

He told them? My plan to go to London after graduation is not known by many, and I prefer it that way. Partly because I don't like talking about my private business with other people. Partly because I have no idea if I'm really capable of it, you know. Leaving everything behind.

It was our secret, Tony's, Lucie's, and mine. Well, and my father's, because I need his permission. So I don't know how I feel about Tony telling everyone.

"I don't know, maybe." I stare down at my feet. "It's definitely still on the table."

I'm expecting my friends to start shouting in protest, but to my surprise, Tony keeps silent and starts buttering himself a piece of toast. Lucie watches us intently, in silence, even though two weeks ago she was pestering me to apply at the same university. I even told her rockstars don't go to university, which Tony approved, but it didn't make her laugh at all at the time. I guess I'm on my own, then.

"I was talking to a friend last night," Tony's father explains. "He says he'll have a room to rent when his current tenant leaves at the beginning of July. I told him it could be of interest to you."

I glance at Tony for support, but he's buttering his toast and not looking at me.

"Nothing is certain yet. My father hasn't exactly given me permission to go."

That's not exactly true, but not exactly a lie either, so that makes it okay.

"Well," Tony's dad says as he gets up. "Just let me know whenever you're sure. I'll talk to my friend about it."

"Thanks."

Tony's father leaves us to our breakfast. We're a little too quiet in there for a few minutes. Perhaps we're just tired. That's probably it.

Simon breaks the silence when he and his blonde walk past the kitchen door on their way out.

"Happy new year!"

They exchange a few words with Tony and Lucie while I'm pondering if I should go home and get started on my homework. When the door slams shut after them, Lucie turns to Tony, her mouth agape.

"Is that who I think it is?"

Tony nods. "No comment."

"Who is this?" I help myself to more coffee. "She famous or something?"

Lucie throws me a look. "That's Gretchen, Lou."

"Who?"

"Julien's girlfriend."

"Ex-girlfriend," Tony says.

"Who?"

Who are these people? It doesn't ring a bell.

Lucie rolls her eyes. "Lou sometimes I think you're completely blind."

Tony gives a cackle. "That's the sunglasses."

"Gretchen," Lucie says, sounding impatient, "was with Julien for years."

I look up, coffee mug halfway to my mouth. "Wait, Julien? Your brother's best friend?"

Tony looks annoyed. "Yeah. That caused some drama."

You bet that it caused some drama.

"They used to go to my old school," Lucie says. "Such a cool couple."

"What happened to him?" I ask. "To Julien, I mean. Is he okay?"

Tony shrugs. "I don't know. They're not exactly talking anymore."

"That's really sad," Lucie says. "They were inseparable."

"It's not like my brother could help it." Tony turns his back to us and begins stacking dishes into the sink. "They fell in love, there's nothing they could do, you know."

Tony doesn't like injustice. He wears T-shirts with Karl Marx's face on it. He also pretends to hate Kiki, his ugly mutt, but will try to break both your legs if you make fun of his *little cutie*. So it strikes me as curious that he doesn't have more to say about it. That's probably because his brother, in his eyes, can do no wrong.

In any case, the subject is dropped and another matter arises. Which of the Blu-Rays Tony got for Christmas are we going to watch today? My motivation to start over, go home, and do some homework is quickly thrown out the window. Before the hour is over, we're all tucked under blankets in Tony's bedroom, homework completely forgotten.

It's dark when I make it back home, two movies and three joints later. Paris isn't a large city, and Tony doesn't live too far, but who has the energy to walk on the first day of the year? Certainly not me. I hop on the first bus I can catch, put on my music, and stare out the window at the endless succession of old buildings. The few people I see walking home look already cold and tired. Guess what? It's only the first day of the year.

When it's my time to get off, a girl by the exit catches my eye and smiles. I forget to return the favour.

I live in the 5th arrondissement of Paris. It's like a district. In my opinion, it's the best one, but depending on where you live, you might beg to differ. Outside my own six storeys high Haussmann building located on rue Larrey, with an old door that is either not opening or slamming right into your face, the kids are playing in the cold around the old Coccinelle no one ever seems to drive. Little Jérémy, who lives on the ground floor with his parents, stops me to show me his new skateboarding skills. I watch him for a minute, longing for my bed.

"You're getting really good at this."

"Thanks, Lou. Come on, stay a bit longer!"

I hung my head. "Sorry, not this time. My dad's waiting for me."

Our fists bump. He goes back to his friends, I enter the code for the door. Today, it opens without problem.

Our flat is on the third floor, no lift. We always hurry up the stairs a little faster when coming up to the second floor because the old lady who lives there has a habit of flagging people down and asking them for favours. I'm so good at dodging her than I haven't been asked to do anything, ever. My father isn't so lucky. That's his fault, though. He's too slow, not reactive enough. He was also too slow to react when my mother decided to leave us. Sometimes I think if he had noticed or fought back she would still live with us today, but she left, and there's nothing I can do about it.

Dad hears me enter the flat and calls my name. I peer into the small living room, find him sitting on his own on the small sofa, watching a game show on the telly, an airplane magazine on his lap. His face looks tired behind his reading glasses. Just seeing him looking tired irks me. He owns a small company of cleaning products, but looking at him, you'd think he's just come back from the war. Perhaps he's just depressed. There's nothing glamorous about cleaning products after all. But it does bring money on the table.

I kick my shoes off. "Happy new year."

"Happy new year."

I hesitate as I remove my coat and hang it on the hook, away from his gaze. "Did Mum call?"

"No." He clears his throat. "There's food left in the fridge if you want."

"Thanks. I ate at Tony's."

My father heaves a deep sigh. "Tony's parents see you more than I do."

I lean against the doorjamb, feeling awkward. My father's expression betrays nothing. That's usually the extent of our conversations, so I'm a little out of my depths. Then something comes to mind.

"Tony's father said he knows of a place for me to rent in London this summer. I'm thinking of taking it."

My father says nothing, only stares at me blankly the way he used to stare at my mum when she was complaining about him.

"I said you could go only if your grades pick up."

I better not tell him I haven't done any homework yet. Leaving him in front of the telly, I retreat into my bedroom and toss myself onto the bed.

Above me, the ceiling's paint is cracked. It's been for years, but it's not so bad that I felt compelled to do something about it. Plastered on every inch of the walls, a flurry of posters picturing men in dark clothing and surly faces are watching over me. Among the mess littering the floor, my backpack lay unopened since the last day of school.

I only have to reach for it, open it, read the list of homework. Perhaps I'd find the motivation to do the simplest of exercises. Or… Maybe not.

Instead, I fish my phone out of my pocket and start texting Lucie.

3

THIS IS WHERE IT GETS WEIRD

Less than a week later, on a dreary Monday morning, freezing my ass in my leather jacket, I spot Tony and Lucie huddled together against the cold outside the gates of Colette International, smoking a cigarette.

Tony assaults me before I can reach into his pack of cigarettes. "You're late!"

"Am I?"

Lucie chortles and smoke comes out of her nose.

"Why are you always so late!!" Tony's voice sounds uncharacteristically whiny.

I peer at his long face from behind my sunglasses and gesture at my baggy pants and worn-out sweater. "This doesn't happen by accident, you know."

I expect him to laugh, but he just stares at me, wild-eyed. Lucie, on the other hand, plants a Marlboro-flavoured kiss on my lips.

"What's up with you?"

Lucie sighs. "Tony hates school."

"Rockstars don't go to school," he growls.

"Hear, hear, my friend."

I cannot agree more. It took all of my motivation in the world and then some to drag myself out of bed this morning.

Lucie ruffles through her backpack. It's a cute little polar bear with beady eyes. "Give me a cigarette, my love. I seem to be out."

It might be nothing, but I know better than finding Lucie's backpacks just *cute*. They are usually an indicator of her mood.

Watch this. Cute little polar bear? Sounds innocent, right? Wrong! It usually means it's winter, it's cold, and I better not test her patience too much. But the polar bear is also wearing a pink ribbon, which means I can be a bit of a dick today and she won't give me too much of a hard time.

But today it's not the empty black eyes of the stuffed backpack which worry me but the book inside that catches my eye. A bland book with a boring guy on the cover. My stomach sinks. Last week was just a blur of movies, video games, late lunches and joints, so many joints with Tony and Lucie, our favourite bands playing in the background.

"Shit."

Watching my face drain of colour is entertaining enough for Tony, who drops the surly act.

"What did you do this time?"

"It's what I didn't do. I forgot to read the book."

Part of me wants to blame them for keeping me away from my student responsibilities, but even I have limits, you know.

I put my head in my hands. "So, you know, Dorian Gray? I may have forgotten to read it."

Tony erupts in laughter. "You're so fucked! Paquin will read it on your face, and you'll be interrogated for sure."

"You think?"

Lucie nods in agreement. Paquin is this old bat with bleached hair who teaches English Literature with an outrageous French accent. Every time she catches me cringing, she interrogates me.

"How's my poker face?" I ask, feigning the confidence of a student who's read ALL the books.

Tony stares intently into my face. "Damn you, it's good."

"Beautiful," Lucie says.

"With his luck, she'll forget he even exists." Tony flicks the butt of his cigarette away. "Lou always gets what he wants."

That's not true, and I don't like the look on his face as he says this. But before I can ask for precisions, Lucie glues her body to mine.

"Let's use the last two minutes before class to make-out in our usual spot."

"Tempting," I say. "Truly. But I have to use the toilet first."

Tony shakes his head. "You live ten minutes away, and you couldn't go on your way out?"

I throw him a look over my shoulder as I walk away. "I was late, remember?"

Colette International is a relatively new building nestled between two old ones in an even older street, Rue de L'Ecole. A modest white building stands behind the black front gate. Inside, everything is painted white with a touch of electric blue, from the tiles in the bathroom and the doors, to the legs of the tables and chairs, even the handles of the cupboards. Someone had probably made a deal for cheap white and blue paint, and here we are. It's the same in the boy's toilets. Sparkling white tiles and a splash of blue on the stall doors. This is where I hide, the last stall on the left. I do not do my business in front of other people.

I wonder if I have time to do a quick joint before class. It's probably a terrible idea anyway. Paquin will see my blue eyes turned red and she'll have me whipped in front of everybody.

When I come out of my stall, some bloke is standing in front of my favourite sink, the closest one to the good soap dispenser AND the good hand-dryer, the one I call The Champion. I don't mind other people using it, but this guy isn't doing anything, he's just standing there with his head down.

I walk over to the next sink just as the bell rings, announcing the beginning of class, and my future humiliation at the hands of Madame Paquin.

Looking up in the mirror, I see it. Defeat plain on my face, on the very first day of term. Hiding in the bathroom instead of making out with my hot girlfriend. Well, I'm going to get destroyed, but I don't have to look bad while she tears me a new one. *C'est la vie.*

I shove a stick of gum into my mouth and rearrange my hair, humming to myself a Good Charlotte song. Sorry, what's that? My gum is begging me to pop a nice fat bubble and I get to it, still humming... Feeling a sort of paternal pride for this bubble which is coming out so beautifully and promises a nice loud pop. I don't immediately notice, but eventually, it hits me. The bloke next to me hasn't moved. And worse, he's staring at me.

What's up? Did I give him the impression that I congregate with strangers in toilets? I think not. I slide my sunglasses down a notch to give him a withering look. You know, the kind of look you'd toss any stranger who's hogging the good soap dispenser and not moving it along. And then, a pair of bright green eyes stare straight back at me from under an organised mess of shiny dark curls.

"Hello."

Like the gun they use at the Olympics, my bubble pops, startling me into action. I start pumping the nearest soap dispenser frantically. I will not get caught in a socially awkward situation on the first day of term.

Of course, the dispenser's empty. I knew that already, since this chatty guy standing next to the only one that properly works, and he's not moving. Why is he not moving? And why won't this soap dispenser take pity on me? I have a feeling this guy's watching me struggle like an idiot with a smile on his face.

Eventually the saddest squirt of soap lands into the palm of my hand.

"Do you..." he starts, moving aside to reveal the Champion.

I grunt more than speak back. "I'm fine."

I finish my business in the blink on an eye, and by that I mean wiping my hands on my jeans, grabbing my stuff with shaky hands, and tearing out of the bathroom without a look back.

How rude are people, really?

Tony and Lucie are waiting for me outside. Tony sees my pack of gum and takes it from my damp hand. Goodbye, old gum. I shall never see you again.

"You look worse than when you got in." Tony shoves five sticks of gum into his mouth. "Did you get molested again?"

Lucie's brow furrows. "Again?"

"Why are you eating so much gum before class?" I snatch the

pack of gum back from Tony's hand. It's empty. "Paquin will ask you to throw it in the bin."

"It's an act of rebellion, Lou. You should try it, it's good for you."

"Again?" Lucie says, tugging at my sleeve.

"Don't listen to this guy." I take her hand and start pulling her toward the classroom. "He's full of shit. Let's move, we're going to be late."

The stranger will come out of the bathroom, and I definitely don't want to see him.

Tony slaps me on the back. "And Paquin will skewer you even more if you're late."

Actually, I'd be fine never to see the stranger again, or be doomed to remember this terrible moment. He was British. I heard it in his accent. Let it be known that I am NOT moving to London if people act like this in public toilets.

We make it on time to the classroom. I assume my spot at the back of the class, a punishment for previous *inappropriate behaviour* which included:

- Asking Madame Paquin why we always read boring-ass books.
- Drawing something crude on the whiteboard and laughing like a caveman (her words).
- Failing to hand over an essay on Shakespeare and justifying it by saying: "Rockstars don't write essays on Shakespeare."

Now I sit all alone at the back of the class, from where I have an amazing view of Tony and Lucie, who share a table together and like to laugh in their fists when I get interrogated. But my seating arrangement also has its benefits. Lars, my favourite Danish guy, is seated right in front of me. He's freakishly tall, and I use him as a shield to hide from Paquin.

The nightmare quickly starts. Not two minutes after she entered the classroom, she requests one of us to summarise the book. I watch helplessly as Lars chooses this moment to bend over to retrieve his book from his backpack, leaving my dumb face in plain view of Paquin.

"Monsieur Mésange."

Tony's strangled laughter reaches my ears. I promise him an act of swift revenge, somehow, someday.

"Monsieur Mésange," Paquin repeats. "Why don't you sum up the book for me?"

Everyone turns to look at me, which just makes it so much better. I clutch the side of my table, a bitter taste filling my mouth.

Not that I know for sure what Paquin does during the holidays, but I suspect it's mostly meetings with her coven like the reputable witch that she is. Don't tell me it was instinct that whispered to her I was the one to interrogate this morning. I call it wizardry.

Like a sign of providence, a knock on the door interrupts my ordeal. I promise to start worshipping Jesus if this person gets me out of this nightmare. The door opens and my jaw drops when the guy from the toilet sticks his face in the opening.

Paquin slams her copy of Dorian Gray on the desk, her face flushed. "You're late!"

A slight frown mars toilet guy's face.

"Actually, I'm new," he says in his British accent.

A few laughs scatter the classroom, especially from the girls. Sacha's face has a suspicious glow to it, and I'm guessing it's not from Paquin's barking. Toilet guy takes his sweet time to come inside and hands Paquin a note. She reads it and gives him a once-over.

"Michael Parker."

He nods, sending his curls bouncing. A few girls give another round of giggles. I lean back into my chair, annoyed.

"Take a seat, Michael."

There's a flutter of sound around the classroom as several ladies shuffle onto their chairs, now regretting having their best friend next to them when New Guy could be taking their place.

There are three available seats in the whole of the classroom today. But for some mystifying reason and despite the deep scowl on my face, New Guy seems to think I'm the right choice for him.

Is it because we just met in the toilet? Does that mean we're connected now? Is this how British people make friends in England?

27

Staring at blokes in the reflection of the mirror in public toilets? Am I the only one who thinks that's odd?

There's no avoiding it. New guy walks all the way to the back of the class, removes his coat, and takes the chair next to mine. Somewhere in my field of vision, Tony's face is split open in silent laughter. Mature, real mature Tony. I click my tongue disapprovingly for good measure.

"So, Michael," Paquin says in her horrid accent. "You are British."

He puts his hands on his lap. "Guilty."

"Welcome, Michael. Your neighbour, Monsieur Mésange, was about to give us his impressions on *The Picture Of Dorian Gray*."

Damn that witch. I feel Michael's eyes on me, as well as everybody else's. Perhaps if I pretend to be caught in a fit of coughing, I'll be able to buy myself some time.

"Today, Monsieur Mésange?"

Tony is gesturing me to move it along. I'll kill him, I swear I'll kill him.

I jerk my head toward toilet guy. "I was interrupted, now I've forgotten everything. Why don't you interrogate him? It's kind of his fault, after all."

Paquin sighs while the rest of the class laughs, either with me or at me. Hard to tell.

"Michael is new. He hasn't read the book."

Michael stares at my copy on the table. "Actually..."

What? What? You've read it? If you answer for me, I might forgive you the toilet scene. But before my hopes get up, Paquin raises her wrinkly hand and smashes them.

"Monsieur Mésange will tell us his impressions on the book."

Right. If she wants to play, I'll play. All eyes are on me. It's not like I have a choice. What did Tony say to me once? Fake it till you make it.

"I liked it." I sound confident enough. Not too confident. Just enough.

"Why did you like it?"

"I really liked the beginning. You know—with the portrait."

More laughter follows. Paquin approaches me, hawk-like.

"Have you read the book, Monsieur Mésange?"

As laughter increases, my temperature rises and my carefully crafted careless persona is about to be crushed, I meet Michael's gaze and hate, absolutely hate, to find pity in there. I don't know this guy, he's not my friend, and he has no right to stare at me like that.

I draw in a sharp breath. "Sure."

"How does it end?"

Paquin's hawk eyes are extremely intimidating. I give a sad attempt at a laugh.

"I wouldn't want to spoil it for the others."

"Everyone here has read it!" She throws her own copy of the book at our table. It bounces off. Michael catches it before it lands on the floor. "But it seems *you* haven't, young man. Or tell me. How does it end?"

On my right, Michael is trying to distract me. His hands, under the table, seems to mime either stabbing or something wildly inappropriate. I spear him with a glare and he stops.

"He dies," I tell Paquin. "He dies at the end."

"How?"

"He was…" The hell with it, I have no clue. This book doesn't even have one decent film adaptation. Remembering what Michael did under the table, I tempt my chance. "He was stabbed."

Paquin's face splits in a malevolent smile.

"You know, Monsieur Mésange… It truly baffles me that you wouldn't even think of searching for the summary of the book on the internet before you came in here. Your lack of resourcefulness is astounding." She retrieves her book and squeezes it between her clawed hands. "As a result, you must bear the consequences. I will write to your parents about your lack of concern for rules and your refusal to do basic homework."

At least Tony has stopped laughing and has switched to painful grimaces instead. Lucie's eyes are brimming with empathy, which means I'd get some proper comforting later. So it's not all that bad.

Enjoying the effects my humiliation had on the class, Paquin slowly slinks back to her desk.

"This year is important. You must pass all of your exams, including English Literature. Enough with the slacking. To show

how serious I am, I'm giving you six weeks to write a proper essay on *The Picture of Dorian Gray*, using a list of questions as a reference. You will work with the person sitting next to you. No exceptions, Monsieur Mésange," she adds, watching my horrified face. Her gaze softens when she turns to Michael. "I'm sorry Monsieur Parker. I bet you regret having picked this particular seat."

Michael looks like he's never had a regret in his entire life. Perhaps he's mentally impaired. Suddenly feeling very weak, and now properly shielded by Lars, I turn away from him and rest my burning face on the table.

When Tony turns around to check up on me, I pretend to shoot myself in the head.

4

NOT MY KIND OF MUSIC

The next two hours occur without incident, but my cheeks are still tingling from Paquin's harassment, the memory of so many laughing faces, and New Guy's pity-filled gaze.

I spend most of the lesson staring at Tony and Lucie's back and hating everything about the way they laugh at each other's jokes or whatever they're writing or drawing in the margin of Lucie's binder. My heart hammering in my ribcage, I long for the end of the day. And it's only the first class of the term.

Michael is really into Paquin's analysis of Dorian Gray. After he asked me to borrow my copy, I could only oblige. I slid the book his way without a backward glance, and he hasn't looked up from it since.

He's so into it that he's almost leaning flat on the table, his nose inches from the page, and from time to time, he smiles at the mention of so and so, just as though the characters on the page are his mates and they just said something funny.

I get it, he's a total nerd, and I should have never been paired with him. Since I met him, my partner has always been Tony. I should be sitting with him right now. I hate myself for having misbehaved so much in the past term. If I hadn't been punished, none of this would have happened. Now I'm stuck with chatty toilet guy.

Michael.

When I catch him turning the pages of my cheap paperback as though it's the first edition of the Gutenberg Bible, I decide to break the spell, because it's just embarrassing.

"So…" He startles at the sound of my voice. Great. I frightened him now. "You like books."

His eyes don't look up from the page. "Everyone likes books."

This makes me snort quite loudly, earning me a silent warning from Paquin. Not everybody likes books, bro. I can't remember the last time I read a book that I actually enjoyed.

I used to have books, though. Tony saw them the first time he came to my place, his hands full of CD's, and chastised me for having them. I lied, pretended they belong to my little cousin, or that my mother owned them, I don't recall.

"From now on," he'd said, kneeling before me, "I'll be in charge of your education." The next day I put them in a cardboard box and stuck them under my bed.

I stifle a yawn. "That's going to be handy, you being a fan of books and all."

He abandons his precious reading to slip me a glance. "What? Why?"

"For the essay."

"I guess." He dips his nose back into the book.

Out of boredom, I start listing all the ways this guy and I are completely different, and how there's no way on earth we could be friends.

From his freshly shampooed dark curls to the fancy boots he's wearing, we are utterly different. Oddly enough, he smells like fresh apples. I don't even own a bottle of perfume or aftershave. His hands are clean, his fingers long. My own hands are inexplicably smeared with ink and all I did was write the name of the book on a blank piece of paper. For a guy, his eyes are quite large, and his eyelashes long and dark. His clothes are nothing like mine; he probably dresses like his father. And the way he treats a battered copy of a book, like it's precious. Spoiler alert: I don't even bother opening them.

After watching him closely for half-an-hour, I'm convinced this essay is going to be more of a chore than anything I've done before.

The bell rings, delivering me from this nightmare. I spring to my feet, ready to GTFO, but Tony is at our table in seconds, followed by Lucie readjusting her hair. Don't think I missed it.

"So," Tony says, twirling my pen like a baton and dropping it. "That was humiliating."

"Yes, thank you, Tony."

Michael appears between us, holding my pen. I snatch it and toss it in my bag, eager to leave quickly, put as much distance between him and I. But Tony turns to Michael, eyes brimming with interest.

"So, Michael, is that right? British, right?"

"Guilty on both counts."

Lucie flashes him one of her best smiles. But he's already said that at the beginning of class. Not very original, is he? Especially for somebody who loves to speak to strangers in the toilets.

"What brings you to Colette?" Tony asks.

Lucie gives Michael a thorough look which makes me think she wouldn't mind spending time locked in the toilet with him.

Michael puts his hands in his pockets. "My mother has gotten a job in Paris for the next few months. I thought it'd be a great experience to join her."

It's as though he can feel Lucie's eyes on him, because he starts shuffling his feet nervously and points at her polar bear backpack.

"Cute."

She beams, but Tony doesn't look so convinced yet. Bless his magnificent long face.

"You left your school and your friends in the middle of the year to come here?"

"I guess I like to live dangerously." He glances at the door on the other side of the room.

"Cool. That's cool." Tony has never found anybody cool except for Lucie and me. I watch him extend his hand, bewildered. "I'm Tony."

"I'm Lucie," my girlfriend adds, a bit too pink for my liking.

Michael finally cracks a smile, which slips at the sight of my scrunched-up face. Tony slides in front of me, obscuring me from him.

"So, Michael. What kind of music do you listen to?"

Oh, nice one Tony. Tricky question. The make or break of any infant of a relationship with him. And therefore with myself, of course. Michael doesn't know that. He's staring at us as though he finds the question a little odd.

"I don't really listen to music, actually."

Lucie gasps audibly in the empty classroom. "You don't listen to music?"

Tony's eyes narrow. "Everyone listens to music."

Tony believes that what you listen to says a lot about who you are. Like listening to French variety makes you a loser, by default. Listening to RnB or pop makes you a trend follower, and listening to classical music makes you a career politician. Avoid these people at all costs, Tony would say.

Tony's intense.

"I just don't," Michael says.

There is a silence during which we all exchange stares that are way too uncomfortable for my opinion. Michael's statement is hanging in the air like a murder confession. With that, all my worries vanish. There is no way Tony will let him into our little group, and I'll never have to deal with his annoying curls.

Eventually even Michael has gotten the gist, because he gestures toward the door.

"I should go. I've no idea of the layout of this place. I don't want to get lost again."

Before we can protest, not that I ever intended to personally, Michael clears his side of the table by sweeping the contents into his backpack with one hand and hurries out of the classroom.

Lucie stares after him. "We could have been nicer, really." She worries her bottom lip. "We scared him away."

"Good," Tony says, stretching his long arms. "What kind of person doesn't listen to music? Serial killers, I think."

Tony, as always, is right.

"I don't think so." I close my bag and start moving toward the door. "That would be too interesting."

"Oh, you're right. Can't have more than one serial killer per school. And we already have Madame Paquin."

Outside, the corridor is packed, and I have to wrap an arm around Lucie's shoulders to shield her from taller brutes.

"Who has Paquin ever killed?" she asks. "Allegedly, of course."

Tony ruffles my hair. "Our dear Lou-Lou, repeatedly, in the past two hours."

"Arsehole." I punch him in the shoulder while he laughs uncontrollably.

No time for more conversation as we reach our next class, History. After two hours of pure bliss where no one even thinks of interrogating me, and where I'm safely seated next to Tony while Michael ends up next to François, we drag our exhausted bodies outside for a cigarette before storming the cafeteria. It's freezing, and the sky looks as gloomy as a January sky entails, but at least there's no wind today.

Looking over my shoulder I see Sacha, Yasmine, and François have wasted no time pouncing on my toilet guy. I don't know who's acting more flustered. François, who in all the years I have known him has never had a male friend, or Sacha, who's had more male friends than anyone should.

"Do we have time for a joint behind the bushes?" I ask, tying up my hair in a low ponytail.

"No." Lucie pulls me to her. She kisses my cheek, my nose, my lips, and before long, she's all over me, laughing into my mouth, smelling of La Petite Robe Noir and tasting of cherry lip balm.

Tony's voice distracts me. "So, Lou. What do you think?"

"Of what?"

I pull two cigarettes from my pack. Lucie takes one and lights mine.

"New guy. You spent two hours with him. What do you think?"

I choke on the smoke. "What do you mean, what do I think?"

"Should we invite him to hang out after class, could he be one of us?"

"Tony, he doesn't listen to music," Lucie says, and I feel a rush of passion for her.

"Sure, true, but if Lou thinks Michael's awesome, then we'll have to make an effort. After all, we can teach him about music. Your precious Lou knew nothing of the good stuff before I peeled him off the streets like a stray puppy."

"Thanks, really."

"That's true. You even looked like one. So?"

Staring in Tony's laughing dark eyes, an unusual resentment fills me. He acts as though he's playing out a joke he isn't letting me on. What is he playing at? I don't like to be left out. I don't like it at all. Bitterness overtakes me.

"Look, I've got to get out of this deal with Paquin." I surprise myself with the harsh tone of my voice. "I don't even want to do the essay with him. Michael. Even his name sounds lame. If you think I'll stoop so low as to hang out with this total nerd, you clearly haven't taught me anything at all."

I was expecting a reaction, sure. But not the one I got: Lucie's eyes widening and Tony's mouth dropping open.

"What?"

They're looking at something located right behind me. With a mounting sense of dread, I turn around…

It's Michael. He's standing right in front of me, my copy of Dorian Gray in his hand. Unhelpfully, Tony lets out a nervous cackle. Lucie buries her fist in his hip.

"Dickhead," she says.

"I took your book by mistake," Michael says, his face blank.

I can try to convince myself he hasn't heard anything, but that would be delusional at this point. I immediately push my sunglasses up my nose to conceal my mortification, but in the centre of my white face, my cheeks are burning with shame.

"Thanks."

Michael turns around without another word. Behind me, Tony's chortling like a kid. Lucie chastises him. I stare after Michael, an odd feeling swirling around my stomach. Sacha, François, and Yasmine welcome him back. Sacha links her arm with his and leads him toward the cafeteria.

"Well done," Tony tells me. "Now you better hope he's not a serial killer."

With a frustrated sigh, I stuff the book into my backpack. This day cannot be over soon enough, but I still have a whole afternoon ahead filled with opportunities to make an absolute fool of myself.

Why should I care if I hurt his feelings? I don't even know him. He didn't care about my feelings when he tried to chat with me in the toilet. But how could he have been aware of my social anxiety? I'm pretty decent at hiding it. All you need is sunglasses during the day and alcohol during times-out.

Despite my initial fears, the day goes on without any more incidents. Not once does Michael even look at me or speak to me again. Amazingly, Lucie and Tony seem to have completely forgotten he exists or that I said these stupid words while he was in earshot.

Still, I welcome the end of lessons with relief. Under the cover of dark, Tony, Lucie, and I share a quick joint near the school bins, and I wave them goodbye as they hop on the bus toward their home.

I live too close to Colette not to walk, even in the cold. I don't mind it. I put my music on and keep my head down, that way I don't even meet people's gazes.

The only time I look up at a red light, I notice with surprise Michael walking in the same direction, only on the other side of the road. Are we neighbours? He spots me, too, but pretends he doesn't. I know he did, though, because he picks up the pace to put some distance between us. A faint feeling of shame settles on my chest. It might just be the weed.

Sticking my earplugs into my ears, I turn the music on. When Michael saw me earlier in the mirror, he probably thought I was a decent guy, so he went to sit next to me. And I am a decent guy. I wish I'd said nothing. I get so worked up performing for Tony sometimes that I act like a complete bully. Now I wish I hadn't.

But still, it doesn't matter what he thinks. I don't know him. He doesn't like music. I only wish he hadn't heard me because he'll get the wrong idea about me, think I'm some kind of asshole, and though I do stupid things from time to time, I don't think I'm an asshole.

Something nasty awaits me at home. My father is seated at the kitchen table, his usual spot to berate me whenever he feels the need to, which doesn't happen often, but always results in uncomfortable and awkward cohabitation for the following weeks.

"Mrs Paquin wrote to me."

"She did threaten to do that," I say with a smile, the weed clouding my judgment. I had completely forgotten about the old bat's threat.

"Does that make you laugh?"

I stick my hands in my pockets. "Not particularly."

My father takes a deep breath. He's as bad in the role of the mean dad as I am at playing the good son. I actually feel sorry for him.

"You had two weeks to read that book. Two weeks. That's plenty of time." He rests his forehead in his hand, as though the conversation is already taking its toll on him. "You never try. Never make an effort of anything." He looks up, his face twisted in a grimace. "God damn it, Louis, you don't even wash your hair anymore."

I rake a hand through my hair, mildly offended.

"That's grunge."

"That's not grunge. That's disgusting."

You know what? I think François told me the exact same thing last week. How uncanny.

My father rises from his seat, his eyes narrowing. "And are you high right now?"

"Nope." I quickly stare down at my feet.

"You better not be."

His lips tighten in a white line. He slowly rubs his palms together, a thing he always does when he wants control of his emotions.

"I tell you what, Louis. Paquin told me about your essay. If you don't get top grades, you can forget about going to London. And that goes for all the other subjects too, you know. There will be no London as long as you don't try a little."

I actually don't know what to say. He's never threatened me with anything before, and despite all the protests that come to my head right now, a part of me knows full well that I screwed up with this Dorian thing. I could yell something, like 'it's not fair!', or 'Mom would never do this to me'. I don't feel like it today.

Dad moves to the sink. "Go do your homework. I'm making dinner."

Perhaps I should show a little more backbone. Rage Against the Machine, you know. So he could tell his friends we had a big fight, and he came out on top.

I lift my chin up. "I'll be eighteen soon, you know. And then I can do what I want."

My father turns to me, frying pan in hand. "Not with my money, you won't."

That's good enough. Now I can turn on my heel and stomp to my bedroom, even slam the door.

Dinner happens in heavy, resentment-laden silence, each of us buried deep into our thoughts. My father wonders if he went too far, if he should've raised his voice at all, if he's worthy. Or perhaps he's just wondering what's on telly tonight.

Personally, I'm just wondering how I'll possibly get top grades on an essay about a book I haven't read, written with a guy who hates me.

A guy who hates me because of me.

5

SO, I'M IN A BIT OF A PICKLE

At the end of the week, it's clear Michael has forgotten all about my existence, or worse, that he'd rather not think of me. Not a single glance or a word from him since he heard me call him a nerd. Talk about holding a grudge.

And here's the really annoying thing. Michael likes everyone, and everyone likes him. He's more popular in his first week than I've been since I set foot at Colette's, since I was given a makeover and gifted my infamous sunglasses. The Golden Fork doesn't let him out of their sight, but teachers and students alike seem to think he's the coolest guy on earth.

Lucie caught me staring at him through squinted eyes on more than one occasion and says I should forget about it, that he'll get around it eventually, and I'll be able to submit my essay. They have never spoken again since Monday, but like everybody else, she thinks he's sweet and amazing and talks like she knows him. Perhaps he's a wizard too, and he has bewitched everyone, and Tony and I are the only ones who can see clearly.

Because yes, Tony's the only one who remains unmoved by the cool, sweet, bouncy curls persona, still begrudging him his lack of music education. A part of me is simply pissed off at the sight of him. I can't fully explain it, but I resent that no one can resist him, not even Paquin, just as I resent his dignified response to my stupid attitude on our first meeting.

Why should he be so cool about what I said? Didn't it even matter to him? He acts like nothing can touch him, but he refuses to even acknowledge my presence. Aren't we supposed to work together? How am I supposed to hand in my essay if he won't even look at me?

What's so special about him, anyway... I don't get it. Everybody seems to adore him. I spent years working on my style, my hair, the careful juxtapositions of accessories, aloofness, and taste and repartee, and this toilet stranger comes in and sweeps them all away. What does he have that I don't? And why, why won't he talk to me?

He thinks he's so much better than me because he reads books and I'm just a slacker and a stoner. But he knows nothing about me. I've got skills, you know. Somewhere. I'll show him one day. I'll show him he's wrong about me.

On Monday, feeling harassed after a full weekend pulled between my nagging father and my high-maintenance hot girlfriend, and after two-hours of English Lit glaring at a stubbornly silent Michael from the corner of my eye, I decide this is enough. I simply cannot take it anymore. I have no choice but to open my heart to Tony.

"So basically, you are fucked," Tony says, cheerful, when I'm done explaining everything.

"Ok, just don't... look so happy about it, thank you!"

Scowling, I flatten myself against the wall to let a group of giggling girls pass. Lucie has abandoned us, fled to the girl's toilets. I only notice now that Tony's wearing a skirt over his black jeans, but I know better than to ask. It's probably an act of rebellion.

Tony unwraps an enormous lollipop and sticks it into his mouth. "What are you going to do?"

"I guess I have to find a way to make him do the project with me, you know."

"The serial-killer kid?"

The lollipop is very distracting and gets on my nerves.

"Let's drop that one. He really doesn't look like a serial killer."

"Neither did Ted Bundy, Lou."

I make a face that makes him laugh. He slaps me across the back.

"Don't worry. Many serial killers are great with books. I saw it in this documentary. He might even write a brilliant essay, you know."

"But I just told you. Since he heard me, he——"

Tony gives a huge eye-roll. "Who cares? He's one of the Golden Fork by now. Probably forgot all about it."

"Then why would he hate me?"

The annoying lollipop makes a disturbing popping sound when Tony pulls it out of his mouth.

"You know what?" Tony says, waving it under my nose, "François probably told him you were a giant asshole."

This makes me snigger. "François doesn't think I'm a giant asshole."

"Yes, he does, actually."

I look at him in disbelief. "Excuse me, what?"

François? Hating me? I thought he thought nothing of me, just as I thought nothing of him. How dare he? There's nothing worse than finding out somebody hates your guts for no reason. Even if you personally think he's a massive dildo.

"Why the long face?" Tony laughs at my expression. "François is the worst kind of bland, watery dish you can find in a typical affluent high-school."

"All right, enough, enough."

Tony's right. After all, François is nothing to me. Thank goodness he's always here to remind me to keep my cool. I get so worked up over nothing, sometimes.

"But how does that help me?" I manoeuvre back toward our conversation. "I'm even more double fucked now. Michael won't want to help me."

"On the contrary." With great flourish, Tony brandishes the lollipop and almost strikes me on the nose. "Michael was assigned by Paquin to help you. So after school, go and tell him you're fine to just have him do the assignment alone, and you'll just copy it."

"How will that make him think I'm not an asshole? It seems it will make things even worse."

"It won't make him like you," Tony says with a pointed look. He gives my shoulder a paternal squeeze. "But you'll get the assignment done with no effort, and you'll be able to go to London after graduation."

Something doesn't feel right about what he just said.

"I thought you didn't want me to go."

Tony gives me a blank look. "I want you to do whatever you want, Lou. Achieve your dreams." He scratches his cheek thought-fully. "London *is* a great city. Home to some of the best music in the world. You'll find the best hangouts in Camden, probably party with long-haired hippies named Duncan, and you'll have a blast. What do I have waiting for me here? Joining the plebes at some random university and getting some one-on-one quality times with fucking Kiki."

"You love Kiki."

"Everyone loves Kiki. That's not the point."

There's a brief silence, during which I try to meet his eyes. "You could come to London with me, you know."

We're interrupted by Lucie storming out of the bathroom. She swings her backpack over her shoulder; it's a mouse wearing a tweed coat. I do not know what this one means, and I suspect no one does.

Lucie plops a kiss on my cheek as Tony sticks the lollipop back into his mouth.

"Sacha's in there. She is head over heels for the new guy."

"Really?" Tony looks astonished. "I simply don't get it. What's so special about him?"

"I don't know." She's not as expert a liar as I am. Her glowing cheeks will betray her anytime. "He's kind of handsome, I think."

You think. I say she has given the matter some serious thought. I find it suspicious that anyone should spend so much time obsessing over one person. I'm just saying.

Lucie pokes me in the shoulder. "Anyway, she asked me to ask you to ask him" — she has to catch her breath here — "if he's inter-ested in her."

I can't help snorting loudly. "You know Sacha likes anything that moves, right?"

Tony guffaws in a beautiful demonstration of *cavemanship*. "Oh,

Lou, my beautiful Lou. Are you still upset that Sacha broke up with you when you were thirteen?"

Hang on, here. Sacha and I do have a bit of history. We used to hold hands in kindergarten, and I was the first guy to French kiss her during that fateful night at Deborah Ramage's birthday party when we were, in fact:

"Twelve, not thirteen." I shoot him a resentful glare. "And we were never together!"

Tony stares at my scrunched-up face with laughing eyes. "You're so sensitive, Lou."

"Just get your facts right."

I'm so annoyed, I don't know why. Tony annoys me. His lollipop annoys me. Lucie's mousy backpack annoys me. The tweed on its back annoys me even more. And Sacha's request in unbelievably rude and entitled.

My stomach starts churning unpleasantly in a classic attempt by my anxiety to remind me it's still comfortably nestled in the depth of my brain, sipping tiny Margaritas from tiny cups with tiny umbrellas in it.

Lucie gives me a look, and I give her a look, and I can see from the way her face turns sour that she assumes I'm thinking of Sacha's lips, while in fact, I'm just wondering if she's packing Advil in that mouse of hers.

As a result, she's moody the whole rest of the day, but I don't really worry about it. I've got a lot on my mind today wondering especially what I'm going to tell Michael when I get my hands on him.

At the end of the day and with a good luck pat in the back and a wink from Tony, I set off a short way behind Michael, my pulse racing.

I have never stalked anyone before. I can see myself stalking Tony during the burgeoning first days of our friendship, but thankfully, I never had to. Surprisingly enough, Tony was as interested in me as I was in him. If anything, he's the one who followed me around and barged into my flat uninvited.

Anyway, the feeling's just awful. There's no way I'm not going to make a complete turnip out of myself. While sober, my comfort zone comprises less than a dozen people. Anything more and I start fanning myself like a character from a Jane Austen novel. I unwrap a stick of gum. Chewing usually helps to steel myself.

Ahead of me, Michael is on his way toward the Cardinal Lemoine metro station, unaware he's being watched by some maniac. My palms are sweaty, reminding me of the first time I invited Lucie to my place and I had to hide them in my pocket so she wouldn't think I had an awful skin condition. Picking up the pace, I push my sunglasses up my nose, this time not in the spirit of concealment but to look a little more intimidating.

Michael is a stroller. He walks like a wandering tourist on a slow August afternoon, stopping often, smiling at everything. Why should he be so happy? I bet you he's congratulating himself of not talking to me all week.

Thankfully I know exactly what to do to rip that smile off his face.

"Michael."

My throat is dryer than I thought and my voice comes out as a croak. Michael turns around. His expression betrays his surprise.

"Hey."

We both spoke at the same time. My pulse quickens as a blur of pedestrians hurtle by.

I can do this. I can persuade some guy to do something for me. I've done it before. I don't get why I should feel so breathless about it. It's just that, I didn't remember him being that tall. He's got a good ten centimetres on me. This alone should be forbidden.

Michaels seems tense, looks over his shoulder, doesn't meet my eyes. Perhaps he's afraid of me. Why should he be? I'm about as dangerous as a feather duster. Come on, you've rehearsed that, just say the line.

When I open my mouth, my gum inexplicably decides to take a plunge down my throat to choke me. I start coughing uncontrollably.

Two bright green eyes come into my blurry field of vision.

"Are you all right?"

The gum's gone, swallowed, destined to inflict god knows what damage to my internal organs. Michael is staring at me like I might drop dead in the middle of the street and he doesn't have time for that.

"I was saying…" Forcing a smile, I straighten up. "Do you live nearby?"

He does a strange thing. His eyes slowly dart left and right, like's he's pondering whether to bullshit me or not. That's right. As I stand right in front of him.

"Yes. Why? Do you?"

"I do. Near Place Monge."

"So do I."

"That's great!" That came out a little too loud. Better tone it down. He's going to think I'm a phony. "We can walk together then."

"Sure, whatever."

Michael pulls at the straps from his backpack, his lips pinched, and resumes his walk. I catch up with him in a few strides.

This is not going the way I wanted it to go. He's clearly not warming up to me. Perhaps I could talk about the book. After all, that's the one thing I know he likes.

"So, you know…"

He slips me a curious glance. I have to pick up the pace just to keep to a level with him.

"The book."

He doesn't say anything. All right, I will.

"I was thinking, since you know all about it…"

The corner of his mouth lifts into a half-smile. He slows down, then stops in the middle of the sidewalk.

"You know I don't even know your name, right?"

"What?" I say, stunned. "You don't?"

First of all, this demonstrates once and for all the conservative nature of our presence log, when teachers only use our surnames. Second, this means I've successfully evaded interrogations since the day we met, which is no small feat. Lastly, and I'm utterly bewildered about it, this means that however rude I was to Michael on his first day, he hasn't told anybody. Or François would have been delighted to tell him how much of a dick he thinks I am.

Nobody knows of my shame but he, Tony, Lucie, and myself. A wave of relief washes over me. I immediately extend my hand.

"I'm Louis. But everyone calls me Lou."

Michael takes my hand and gives it a vigorous shake. The intensity of his gaze forces my eyes down to our feet. My Vans are disgusting compared to his boots. I keep my eyes low as we set off again.

"Why does everyone call you Lou?" Michael asks, avoiding with grace the rush of men and women streaming out of the Cardinal Lemoine station.

I have to perform a ridiculous twirl to dodge a stout woman charging toward me.

"Tony says Louis reminds him of the Sun King, and he was a prat. Meanwhile, Lou Reed was a rockstar."

Tucking a strand of hair behind my ear, I wait for Michael to tell me how cool Tony is. He doesn't. Instead, he furrows his brow.

"Can I call you Louis, then?"

I'm that close to tell him he can call me Lucie if he promises to write this stupid essay with me. But I nod soberly instead.

"And you can call me Michael."

I cock my head. "I could call you Mike."

"I prefer Michael."

Have I vexed him again? I glance at him, alarmed. But his face is relaxed, turned up toward the inky sky.

We tread down the busy streets in silence for a while. The window displays, still packed with Christmas decorations, glitter merrily as though the holidays are just around the corner. They are, after all, but in the past. I wonder if Michael likes them. And I wonder... Where will I be next year when they are put up again?

Suddenly, Michael grabs my arm and brutally jerks me toward him. A cringeworthy squeal escapes my lips. When I whip around to ask him what his problem is, Michael, unperturbed, points at a dark shape on the ground. Confused at first, I finally see it. A dog poo the size of India, in which I almost buried my foot.

"You saved me..." I stare at him in awe.

"You should probably lose the sunglasses." He scratches the

back of his neck. "It's dark, I don't know how you can see anything at all."

I don't, I don't see anything. These glasses are not meant to see, but to be seen with. But he's right, so I remove them with fumbling fingers. My face instantly feels naked, vulnerable. Even more so when Michael looks right at it.

My mind races as I'm flicking through different appropriate subjects to engage in small talk. What do I know about him? British. Toilet. Curls. Lots of it. Mum. He said he's got one, right?

"So, ahem, you said you moved in with your mum, is that right?"

For the first time since I met him, a proper smile appears on his face revealing a row of perfect teeth. So much for British stereotypes.

"Yes, she's a theatre actress. She's starring in that new play over at the Paris Theatre."

"Theatre actress?"

He nods. I never thought one could actually live off that. That has to be more interesting than selling cleaning products. I start patting my jackets for my pack of cigarettes while searching for my next question. I offer the pack to Michael, but he shakes his head. As I light the cigarette, the next question comes quite naturally.

"Where do you normally live?"

"London." He tilts his head. "Kensington, to be precise. Do you know it?"

"No. I've never been to London." I'd like to tell him I'd love to go, but he will think I'm trying too hard. I have to tread carefully with him. "But I'd love to travel out of here one day. See the world, meet other people."

Michael stays silent for a while. He thinks I'm an idiot, doesn't he? I feel like an idiot. I was supposed to persuade him to do this essay, not bore him to death with details of my life.

"You know—"

"Anyway—"

Shit. We spoke at the same time again.

Michael holds out his hands. "Sorry, go ahead."

"No, you go ahead."

"No no, I insist."

"Anyway…" Why is this so difficult? My throat is turning to cement for no reason. "London has a great rock scene, and that's all that matters to me."

"Right!" He points his finger at me. "You're in a band, aren't you?"

Every time.

"No, I'm not."

"Oh, I thought you were."

A part of me is elated he thought so. The whole attire does give people this impression. But before I can auto-congratulate myself too much, we have arrived at Place Monge.

"I'm going this way," Michael says. "I'm on Pestalozzi."

"Nice, I'm on Larrey."

There's a silence. Michael does this thing again. Looking left, and right, then at me, like he's trying to make a decision. Then he blurts out:

"Why did you decide to talk to me?"

Huh, hello, what kind of question is that? What happened to the good old superficial small talk, heh? There are rules, Mister, rules to which we—

"So?"

And he insists.

My throat is suddenly in need of much clearing. "I saw you and I walk in the same direction, so…"

"So what? You seemed to want nothing to do with me the other day."

Right. He's into dropping bombs, then. I should have known that much. He's British, after all. Ok, fine, the truth then.

"We don't really have a choice now, do we? We have to work together, or Paquin will give us both a bad grade."

I realise now I've completely forgotten Tony's plan to ask him to write the essay on his own and slap my name on it. There's still time to ask, if he refuses me. I mean, to work with me.

Michael seems to think about it.

"Come on, it will be easy for you. You seem to know all about it. You had to read it at school in London, didn't you?"

Michael's eyebrows knit together. "I read it for pleasure. The first time, at least."

"For pleasure, really?"

I can't help laughing, but I swear, I didn't mean anything bad by it. He's so very touchy.

"You should try reading it, really," Michael says. "Not because some teacher you'll never remember asked you to. But because you want it. Didn't you say you wanted to see the world and meet other people? Reading a good book can do that for you."

My shoulder lifts in a half-shrug. "Tony says rockstars don't read books."

It's Michael's turn to snort in derisive laughter. "That's the stupidest thing I've ever heard. I bet you the best ones do."

It's my turn to feel offended. Michael thinks he's so much better than us, huh? Because he lives in Kensington, wherever that is, and reads books and has a mother who not only reads books, but learns them by heart.

And Tony and I, we're just dumb freaks in leather jackets. My eyes narrow, and my jaw wires shut in boiling resentment.

Michael looks confused and eager to go. "I have to go, but I'll see you around, then."

"And the essay?"

He nods. "Don't worry about the essay. I know we have to do it together." With a little wave, he carries on down the street, and I take a left.

So, he knew we had to work together, and he knew he would have to do his part. Took his sweet time to get in touch with me about it, though. And by the way, I did all the work. I came to him, stalked him in the dark and made small talk, and all he did was nothing. It's like he was waiting for me to come after him, you know.

Weirdo.

Well, in any case, mission accomplished. We'll do the essay together and he'll use his big smarty brain and... And it will be a success. No biggie.

Then why am I so emotional? So what if he hurt my pride a little? I did the same to him when I called him a nerd, and he seems to have gotten over it.

Perhaps he's just a better guy than I am. That wouldn't be too difficult.

Or perhaps I want to prove him wrong. Perhaps I want to show him what I've got. If he thinks I can't read, then he's in for a surprise. I've read books before, I'm not a complete idiot.

The first thing I do ten minutes later when I launch myself on top of my bed is to retrieve Dorian Gray from my backpack.

The bloke on the cover and I exchange a stern look. Then, after drawing a long, steeling breath, I open the book on the first page.

6

I'M TRYING OUT NEW THINGS

Well-rested after seven hours of uninterrupted sleep and the powerful knowledge of having surpassed myself, it's in high spirits that I wake up the next morning next to Dorian Gray still open to the last page read.

My father's eyes widen in shock when he sees me slink out of my bedroom an hour earlier than usual. He probably thinks his little speech is the reason for my early rising, but he's wrong.

It's not his anger, but mine, that got me up so early. I'm going to show Michael how wrong he is about me and that I'm not just really handsome, but also super smart.

OK, fine, that might be a bit much. But my mind's made up. I'm determined to innocently stumble upon him on the way to school to tell him I've read a quarter of the book by myself and without a glance at the pictures. Not that I want to impress him. Just to show him I'm not the idiot he thinks I am.

"Are you ok this morning?" My dad asks when I sit at the kitchen table. He pours me a healthy dose of black coffee. "You look feverish."

"I'm fine. There are just many, many things to do. Busy year. Lots of work to be done."

If I leave now, I'll probably catch Michael. He looks like the type of bloke who's early for about anything with spare time to read the paper before leaving the house like some sort of 1950s nuclear-family-super-dad.

My dad watches me devour a piece of toast and take a large swig of steaming coffee. It's like lava. I'm pretty sure it will melt my organs on the way down.

"What news about your essay?" he asks.

I get up, eyes streaming. My backpack and sunglasses are waiting for me under the coat rack.

"I'm working on it tonight." Probably. "Might be late."

My burnt tongue is still prickling when I shut the door behind me.

It's with a good song on my lips that I careen down the stairs, backpack swaying on my shoulder, until a vision of horror stops me in my tracks.

The old lady from the second floor is there. Clad in black slacks and the pinkest blouse, arms folded over her chest, she's staring right at me.

"Good morning, young man."

We gaze at each other through squinted eyes, sizing each other up.

Oh, I knew. My time was bound to come one day. Like the brave young men of her generation who evaded the war long enough and eventually were called to the front. I had been too good at dodging her, and part of her always wanted to get me for it.

Bad news for her, people don't go to war anymore, they go to school, and she doesn't have to know how early I am.

Ostensibly checking my phone for the time, I mutter *good morning* back.

She studies me through her sharp brown eyes, her bob of white hair perfectly framing her wrinkled face.

"You look like you certainly have the time to help an old lady."

Do I? Do I? Really? That's funny. Was I not literally running down the stairs? Emphasis on RUNNING?

But she's so tiny and wrinkly… What would happen if I refused her? I don't know what she needs help with. Heartbroken at my refusal, she might attempt the job herself. Then she'd break her hip, and I'd never forgive myself.

Throwing a longing look down the stairs, I advance toward her. "What do you need?"

Her eyes light up. "It's nothing. I just need you to take a box out of my closet. It's too heavy, I can't lift it by myself. But for someone like you, it won't take a minute."

Dragging my feet, I follow her into her flat and in through a dark, narrow corridor. She practically hisses at me when I bump into one of the million and a half picture frames she's got hanging on each wall.

I was half expecting the old lady's home to smell musty, like old people, or worse, like cat pee, but it smells just fine. She probably doesn't even own a cat. I only wish she'd walk faster. I've got things to do, curly haired people to talk to. She probably cannot comprehend it at her advanced age, but I've got a life.

At the end of the corridor, the door to her living room is ajar. I catch a glimpse of a cosy looking rug and a squashy-looking sofa and piles and piles of bits of paper littering the handsome carved coffee table. But we're not going in there. Old Lady turns left into another, shorter corridor and pushes open the door to a medium-sized bedroom. The heavy velvet curtains are drawn, conferring the room a gloomy feeling.

I stroll in, both hands on my hips. "Jesus… Did somebody die in here?"

She gives a dry chuckle. "You could say that."

All right, I see, she's pulling my leg. Or the box she wants me to lift contains somebody's decaying body. Above the bed, an old clock informs me that I've already wasted too much time. Michael might have already left. Who knows when I'll have another opportunity to shove my achievement down his throat. The impatient click of my tongue earns me a disapproving glare.

Old Lady points at the massive wardrobe on my right. "The box is in there. Top shelf. You can't miss it."

I shuffle hesitantly to the imposing wardrobe, put my hand on the handle, turn around. God knows what's in there. What if I come face to face with some… old lady things?

She waves for me to get on with it. "Go ahead, it's not going to bite. But don't drop it, or I'll skin you alive."

Ok, I see. You're a funny one.

"Can I at least have some light or something?"

"No."

My grimace makes her scoff. "Don't look so miserable."

"I'm not miserable. I'm just... busy." I remove my sunglasses and hand them over to her. "Here, hold this."

Old Lady takes them with an amused look.

"Busy or not, you're young, you're supposed to have a good time."

Rich. I was having a great time before she forced me into unpaid child labour.

"Look, if you don't mind..."

My phone starts vibrating in my pocket. I ignore it and pull the handle. The door creaks open.

Thank goodness, no threatening old lady things, but coats and things like that. But despite standing on my toes, I can still barely reach the top shelf. I start feeling around for the box with my fingertips, while she watches me, her eyes twinkling. She's having fun, watching me poke around her wardrobe in the dark.

"I have to go to school, you know," I say, mildly offended. "What about my bright future?"

She lets out a stifled laugh. "Is it school that makes you so miserable?"

Inside my pocket, my phone won't stop vibrating, adding to my irritability.

"I am not miserable!" I throw her a nasty glare over my shoulder. "I can't feel it. Where is it?"

"Perhaps a little deeper."

"Look, I don't know how tall you thought I was, but it's not — oh." At last, I can feel the edge of a cardboard box deep into the wardrobe. "Okay, I almost got it. Where do you want it, by the way?"

"What? You're mumbling. I can't hear you."

"Where do you want it?"

Her white head appears next to me. "Leave it on the bed. If you ever manage to get it out, I mean."

For fuck's sake. Grasping the box as firmly as my extended fingers allow it, I give it a good pull. It's heavier than I thought. What does she have in there? Gold bars? Who knows. Maybe she used to work for a cartel or something. Am I to become an accomplice? Perhaps she'll give me a bar as a thank you.

The box is stuck. Straining under the effort, I pull and twist and pull some more, until it suddenly breaks free, sending us both, the box and I, flying backwards. The old lady lurches forward, seizes the collar of my leather jacket and twirls me around. Before I know it, I'm falling back into her open wardrobe. One of the gold bars jumps out of the box and lands heavily on top of my head. Mercifully, her pile of fluffy coats stops my fall.

The old lady laughs at the curse that escapes my lips.

"Careful, you wouldn't want to get stuck in there." She helps me up and out of the wardrobe.

I look down at the thing that struck me. It wasn't a gold bar. It was an old metal box, but it felt just the same.

"This thing almost gave me brain damage. My father would have sued you."

She waves her hand dismissively. "I'm not afraid of your father."

Well, can't exactly blame her for that.

And all the while, I haven't dropped her stupid cardboard box, and my phone is still vibrating in my pocket. It stops just as I drop the blasting thing on the bedspread. Then I take notice of the clock above the bed. If that's the time, I'm officially late now.

Thanks, thanks a lot, old lady.

Wiping my brow with one hand, I take my phone out of my pocket with the other. The harassment was from Lucie. She wants to know what to do this weekend. Why? Why? I'm about to see her in about ten minutes.

"All right," I say, turning on my heel to face my tormentor. "All done."

She's gone.

What if she's looking for other chores for me to do? Hell, no. I need to get out of here, now.

Retracing my steps quickly through the corridor, my hand is already on the front door when she calls out.

"Wait. I've got something for you."

My fingers freeze around the handle. That's actually really nice. I wait in silence as she ambles toward me.

"Thank you for your help," Old Lady says. She presses something into my hand. It's round and heavy, so fat chance for a twenty euros note. I stare down in disbelief: it's a bottle of shampoo. "It looks like you really need it, dear."

"Are you for real?"

I almost broke my neck retrieving her gold, and she insults my lifestyle?

"Don't forget these either."

My sunglasses are dangling from her tiny fist. Snatching them, and not without one last glare, I leave her chuckling in the middle of the corridor, not bothering to shut the door behind me.

On second look, I can at least appreciate that her shampoo looks high-end, Champs-Elysées super-shampoo sort of stuff. With a groan, I stick it in my backpack.

Once outside, a feeling of disappointment settles on my shoulders. I'm late again. Way too late to meet Michael anyway. My plan to impress him, I mean to show him I'm just as capable as he is, has turned against me.

But to my surprise, just as I reach Place Monge, Michael is right on the opposite sidewalk, walking at his own pace, not a care in the world.

I double-check through squinted eyes. Is it him? I recognise his set of long legs, long coat, and dark curls. It really is Michael, on his way to school.

LATE.

Haha! Who's the loser now, right?

I start lumbering toward him, clutching my baggy pants as I go.

Michael doesn't seem to know he's late. He's looking up at the sky, a contented look on his face. The clouds part at this exact moment, bathing his face in bright sunlight. I slow down and call his name. He turns around, his eyes scanning the street.

An obscure, deep-seated and foreign part of me flutters to life. From it, a shy question arises, confusing me.

Will he be happy to see me?

But his face only tenses when he recognises me.

I reach him, panting. "I'm late."

With a dubitative frown, he looks down to check his watch. "I'm not, though."

"What?"

I pull out my phone once again to check the time. It's fifteen minutes earlier than I thought. Damn this old lady! Her clock must have been defective. But it's not completely her fault. It was probably as ancient as its owner. That must be it.

"We're not late." Michael looks at me with concern. "You don't have to worry."

"I'm not worried."

His mouth twitches, then he bites his lower lip as though to stifle a laugh. I forget what I wanted to say. It was probably not important.

We start walking in silence again. It makes me feel self-conscious. I don't like it.

"I only thought I was late because I was helping my neighbour with something and…" I hesitate to tell him the whole experience. Normally I would tell Tony first thing, but I don't want Michael to think I'm an idiot. "She's an old lady, so it took a while."

Michael stares at me with surprise. "You were helping an old lady? That's so nice."

"Oh, it's nothing you know. I do it all the time." I hide my face behind my scarf, ashamed of my blatant lie. "Anyway, that's the only reason why I'm late."

"I usually leave earlier as well," Michael says, "but I got distracted this morning."

"Why, what happened?"

"Nothing as nice as helping my neighbour, I'm afraid. I was just talking to my mum, and I lost track of time."

The massive snort that comes out of me probably won't do me any favours. But I couldn't resist.

"Did I say something funny?"

"You lost track of time while talking to your mum?"

"Sure." He seems half-amused, half-exasperated by my astonish-ment. "I love talking to my mother. She's brilliant."

Now we both stare at each other in disbelief. I cannot compre-hend that anyone would want to spend time with their parents. He probably doesn't get what sort of animal wouldn't want to.

"You don't talk to your mum?" he asks, frowning.

"Not really, no."

And it's better this way.

"Then I'm sorry for you."

"Don't be," I say, shrugging. "Not every family's the same, that's all."

"I guess not." I can feel his eyes on me for a brief moment.

The silence between us growing oddly thick once again, I decide to get straight to the point.

"Should we meet tonight, work on the essay then?"

"Oh, about that." He offers me an apologetic smile. "I forgot to tell you, I don't have the book, I left it at home. I mean, in London."

"Right."

"I need to buy a new one, but I haven't had time yet. So, before we start…"

"I know where you can get one," I say quickly. "I'll take you after class if you want."

Look at me, helping a mate out. Shopping for books. It really is a new year.

"Sure, great!" Michael seems very enthusiastic about it and even picks up the pace. "Let's meet at the school gate after class then?"

"No!" I have just realised something. "It's better if we meet at Place Monge. But believe me," I add, when he begins to frown again, "this place will blow your mind. It's the best bookstore in Paris."

I'm half-expecting him to say he's surprised I know of one book-store in Paris. I'm waiting. He's going to say it.

But no. He says nothing.

When our eyes meet again, his expression is perfectly relaxed. But before I can return his smile, I hear Lucie's voice calling me. I look around and am shocked to see her and Tony waving at me. Are we already at the school gate?

We walk over to them. Tony, looking bored, tosses his cigarette in my direction but it lands right between Michael's feet.

"Funny!" My voice sounds a little squeaky. "We ran into each other on the way."

Michael politely salutes them, but immediately leaves us to join Yasmine, Sacha — who looks completely flustered when he kisses her cheek — and François, who's glaring at me for no good reason.

"So," Tony says, as Lucie grabs my face and crushes my lips against hers, "what happened last night?"

I wipe my mouth across my sleeve. "What? What do you mean?"

"Did you get him to do the essay for you?"

"Close enough. I'm gonna work on it too. Tonight. But—"

"We were supposed to meet tonight. Play CS together."

I had totally forgotten.

"Look, I've got to do this thing, or my dad will ground me until the end of the exams."

Tony turns to Lucie, who's fixing her lipstick. "I'll hang out with you instead, then." She nods and smacks her lips.

I toss an inconspicuous look over my shoulder. Michael is laughing at whatever Sacha's is blabbing about. She expertly shakes her mane of light, shiny brown hair.

I wonder if an old lady has ever offered her shampoo.

7

WHAT DO DORIAN, SHAKESPEARE AND FRANÇOIS HAVE IN COMMON?

Tucked away near Notre-Dame, The Shakespeare and Co is for avid book readers almost as famous as the cathedral. Michael's joy is already palpable when he first spots the green facade, and I get to feel a little proud of myself. Not that I particularly care about Michael's opinion, but I want him to know I am perfectly able to find the coolest places in the capital.

Casually twirling my sunglasses between my fingers under the awning, I watch him pick up volumes from the heavy wooden crates with sparkling eyes. To top it all, the sun's still out, bathing everything and everyone with its warmth.

"This is fantastic," Michael says, caressing the spine of a musty travel guide.

I can't help but laugh. I've never met anyone who enjoys anything the way he enjoys seeing books.

"Wait until you go inside."

I thought this day would never end. Three hours of maths this afternoon did nothing to help pass the time. It's not because I'm naturally good at something that I particularly enjoy it. There was little else in my head than meeting Michael after class. But it's only because I was nervous to get away from Tony and Lucie before they insisted to accompany us here. Having Tony in a bookstore is a synonym for disaster. Every title would mean something funny or dirty to him. Then Michael could congratulate himself thinking we're cavemen, and I can't allow it.

Once inside, and despite the swarm of tourists and locals haunting the tight spaces, Michael's enthusiasm grows.

"This place looks straight from Harry Potter."

With its crooked shelves and narrow aisles, its quirky decor and tiny reading nooks, the bookstore does have a magical aura and could perfectly have been found in Diagon Alley.

"Harry Potter, huh?"

I have read that one. Who's illiterate now? And I enjoyed it too, not that anyone knows about it.

"So..." I say, running my fingers along a set of nameless spines. "How do you like Paris so far?"

Nice. Interested without being inquisitive. I should become a detective.

The corner of Michael's mouth curls up. "I've been here before, on holidays, but it's not the same."

Noncommittal answer. Perhaps he doesn't want me to get to know him. I earned this by insulting him on the first day. But all this aura of mystery only makes me want to prod until I get to the bottom of it.

A book catches his attention; he flicks it open and grows quiet. Meanwhile, I'm constantly asked to move aside by impatient customers who are, for some mysterious reason, all interested in the Greek Mythology section behind me. When I finally get some peace, I try another angle.

"I see you've made friends already."

Michael's green eyes appear from the top of the book, an eyebrow quirked.

"Hm?"

"You've got friends already. Like Sacha."

"Yes." Sacha's name brings a smile to his face. "They're nice."

I'm getting a little warm in here. Not big on tight places. I start fanning myself with a battered copy of Bel-Ami tossed on top of an overflowing crate.

"Excuse me."

Another patron makes heavy eye contact with me. I edge closer to Michael.

"Sacha seems to like you a lot."

Michael puts the book down. "Does she?"

Men. All the same. Am I right?

"Yeah, that's obvious."

"That's nice to hear."

Is that it? He's good at keeping his true feelings out of sight, I'll grant him that. A group of giggling teenagers too large for the narrow space forces its way with substantial use of their elbows and shoulders. Michael and I find ourselves slammed against best-selling fantasy.

"It's getting tight in here."

He doesn't answer, turns around at the first opportunity, leaving me gasping for air.

"You don't like to talk, do you?" I ask, chasing after him.

Michael shrugs. "I like to talk. I just don't have anyone to talk to."

Another bombshell. If he's looking for a career, may I suggest the Royal Air Force?

I guess I had it coming; I asked. But who tells the truth without so much as a warning? I would never bare myself like this, confess that I have no friends. His neutral expression suggests he's not doing it to get sympathy.

I know a little about loneliness, and I don't wish it on anyone. If Michael wanted to talk to me, I think I'd let him.

"You can talk to me, if you like."

My tone was the perfect balance of kindness and camaraderie. Nothing improper. By the look Michael throws me over his shoulder, he's understood my meaning.

"Thanks, Louis."

A faint thump catches my attention. I've dropped my sunglasses. I retrieve them and put them back on. When I rise, I'm alone in the chattering crowd. When I find Michael again after two wrong turns in this labyrinth, he's laughing quietly in sheer, childish joy, drumming his fingers along the cover of an old book. He's definitely strange, there's no other way to put it. But I don't really mind that much. He's kind of easy to be around, at least.

We begin to explore the shop in a way I have never bothered to before. Michael points to me his favourite novels as he sees them. Sometimes he stops, eyes glinting, in front of a rare edition of a volume he loves. His father, he tells me, teaches philosophy at a London College.

"Books are practically my best friends," he says, with an affectionate sigh at the sight of the first French edition of Pride and Prejudice.

He looks at me, cheeks pink, as though he just confessed being into hardcore porn or something. I pretend I'm looking elsewhere.

"I know Jane Austen." I make a show of being absorbed by the letters on the cover of the manuscript "My mum used to watch period dramas on TV, and I watched with her."

"Did you?"

I can tell Michael's amused, but there's no mockery in his face.

He leans in and lowers his voice. "I still watch them, you know." He waggles his eyebrows.

I can't help laughing. That says a lot about him, Tony would say. But Tony's not here. And that's fine.

We move on to another shelf, then, another. After a while, it occurs to me that I'm having fun. It's strange, I didn't expect any of it to happen, even less with a guy like him.

Some classics I recognise and let him know all about it. It seems that Michael knows every book and every movie adaptation of it. Every time we pass a volume he loves, his eyes catch fire. He's not an ugly guy, I can concede that. Nothing wrong about admitting it.

"I've never met anyone who knows so much about books."

Michael seems embarrassed. "Well, I don't have many things to do, I guess, so books are my thing."

What is my thing? Video games and weed? Kaiser Chiefs? Lucie? His passions are just as good as mine, if not better. I feel sorry I made fun of him now, but I don't know how to say it.

"You know… I could use picking up a book once in a while."

Did he get my meaning? Can he hear how sorry I am? I don't know. He turns his face away.

"And I could use a night out once in a while, you know."

Perhaps he did get it, then.

"I can help you with that."

Crap. I spoke a little too fast. Michael, hanging out with Tony and Lucie and I? Neither Tony nor Michael would ever forgive me. A familiar heat warms my cheeks. Michael acts like he hasn't noticed and plunges deeper into the aisle.

We carry on walking from shelf to shelf for several more minutes in silence, then Michael stops in an unusually quiet, cosy-looking nook to admire a collection of Shakespeare's sonnets. I slump against the shelf next to him. This is the sort of place where sneaky lovers steal a kiss beneath the beams. Michael idly turns the pages of his new find while I pretend to read the titles on the nearest volumes.

He breaks the silence first. "What's the story behind the sunglasses?"

"The story?"

"They never leave you. Even when it's dark," he adds, his tone teasing.

I remove them to better admire them and realise I'm still holding Bel-Ami. "They're important to me. They were a gift."

"Who gifted them to you? Your girlfriend?"

I laugh quietly. "Lucie wouldn't know which model to pick from. She'd get me really crazy or girly ones, you know." Michael doesn't answer, turns around to peruse more books on the shelves. "Tony bought them for me. He found them at a flea market. Why? Do they bother you?"

"I never said that." A moment of silence while he scratches the back of his neck. "Tony is your friend, right? With the dark hair?"

"Yes."

I'm surprised he doesn't remember Tony. Everyone does. Tony leaves a strong impression, whether you like him or not. Usually the latter.

"You know, I think we're in the right spot." I say, with a nod toward the crooked "English Classics" sign above Michael's head.

"How did you meet Tony, exactly?"

"Oh! This is a great story, actually."

I'm glad he asked. I enjoy talking about Tony. I think it's the perfect opportunity, now that Michael is browsing the shelves, looking for his Dorian Gray.

"I'm all ears," he says.

"Well…" I take a seat on the bench behind him. "It was when we started at Colette. History teacher organised a school trip. A visit of the Louvres. I had decided to show up late, almost at the end—so I wouldn't die of boredom. The teacher was confused, because he could swear I wasn't here when the group started the visit, and he wanted to tell my father about it."

Michael turns around to flash me a smile. "You don't like to play by the rules, don't you?"

That's right! My face grows hotter.

"You could say that. Anyway, I told the teacher I was here all along, he simply didn't notice me. Tony appeared out of nowhere, covered for me. He was really impressed by my lie."

Michael nods thoughtfully. "Great story indeed…"

I think he's making fun of me. He is, isn't he?

"But that's too bad you didn't get to see the Louvres," he adds. "It's the first thing I did when I arrived."

I shrug. "Tony says rockstars don't go to museums."

Michael slips me a curious glance.

"Do you want to be a rockstar?"

"What do you mean?"

"Do you want to be in a band, be a singer or a musician, play rock music and go on tours? That's what I mean."

I wave my hand dismissively. "Our thing is more of an attitude, really. You don't have to sing to be a rockstar, we don't think. It's a whole philosophy. About, you know, being different, being… free."

Michael turns to me, smiling. "Live. Live the wonderful life that is in you. Let nothing be lost upon you. Be always searching for new sensations. Be afraid of nothing."

Why does this sound familiar and churns the gears of my stomach?

"It's from Dorian Gray," Michael says.

"Oh, right."

"Not far removed from your own philosophies, is it?"

Yes, sure. I'm baffled that he should pay so much attention to my stupid philosophy. He stares at me, expecting me to say something else, but I don't feel like going into the details, especially without Tony around. He's better at explaining it than I am. I feel I would just make a fool of myself.

"My cousins are in a band," Michael says at last. "They're not half-bad. I think they could make it big one day."

What is that supposed to mean? That I won't make it big? Or just simply that he likes artists?

"Oh, got you!" He whips around, brandishing *The Picture of Dorian Gray*.

I get up. He closes the distance between us in two strides.

"This place is wonderful. Magical," he whispers, eyes glinting. "It brings all sorts of wild ideas to my head."

He opens the book and starts reading a passage at random, seemingly unaware that we're going to have to go through this crap many times as we work on the essay. His bent head, so close to my own, gives me a perfect view of his dark curls.

I wonder what they feel like.

The flashing thought rips through me, thunder-like. Then it's gone.

"Don't you think it's stifling in here?" Raising Bel-Ami between us, I begin to fan myself. The man's face on the cover stares at me with disapproval.

"Are you going to buy this?" Michael asks.

It's at this exact moment, and in this relatively awkward position, that golden child François glides out of nowhere, all pastel jumpers and toothy smiles.

"Hello, there!"

I had not missed his horrible French accent.

François approaches, carrying his coat on his arm. There's not a drop of sweat to him.

Now sweating buckets and staring at his overjoyed goat-like face with a clenched jaw, I realise I never knew how much I disliked François until now.

"François!" Michael shakes his hand with a look of delighted surprise, the kind of expression you reserve for people you haven't seen in a long time and you really, really didn't expect to meet at a bookstore, you know, not for fucking François whom he heard butcher Spanish not an hour ago. "What are you doing here?"

François attempts a casual shrug. "Just hanging out. I love books, you know."

"I love books too," Michael says.

Oh, come on. What the hell is this? It's obvious what he's doing here. He's stalking Michael. He's a stalker. I'm seething.

"I know, it's crazy, right?" François throws his head back and laughs.

This is stupid.

"And what are you doing here?" He asks in the tremulous voice of the unskilled liar.

That means he knew exactly where Michael would be at this hour.

"Haven't I told you this morning?" Michael asks, frowning.

"Must have told someone else…" François's face grows as red as shame itself.

"I thought I told you. Louis says he was taking me to the book-store to get a copy of Dorian Gray."

François peers at me through squinted eyes. "Oh, Louis! I couldn't see you in there, with all these books. I hope you're not feeling too much like — how do you say — a fish out of water."

He pretends he's happy to see me through a great deal of teeth-flashing. All that comes out of my mouth is a grunt. Michael is standing between us, a slightly frozen smile on his face as though the meeting of his two best friends is, despite his deepest wishes, not going as well as he hoped.

François reaches for the books in his hand.

"What do we have here… Oscar Wilde and William Shake-speare! I know them."

He butchered both of their names with his impossible accent, but I guess it's not totally his fault. He's lucky Tony isn't here, that's all. The implication that he knows them, however, is unacceptable. I'm by far the laziest student in my class and even I know who these two authors are.

Michael attempts to take his books back, but François clutches them to his chest.

"I love Shakespeare's sonnets!" he cries. "Did you know Shakespeare was gay?"

I snort loudly enough for an old patron to glare at me in outrage.

"Nonsense."

"He was."

"Wasn't."

"Why not!" François angrily stomps his foot.

Michael's eyes dart from François to me, wide and afraid.

"Well," I say, "he was married, for one…"

"That doesn't mean anything," Michael says. "Lots of gay men were married."

"Have you even read his sonnets?" François says, blinking fast.

"Do I look like a guy who reads medieval poetry?"

Michael looks away.

"He wrote poems to the man he loved. It's all in here." François waves the book in front of my face. I use my Bel-Ami to ward him off.

"They were probably just friends."

Michael gives a little laugh. "Do you write poems to Tony?"

"What? No. No!" I ball my fists when François slaps a hand over his mouth. "No one writes poems nowadays. People are lucky enough to receive a text."

François, smirking, turns to Michael.

"Anyway, Shakespeare might not have been gay, but I am."

Gripping Michael's arm with claw-like fingers, he erupts in laughter as I watch, stunned. Michael joins in mildly, as though François's revelation is yesterday's news.

But is it?

François is gay. Why does this surprise me? And yet I feel like I was supposed to know. Staring at François's laughing face, I try to imagine a François who would be gay, and one who wouldn't be. But all I can see is François's stupid face, the way his fingers curl around Michael's arm.

"I'm gonna wait for you outside. I can't breathe in here."

I don't wait for their reaction. With little regard for other shoppers, my blood pounding in my ears, I retrace my steps toward the exit.

Outside, a breeze of cold air soothes my burning face. I dig up a cigarette, light up, take a long drag. What happened in there? They're going to think I'm some sort of homophobe. I cannot explain, even to myself. I'm the same way with people who act all cheesy when they're in love. It annoys me to no end.

François has no class, no shame. To scream things like this from the rooftops. It's vulgar, even. Whatever he does shouldn't be any of our business, should it?

None of our business.

Why is he here anyway? He was definitely following us. "I love books" my ass. No. He had a motive in coming here, and... and...

And it just dawns on me how thick I can be sometimes.

If he's after Michael, does it mean that...

Is it possible that...

Is Michael gay too?

8

WHAT'S YOUR NUMBER?

We walk the way back in silence. Hidden behind my shades, sneaking side glances at the quiet Michael next to me, I can't help thinking about gay François. I picture them both tucked away in the reading nook at the Shakespeare, having it out. It sure churns my stomach to imagine them together.

I might be a homophobe. Damn it. There's already so much wrong about me, now I'm a homophobe? Life's not fair, really.

François is gay. That, in itself, doesn't exactly come as a surprise. The fact that he's stalking Michael doesn't come as a surprise either. It's not like the guy's ugly. Even as I speak, sunlight bounces off his curls in an attractive way.

Now, the important question is: Is Michael gay?

If he is, is he interested in François?

But why should I care? I'm being ridiculous.

Or am I?

After all, the first time I saw Michael, wasn't he looking at me strangely? And in a public toilet!

I'm the one who took him to the best bookstore in Paris, by the way. And honestly, am I not better looking? Not that I would… But if Michael is gay, shouldn't he be attracted to me?

That's it, I'm officially losing my mind. All because of François. I never thought I'd live the day.

Rewinding to the last words we shared outside the Shakespeare, I start over-analysing everything. How they got out of the shop, laughing at some secret joke, and the way François kept leaning toward Michael conspiratorially.

"Didn't buy anything, François?" I took an enormous drag of my cigarette.

"Not today." He was smirking. "I come here all the time, though. The staff knows me."

I said nothing, but my leg started twitching. So what if no one knows me? Michael doesn't need any help to pick up a book, he's not mentally disabled as far as I know!

François rearranged his perfect strands while staring at my limp mop of hair, then point-blank asked Michael out, wanting to know if we would go to the cinema and watch a movie with him. "We," he said, staring pointedly at Michael.

"We have to work on this Dorian Gray thing," Michael said.

François made a face. "You can do it later. There's time."

Rich, coming from the teacher's pet who never fails to submit all of his work in advance. I shoved two sticks of gum into my mouth to keep myself quiet.

"I'd rather be done with it," Michael said.

Yes, he said that. I started fuming. Why not go around town wearing a sign saying 'I was forced to work with this idiot, please send help' while you're at it? And all the while I thought he started to like me.

François gave us a fake smile, frozen at the edges, and said his goodbyes. Michael and I have walked in silence since, occasionally exchanging looks, but for once I'm happy no one's trying to break the silence.

When we reach Place Monge, Michael stops.

"Where do you want to go?"

That's a valid question.

Not that I'm trying to impress this guy, but considering the state of my bedroom, or the fact that my father barely categories as a life form, I'd rather keep my home life a very well-guarded secret.

Besides, going to Michael's seems like the perfect plan. If his bedroom walls are covered with posters of men, then I'll know he's gay, and I can move on.

"Can we go to your place? Mine is a proper mess."

Michael leads the way, smiling. "If you're lucky, you might even meet my mum."

Ok, gay or not, it's definitely a weird thing to say.

Michael's flat looks like a model home, like it was decorated only to take pictures for a magazine, and it wasn't really made to live in. Perhaps it's because they just moved in and their stuff isn't there yet. Or perhaps they're renting it as such.

Save a few plants and generic books with nice pictures of boats on it, most shelves are bare. Everything's maddeningly neat, and the cream linen sofa looks so perfect that I would never dare sit my ass on it.

The exception is the kitchen, where the breakfast table is still set, with half-empty plates and crumbs and pieces of fruit scattered everywhere. I can't help staring at every item, every shape and texture, something that would scream 'I'm gay!' or 'my son likes dicks and I'm totally okay with it', that sort of thing.

Do I feel dirty and borderline homophobic doing that? Yes, you bet I am. I could just turn around and ask Michael if he's gay, after all. But then he might get the wrong idea. Like I fancy him, and all. I just feel I should know if he is, since we're doing the essay together. I wouldn't want him to get his hopes up.

As I'm browsing for clues through what I hope are discreet glances, I eventually take notice of a woman with a heart-shaped face standing in front of the sink and staring right at me.

Gulping, I straighten myself up as Michael runs to her and hugs her in the middle of the kitchen. I turn my gaze away until they're done patting each other's backs.

"Mum," Michael says, as the woman looks at me from head to toes. "This is Louis. I told you I had to do this essay on Dorian Gray, didn't I?"

Michael's mum is definitely an old woman, perhaps even in her early fifties, but she has a handsome face. Behind her black glasses shine a pair of very bright green eyes. Her dark hair is cut short, in a boyish way, but one thing is certain: she doesn't have Michael's curls.

Is his father home too? I begin craning my neck to look around the flat, just in case Michael's father is hiding, curls and all, behind the sofa.

Michael's mother introduces herself as Anne and extends a hand. I remove my sunglasses and shake it gingerly, hoping my face isn't as red as it feels, or my hair as dirty.

"Nice to meet you, Madame."

"You can call me Anne."

"He's French," Michael says, inexplicably.

Mrs Anne laughs at his comment. "Indeed he is."

What is that supposed to mean? Do I have a French face? François has a French face. I don't want to look like François. But I don't ask out loud, so she walks over to the kitchen table and shoves a handful of half-walnuts into her mouth.

"Dorian Gray, you said?" She speaks with her mouth full. "Interesting stuff. *The only way to get rid of a temptation is to yield to it.*"

Michael scratches his chin. "The teacher assigned us do it together."

Here we go again. You know, blaring from every rooftop that you were forced into this is not going to improve our chance to work together, but go ahead. Say it! I'm not your type, obviously.

Anne hasn't taken her eyes off me. It's the hair, isn't it? Fourth time's the charm, I do promise myself to take better care of it.

"Would you boys like something to drink?"

Michael turns to me, I nod and shrug at the same time, noncommittal.

Anne cocks her head. "Tell me Louis, are you a coffee person or a tea person?"

"Coffee, obviously." I hesitate. "Tea's for British people, isn't it?"

My answer, though delivered politely, only serves to make her laugh. With a pointed look at his mum, Michael waves at me to follow him.

"We're going to my room."

Michael's room is located at the end of a long and squeaky corridor. His bedroom is also bare. A queen-size bed with navy blue sheets and neutral pillows sits in the corner of the room, close to an oak desk. A matching wardrobe stands on the opposite wall.

It's too neat to be real. The only thing on the wall, above the desk, is a poster about a Chopin concerto occurring next month at Opera de Paris. Unless he's sexually obsessed with Chopin, or pianos, I still have no clue as to where Michael stands on the spectrum.

He shuffles his feet, an apologetic look on his face.

"We've just moved in. It doesn't look like home yet."

Thankfully, he has no clue as to what I'm thinking. Nothing in this room could tell me anything about himself, let alone how gay he might be. It's the plainest most boring teenager room I have ever seen. No way this guy is gay. Not that I was expecting glitter bombs and butt plugs, but shit, come on, a minimum of effort would have been nice.

Where's the life? What are you hiding? Who are you, Michael? What's your favourite colour, the name of your first pet, your worst memory? When did it all go wrong?

"We only took two suitcases each," Michael says. "We didn't really plan beyond that."

He's frowning at me. I frown back. What does he expect me to say?

"It's, ahem… It's great that you can pack so efficiently."

"Hm… Thanks."

Still frowning, Michael offers me to seat on his bed, by his desk. The only thing on there is a laptop.

I wonder if he has Facebook. His profile would surely show pictures of girls, or boys. But he would need to add me first. There's no guarantee he will. He has not, after all, offered me his phone number either.

If he is gay, he isn't into me. A small part of me finds this unacceptable.

Mrs Anne knocks on the door and enters, carrying a tray of coffee and biscuits. She puts it down and hovers by the desk, a bright smile on her face.

"Good luck, boys."

She's not showing any sign of leaving. Michael notices too.

"Thanks, mum. We'll see you later."

"Right. Just let me know if you need anything."

"Will do."

I pop my gum just loudly enough to make her jump.

"Are you staying for dinner?"

I can't help snorting a little. Just a little. A little snort. "No, I'm good thanks."

Michael looks embarrassed for the first time. Watching his face flush is sort of exhilarating. I don't know why I was thinking he thought he was better than me, or Tony. He's probably just as screwed up as the rest of us. He's just better at hiding it.

Mrs Anne closes the door behind her, all smiles.

Michael hands me a mug of coffee. "I'm so sorry, she just likes to… hang out, you know."

"That's all right." I point to the poster of Chopin above his bed. "You do like music after all."

He gives the poster an anxious glance. "You can understand why I'm not advertising this."

"Are you worried about what people say? Worried they'd take the piss?"

"They do. You did." He rubs his palms against his thighs.

"Did I?" I pretend to inspect my nails.

"You called me a total nerd. You said you would never stoop so low as to hang out with me."

Our eyes meet. I start blowing on my coffee, fast. "I wasn't sure you'd picked up on that."

"Look, I get it, okay? I'm boring. I'm not into whatever it is that you like. I care more about books and movies than parties and girls."

Girls? Did he say girls?

"You're not boring." I surprise myself to come so quickly to his defence. "You know, about that day… I was having a bad time. Paquin has been on my case since the start of the year, and Tony was pulling my leg, and—"

"That's quite all right." His tone indicates me he'd rather talk about something else. "You're not the only person who made

76

comments, you know. I've heard it all before. Though not usually on my first day."

"Do you often talk to strangers in the toilet on your first day, though?"

"What?" He gives me an incredulous look.

"That was weird, it freaked me out!"

"Why?"

"I don't know. People making eye contact and talking in public toilets make me uncomfortable."

He laughs. "I wasn't trying to make you uncomfortable. It was my first day, I was nervous, you came in here, you seemed cool, so when you looked at me, I said hello, you know."

He said I looked cool. Just to be clear.

"I looked at you?"

He nods. "You definitely looked at me."

"Probably only to warn you to stop looking at me."

"I wasn't aware that I was looking at you." He slams a hand on his forehead. "I must have been lost in thought. I'm sorry. I feel like an idiot now."

"That's fine, come on." I don't want him to beat himself up for this, especially not because of me. "Think about it. Now the tension's out of the way, we can move on."

He smiles. "We can even be mates, if you want."

"Sure, but not in public."

Silence.

Why the fuck did I say that? That's the gay stuff I can't shake, François's fault. I didn't mean to say that. Why am I even allowed to live?

Michael's jaw has slacked as though he can't believe what I just said, but just got another confirmation that I'm a small dick in a bag of bigger dicks. I want to throw myself out of his window, but he lives on the second floor and there's no way the fall would kill me.

Now why would Michael be into me after that? He may have liked my reflection, but the real deal is something else. I insulted him, stalked him, made a fool of myself in front of François, and now I've insulted him again. Even if Michael was the gayest man in the galaxy, there isn't the smallest chance of him being interested in someone like me.

It's not my safety I should be worried about. It's my honour.

"What I mean is… My friends are pretty, hum, possessive, and they don't…"

"So you do think I'm boring."

"No!" In my panic, I can't find a nice, white lie to say. The truth comes rushing out, and I can only witness in horror. "I just — I don't want you around them. Tony can be a bit… wild."

Can't exactly explain that hanging out with Tony would scar Michael for life and then fat chance he and I could ever be mates.

Michael's face is twisted in a painful grimace. I can see he's trying his best to move on from this weird conversation, and he's trying even harder not to call me an asshole.

"Ok. Let's get started on this thing."

I get it if he wants to be done with me as soon as possible. I won't hold it against him.

Michael stretches his long limbs and cracks his neck. I guess there would be worse things in the world than kissing this guy. I could almost understand François, if he wasn't such an impertinent snob.

"Yes?" he suddenly says, looking at me.

He has seen me stare. He has seen me stare. Abort!

"Your mum's nice!"

That's the best I could find.

"Isn't she?" Michael's face softens. "She's brilliant."

I've never heard anybody call their mum brilliant. Tony's mum is close, though. She's a funny woman. But Tony thinks she's annoying too, sometimes.

Avoiding my gaze, Michael drums his fingers on his desk. "And your mom… How is she?"

He's just asking a question. He doesn't mean anything by it. He doesn't know how little I want to talk about it. But after the way I treated him, I owe him a fair answer.

"She lives in the South. I hardly ever see her. That explains why I'm acting so unhinged most of the time!"

I meant it as a joke, but still. I don't feel like seeing pity in his eyes, so I look down at the tiny nightstand I hadn't noticed before. The picture of Michael and his parents at the beach on top of it catches my attention. Michael's curly hair was much longer, his laughing face younger. When I spin around briskly, the real Michael looks away. Was he staring at me?

"I'm sorry," he says.

About my mum? Or about staring at me?

"Why? I'm perfectly fine." I hesitate. "She calls for my birthday, sometimes. Plus I met Tony a couple of years later, so…"

"Tony's your best friend."

"Yep."

I wish he wouldn't look at me so much. I'm no good for eye contact without my sunglasses. Whatever riches people want to read in other people's eyes, they won't find in mine. But then, Michael startles me by slamming his Dorian Gray on his desk.

"So! *The Picture of Dorian Gray*. You have to read it."

Ha! The moment has come for me to unveil my awesomeness. He still thinks I'm a total loser because I haven't done my homework. After all, he hangs out with the likes of François, who knows the Shakespeare's staff and can get him 'special editions'.

But hear this, Michael:

"I read it last night."

A look of delighted shock brightens his features. Yes, I did that.

"You have read the whole thing last night?"

"Well, no." Way to smash my achievement, Duncan. "I've read about a quarter of it."

"That's great!" He starts gesturing excitedly. "Because half of Mrs Paquin's questions are about the beginning, and when you're through, we can meet again, and we can start on the actual essay, and — and…" His shoulders sag. "You probably think I'm a total nerd again."

"Hm?" All I heard was *great*. "What? No. I mean… Yes. Yes you're a nerd, but you aren't boring. I was wrong to say this—and you know what? I don't know if you picked up by now, but I'm shit with words. Everything comes out wrong. I'm sorry."

He folds his arms over his chest, his bottom lip stuck between his teeth. "I have never been apologised to by a rockstar before."

"First times for everything, baby."

He laughs, so I follow, but my laughter turns nervous pretty much instantly when I realise how dirty everything I say sounds. He doesn't seem to notice. He switches his laptop on.

We work better together than I would have expected. Not once does he make me feel stupid or useless, despite the startling difference between our educations. I feel at ease, so much, even, that I totally forget to worry about whether he's gay or not.

Slightly astounded that anyone could make Paquin's homework interesting, it takes me a long time to get back home. I find myself stalling to admire my city for the first time in years. I'm even looking forward to having English literature on Friday.

Michael doesn't have Facebook, but his phone number is now safely tucked away in my pocket.

I hope he'll understand what I meant earlier. I hope he'll understand. There are things simply too precious to share.

9

RUFUS GOT TO IT FIRST

I don't know if Michael is gay, but if he were gay, I hope he'd
pick me.

Ok, ok, let me rewind here. I'm only saying this because, after
several afternoons in his company, I believe we really get along, and
I believe he really likes me, or the version of me I allow myself to be
around him, you know.

Clad in my rockstar uniform and stealing glances behind my
oversized sunglasses, a cigarette hanging from my lip, a quick joke
and a snarky attitude always at hand to make him laugh, that sort of
thing. He said it to me once, he said, "You look so carefree, I wish I
could be so carefree," and I could have wept, because I have
successfully hidden from him my constant anxiety.

January passed in a blur. In a remarkable feat, I finished *The
Picture of Dorian Gray* in record time, aka less than a week. Even more
impressed upon hearing it, Michael offered to meet once a week to
work on the essay. We're both too busy to hang out more, though I
wouldn't mind if he were less solicited.

Our essay will be superb. Michael's smart, he sees things that I
would never notice in a million years, but he says it's because he's
English, and if I were too, I would pick up on certain things. He
says despite my years at Colette, we still don't speak the same

language, and it shows. I asked what he meant by that, but he never answered. Answering my questions is not Michael's strong suit. Perhaps if I bothered asking more of them...

Despite his enigmatic ways, I feel I'm starting to get a good idea of Michael, and I'm amused to recall he once called himself boring, because he's nothing at all like that. I have spent enough time with him to have picked up a few things.

Michael is kind, really kind. Not faking it, kind. You know like some people are 'nice', but they're not 'kind' and the difference is subtle, but it's there. Nice people want you to think they care. Kind people actually do. Michael worries about people's wellbeing like Tony worries about the future of Babyshambles. That means a lot.

Michael's the sort of person who hangs out with his mother, picks up anything you drop before you notice its absence, and gives directions to strangers on the street, even if he's new to the city himself.

Michael's easy to be around. You could say he's low-maintenance, but he wouldn't like you talking about people like that. Smiles come easy to him, and he never opens his mouth to say anything vile. He lets people rant on about things he doesn't even like himself. He allowed me to talk about Franz Ferdinand's last album for twenty-five minutes once, before gently reminding me to get back to work.

And he doesn't mind trying new things.

Michael loves Paris, really looooooves Paris. Every bridge must be stopped at and its architect praised, every cobbled alley commented about, every plane tree admired.

At first, I thought he was odd, and Tony might be right, he could be a serial killer, but now I find myself stopping in the middle of a busy street to admire an old mosaic or a lamp post, and I've realised I've taken my city for granted for too long. I told Michael I spend more time smoking plants than admiring them. The way he laughed! Faint dimples appeared in his cheeks and looked very pretty. I became agitated, but as I was wearing my sunglasses, he didn't notice.

Michael is so delighted by Paris that he doesn't even mind the smell of piss in the metro or how rough the hordes of suburbans rushing home at night can be.

But the strangest thing about Michael is that he genuinely seems to like me. Ok, granted, he likes everyone, and everyone likes him which is very annoying. Well, Tony doesn't like him at all, but it's probably because he's a contrarian and also because I have twice cancelled plans with him to work on the essay, and he didn't like it.

Despite Michael's good nature, I still believe he favours me a little.

Last time we met at his place, we talked about our future. Michael's got bright ideas about his, as you can imagine.

"Perhaps I'll go to film school." He was swaying on his chair, dangerously close to tumbling backwards, as I stared, slack-jawed. "Where are you going?"

"I don't know what I'm going to do."

I realised a little too late that I had said the truth, without even thinking twice about it. But Michael didn't think of being judgmental. He waited for me to gather my thoughts while the chair seemed hellbent on keeping upright just for him.

"I thought I might travel, you know."

He nodded. "That's a great plan, do you know where?"

He lifted his pencil to his mouth, chewed on the tip, glanced back at me when I didn't answer. I shook my head. I wouldn't want him to think I could be going to London. He might get the wrong idea.

I've never quite met anyone like Michael before. Part of me wants to impress him, another to never see him again. And yet I always show up to our meetings with a trepidation that English Lit never birthed in me before.

Michael is my well-guarded secret. Tony would make fun of him or grow jealous. And despite her best intentions, Lucie would want to twist him around her finger. Is it wrong of me to enjoy someone's company without having to justify myself?

Every hour spent in his company rushes by really fast. I like the way the corners of his eyes crinkle when he sees me, the way his eyes are always on me, saving me from more than one massive dog poo and always seeking even for my most random opinion.

Michael likes me, and I like Michael. It's an unspoken truth, our truth. Sometimes I think we're the best of friends. I wonder what would have happened if I'd met him before Tony found me. New questions arise, and I'm nowhere near getting answers.

But I know this.

A person like me, whose stomach is quick to turn and whose imagination always rushes to the worst conclusion, has been able to find peace in the company of another bloke. A simple guy, whose laid back attitude has almost become an inspiration.

Today is the last time Michael and I are to work together. If you ask me, I would tell you the essay was already perfect a week ago, but Michael insisted to go over it once again, and I don't mind at all. Anything for my grade to be perfect, of course.

Chemistry is cancelled, our teacher is sick. Our teacher is often sick — with us — but as a result, we have decided to spend the afternoon working at Le Censier, a bistro in our neighbourhood.

The day is unusually beautiful and warm. I'm running a little late. I wanted to exchange my sweater for a T-shirt and collect myself before meeting him. I have been worried about the future of our relationship, now that the essay is over.

By relationship, I mean friendship. Of course.

Michael is gathering two tables together. He accidentally slams his knee into the table leg when he sees me approach. It's probably because I'm lumbering to hold my baggy jeans together, or anyone on the street would get a sight they never asked for. He starts laughing. Nothing mean about his laugh. His eyes fall on my jeans. I quickly pull out a chair in front of me.

"Why?" he asks, moving his bag to give me more space.

"Why what?"

The waiter arrives, we order coffee. I repeat my question. Michael shakes his head. He's still laughing.

"You dress like an old man's idea of a kid."

What's that? I throw myself on the chair, give him a withering look from behind my sunglasses.

"I dress like Kurt Cobain, man."

"Who's that?"

Who's that. Cute. He's joking, right?

"Are you serious? He's only one of the biggest rockstars!"

Michael flips his laptop open and our essay appears on the screen. It does look perfect as it is. Just perfect.

"Why do you dress like this Kurt guy? You love him or something?"

Ok no. Just no. The way he says that upsets me. I must defend myself, or he'll think I'm some cheap-ass groupie.

"I don't love him per se. But I look like him, so I thought it made sense, you know, to play with it."

He cocks his head. "Oh, so you dress like someone you don't even like because you look like him."

"Well—"

"Isn't it like, erasing your whole identity? Which is exactly the opposite of your rockstar lifestyle?"

Hang on. He's not supposed to see the glitch in the Matrix. Soon he'll start to psychoanalyse me and he'll never speak to me again.

I throw my head back and laugh. "Can we stop talking about my fashion sense? You're not Karl Lagerfeld, as far as I know. He's a fashion designer, by the way."

Michael says nothing while our waiter returns with our coffees, then he gives me a look. "I know who Karl Lagerfeld is, Louis."

I love the way he pronounces my name, Lou-ie, like the 'L' is a string he particularly likes to pluck.

Since we rarely meet around other people, when he says my name like that, I keep asking myself if he's the same with everybody, or performing just for me. Then I start wondering if he's got somebody, somewhere. Perhaps he swings both ways. Will I ever know? I should learn not to care about such trivial things.

Michael is shooting me insistent looks and eventually tears me from my thoughts. A little rattled, I drink a large swig of scalding coffee to look inconspicuous.

"Do you like his music, then?" he asks.

"Who, Kurt? Yeah, sure, but he's not my favourite."

Michael edges closer to the edge of his seat. "Then who's your favourite?"

He couldn't have pleased me more even if he got down on his knees and called me Jagger.

"Wait, I'll show you."

Immediately, I jump off my chair to get my iPod out of my bag. When I turn around, the device in hand, I trip over the leg of my chair and land almost face-first onto his lap. My sunglasses slide off my nose, he catches them just before they hit the ground.

As stated previously, Michael's a kind bloke and as such he doesn't complain, even as he manoeuvres my sorry ass back into my chair. But from the look on his face, I can tell that I have probably broken fifteen unspoken rules and the Queen would have me put down if she knew.

After we're done making fun of my stunt, his laughter a tad nervous and mine two octaves too high, I stick an earbud into his ear, and play Kaiser Chiefs' *Ruby*. It's a little loud, and I'll be a little deaf later in life, but who cares? People have less interesting things to say than Kaiser Chiefs. Michael grimaces at first, but when I inch closer and put the other earbud in my ear, he grows perfectly still.

"It's nice, I like it," he says after a minute.

"You do?"

He gives a nod of assent. Perhaps it's a lie, to make me happy. I can't tell the difference, so I hold on to our earbuds.

Our faces are really close. I can see every speck of gold in his green eyes. I expect he can see the same in my blue ones. Where the fuck are my shades? I look away. He does the same, glances down at my arms first, then at the iPod I'm holding between us.

When the song is over, we part from each other. Michael looks agitated. He does this thing of chewing his bottom lip when he's thinking hard about something.

"Do you want to…"

"What?"

Whatever he's about to say, my answer's already YES, but despite my pleading eyes, Michael doesn't finish his question. His face softens and relaxes at the sight of something behind me. What the fuck could be more important than talking to me at this exact moment? I turn around. It's Yasmine, walking her big Malinois on a tight leash.

I'm acquainted with that beast, and accordingly, I withdraw my legs under my chair. Yasmine stops at our table, pulling the dog closer. The dog and I stare at each other. He starts panting. Instinctively, I reach for my sunglasses and put them on.

As usual, Yasmine looks unimpressed, too cool for school. She leans down and pilfers one of my cigarettes.

"You guys are still working on that thing? Sacha wanted to go to the movies."

Michael stretches his arms behind his head. "I told her I had to finish this."

"You're trying too hard, it's only for Paquin."

She blows smoke out her puckered lips. Her dog begins sniffling under our table. Unnoticed, I squeeze my thighs together.

"I don't think I've ever been accused of trying too hard." I arch an eyebrow, pretending to be amused. The dog's snout brushes against my knee.

Yasmine's smirk tells legions. Michael casually sticks his hand under the table and pets the dog's head. The beast shuts his eyes, satisfied.

Yasmine, who rarely smiles in public, gratifies Michael of her sweetest specimen.

"Rufus doesn't like anyone, usually."

"He's adorable."

He's a lunatic, I swear! Michael is too innocent to know this. But of course, Michael has superpowers, everyone likes him. A rattlesnake would remove its hat to salute him. If they were wearing hats, that is.

Yasmine leans over the table and starts reading Paquin's list of questions.

"You missed one," she says.

"What? Which one?" Michael bends over the list.

"Here. Question 4: Which event causes Dorian to alter his life?"

Michael looks all flustered to have missed a question. The dog watches him quietly through his dark brown eyes.

"It's getting really hot." He wipes his brow with the back of his hand.

"Of course," Yasmine says. "You're wearing fifty layers." She points at her cropped top and high-waisted jeans.

I put my coffee cup to my lips. "She's right."

Just like that, Michael pulls away from the table, grips the hem of his sweater and gives the whole thing a good yank upwards. He accidentally lifts his T-shirt as well, revealing a flat tummy and an inch of neon blue underwear.

It's as though I received an electric shock. Something springs up within me, rises every hair on my body. Coffee catches in my throat, sending me into a coughing fit.

Yasmine turns to me. "Jesus! You're ok over there?"

"That's really hot." Eyes streaming, I point down at my cup of coffee.

Naturally, the dog pounces on me, barking, and sticks his snout between my legs. Michael stares at me, open-mouthed, while I battle with the beast under the table.

About ten seconds too late, Yasmine finally retrieves him and leaves us, laughing all the way.

There are drops of coffee all over Michael's laptop and my embarrassment is so bad that it takes all of my willpower not to throw myself under the first passing car.

"What's wrong, Louis?" Michael looks concerned.

"Nothing. Why are you asking this?"

"You look very anxious."

"That's not true."

What the hell was this? What is happening to me? I'm shaking. I could always tell him I have epilepsy. That might work.

Michael is pinching his lips. "You're the most anxious person I've ever met."

"I'm not."

"I'm not saying it's a bad thing."

I clear my throat. "I'm not. It's just... I don't see what more we can do for the essay, and I'd prefer to go home, so let's get to it, so I can go home."

Michael scratches the back of his neck. "You can go, if you want. There are only a few typos to fix. I can do that myself."

"Really?"

"I'll take care of it, you go."

His evident concern for me makes it all the more devastating, but I cannot stay around him any longer. I swing my backpack onto my shoulder, and after one last wave goodbye, I sprint back home without a look back.

10

HIT ME WITH YOUR BEST SHOT

"**A**re you deaf or what?"

Tony slaps me across the back, tearing me from my thoughts. I stare at his amused face, then around me. We're in the gymnasium's changing rooms. Everyone's dressed for the volleyball class starting in five minutes, except for me. My backpack's open, my gym clothes bunched up in there amidst random papers, old pens and pieces of rubber erasers.

"What?" I bark, rubbing my eyes.

I haven't been myself this morning, ever since I woke up sweaty after four hours of awful sleep and a bunch of nonsensical dreams.

Tony, looking too skinny in his sweatpants, studies me through narrowed eyes.

"You're hungover."

"I'm not."

"You are. You went out yesterday? With Lucie?"

I love Tony, but sometimes, he gets on my nerves.

Without any hope for success, I attempt to shove my foot into my trainer. "I wasn't with Lucie. I was at home."

"Then why didn't you come to my place? My mother made lasagna. You love her lasagna."

Because! I was laying in bed in the dark, having all sorts of weird thoughts about Michael. I'm sure he'd love to find out that seeing another bloke's underwear gave me a boner and that Yasmine's Malinois almost chopped my dick off.

I'm slowly losing my grip on reality. This morning, I was that close to run to people on the street and ask: "Tell me, am I gay??"

"Sorry, Tony. I'll come next time."

"There are leftovers, you know. You can come tonight."

"Fine, tonight."

Tony stomps his foot. "Perfect, but in the name of sweet baby Jesus, hurry! If you move it, we can share a joint by the dumpster."

I stare down at my halfway laced-up trainers. "Nah, I'm good, thanks."

"What's wrong with you?"

Tony slaps his hand against my forehead. I push him away.

"Nothing. I didn't sleep well, that's all."

When I lift my own T-shirt over my head, I can't help but shiver at the memory of Michael's flat stomach.

I haven't spoken to him since. Sure, I saw him on Monday when we submitted our essay in English Lit. But I kept to myself, and as I was being stubborn in my silence, he didn't insist, left class without a word, and I was left to repeatedly bump my head against the table until Tony came over to get me.

I shouldn't worry too much about it, I know. I'm almost eighteen, I've got hormones on fire, as the experts say on TV. I saw a flash of skin and my body reacted. It doesn't mean I'm into guys. Just one look at Tony's long face and dangling arms and I'm missing Lucie's striking beauty.

But something is messing with my brain. I haven't been feeling right lately. Because if it were just this incident, right, but it's not. Was I just not, the other day, marvelling at the elasticity of Michael's curls? Is that really a straight thing to do? I could ask Tony if it ever happened to him...

Tony tosses my shirt at my face. "Wake up!"

Forget it. There's no way I can ask him anything. He would never shut up about it.

"Sorry, sorry." I put the shirt on hastily.

"Lucie's waiting outside."

"She can wait a second, can't she?"

"You're so annoying this morning." Tony never gets the hint to shut up. "Are you on your period or something?"

"You're so funny." I rise from the bench and jab a finger in his chest. "Remind me to consult you next time we have an essay on sexism."

"Oh!" He clutches at his chest, pretending to be shocked. "Excuse me?"

"I told you I haven't slept!"

"Confess, it's because of the new guy."

My heart jumps in my throat. "What? Why?"

"Is he that boring? Did he suck the life out of you?"

Once again, Tony's got it wrong.

"Just drop it, okay?"

Tony's too entertained by my bad mood to drop it. I can see in his black eyes that he's about to add something, and I already want to punch him in the face, but at this exact moment, Michael charges into the changing rooms, closely followed by François. They're both flushed, as though they've raced the whole way here.

Seeing me with my jaw hanging open makes François look particularly chipper.

Michael barely registers our presence, hurriedly opening his backpack to retrieve his gym clothes. When I realise what he's about to do, I brutally shove Tony toward the exit.

"Come on, Lucie's waiting outside!"

Once the door is safely shut behind us, I release a breath. The last thing I need is another glimpse at Michael's underwear. When it comes to the sensitive subject of my genitals, I'll take Yasmine's Malinois over Tony's laughter any day.

Volleyball class is just as it sounds. The class is taught — if you can call it teaching — by Mr Granger, an overweight man in his early thirties, whose baby face is always red. If Granger has given up on life by becoming a PE teacher at Colette International, he has not given up on terrorising generations of slackers through his harsh grading.

Needless to say, he hates Tony and I most, especially since that time Tony tried to convince him he had developed the ability to menstruate overnight, and therefore couldn't attend swimming lessons.

Volleyball is pretty straight forward. Granger splits us into teams, and we face each other while he watches lazily, drinks coffee, and types on the keyboard of his old Pocket PC.

There's no way I'll distinguish myself as a brilliant athlete today, so I'm not expecting a good grade and I'm not too anxious about it.

Lucie's great at volleyball, she can throw a nasty punch, and I'm not the only one who gazes at her longingly while she plays. She trots toward us in her gym shorts and swaying ponytail, meaning business, and hands me a hair tie.

"So you don't miss the ball this time."

It happened once, okay? My hair fell over my eyes like a curtain, I missed the ball, and our team lost. She never got over it.

"Why are you helping me?" I gratefully accept the hair tie and begin pulling my hair back. "You're on the other team."

"Exactly. I don't want to have to watch you fail miserably."

When I'm done tying my hair in a low ponytail, Lucie watches the result with glowing cheeks.

"Your hair looks so good these days."

"Jesus Christ!" Tony says, bending close to the top of my skull to take a better look. "It's true, your hair's been weird all week. You're washing it, aren't you?" He puts his hand on his hip, looking thoughtful. "You know, that's not the only thing different about you." He turns to Lucie. "The other day he stopped at the Papeterie outside my flat and bought a binder and notebooks and shit."

"What?" I try not to sound too defensive. "I needed new supplies."

"Lou, you never even take notes."

"You don't, baby," Lucie says, laughing.

"I do now." My cheeks heat up. "I need good grades, you know, for London."

A brief silence settles between us. Then Tony lunges at me and ruffles my hair.

"I'm sorry," he says, his face split into an evil grin. "That was too tempting."

Lucie, laughing at my disgruntled face, blows me a kiss and

walks over to the other side of the net, where Michael is also standing, flanked by Sacha and Yasmine. Sacha looks angry and Michael is pretending to be absorbed by the structure of the net.

I jerk my chin toward Sacha. "What's up with her?"

Tony rolls his eyes. "She's mad at New Guy."

"Michael?" My heart thumps. "Why?"

"Who gives a shit? Some girl stuff." He laces his fingers behind his head. "I tell you what. I'll tell you everything if I can bum a cigarette later."

"Fine. Now, tell me. I can't wait for you to explain to me how you became an expert on 'girl stuff'."

He lets out an enormous bark of laughter. "Ha! What do you think?"

"Lucie told you, and you thought the information too irrelevant to share with me."

"Bingo."

Amused, I shake my head. "So, what's up with Sacha?"

"She thought she could get herself a nice juicy slice of British pound cake, if you know what I mean?"

"You are so gross."

He shrugs. "Anyway, it's not gonna happen."

"Why not?" My heart rate kicks up another notch. "She is… ahem… great."

I'm such a hypocrite. Tony's eyebrows rise to his hairline. He seems to agree with me.

"Sure, Sacha's great. Anyway, New Guy's got a girl back home."

A little glass bubble shatters in the confines of my chest. I glance up toward the windows above the stands, the milky-white sky staring back at me, indifferent.

Michael's got a girl, back home.

"So," Tony says, now making ridiculous poses to stretch his legs. "Sacha's pissed off, she's wasted a lot of energy on him since he arrived, and it was all for nothing. And Lucie comforted her, even though Sacha is a bit much. But I was telling Lucie, you know what? We know her, she'll bounce back, she'll find a way to get around that small complication."

A small what?

Well, it's not like I never thought it was possible. It's just that…
you know…

He never told me. Why wouldn't he tell me? He's acting like
we're best friends, but he didn't tell me he had a girl back home.
What's her name? What does she look like? Unsurprisingly, my
imagination kick-starts with no regards for the truth, and the image
of a brunette in a schoolgirl skirt and tweed jacket, striking sexy
poses for him on a velvet bedspread, flashes before my eyes.

Michael has a girlfriend. I could have asked him this question a
million times. He would have told me, if only I'd asked. All my
stupid little questions would have been answered, and we would
have moved on.

Michael isn't gay. Sorry, François. He's got a girlfriend, sorry,
Sacha.

Now I can stop acting crazy. No more asking myself weird questions which fuck with my brain, my sleep, and occasionally, my
manhood.

All is well in the world.

Rubbing my hands together, I jump into the game with a
newfound determination.

Ten minutes later, they're destroying us. The third time François
slams into me, allegedly to get the ball, but I think it's just good old
sabotage, I'm ready to throw in the towel. My already thin motivation to honour my team has pretty much evaporated. I remove
myself to the back of our team to watch better athletes than myself
take care of business.

On the other side of the net, Lucie, her face glowing, is an absolute beast. Everyone watches in awe and no girl in their right mind
is tempted to comment on the sweat pooling down at the small of
her back. Behind her, Michael looks taller than the others, second to
Lars. But contrary to Lars, he's too much of a gentleman to stare at
Lucie's ass. Sacha, on the other hand, won't take her eyes off of his.

Classic.

Tony joins me, breathing hard.

"Fuck this." He leans against me for support while he adjusts his
shoe.

"My thoughts exactly." I sound bitter.

Tony points toward Lucie. "She's so good, though."

"She's perfect."

Tony adds something, but I'm not paying attention. Sacha is approaching Michael, a determined look on her face.

She raises herself on tiptoes, whispers something in his ear. Michael's eyes widen, his mouth stretches into a smile, he laughs. Then, quick as a fox, he spots the ball François is hurtling at him and throws it right back at him with great agility, scoring another point. His team cheers. Lars headlocks him, buries his chin into his hair to congratulate him. Some people know absolutely no boundaries! Who does he think he is?

Michael doesn't seem to mind. He pulls at the band of his sweatpants with one hand and uses the other to wipe the sweat off his forehead. Sacha's burning eyes are not leaving him.

It's a shame, really. Isn't it, Sacha? A real shame.

Tony tugs at my sleeve. "Come on, let's go."

"Sure."

Sacha walks over to Michael again. A bead of sweat glimmers at the edge of his full eyebrow. Slowly, he lifts his hand and runs his long fingers through his dark, glistening curls. His nostrils flare with each of his strained breaths. His sharp green eyes never leave the ball.

Sacha speaks. Startled, Michael jerks his head back, sends heaps of curls bouncing like a flock of fat little lambs, and—

WHAM!

Something hits me square in the eye with the force of a wrecking ball, and flattens me to the ground, knocking the air out of me. Bouncing lambs give way to an explosion of stars. Somewhere around me, the sound of Tony's laughter and Granger's whistle reach me.

"Whatdijfoirgjthappened?"

I seem to have lost the ability to form words. Probably because my brain has been punched out my skull.

Tony's blurry hand appears in my field of vision. After two failed attempts, I manage to grasp it and pull myself up. My teammates gather around us, some shaking their heads, some trying hard not to smirk. Lucie goes over to our side, takes one look at my face and gasps. A part of me shamefully relishes the attention.

"Watch the ball, you dumbass, not the players!" The teacher comes running and snarling, then skids to a stop once he sees my face. "Well, hem… What are you waiting for? Go to the infirmary, now!"

I feel strangely calm and put together, despite all of this. Perhaps getting hit in the head was exactly what I needed. I turn to Tony. "Does it look horrible?"

He slams his hand on my shoulder, looking proud. "Yes! I love it."

"What happened?" I lift my hands to my face. Everything seems in place. "Who hit me?"

"Fate." Tony points at the ball at my feet. "You were staring at Sacha's tits, confess. The Gods have punished you."

"You were what?" Lucie says.

I let out a groan of dismay.

"Don't worry. I'll have concocted a great backstory for you by the time you return." Tony uses his fingers to make imaginary quote marks. "Like 'Charismatic hero takes on a gang of fascists to topple the patriarchy', something like that."

"You're a true friend," I mutter, leaving him with a confused Lucie.

I take my leave and my secret with me, but ventures one last look over my shoulder before leaving the gymnasium. Tony is making a faithful impression of the ball hitting my face, Lucie looks torn between amusement and horror, and further away, Michael is standing on his own. Our eyes meet.

My stomach makes an unpleasant jolt. Not only did the ball not fix my little problem, it seems to have made matters worse.

Back at Colette's, Sana, the veteran nurse, straight out laughs in my face.

"Were you looking elsewhere or is it just pure incompetence?" she asks after two minutes of uninterrupted laughter.

I slam both hands on her desk. "Will you check on me, or should I drag myself to the E.R. and have my parents send an email to the headmaster?"

"All right! No need to be cheeky."

Sana sits me down and waves all sorts of tools in front of me, and is all like "Can you see this?" and "Can you feel this?" and "Do you feel normal?" and I want to scream: "No! I'm still thinking about Michael!" but I don't say a word, of course.

She soon declares me safe to go back to class, that only my pride will suffer long term damage. I do want to bite her head off, but she hands me a lollipop on my way out, so I thank her and slink out of her office with my reward clutched in my fist.

I do feel different. More confused, more miserable than ever. I know I wasn't looking at the ball. And I know *why* I wasn't looking. Did it take a volleyball in the face for me to confess that I'm jealous? That I'm annoyed? That I feel cheated, even? That Michael's girlfriend feels like a huge smudge on my carefully constructed friendship with him?

I don't know why, I had a strange feeling that he and I, we were different. That we were on to something special. A secret, perhaps. And perhaps I'm mad, yes, that he didn't tell me about his girl, and it's not just because it means he doesn't trust me. It's something else. Something heavy and charged is swelling within me, like dark clouds before a storm. Soon there will be thunder, I know it, but it doesn't mean the first crack won't make me jump out my skin.

Dragging my feet across the playground, the cold winter wind beating at my ears, I don't hear the voice calling out to my at first.

"Louis!"

Louis, not Lou. My breath hitches.

I turn around. Michael is running toward me, still dressed in his gym clothes. My heart jumps, both in elation and seething anger.

"Michael?"

He stops before me, panting. A tiny bead of sweat is perched on the curve of his upper lip. Two very conflicting thoughts burst into my mind. Shove him, call him a traitor. Pull him closer and check for myself what his sweat tastes like.

"I was worried you were really hurt. Granger was worried too. He sent me to check up on you, just in case you might want to sue him or something."

"He sent you?"

Michael nods. "Yeah, he said I seem to have my head on my shoulders."

I stare down at my shoes.

"Are you going to be okay?" he asks, stepping forward.

I recall Sana's parting words. "No lasting damage, except to my dignity."

Michael laughs, sending tingles through my fingertips. I ball my fists and stick them in my pockets.

"You're always so hard on yourself."

"That's because I'm useless."

"I see you've made my point."

I say nothing, because the way he's looking at me is confusing the shit out of me.

He *has* a girlfriend. He has a *girlfriend*. Stop making everything about you, Louis.

Michael takes another step forward. "Here's the thing — Wait."

His hand reaches toward my face. My heart starts pounds madly in my chest.

Michael's fingers briefly graze my hair, sending a jolt of electricity that sparks life throughout my entire nervous system. My hair falls back on either side of my face. Michael withdraws his hand and dangles Lucie's hair tie before my eyes.

"You were about to lose it."

"Just about, yes." I choke on a laugh. "You were saying?"

His hands tightly squeezed together, Michael steps back. "What are you doing tonight?"

I stare blankly at him for a moment, trying to unpack what's going on, if I do have a concussion after all. But stars and volleyball aside, I'm thinking real fast, am I reading this right? The way he shuffles his feet, kicking pebbles out of the way, not meeting my eyes…

What is happening?

"Or…" Michael says. "It's fine, if you don't… Or if you have other plans. Or if you prefer to hang out with Tony."

Tony? Who's Tony? Never heard of him.

"No. We can hang out. I don't have any plans."

Shit! I do have plans. Damn it, Louis! I'll just have to cancel them.

Michael doesn't look so convinced. He leans in, filling the air and my sensitive nostrils with the scent of fresh apples. Imagine being buried nose deep into the crook of his neck. Imagine that.

"You left so strangely last time we hung out."

Oh, right. The underwear incident. Old news. Haven't been thinking about it for ages. I give a little laugh.

"What can I say? I'm a little strange."

"Perfect," he says, not skipping a beat. "I like strange."

What does this mean? Does he like strange things? Like weird-ass ice-cream flavours? Amusement parks? Or worse: Disney? Or does it mean he likes me, particularly? Me, me, me!

"Strange means you can stomach this Korean movie I want to show you. They show it at the cinema on Mouffetard."

"Ah, right."

My stomach sinks. It awfully feels like I've been demoted from my position of mysterious rockstar, and relegated to the freaky part of the spectrum, with mimes and people who scrapbook.

"Are you sure you're up for it?" Michael asks.

I let out a snort of derision. His concern sounds a lot like he doesn't think I can sit still for two hours to watch a foreign movie. Well, what do you know? I have done it, I have watched *The Two Towers, Extended Edition.*

"Yeah, of course, why?"

Michael points at my face. "You got hit pretty hard."

Vividly aware of the pain in my eye cavity, I dispel his concern with a wave of my hand.

"That? It was nothing. I'm fine! I can totally watch a Crimean movie."

"Korean."

"Yeah, that too."

Michael's face splits into a blinding smile. "Brilliant. Let's meet at six then."

He walks away. His perfume lingers in the air, my heart is still thumping, my thoughts still reeling.

Ok, I need to calm down. I just found out he was straight, and that he had a girl. It's just a movie between friends. I'm not even gay, by the way. Remember?

Oh, and I too, have a girlfriend by the way. And... we love each other.

I'm feeling quite light-headed. It must be because I was just hit by a volleyball. It's quite possible I'll never recover, mentally.

11

IS IT YOU OR IS IT ME?

It's as though I can see myself acting out of character but cannot do anything about it. I know I shouldn't lie to my friends, and I know I'll get into trouble if I keep doing this. But I simply cannot stop myself.

At six o'clock sharp — well, actually I was seven minutes late, which isn't at all bad for a fiend like me — I meet Michael in front of L'Epée de Bois, the small cinema Rue Mouffetard dedicated to movies no one in my class ever bothers to watch, except Michael.

I'm nervous. Michael, of course, isn't. We share a few words about homework, and I ask about the movie we're about to watch. It's better if you don't know anything, Michael argues. The surprise will only be heightened. All right. He smiles. I smile. He sticks his hands into his pockets. He looks nice, tonight. I turn away, light a cigarette. More smiles.

What are we becoming to each other?

Do all the smiles and looks we share mean what I think they mean? Michael might well have a girlfriend, this doesn't help a nagging question bouncing around in my head.

Did he ask me out as his English Lit mate or has he too, lately, felt as though some strange tension was growing between us?

Is he, like me, afraid of the truth? What would happen if tonight, we both decided to find out? What would it mean?

We buy our tickets at the small kiosk. Michael opens the door to the screening room.

"You go first."

"You must be popular with the girls," I say stupidly.

He darts me a quick glance, but doesn't answer.

Michael is excited as we take our seats in the small, nearly empty room. He promises a great film. My mind is racing. Has your girlfriend seen this one? Or is it a special event only for the two of us? What kind of person is she?

I bet she has a great mane of wavy, shiny hair. And she wears a schoolgirl uniform. She probably recites him some poetry before bed. And why does it matter, anyway? I'm not gay.

I clear my throat. "Do you take your girlfriend to the movies, sometimes?"

Michael flashes me a look of alarm. "What?"

Suddenly, I understand how delicate this balance is. He cannot know that I have these weird ideas. If he knows and doesn't share them, a lot of terrible things will happen. I make a choice, resolutely and bitterly, to stay quiet about the matter, but at the same time secretly decide to interpret Michael's choice of a movie as a sign for the direction in which our friendship would go, if Michael could influence it.

Michael answers my question in a muted voice. "I've never shown this one to anyone."

When the screen lights up, so do Michael's eyes. We exchange a smile before the room turns pitch black.

The movie is called Old Boy, and it's a brutal explosion of style and violence. If Michael's intention is to kidnap and imprison me for fifteen years, resulting in heavy trauma, then I daresay the choice of the movie is flawless.

Twice Michael darts side glances at me during the film; I faintly register it. When the movie ends, I'm speechless, and Michael looks uneasy for the second time since I met him.

"Did you like it?" he asks in a whisper, his eyes wide.

Too mesmerised to speak, I answer with a shrug. Michael's shoulders sink. He rises from his seat. I hurry after him.

"I loved it. It was great."

Michael opens the door and gestures for me to go first.

"Liar," he whispers, right into my ear, as I walk passed him.

He must have accidentally touched a nerve, because my whole body twitches. Forgetting how to breathe, I jump back and flatten myself against the wall.

It's definitely the ball. It must have broken my brain when it hit my head.

Michael pretends to not notice how I flinched away from him. We leave the warmth of the cinema for the reality outside. I don't know what's the most brutal. The wind clawing at my face and my hair, the traumatising movie I just watched, or how twitchy and electric everything feels around him, like I'm about to burst at the simplest touch.

Michael proposes we talk about the movie, so we take refuge from the cold at Café Mouffetard.

Despite my blatant lies, the memory of what happened last time we had coffee together is still burning my face when I think about it. But this time, small chance of Michael getting undressed, because it's freezing.

And yet: Michael opens his coat with shaky fingers, blows on his hands, avoids my gaze. Is it me, or is he nervous? Or it's me who's nervous, and I paint everything with my own anxious colour palette.

"Are you all right?" I ask.

"Always." He meets my eyes. And smiles.

Better excuse myself before I say something stupid.

I move fast, before he can stop me, my blood pounding in my ears, and take refuge in the gents.

I've been here before. I know the layout of the place. But tonight everything feels unfamiliar. I'm coming apart at the seams. The mirror reflects my face, tense, red. Another question comes crashing like an unstoppable wave.

If tonight, Michael wanted to kiss me, would I let him?

It's a crazy question. I've got no answer for you, mate.

Probably not, anyway. Because I'm not gay.

A splash of cold water on my face has the effect of a slap and pulls me out of my own head.

All right. You can do this. It's only coffee, you know. Not a blowjob. It's coffee with your British friend. All is fine and dandy.

When I come back, coffee's already served, though I don't remember ordering. Michael interprets my incredulous frown as a need for explanation.

"I took the liberty… so it would have time to cool down."

My frown only deepens. He adds:

"So you wouldn't burn off your tongue, like last time?" He makes a face that's supposed to be like mine when I choked on my coffee that time when Yasmine was there.

I begin to laugh, a quiet, awkward little giggle that sounds like I've just been talked to by the hottest jock in an American movie. Michael joins in my laughter, though with reserve.

His dimpled smile brings me my answer, as uncomfortable as it is.

I *wish* he wanted to kiss me. Not only would I let him, but I'd probably enjoy it more than I want to admit.

I realise I've been staring. Must find something to say before he thinks I'm brain-damaged.

"I'm worried about the essay."

"Why?"

"I'm not convinced it was good enough."

Michael shakes his head. "It was perfect. We went even deeper than was required. Yasmine was right. It's only for Paquin. It's not that important."

If it's not that important then why did we spend so much time on it? Nit-picking every turn of phrase, checking every word? The essay has been the most important thing in my life lately. I want to do it justice.

But Michael doesn't care about the essay, apparently, nor does he want to talk about it. He's tapping his teaspoon against the rim of his cup of coffee.

"I'm more worried about volleyball, honestly."

Worried about volleyball? No one ever worries about volleyball, except perhaps volleyball players at an international level. And their coach. Perhaps their mothers. Not a whole lot of people, you see.

"Why are you worried about volleyball?" The hint of disappointment in my voice gives it a bitter edge. "I'm the one who got hit in the face."

Tony would have laughed, but Michael looks mortified.

"It barely shows, you know."

"I know."

I probably have internal bleeding, considering the thoughts I'm nurturing toward him right at this moment. But without a black eye, good luck getting sympathy votes from the other teachers who might have thought I have problems at home.

"Why are you worried about volleyball, anyway? You're good at it."

Michael watches me take a large swig of scalding coffee with an arched eyebrow.

"You think?"

"Yeah, I watched — I mean, I saw you play, you were good."

"I'm... adequate." He finally stops banging the teaspoon against the cup. "Lucie's really good. Very impressive."

Why are we talking about Lucie now? The only time I get to not talk about her is when I'm with him. It's like he's determined to do the opposite of what I want him to do.

"Yeah, she's good at many things, you know. Like Spanish."

Michael hangs his head. "Have you known her for long?"

Now I'm starting to worry he's into her and has lured me out of my flat to gather intel about her. It wouldn't be the first time this happened to me. Way before I met Tony, my only value seemed to have been a reminder to all of my friends of how better they were than me.

"No," I say in a low voice. "We met in the fall, at the beginning of the school year."

Michael nods, but doesn't add anything. Another silence stretches between us. Does he, too, wonder what it would be like to kiss me? At times, I can almost swear he wants me. Other times, like now, he's like a mystery book in a language I can't read. He makes me want to scream into a pillow.

"Are you and her very close?"

I sneak a hand under the table and dig my nails into my knee until I feel composed enough to answer.

"Why do you care about Lucie?"

A flash of alarm in his eyes. "I don't know. I was just making conversation."

"Sure."

Perhaps he's lying, perhaps not. I don't mind humouring him. There's nothing special about Lucie and me.

"We met at orientation. She said I was hot. I thought she was beautiful. We talked about music, the next day we were dating."

Michael makes a face. "How romantic."

Dear Michael, let me tell you something. Romance is overrated. This great outpouring of mushy emotions, private information recklessly undisclosed in an attempt to manipulate and seduce the other, the hushed concealing of the worst things about yourself to highlight the best, all of these efforts, these battles against oneself to grow and share and for what?

To end up just like the others, eventually dumped and feeling smaller for having revealed too much for too little reward.

Well, no thanks.

But I stare into my cup of coffee and I say nothing. The waitress comes to our table, asks if we want anything else. Eager to put an end to this masquerade, I ask for the check.

"The truth is," I tell Michael when she's gone, "Lucie doesn't even know who I am. Does that tell you how close we are?"

"What do you mean, she doesn't know who you are?"

I shrug. "I've never actually told this to anyone."

Michael's face takes this very solemn expression, as though whatever I'm about to reveal is a top-secret of the utmost importance, and will determine the future of our species. I appreciate him. I really do.

"So, long story short: I slept with someone last summer."

Michael furrows his brow but doesn't say anything.

"I wasn't even aware of Lucie's existence then. So it shouldn't be that big a deal, right? But it is. Everything always is. I'm a private person. I like to be able to keep some things to myself. But I slept with this girl and never told anyone. But now, Lucie, she thinks I'm like her, and she wants us to, you know…"

"Oh," Michael says, leaning back in his chair.

"And Tony—"

"Wait. How is that Tony's business who you sleep with?"

"It's not, not really, but you know how it is."

"No, I really don't."

"He's my best friend. We're supposed to tell each other everything. I know he's telling me everything… I mean. He used to. Now he has secrets of his own. And I — I try really hard not to mind. But this information, it has so much power over things, and I hate it. I just slept with someone, and I feel like a criminal now. I'm stuck. I waited too long to tell them and they'll think I have something to hide, and… And every time she wants to touch me I freeze, and I deflect, and I hide from her. She's probably growing suspicious by now."

Michael starts chewing on his bottom lip. Then Vivaldi starts blasting out of his pocket. Michael digs up his phone, checks the screen, doesn't answer.

"Sorry about that," he says. "And let me tell you this. If they love you, they should understand. They should try to put themselves in your shoes, and they will understand why you decided not to tell them."

"You're right. I guess the hardest part is to start the conversation, am I right?"

He didn't flinch when he found out Lucie and I had not had sex yet. Gave nothing. But now, his whole face flushes, and he lets out a laugh that sounds a little insincere. For an instant, I even think he's about to clap me on the shoulder and call me mate. But we're saved by his phone, which vibrates loudly under the table.

Michael, again, doesn't pick up, but sticks the phone back into his pocket with a strained smile.

"Sorry."

It's a good opportunity to fish for answers.

"What about you, then?"

"What about me, what?"

"Are you close to your girlfriend?"

Once again, his phone turns to life. Michael retrieves it from his pocket and shows it to me.

"She's still calling." The screen says 'Abby'.

My stomach drops. It's one thing to hear about a distant girl-friend stranded on an English moor or something, it's something else to have her invade our little conversation.

"You should pick up." My voice comes out a little strangled.

He shakes his head. "I don't like talking on the phone while I'm sitting with somebody. I find it rude when others do it."

You're so nice. I wonder what you taste like.

Michael watches me with a little smile. I decide to put my hands on my lap under the table, should I get too tempted to do something stupid.

"You know," he says, "now that you've told me your secret…"

"Did I?"

If only he knew. I have more.

He puts his chin in his hand. "It's only fair I tell you one too."

I agree! And show it with vehemence by nodding enthusiastically. Perhaps he'll tell me Abby is not real. That she was a device to make me jealous.

I am losing my mind, aren't I?

Before Michael can speak, *another* woman, our waitress, interrupts once again. She hands me the check without a glance, too busy admiring Michael.

"What an adorable accent," she says, when he thanks her in French. "Where are you from?"

"England," he says, all dimples and shit.

They start talking. Suddenly, she wants to know all about him. She even leans on the table, putting herself between us.

There are too many women in our lives. It's maddening. She doesn't turn when I put the money on the table, or tell her she can keep the change, but she takes my receipt and writes her name and number on it, saying she'd be happy to help, if he ever needs a tour guide.

I am NEVER coming back here.

When she finally gets back to work, skirts swinging, Michael is looking down at his empty cup and is not smiling anymore. And I'll never know what he had meant to say.

We leave the coffee place and make our way back home in silence. The streets are quieter outside Mouffetard at this late hour. It should be relaxing, but I'm way past hoping for relief tonight.

When we enter Rue Pestalozzi, I feel a sharp pang of disappointment. Soon Michael will be out of reach, and I'm nowhere nearer understanding what is happening to us, or at least, to me.

"You know…" Michael says.

"Yeah?"

"My girlfriend…"

Michael's phone goes off again. For the first time since I've met him, he blurts out a curse.

"This is mad," he says, squinting at the screen. "I never get any calls. I hate being on the phone, I hate it so much."

"Please, please answer." I can see Abby's name on the screen. "If only for a minute."

He answers, listens for a moment. Then he says he'll call her back in a minute, yes, an actual minute, don't worry, before hanging up.

"Sorry, Louis. It's going to take more than a minute."

I can't show him I'm sad or disappointed. He doesn't need any of my shit.

"That's fine. I have to go anyway."

Then I remember the receipt in my pocket. I fish it out and hand it over to him.

"You want it?"

He takes it with a blank expression and crumples it. "You know I don't."

"You're not asking me if I want it?" I playfully dig my finger into his shoulder.

"Why? You have a girlfriend."

Ouch. The tone of his voice. I really don't know what I was expecting.

"Oh, right, of course."

Poor Lucie. She deserves better too. I haven't been thinking much of her lately, all because I'm losing myself to some kind of weird fantasy. I don't know who I am anymore.

Michael and I part ways with a few generic words, and I walk home, alone.

He did not kiss me, in the end. Didn't act like he wanted to, not really.

And that's fine.

Enough of this, already.

We're good friends. Am I so screwed up that I start floundering at the first sign of affection?

Perhaps a kiss would have been too much.

Perhaps it wouldn't have been enough.

12

I'VE GOT THIS

W e've all been there.

It's what I think, on my way to school the next morning, watching people as they walk to work, their face unreadable for some, their secrets safe, for most.

We've all had that mild crush that turned out to be a better friend. Once, while drunk or high, you might say: "Hey, did you know that when we first met, I had a crush on you?" The other person might say: "Wow, that's funny!" and all is well in the world, or they may say, "Well, you know what? I had a crush on you too!" and then your friendship will or will not be altered forever.

To make up for the cold temperatures, the sun is making an apparition. And it's not just the sky that has cleared. I've gotten my shit together, I can feel it.

In my case, my "crush" on Michael was a little unusual. Him being a Michael, and not a Michaela, that's why. But now that everything is clear between us, he has a girlfriend, she's real, and I have a girlfriend, to whom I'll soon tell the truth about me, so, all in all, everything's peachy.

My mild little crush was never really a crush, to be honest. I must have been bored. Consumed by my secrets. Too anxious, as usual, to understand the difference between what's real and what's not. I've confessed to Michael last night, and the burden on my shoulders feel considerably lighter.

Let's see it that way: If I'm so worried about my girlfriend breaking up with me, then it's obvious that I'm not seriously considering kissing someone else.

Especially not a GUY.

You know when I said I wanted to be different, it's not what I had in mind. I meant becoming a charismatic leader, perhaps a CEO, hopefully an artist. I didn't mean running around in circles and pulling my hair, wondering if my great speciality is being attracted to men. That's not it. That's not who I am.

Crazy what a flash of underwear can do to a boy my age. I must be particularly healthy. Now that I think about it, imagine all the stuff that must be going down in boarding schools and university campuses.

In military bases.

Especially in military bases…

But perhaps I should stop thinking about what goes down in military bases. If people knew, they might get the wrong idea.

Anyway, it's all good. Everything's great. Just like every other Friday, I take my seat next to Michael in English Literature, amidst the bustle of students debating their plans for the weekend, and drop my shades on the table.

Michael asks about my morning. Michael has a girlfriend named Abby. He's not gay.

Nothing weird has ever happened between us. We're just two friends who like talking to each other and sometimes want to touch each other's hair.

"I was hoping to see you on my way here," I say. As a friend, of course. "But I was running late."

"You're always late," Michael doesn't look mad. He looks, as always, elated to see me. "I met with Yasmine, we walked together."

We're such good friends. If I couldn't see Tony from the corner of my eye, I would call us the best of friends.

"I've got something to show you," I say, opening my binder. "Look what I did last night."

I have spent hours painstakingly copying and organising my

notes since the beginning of the year, and it shows. My handwriting has never been so neat or my notes actually inserted into the binder.

"They're perfect." His enthusiastic reaction sends a pleasant chill through my spine. "It must have taken you all night."

That's irrelevant.

"And what did you do last night?" I ask, keeping my tone polite and detached.

Michael worries his bottom lip as he recollects his thoughts.

"I had a late snack with my mum, then I went to bed with a book."

I see he'll give me nothing unless I directly ask for it. I close the binder with a snap.

"How did it go with Abby?"

I dislike the resentful look on his face, as though he doesn't particularly appreciate when people pry into his private business. But he recollects himself quickly, leans in, the air between us charging up with some invisible current, and whispers:

"Abby really is—"

"Silence, please!"

Paquin has entered the classroom, her arms charged with papers, and everyone grows quiet.

My fist slams on the table. I'll never get to hear that one either. That's just grand. Michael offers me an apologetic smile and leans away from me. The air is now nothing but air, with the faint lingering scent of apples.

It just so happens that the papers Paquin is holding are, in fact, our Dorian Gray essays. My heart leaps hopefully. I watch with growing trepidation as she distributes them.

She deposits one between Tony and Lucie with a disapproving look. "You could have tried harder. Especially you, Lucie."

Lucie not giving her best on a Literature essay is odd. I guess I'm not the only one who has been distracted, lately. I would know what she has on her mind if I'd paid more attention to her. And I will, of course, on the advice of my very good friend Michael.

Paquin turns her back on Lucie and Tony, who don't look at all disappointed, but instead are laughing as they fight over the copy. From here I can't read their grade.

When Paquin stops in front of our table, my pulse is racing. She won't be able to resist making a snarky comment. She never has. Quite my fault, yes, since I started off the year writing something idiotic on her whiteboard, never to be allowed the use of a magic marker again.

Beside me, Michael is waiting patiently, showing perfect confidence in the work he provided, and perhaps, I dare to think with a jolt of the heart, in me.

"It seems I've found the best partner for you, Monsieur Mésange."

There you go. The snark. Laughter in the classroom.

I extend my hand to accept the copy she's handing me, but she resists, and I have to pull harder. When she lets go of the copy, she's laughing.

I stare down at the piece of paper, my heart racing. Red ink usually so angry this time spells a proud 19/20.

I've never, never had such a mark. Which is why I react like an idiot.

"Nineteen? Why not twenty?"

Paquin turns around, her plucked eyebrow arched. "Because, Monsieur Mésange, perfection doesn't exist."

Michael takes the paper from my hand. Our fingers brush together.

"Like hell, it doesn't," I mutter, shivering.

"I'm not gonna say I told you so," Michael says, mischievous.

"You just did!"

He's right. We did good. We did great, actually, almost perfect. 19/20. We are undeniably a good match. By that, I mean team. We're a good team. Work team.

Michael drops the essay into my open backpack. "Show it to your father. He'll be pleased. Do you think he'll let you come tonight?"

"Tonight? What's going on tonight?"

"Sacha's party."

My smile falters. "Sacha's throwing a party? That's news to me."

"You didn't know?" Michael's face blanches as we both realise I was not invited.

What's going on? Sacha's throwing a party, and I'm not invited? That has to be a first.

Sacha likes me, she always had a weakness for dorky little me, and now more so since I've grown into something more presentable. She likes me so much that she even puts up with Tony, whom she thoroughly dislikes, and always invites us all to her parties. So, in the words of a great saint: What the fuck?

"I probably misunderstood," Michael says, embarrassed. "It's probably not even a party. I always misunderstand everything."

Does he, now? His top grades, social skills, and his acute understanding of how to style his hair beg to differ, but okay.

"Since when have you known about it?" I try to control my voice to sound less dejected than I actually am.

"Only yesterday. It's probably nothing."

At the front of the class, Paquin has the name of the next book we are to read during the fast-approaching holidays. Wuthering Heights. I absently make a note of it, too distracted by my disturbing news.

As soon as the bell rings, I breathlessly leave Michael behind to pounce on Tony and Lucie.

"Have you heard about Sacha's party? Sacha's throwing a party, and she didn't invite us."

Tony and Lucie exchange looks.

"Whatever," Tony says, jamming his notebook in his backpack. "It doesn't matter."

"But—"

"Honestly, I always wondered why she invited us in the first place. We've got nothing in common."

I can always rely on Tony to be unhelpful, at least.

Lucie sighs and takes my hand. "It's not the end of the world. You can come to my place instead."

"What, and leave me alone?" Tony says, scowling.

Don't worry, Tony. If I go to Lucie's place, I'm going to find myself in a very complicated situation, and I'll have to confess to being a liar, or worse, lie some more to cover my first lie, and I don't think I can do that, to her and to myself.

"Come on," Lucie insists. Her tone is strangely pleading. "Come to my place."

The polar bear backpack is back. I better choose my words carefully. She didn't use to be like that. Whatever happened to us? I was perfectly fine holding hands and making out on public benches for the rest of eternity. Eventually, sex gets us all.

"I think I'll just stay home." I let go of Lucie's hand. "Do some homework."

Her eyes narrow. "You? Doing homework on a Friday night?"

"Well, yes."

"Then why are you whining about Sacha's party?"

"I'm not." Even I know that this lie is pretty obvious. "I've got to keep my grades up, you know, to go to London."

They exchange another glance they think I didn't catch.

"This book isn't going to read itself," I say, pointing at the whiteboard as we exit the classroom.

"We have four weeks to read it."

"Yeah, and remember what happened to me last time when I didn't finish it. Remember?"

"Yeah," Tony says, laughing. "You got paired up with Mister Clean."

"Don't call him that."

My harsh tone plunges Tony into silence for a minute or so. But once outside, he lights up a smoke and turns to me, his lips pursed.

"Fine. Stay home if you're in this shitty mood. I've had enough of you lately."

Lucie fumbles with her own cigarette, watching us anxiously.

"Sorry," I say, quite low.

But truly, I don't mean it, and I wish he'd apologise, for once.

Hours later, at home, all I can think of is this party to which I'm not invited, where Michael will probably be. Tortured by ideas of how loose Michael might be after a few shots, I'm that close to start banging my head against the walls.

Even more so when my father, upon seeing the copy of the essay I left on the kitchen table, knocks on my door to congratulate me.

"Continue like this and I'll speak to Tony's father myself about getting you that flat."

"You would?" I ask, surprised.

He nods. "I would."

He looks around my bedroom and his mouth drops open. I may have cleaned it from top to bottom last night, before deciding to compile my English Lit notes.

"Are you not going out tonight? To celebrate? You can stay as late as you want."

My father has never encouraged me to celebrate anything, ever. It had to happen the night of the only party in the world to which I'm not invited.

Groaning under my breath, I retrieve my phone from my pocket to text Lucie.

> LOU:
> HOW COME SACHA IS THROWING A PARTY, ANYWAY?
> WHAT'S THE OCCAS'?

LUCIE:
WHY DO YOU CARE? IT'S GOING TO BE BORING. FILLED WITH HER SNOB FRIENDS AND THE GOLDEN FORK. YOU DON'T EVEN LIKE THEM.

I do like one of them. My friend, Michael.

> LOU:
> I DON'T CARE. I'M JUST CURIOUS.

Lucie types for a long time while I wait, chewing on my cuticles.

LUCIE:
SACHA WANTS TO GET WITH MICHAEL TONIGHT.

My breath catches. I start pounding on the keys.

> LOU:

LUCIE:

A GIRLFRIEND? YEAH, BUT SHE LIVES IN LONDON AND SACHA DOESN'T
CARE.

Sacha, you witch.

So, this party is an entrapment, isn't it? Luring poor innocent
Michael to your den, and fill him up with disgusting Malibu-based
cocktails until he miraculously develops feelings for you!

I can't let you do this. It's immoral. I've got to get in there first.

I mean, to protect him.

LOU:

WHY DIDN'T SHE INVITE US? SHE ALWAYS DOES.

Lucie takes forever to reply, which is frankly maddening.

LOU:

HELLO?

LUCIE:

I DIDN'T SEE YOUR LAST MESSAGE. I DON'T KNOW. PROBABLY
BECAUSE OF FRANÇOIS. APPARENTLY HE DOESN'T LIKE YOU.

François? François again? What did I possibly do to this guy? I
fall back onto my bed, my head reeling. Then my phone beeps
again.

LUCIE:

ARE YOU SURE YOU WANT TO STAY HOME TONIGHT? I TOLD YOU MY
PARENTS WEREN'T HERE.

My Lucie is becoming really obsessed. I mean, what does a guy
have to do not to sleep with his girlfriend these days?

LOU:

Poor Lucie. I should tell her the truth. I should tell her now. It's not too late. She might not be that angry about that girl I slept with last summer. I can tell her I don't even remember doing it. It's the absolute truth. It only happened once we were very drunk. She said she had a great time, and I believed her, but Lucie doesn't have to know that. If she forgives me, I can walk over to her place. We could have sushi, share a bottle of wine, watch a movie. I could finally spend the night...

But why am I not invited to this party? Why does François hate me? I can't get it out of my head, it's so infuriating!

Damn them all. The Golden Fork is the worst. Only Yasmine is worth saving. And I'm not only saying this because I'm terrified of her.

What if it was all related to Michael? After all, what do Sacha and François have in common? They both want Michael for themselves.

And why would they get rid of me... unless I was, in fact, their competition?

It's official. I must crash this party.

At the very least, to warn Michael, or he'll find himself pulled in both directions. He's my friend, that's the least I can do.

But what about Lucie? I just made a promise to be a better boyfriend and tell her the truth.

I can always be a better boyfriend tomorrow. When I have time to think about what I'm going to say. So many things can happen between tonight and tomorrow... I'm sure by then I'll find the words.

But right now, I must get to Michael before he does something he might regret.

Of course, I must find something to wear first, and it would probably do me some good to clean up a little. After all, Sacha and François might be less inclined to toss me out if I look like one of them.

What does Michael wear at parties? He will probably show up in one of his father's suits, outshining everyone in there and causing

François to pass out in the kitchen. How does one have this sort of power on people? If I had nice clothes, I could show François who's boss too. He may have an expensive hairdresser and a range of skin-care, but he's freckled and insufferable.

For the first time in years, I use my voice to call my father in the other room. He trips over something on the way and the sound of a pile of aeroplane magazines toppling over reaches me. Two seconds later, he's in my room again, looking frightened.

"What's going on? Are you all right?"

I pretend to wipe a speck of dirt off the surface of my desk. "Do you have a nice shirt I could borrow?

Despite his initial surprise, my dad does his best to pretend my request isn't unusual. We walk over to his bedroom. He explores the depths of his wardrobe, while I pretend not to notice my parents' wedding picture is still on his nightstand. Is he hurting about it, or has he simply forgotten to remove it? Eventually, with a little smile, he pulls out a carefully wrapped navy shirt.

"What do you think?"

I'm actually astonished at how nice it looks, for something belonging to my old man.

"It's great, thank you."

"It was your mom's favourite."

Why does he always have to ruin everything? With a sigh, I take the shirt from his hand and retreat to my bedroom. We are not going to talk about this now. For years we have not brought it up, establishing this perfect silent relationship between us, should the subject arise. Not about to break it now.

"It's your birthday soon." My father sticks his head into my room as I put on the shirt. "Do you know what you'd like?"

I had completely forgotten about this. Who has time for birthdays when Michael is in danger?

"Oh, you know…" My trembling fingers fumble with the buttons. "It doesn't really matter."

Granted, I'll have to think of something before he panics and gets me something stupid. But not now. Now, I've got to rescue my pretty friend.

My father's shirt fits me well. Paired with black jeans and my leather jacket, I look perfectly respectable. I only need my sunglasses.

They're not on the desk. They're not in my pockets. They're not hiding in the folds of my bedspread. Then where the hell are they?

Pressed by time, my heart racing, I overturn my backpack, flip over my mattress, wrench open every drawer, turning my neat bedroom into a battlefield,. My shades are nowhere to be found.

What can be worse? Tony's gift to me hasn't left me in more than two years. I never go anywhere without them, and I would never envision crashing a party without them. But the clock is ticking. With every minute Michael is getting drunker and looser. Who knows in which state's he'll be in an hour? Whether he ends up in Sacha's arms or François's, one thing is clear: I can't let that happen.

Downcast but still determined, I make my way downstairs. Old Lady is there, picking up her mail.

"Don't you look nice!" She gives me a once over, a pile of letters clutched in her hand. Her gaze reaches my face and she grimaces. "Except your face. Your face looks miserable."

"And you're old."

She scoffs. "Perceptive, for a little shit."

I point at her pile of mail. "Who picks up their mail at eight o'clock on a Friday evening anyway?

"I do! To avoid little shits like you."

All right, fine! She can be funny. I concede a smile.

She ambles toward the staircase. "Why are you so miserable tonight?"

My long harrowing sigh makes her laugh some more.

"For your information, that's why I always wear my sunglasses. It hides a part of my face, you know?"

"The most miserable looking."

"Whatever. Anyway... I've lost them."

"And?" She puts her hand on the handrail.

"I never leave without them. They're a part of me."

"So why don't you get a new pair?"

I hesitate. "It's not the same. They are a part of my identity. Can I get a new identity?"

It's her turn to sigh, as if my despair is just boring to her. But then she gestures for me to follow her upstairs.

"Come with me. I've seen you wear these blasted things even during the darkest of nights. Tripping over these very stairs."

"They make me look good."

"For whom do you want to look good, the stairs?"

I follow her up the staircase, my arms spread out, worried she might slip and break her neck at every step. But she seems to know what she's doing.

A minute later, I'm back into her flat. This time, she leads me into her living room. I recognise the comfy-looking sofa and the handsome coffee table. It's littered with trash, but looking lonely in the corner, there's a bottle of gin and a small glass. I give Old Lady a pointed look.

"What?" she says. "At least I'm not miserable like you."

"Can I?" I point at the bottle.

"Help yourself."

I pour myself a shot while she rummages through the large drawer of an antic dresser. Why does she have so much shit on her coffee table? The rest of her flat is pretty neat. Then it hits me. It's not trash… it's…

"Is this?"

Yes, it is. Unmistakable pieces of paper, stickers, ribbons and Washi tapes. The whole armada.

"What?" She doesn't look up from her drawer. "I'm trying scrapbooking."

Clutching a hand to my chest, I toss the shot back, and immediately pours another.

"Scrapbooking is for losers, Miss. You should know that."

"And you would know about losers."

Jesus. She doesn't skip a beat, this old lady.

"There." She hands me a fine leather box. "Don't break them or I'll have you drawn and quartered."

I pop the box open and find a pair of black vintage acetate aviators that would make any of my rockstar idols blush with envy. I turn and turn them around in my hands, speechless.

"Where did you get them?"

She slams the drawer of her dresser shut. "I've had a life, you know! And better friends than yours."

Yeah, probably. I mean, I don't mean that. I don't know.

"They're perfect. Thank you." I put them on with twitchy fingers. "How do I look?"

"You'll have more success than you can handle with these. Proceed with caution."

Best news I've heard today. I put the shot glass, now empty, back on the table.

"Joke aside." Old Lady drops heavily into an armchair. "You do look very nice. Ready for battle."

I slide the glasses down my nose. "For battle?"

"For chasing after your girl."

I shake my head. "I'm not chasing after anybody."

She points her finger at me. "Then why are you dressed so well? And the hair… So clean!"

I plant both feet in front of her and bend down to reach eye-level with her.

"Were you already that curious during World War One or is it recent?"

She snorts and waves me off. "Go on then, don't chase after your girl."

I trot toward the front door, hesitate, swirl around.

"Hey, you know… You're quite cool, for an old lady."

She twists around in her chair to give me a better look.

"My name's Eugénie," she says, "and I'm cooler than you."

13

THIS IS WHERE IT GETS EVEN WEIRDER

W hile riding on the bus toward Sacha's, I realise I'm nervous. I'm feeling rattled, paranoid like the first time I smoked a joint and felt everyone's eyes on me on the metro ride home.

Miss Eugénie's right. Am I, or am I not, crashing a party to make sure my friend doesn't get cosy with anyone? Boy or girl, it doesn't matter, if he should kiss anybody, like anybody, need anybody, then this person should be me.

I've never crashed a party before, but I've seen spy movies, so as I climb the steps of Sacha's building's grand staircase two-by-two — it's better to avoid running into people in the lift — I think I'll be all right. To be honest, Sacha's flat is probably the easiest place to get into. Before I get lost in fantasies to climb up the wall — she lives on the top floor — it makes sense to start with the front door.

Excellent idea, if I could pat myself on the back, literally, I would. Things couldn't get any easier: Sacha's door is wide open, Sean Paul's last hit blasting loud enough from her expensive speakers to shake even the building's walls to their core.

My mouth falls open when I sneak inside. Small gathering, my ass. Everyone from class seems to be here, spread out across the flat, sipping booze from plastic cups and smiling beatifically at each other. Even Lars is here, unmissable by his monstrous size. He flashes me a smile as I attempt to slink undetected toward the living room, so we're cool.

Short-lived, my good luck is aborted when I straight out knock François over in my haste to reach the dance floor. His initial shock at being shoved into a wall over, he recognises me and his face flushes even in the dark. He clamps his hand around my wrist, his pale eyes threatening to pop out of their socket.

"You're here!"

"Not thanks to you."

I try to break free from his grasp but he digs his nails into my skin. Is he seriously considering wrestling me out of Sacha's flat?

"Why did you have to come?" The tone of his voice, overtly whiny, makes my lip curl.

"What? Is it invitation only?"

"Pretty much, yeah."

He lets my arm go, at least.

The truth is, I won't get anywhere by antagonising François tonight. I have to do better, if only for Michael. Pushing my borrowed sunglasses up my nose, I decide to appeal to his kinder nature. It worked for me during the New Year's Eve party.

"Sacha has only forgotten to invite me."

"I doubt that." François's fingers fly to Eugénie's sunglasses. I slap his hand away.

"Hands off."

Come on, François. I don't have time for you. I need to say hello to a guy.

Lunging forward, I make a run for it, François hot on my heels. Sacha chooses this moment to come out of the kitchen and stumbles, already drunk, right into my arms.

"Hey, Lou!" She lets out a small burp. "Oops. Sorry."

François catches up to us and pushes me against the wall. Sacha gasps. François makes another go at my sunglasses.

"Where did you get that?"

I shrug. "I've got better friends than yours."

"What is that supposed to mean?" He looks almost angry.

"I don't know." I flash a smile at Sacha, who grins and literally melts into my arms. To my surprise, François helps me get her to her feet.

"Lou! I'm so glad you made it!" Sacha throws her white arms around my neck and plops a very, very wet kiss onto my cheek. "Nice glasses."

"Thanks. They're vintage."

"And extremely expensive," François gives me a resentful look. "You've really cleaned up, tonight. What's going on? Have you discovered the existence of outlets?"

Sacha bursts out laughing. "Come on boys, be nice."

This is so painful. But on the other hand, as long as they're with me, they're not pestering Michael.

"You always have the best stuff, Lou." Sacha attempts to caress my cheek but scratches me instead.

"I seriously doubt that," I say. "Can I have a drink, Sacha? It seems you forgot to invite me."

"I would never!" She glues herself to me. "Come on, let's go see Michael, he's completely miserable."

"Sacha!" François protests.

He looks completely defeated, but there's no stopping Hurricane Sacha.

We stumble arm-in-arm upon the make-shift dance floor in the middle of the living room. Sacha scans the room for Michael, using her hand as a visor, undoubtedly seeing double. I'm taller, and sober-ish, better fitted at sniffing out Michael in a crowd. It doesn't take too long for me to spot him.

Dressed in this morning's clothes, standing alone by the plant in the farthest corner of the room, Michael dives nose-first into his cup, throws the whole thing back. His eyes squeeze tightly shut as the liquid burns down his throat. The tip of his tongue darts out and takes a swipe at any stray drops. When he reopens his eyes, the mere sight of their intoxicated glint swathes my skin in goosebumps. My arms fall limply to my sides.

Congratulations. Michael can even make drinking out of plastic cups look hot.

Without me to support her, Sacha trips and falls over. Called by an invisible force, I keep moving, slowly closing the distance between Michael and I. At last, he looks up. A slight frown mars his face when his gaze falls upon me. I remove the sunglasses; he knows me.

Do you like me? My expression says.

What are you doing here? His own answer.

When his smile reaches his eyes, something powerful, bright and hot swells in my chest.

I know I have to get closer. I start forcing my way through the crowd of classmates. Move, move aside. On the other side of the room, Michael is picking up, and begins to wade his own way toward me. Soon, we'll be together. Then—

Then, I come face to face with the last two people I ever expected to be here.

My best friend and my girlfriend.

Everything stops. I even forget all about Michael.

I don't know who's more shocked. Well, actually, I do, it's me. I'm shocked and I show it, slacked jaw and wobbling knees, cheeks already burning. Not only caught in a lie, but catching them at it too.

Tony looks almost afraid, but Lucie, my Lucie dares me to say a word, looking at me as though I'm a volleyball she needs to punch as hard as possible. We wait in a supercharged silence, like strange statues among the carefree people laughing and dancing around us.

Lucie's nostrils start flaring. I'm honestly too shocked to find them both here for anger to be my first reaction.

"What are you doing here?" We say at the same time.

I'm first amused at our synchronicity. Her murderous eyes swiftly wipe my smile from my face.

"Answer me," she says. She crosses her arms firmly over her chest.

My throat squeezes tightly shut. "I changed my mind. Didn't want to stay home."

Tony looks down at my shirt in disbelief. "What are you wearing?"

"You changed your mind, but you didn't tell us?" Lucie's anger gives her face a frightening tinge.

128

Am I going to be found out? How can I find a good reason to be here without being found out? Technically, I haven't done anything that bad, yet. But a minute ago, I was contemplating it.

To make matters worst, the object of my obsession crosses the sea of people to meet me, smelling of divine after-shave and cheap liquor, puts his hand on my arm, and doesn't notice Tony's eye-roll.

"Hey, Louis, look what I've got?" Michael's words come out a little slurred. In his open hand lay my sunglasses.

"Did you lend them to him?" Tony asks, his face white.

"No, I didn't." I'm not lying but my voice comes out as squeaky as some Disney mouse.

"No," Michael says. "He forgot them in class."

"You forgot them." Tony shakes his head. "Great."

"Shit happens, Tony."

My reaction takes him aback. His face takes on a hurt look.

"Here," Michael says, putting them in my shirt pocket. "You wouldn't be the same without them."

Tony slips him a glare. "Okay, Dorian Gay, settle down."

Michael stares at Tony in disbelief. Tony stares back, unperturbed.

"Boys! Boys, look at me." Sacha stumbles into our perfect little circle of friendship, pushing Lucie out of the way, determined to be the centre of attention. François is right behind her. This is getting better by the minute. "Did you know… LouLou and I used to be together?"

Groaning, I slap a hand against my forehead.

"You've got to be kidding me," Lucie says, her lip curling.

Michael looks in disbelief. "You two used to date?"

This sudden interest is either for my benefit, or Sacha's. We both know it. Which one of us shall it be? I'm better than Sacha at pretending I haven't noticed.

Next to the sparkling Sacha, François looks like a shadow.

"No," I say, a little too loud perhaps. "We held hands in kindergarten."

"We graduated from that," she says, her voice charged with boozy lust. She tries to hug me but ends up slipping into Michael's arms instead.

What's going on? I promise I've never done anything more than French-kissing her at Deborah's party. We were twelve. I'm innocent!

Lucie pulls me aside, still glaring at me.

"You're a liar, Louis."

Well. This is true. I can't deny it. I wish I was the sort of guy who gets on his knees and begs for forgiveness. But I'm not, and I feel it's unfair to be put on trial here.

"I'm sorry I lied, but—"

"You're a liar!" Lucie's eyes fill with tears.

"But you lied to me too!"

Her face turns white. "What?"

"You didn't tell me you were coming here." I pause, for emphasis. "With *my* best friend Tony."

Sacha, François, Tony, and Michael aren't missing a single beat of this conversation. I came here in the foolish hope to save Michael, and now I could definitely use his help. But from the way he and Sacha are clinging to each other, he's nearly as drunk as she is and can't even save himself, let alone me.

Lucie digs a small finger into my chest. "I offered you to spend the night with me, and you, you only thought about this stupid party."

"You are at this stupid party."

"I was invited, okay!"

"Wait a minute." I look at her in disbelief. "You were?"

"We were," she says bitterly, pointing at Tony. "We didn't want to tell you because we didn't want to hurt your feelings. François didn't want you to come, okay? Everyone was invited but you."

My surprise quickly makes way to bitterness. "That's cool. You decided to come here without me, the both of you. Nice."

"Only after you refused to come to mine again." She rubs her eyes, looks at me, lets out a long sigh. "Fuck this, have fun at your stupid party. I'm leaving."

She shoves François aside, who stares after her in outrage, and forces her way toward the exit without a look back.

Tony first hesitates, and looks like he wants to say something to me. But after a last glance at Michael, he clicks his tongue frustratedly and mutters a "see you around" that doesn't bode well, and goes after Lucie.

My mouth fills with a bitter taste. I shouldn't let them leave together when they're so angry at me. I shouldn't. Something is telling me I'll pay dearly for it, one way or another.

Sacha, on the other hand, wastes no time and hops over to me, clutching me and prodding me like a long-awaited newborn baby.

"Don't be sad, LouLou."

"We kissed once, get over it," I say, annoyed.

"Let's kiss again!"

Sacha attempts to grab my face. I try to keep her at a distance with both hands. Michael takes her cocktail and chugs half its contents down his throat.

"Great party," he says, choking on an ice cube.

Sacha tosses her hair back, confused. Her hazel eyes and little freckles around her nose are very cute. I can still remember her face when we were babies.

"You should take it easy, Sacha. Where's Yas'?"

"Couldn't make it tonight. Family thing."

That explains it. Yasmine wouldn't let her best friend get completely hammered over some guy.

François, however, is stuck in a dark and revengeful place fuelled by cheap alcohol, and he seems to inexplicably hate my guts. He pulls Sacha by the arm and yanks her bodily away from me.

"Good job, Lou!"

What on earth have I done to this guy, honestly?

"Next time you're not invited, make sure you stay that way, okay?"

He trudges toward the kitchen, dragging Sacha by the arm. She blows Michael and me a kiss. I remove Eugénie's shades and, after closer inspection, decide they're too dangerous and better left in their leather box at the bottom of a drawer. I tuck them neatly into my pocket.

Drunk Michael, up close, is a sweaty mess of curls and wide eyes. I'm not saying he's not hot anymore. I'm saying I think I've

131

come down a little. I'm saying my little obsession's about to cost me a price I don't want to pay.

"What's going on?" Michael asks, looking just as confused at Sacha.

"Chaos." I wince at the bad feeling growing in the pit of my stomach. "I'll explain later."

Michael takes another swig of Sacha's disgusting-looking cocktail. "Can I help?"

His eyes are soft, earnest. He's here, so close. The reason I'm not running after my friends right now. I could almost kiss him, right here, right now, in the middle of Sacha's living room, and people might notice, but I'd at least be able to understand all of this, and maybe I could move on.

"Yes. Yes, you can."

Just one kiss, and it would all be over.

But here it is. He's absolutely wasted. Taking advantage of him would simply ruin everything. I came here to save him, not molest him.

I drag him, smiling, across the living room, and throw the contents of his cup in the nearest plant.

"First, don't drink this shit, it will give you a headache."

"We were out of wine," Michael says, following me diligently.

I hand him his coat, hooked neatly in the doorway above a passed-out Lars sprawled out onto the floor. Michael struggles back into his coat.

"Are we going after them?"

"Who?"

"Tony and your girlfriend."

"I don't think so." Lucie's angry face flashes in my head, twisting my stomach. "They wouldn't want to see us right now. Come on, I'll take you home."

"I'm drunk," he says.

He attempts to button his coat but gives up after the first half-assed try.

"That's okay. That's why I'm taking you home."

Wrapping his scarf around his neck, I gently nudge Michael toward the door, when Sacha calls his name.

"You're not leaving, are you?" She comes trotting toward us, her face the picture of drunken disappointment. She shoves a plastic cup full of booze into Michael's hand.

Michael kisses her cheek. "I'm sorry."

"I think he's had enough."

Both Sacha and François glare at me, as though I have single-handedly ruined their night. Their anger somewhat amuses me.

"Look what you did!" I tell Michael, with a nod toward them.

Michael trips over Lars's leg and the cup Sacha gave him tips over, pouring its contents all over his shirt. Michael stares at the stain spreading right above his heart and slurs:

"It's not me, it's you."

"Ok. I'm taking you home before we do any more damage."

A deep feeling of relief washes over me once we get outside. The sky is clear for once, and the stars glinting above seem to be watching over us.

Michael's freezing in his open coat. We stop in the middle of the pavement so I can button it for him.

"When I arrived," I say, "Sacha said you were miserable. What happened?"

"I don't like parties." His voice is too loud. "Or, I don't like people. No, that's not right. I don't know."

The last button dealt with, I smooth Michael's lapel and step back to admire my work. "All done."

We slowly walk toward the nearest bus stop. Michael is silent for a long time.

"I didn't think you'd come," he says eventually.

"I didn't think you were a drunk!"

He snorts and buries his fist into my shoulder. "Sacha was really nice and kept serving me drinks."

I bet she was.

Drunk Michael is hopeless. Soon enough, he almost slams into a lamppost. Catching his arm, I stir him back to safety. He clings to my side, his body warm despite the cold.

"Even drunk," he says, "I wasn't having fun before you showed up."

"Really? But I stayed for five minutes, and I was fighting for four of them."

"Were you?"

I can't help laughing. At his drunken sweetness, at myself, at the situation.

Me and Michael. The best of friends.

We arrive at the bus stop. I drop his drunk ass on the bench and start pacing. Without alcohol to keep me warm, I'm quickly frozen to the bone.

Michael turns to me, his breath like little puffs of smoke in the warm light of the bus stop.

"I want to tell you something."

My heart jumps in my chest. "Could you possibly... tell me tomorrow?"

This is about the worst possible time for confessions right now. Whatever he says to me drunk is not going to be of any use to me tonight.

Michael shakes his head. "I want to tell you now."

"Fine."

I reluctantly take a seat next to him. Michael takes a deep breath, stares down at his shoes.

"My parents are having problems."

That... wasn't what I expected. But it's also not what I feared.

"What sort of problems?"

"I think they wanted to split up. That's why she took the part, so she could come to Paris and, you know, put some distance between them."

Michael's perfect life isn't so perfect after all. Even his parents got fed up with each other, just like mine.

"Did your mum ask you to come with her?"

Michael shivers in his coat. "No, not really. I just wanted to be with her."

I listen, aghast. "You left all of your friends and your girlfriend just to be with your mum?"

I wouldn't even leave Tony one afternoon to spend time with my mum. Hang on. That's not exactly true. She wouldn't leave her friends one afternoon to spend time with me. That's more like it. Michael's mum isn't like that, though. She seems pretty great.

"I guess," Michael says with a faint smile. "Anyway. Now, you know my secret too."

I recall our time at the movies, when he said he owed me a confession. He remembered. That alone brings a smile to my face.

"How did she take it?" I ask.

"She was very happy."

A cloud of fog snorts out of my nose. "Your girlfriend, I mean."

Michael doesn't answer at first. His gaze still locked on his shoes, he runs a hand through his curls.

"Louis."

"Yes."

"You know... my girlfriend?"

The sudden arrival of the bus smashes our little bubble and interrupts once again our conversation. I help Michael to his feet, and we stagger together toward the door.

Michael gets in first, not so assured on his legs. The bus is crowded, noisy, filled with young people excited to go out for the night. My hand, flat on Michael's back, helps to stir him toward the last available seats in the back.

"Are you and Lucie okay?" Michael asks, dropping heavily onto the seat.

I slump down next to him. "I honestly don't know."

The bus lurches forward. Michael and I are so close. A bump in the road and my mouth would be on his ear, telling things no one's ready to hear.

Lucie and Tony are going to need my immediate intention if I don't want to screw everything up. I've got to start thinking about what to tell them now.

"I'm sorry," Michael says.

"I know."

He's drunk. His words carry no meaningful weight. Mine do. He's so drunk, and he suddenly rests his head on my shoulder, his curls grazing my cheeks. He's drunk, but still, my heart starts thumping in my chest, and I have to dig my nails into my knees to resist the temptation to bury my lips in his hair.

Michael moves his hand toward mine. His fingers brush against mine, my breath catches in my throat. He's drunk, he doesn't know what he's doing. But still. In silence, my fingers tentatively slide toward his, deaf to the barking orders from my brain to get my shit together. Two of my fingers intertwine with two of his. February makes way to June, the temperature rises. A hush settles on my soul at the same time my heart threatens to jump out of my ribcage.

Very silently, very quietly, we ride the bus with locked fingers and tight lips, both unwilling to break the charm with stale words.

Michael is better when we get off the bus. He doesn't need my help any longer, but I deliberately keep close, just in case. At his door, he drops his keys. I pick them up and inwardly smile when our fingers touch again.

He scratches the back of his neck. "Thanks for taking me home. Really."

"No problem. I live to serve."

"You're funny, Louis." His smile freezes at the edges. "Everybody likes you."

I can't help laughing. "You're obviously still drunk."

Our laughter fades into silence.

"Can I ask you something?" Michael says.

Time stops. My imagination gets carried away. I picture the scene in my head.

Me, stepping closer. Me, saying, "Yes."

Michael worrying his poor bottom lip, twisting and turning his keys in his hand.

"Tonight... Did you come for me?"

"Yes."

My heart's doing cartwheels, me thinking I might die. Michael leaning closer... our lips almost touching...

"What are you doing tomorrow?" the real Michael asks, bursting my little fantasy like a soap bubble.

I blink fast to recover. "Er... Nothing important, I think?"

Tony and Lucie's angry faces come rushing back into my mind. I screw my eyes shut.

"Can I text you?" Michael asks, lightly touching my arm.

I don't want to look at him. If I do, I'm lost.

"Yes."

We both want to say more, to do more, I think. We're both afraid. We both abstain. We both turn our back to each other, eager for the safety of our homes, where we slip under the sheets and surrender to the night, alternating between states of sheer terror and feverish exhilaration.

14

TIME OUT

When I enter the coffee place, I do a double-take, because it seems colder in there than outside. Or it could be just from the way Tony and Lucie, sitting at a table by the window, are glaring at me.

Tony sent me a message this morning, shortly after I woke up, simultaneously shaken and happy from a good night's sleep, congratulating myself on a morning without a hangover.

TONY:
WE NEED TO TALK.

This being code for I'm going to break up with your sorry ass, I decided to pay real attention to it. I made a mistake last night, chose Michael over them, and here's the reckoning.

I come to the meeting rendezvous, a coffee place between Tony's and my own place, with the firm intention of apologising, and the naive hope to be able to go home early and wait for Michael's text.

Oh, to be young and stupid.

Dorian would get me.

I take a seat on a booth opposite Lucie. My mouth stretches in a yawn.

"Long night?" Tony asks, sarcastic, tearing a good chunk of the croissant laid in front of him and shoving it into his mouth.

Despite their hostile attitude, I choose to believe I'll get out of this place unscathed if I just act like I haven't done anything wrong. Which, technically, I haven't. Apart from lying to their faces about the party last night.

I put my sunglasses, the ones Tony gave me, not Eugénie's chick magnet, on the table before me and flash them a smile.

"I slept really well, actually. You?"

They don't answer, but from Lucie's tinge, I can assume she didn't, in fact, sleep well. The cup of coffee and the croissant in front of her lay untouched, and the way she's looking at me turns my stomach into a knot.

A young waiter arrives at our table, puts a menu under my nose, twisting his long neck to look at me.

"Can I take your order?"

I answer without blinking. "I just got this. I'm gonna need more time."

"I'll be back shortly, then."

With a clipped smile, he spins around and walks off. Instinctively, Tony and I exchange a look.

"This guy looks like a bird," I say.

Tony can't help chortling, his mouth full of croissant. "He does, doesn't he?"

Lucie gives a great sigh, reducing us to silence.

"What's up?" I ask, pretending to read the greasy menu.

No answer. Looking up, I see they're both looking at me intently. My anxiety rises. It dawns on me that I'm on the wrong side of the table.

"Look," I say, in an effort to make things right. "I fucked up yesterday. I should have told you when I changed my mind and decided to crash Sacha's party. But you didn't tell me that you were invited. So, we're even, aren't we?" I attempt to convey with my eyes how sorry I am but how reasonable this demand is.

Tony looks annoyed.

"It's not the same. We didn't tell you we were invited because we didn't want you to feel bad. You, on the other hand, just treat us like shit to spend time with your new friends."

My new friends. Does he mean Michael?

"I left the party two minutes after you, I swear."

Tony gives a dubitative smirk. "Sure."

"I did!" I nod to add emphasis. "You can ask Michael."

The mention of Michael is enough for Tony to toss the last bit of his croissant on the table and point a finger at me.

"That Michael. What's his deal? Is he gay or what?"

Wouldn't I like to know!

Take a ticket and wait in line, bro.

"What?" I nervously scratch my cheek. "Why are you saying that?"

"Nothing. Forget it."

Lucie glances nervously at Tony, who tears another chunk from his croissant.

"You're different," she says. "You seem to want to hang out with them more than with us."

"With whom?"

I'm seriously not getting it, and I'm not hungover.

"Seriously? You literally lied to us to party with Sacha and Michael."

Oh, right.

I respect that she left François out of this, at least.

"Again, I'm sorry I lied, but I don't understand what's the big deal about it."

"You don't see it, that's good for you." Lucie rests her forehead in her hand.

"It's this Michael," Tony says. "I know it."

What do they think they know? They don't know anything. *I* don't know anything, so…

At the same moment, my bird-like waiter comes back, all smiles.

"Have you chosen yet?"

We all stare at him, bewildered.

"Give me another few minutes, please?" Ignoring his scandalised expression, I turn back to Tony. "What's wrong with Michael?"

Tony tilts his head. "Ever since you've started hanging out with him, you've been acting really weird."

"I haven't been... hanging out with him." I clear my throat. "I've been doing homework with him."

"Last night didn't seem like homework," Lucie trails her finger along the edge of her untouched plate.

My pulse quickens. What have they seen?

"What do you mean?"

Tony picks at his croissant until it's ripped to shreds, sending pieces flying everywhere.

"What? Were you planning to do homework with Michael at Sacha's party?"

"It's not just that." Lucie chimes in. "Since New Year's Eve, you're just different. You've cancelled on us half a dozen times—"

"To work on the essay."

Tony gives a mocking laugh. "You've never given a shit about homework before."

"I've never had my father making threats before."

"Threats? Of what? London? You were never serious about London."

This is starting to get on my nerves.

"Oh yeah?" I say, holding my ground. "Sorry, but for a second there, I really thought you wanted me to go."

Tony leans back in his chair, lips pinched. I've touched a nerve.

"You've changed your clothes," Lucie says.

I shake my head. "I wore a stupid shirt to go to Sacha's party. Big deal."

"You wash your hair," Tony adds.

"You can't be serious. You can't hold that against me."

"We're not," Lucie says, voice trembling. "We're just saying, something changed you."

My mouth opens, but no words come out. What can I say? Some of it is true.

Tony leans forward, looking to make eye contact. "It's always Michael this, Michael that. And every time I'm talking to you, I have the feeling you're somewhere else."

Lucie nods. "You don't listen to us anymore."

"You're acting like you'd rather be somewhere else."

"Like last night. You hang out with The Golden Fork. On a Friday night."

They exchange a look that shows how much they think of *that*.

For a moment, no one speaks. My gaze hops from crumb to crumb scattered on the table. I'm starting to understand where this is going, but it's so ridiculous that I can't yet admit it to myself.

"Okay, so you don't like Michael."

Tony scoffs. "Michael doesn't like you, Louis."

"What the fuck is that supposed to mean?" I ask, offended.

"If he liked you, he wouldn't try to change you," Lucie says.

"To mould you to his taste."

"To change your clothes."

"And decide who you hang out with," Tony concludes.

Michael hasn't done any of this. I have done this. By choice.

But if I challenge what they think… I might incriminate myself and reveal more than what I want to reveal.

On the other hand, they're right. I have changed. I have taken decisions that might seem completely crazy to them. The worst of all… I have ditched them to run after a guy. I've never acted like this before.

It's true. It all started when Michael arrived.

Wasn't I perfectly happy before he showed up? The three of us were indestructible. Three rockstars living the life.

Who am I now? The sort of guy who shows up uninvited to a Golden Fork party to hang out with a Golden Fork member. I have repeatedly lied to the most important people in my life, sneaked around town, hoping that a straight guy might give me, another straight guy, a kiss?

Damn it. Michael is the reason for all my problems. He persuaded me to watch a Korean movie! With subtitles!

"I didn't think…" I say weakly. "I didn't think this would matter so much to you."

"We love you," Lucie says, her face so tense she looks on the verge of tears. "It's always been the three of us. I don't want it to stop."

So far, they only think I've been ditching them because I've made a new friend. They don't know about my crazy, completely mental school-girl crush on him. No one knows but Michael. And possibly François. But what proof does he have? Nothing. As for Michael… Nothing ever happened. I can't still get out of there without causing any more damage.

Staring into Tony and Lucie's faces, I understand they're offering me a choice. Tony, shoving the pieces of his croissant in his mouth, cements the matter.

"Honestly, Lou, you can't be serious. It's the Golden Fork we're talking about. Are they really worth fucking us up?"

"I don't care about the Golden Fork."

They don't look convinced.

"We miss you," Lucie says, her eyes red. "I miss you. You've completely abandoned me."

A deep feeling of shame settles over my shoulders. She's right, a hundred percent right. I have.

"It's not normal that Tony takes better care of me than you do," she adds, sniffling. "He took me home last night. It should have been you."

I glance up at Tony, who looks back in alarm. "I mean, get your shit together, man. We shouldn't have to tell you this. It's like we're not good enough for you anymore. If you don't want us in your life, just say so."

I am, I definitely am, on the wrong side of the table. If I don't get my shit together, as instructed, they'll both break up with me. Without me, they'll be just fine. Without them, I'll be screwed. And not screwed in a nice way. Screwed like hanging out like a fool in the corridor watching my mum slam the door behind her, kind of way.

"Are you ready to order this time?"

Startled, I look up to find my bird-waiter back at the side our table, peering at us through his glasses, lips pursed. That's all I can take from him without biting his head off.

"Honestly—" I begin.

"Dude," Tony starts.

"Read the room!" Lucie says.

I hand him back the menu. "Can't you just be lazy and pissed off like the rest of us and take a cigarette break or something?"

143

With a hurt but dignified look, he snatches the menu from my hands and walks away.

"So…" I meet Lucie's eyes. "You want me to—"

"I just want things to go back to what they were."

"I agree," Tony says, picking up the last of the croissant crumbs from his plate and licking them off his fingers. "This only thing is, do you want to?"

From the way they're looking at me, my answer is of the utmost importance. Michael's face swims into my mind, of course, but at this time I can confidently say nothing, and no-one is worse losing them both at the same time.

Returning to things as they used to be wouldn't be so bad, anyway. The only thing Michael does, really, is mess with my head. Last night I ran over town to rescue him from the clutch of another guy. How ridiculous am I becoming? No-one in their right mind would risk their gorgeous girlfriend and their best friend for a silly little obsession like this.

Tony and Lucie's intervention shows how well they know me. It's like I've been awakened from the strangest dream. Did I almost upend my life for a few handsome curls?

"I want it too," I say, wiping my hands on my thighs under the table. "Things, just as they were. I'm gonna get my shit together, I promise."

There is a short silence, then Tony lets out the loudest groan I've ever heard.

"Thank you, baby Jesus!" He claps his hands together. I watch him, astonished. "I couldn't take it anymore. All this bad blood, this hostility! I'm a man of few needs, Lou, you know me! All I ever wanted today is food, a joint, and an afternoon of video games and The Fratellis. And I earned it." He gets up and stretches. "Where's that waiter? Has anyone seen him? Who do you have to kill to get some food in here?"

Tony walks away to search for our waiter. Lucie leaps forward and swallows half my face in a hungry kiss.

"I've missed you." She still looks pale and nervous. "I'll be right back."

She slides off the bench and takes the staircase down toward the Ladies.

Was that all? All they wanted from me was an apology and a promise I would do better? I can literally feel sweat streaming down my back. I really thought they would both break up with me. After this rollercoaster of emotions, I feel strangely hollow.

My phone vibrates in my pocket, startling me. I dig it out of my pockets with trembling hands.

Michael. He wants to know if we are still meeting this afternoon.

My finger hovers over the REPLY button. Yesterday, a message from him was all I ever wanted. Now Michael is like a body I once buried, something I'm afraid will come back to haunt me.

LOU:
I CAN'T.

My reply, so short, has taken me so long to come up with, that by the time I send it, Lucie's back at the table, pointing at my phone.

"Who's that?" She tries not to sound suspicious, but she does.

She doesn't trust me.

It's my fault, I haven't given her reason to. I could, right now, if I could find the courage… Courage is something I clearly lack.

I stick the phone back into my pocket, my heart giving a heavy sigh, my brain telling him to keep quiet. If I tell her, things can get back to normal again.

I've made my bed, and I'm ready to lie in it.

"Lucie… There's something you should know."

15

THOSE WERE THE DAYS

My life without Michael is pretty much what I envisioned, except for the part that I hate everything now.

School, especially, is a blast. Especially since Michael doesn't sit with me anymore. I must say, he accepted my decision relatively well, or too well, depends on my mood of the minute, because it's ever changing. The Monday morning following my conversation with Tony and Lucie, I made it clear to Michael that I didn't want anything to do with him. I didn't speak to him, didn't look at him, didn't answer his subsequent text messages.

For our next English Lit lesson the next Friday, I found him, without surprise but not without resentment, sharing François's table at the front of the class. Michael didn't complain, didn't try to talk to me again. He took my silence as a sentence, and a sentence it was, for me.

Thankfully, the holidays arrived shortly after. Two weeks of freedom, two weeks without driving myself insane, wondering if I should have done things differently.

To the outside world, I'm on top of my game, best friend AND attentive boyfriend. Inside, I'm either completely placid, apathy incarnate, or mounted on springs. Yes, I know, I don't make much sense to myself either.

"If people knew, they'd probably think I'm completely mental,"
I tell Miss Eugénie over tea on the first weekend of the holidays.
"Honestly. If you're bored playing video games and smoking the
same joints, and if you're not sure your sexy girlfriend does it for
you anymore, then leave, go home, ring your mad crush's doorbell,
and tell her you'd like to kiss her somewhere dark and find out once
and for all what the hell is wrong with you. But Tony is everything to
me, and you see, if Lucie and I break up, I'm not sure he'd stick
with me." I let out a dramatic sigh. "Anyway... That's the worst
of it."

Miss Eugénie, her brow furrowed, leans away from the window.

On my advice, she has ditched scrapbooking, in profit of bird-
watching. I guess it makes us friends.

"You think your best friend would leave with your girlfriend."

"Yes, I just told you."

"And you're happy with that."

"Do I look happy to you?"

I'm starting to regret taking up her invitation. When I rang her
doorbell to return her sunglasses, she took one look at my face,
ushered me with an iron grip into her sitting room and ordered me
to tell her everything. Only to say:

"No, you look miserable, as usual."

Miss Eugénie makes a note in her handbook about the
hundredth blue tit who flew by with a little smile. I'm too exhausted
to retort, so she makes a serious face, as though my predicament is
something significant and nothing like the insecurities of a seven-
teen-years-old teen.

"Eugénie?" I sink deeper into the cushions of her sofa. "Have
you ever been in this predicament?"

Her eyes widen. "Torn between two lovers?"

"Attracted to the wrong person." A small crack in the paint of
the ceiling catches my attention. "You know it's wrong or even
ridiculous to be attracted to this... girl, but the more you realise it's
crazy, the more you want to do it, and you can't get it out of your
head."

Miss Eugénie, spotting another bird, lifts her binoculars to her
eyes. "And this girl you like..."

Oh, yes. Miss Eugénie being as ancient as Rome, I didn't tell her I had a crush on a guy. Wouldn't want the shock to wipe out the only person I can talk to.

"Doriane," I say, after a quick rummaging around my head to find my fake crush an English name. "Her name's Doriane."

"You don't know if she ever liked you, and you didn't bother to ask."

"I'm glad I didn't."

"Why is that?"

"Because," I say, in a tone that suggests it makes complete sense, "if she liked me back, then I wouldn't know what to do!"

She snorts. "A part of you would know what to do, trust me on that."

The sofa springs squeal as I jolt upright. "You're a disgusting old woman, you know."

"No, you're disgusting," she says, smiling. "I was talking about your heart."

"No, you weren't."

"Fine. I wasn't."

I start stuffing my mouth with her delicious biscuits while she laughs at her joke. Eventually, she gets away from the window and comes to sit next to me.

"It looks like you put yourself in this situation. And you're the only one who can get yourself out."

"That's it? That's your advice?"

A piece of biscuit gets stuck down my windpipe. Miss Eugénie sighs and pours me some more tea.

"Don't beat yourself up. Everybody lives through the same situation at least once in their life. The world is vast, and so is the heart. This is probably just a fling, you'll get over it in no time. Everything will go back to normal."

"You promise?"

She shakes her head. "No, of course not. Why would I promise you that?"

"So, what happens if it's not just a fling?"

She holds up a finger. "If not, next time, we'll have gin."

Oh boy… Get over it, I did. For the next two weeks, Tony never lets me out of his sight. I believe he's never liked me more than at the point of losing me. He always comes up with plans, meeting for a movie, or play the newest video game, getting our hair cut together, and of course celebrating his and Lucie's birthdays, which are only three days apart. The Golden Fork is not invited to their celebrations this year, and I've got a feeling it's my fault, and mine only.

I'm so good at faking happy, I'm honestly considering becoming an actor. 'Fake it till you make it' has some truth to it. Eventually, I begin to enjoy myself again, one afternoon at a time. The good thing to come out of it is that Tony has stopped saying I always get what I want.

I've also become the perfect boyfriend. Lucie and I go on many walks. We hold hands in the park like cardboard couples from rom-com movies. We stroll along interminable lanes and I try not to think of Michael every time we encounter a plane tree.

I've told Lucie about the girl I slept with. She wasn't happy about it. It took her forty-eight hours to come around the fact that I lied about something which she deemed so important. But then, she came back and apologised for being so insensitive, confusing the hell out of me.

Now that she knows I've had sex before, she doesn't seem so hell-bent on shagging me senseless, and I cannot tell either of them how relieved I am. Sex is the last thing on my mind, and I'm almost eighteen! My body feels shut down, sealed like some ancient tomb.

Lucie's got another obsession: planning my birthday, which happens in April, during the next holidays. I don't care much for it, but Tony and Lucie want to celebrate the fact that all of us will be allowed to drink alcohol in public.

It sounds great, really. I can't wait to be able to drink any time I want, and be happy all the time. What madness possessed me to spend so much time worrying about Michael? Now I'm sure that it was nothing but a fling, and I'll be able to face him without concern when we get back to school.

To my father's satisfaction, I've done all of my homework during the first week of the holidays, working at all hours, even at night, depending on how sleepless I was. I've read Wuthering Heights as instructed and without complaint, and I really could have complained, since I understood half of it, and I'm not even sure about the stuff I understood.

I told Lucie and Tony I needed to keep my grades up if I wanted a chance to go to London after the holidays. Tony asked if I was really serious about it. I said I was. I don't know if I mean it. London might be the worst city for me at the moment. But on the other hand... the idea of going away is definitely growing on me.

And just like that, between games, smokes, walks, homework, celebrations, bird-watching with Miss Eugénie, and banging my head trying to understand Catherine and Heathcliff, the two-weeks break is over.

It's a new, rested, and cured of all insanity Louis who arrives almost on time at school on Monday morning and who doesn't have to sweat over Mrs Paquin's hawk-like stare for the first time ever.

My confidence, just as my self-control, is off the hook. It's early March, and the sun is back. Shades on, I blast through Colette International's front doors practically in slow-motion, and I'm close to starting winking at strangers like in the movies.

Keeping my eyes straight to make sure not to make eye contact with any undesirable, I pay little attention to Tony and Lucie's friendly chatter behind me, until I hear my own name.

"Lou's never been in such a hurry to go to English Lit."

I wheel around so fast that my own hair slaps me in the face. "That's not true."

"Then why are we practically running?" Tony asks, unwrapping a madeleine.

"I know why," Lucie says.

Keeping a straight face, I ask: "You do?"

She advances on me, slyly, her eyes glittering.

"You want to show off because you've read the book on time this time."

"Ha!"

She's absolutely right. I'm a new person, a responsible one, who does his homework, washes his hair, and as of last night, lays out my outfit for the next morning.

"I've read it too," Tony says, through a mouthful of madeleine. "But I can't talk about it. I think I need PTSD counselling now."

"More like you didn't understand what was going on," Lucie says.

"Touché!" He showers us with madeleine crumbs.

Meanwhile, they're not walking fast enough. I clap my hands together to spur them.

"Enough, fools, or we'll be late."

"God," Lucie says, looking over my shoulder. "Is it me or this guy keeps getting hotter?"

"Who?"

Whipping around, I collide into François whom I didn't notice standing right behind me, and sends him flying straight into Michael's arms.

"Watch where you're going!" I bark.

I know who Lucie was talking about, and it wasn't François. With slightly longer hair, his bouncing curls looking softer than ever, Michael is now the hottest thing identified on the planet since that asteroid that wiped out the dinosaurs.

Everything Eugénie promised wouldn't happen happens. Desire ignites in every part of my nervous system, alighting me like a god damn Christmas tree.

"Get out of the way, then!" Yasmine's harsh voice brings me back to reality.

Her black eyes boring into mine, Yasmine dares me to say another word. Sacha, who doesn't mind this sort of thing, pulls me into a hug, then proceeds to kiss us all on the cheeks.

"Lucie!" She says in her usual chirp of a voice. "How was your holiday?"

Lucie, for once, doesn't seem at all happy to see Sacha, and mutters a vague answer. Tony, too, seems to look at her with more contempt than ever. Is it because she let me into her flat the night of the party? Anyway, while Sacha keeps them all busy, I end up sandwiched between François and Michael and begin to sweat profusely. Oblivious to my presence, Michael is searching through his backpack.

"Did you have a nice break?" François says.

At first, I think he's talking to Michael. Or even to Tony. But to my surprise, he's talking to me.

"Hum. Sure. You?"

He glances up at the ceiling as though I asked something stupid. "I went to Florence, so, yes."

"My family's from Florence," Michael says.

"Oh, really?" François says, arching an eyebrow.

"Really?" I repeat, my voice squeaky.

We both glance at Michael with newfound interest, and then at each other, realising what we just did. My cheeks heat at the same time a deep flush betrays François's own thoughts.

Michael, still nose deep into his bag, doesn't notice us. "Yes, on my mother's side."

"Well," François says, still deeply red. "I think it's a wonderful city, and the people! Oh. The people."

Oh, François. I wish you'd stayed there and broken your neck. Would have done us all a favour. But Michael looks up from his bag and gives François the sweetest smile.

Unprompted, François launches himself into a tirade of what he visited, the restaurants he dined at, and the beauty of Italian men. Naturally, I tune him out.

Michael's familiar scent of fresh apples fills the air between us and makes my head swim.

"What about you?" I ask, before I can stop myself. "How was your holiday?"

He glances up from his bag. "Can't complain."

I can't believe I have spent two weeks without hearing his voice. Gosh, British accents should be banned. If Michael had an American accent, I would have never spiralled out of control and questioned my very normal sexuality. I would have felt nothing at all.

Sacha's twittering is over, and she leads the way into the classroom, all the while boring Lucie with details about a concert she went to.

Michael ends up behind me and that's enough to send my hair standing up on their end. Before I can control it, my heart resumes once more its mad hammering. Perhaps it's the accent combined with the smell. Perhaps it reminds me of something. I once saw a documentary about how people are attracted to people who are connected to good memories. Nothing to worry about.

"See you later, maybe?" I feel the ghost of his breath on my neck.

Everything is fucked. Abort—Abort!

Must get as far away from him as possible before I melt into a puddle at his feet. Damn you Eugénie, prepare the gin, this was not a fling, I repeat, this was not a fling!

I take my seat at the back, he remains standing at the front, turns around, meets my eyes, frowns a little, probably because I look like I've just swallowed a shovel and it's stuck in my throat. He then takes his seat next to François, who I swear, is still droning on about Florence, unaware nobody's listening to him at all.

Ok. Calm down. One breath at a time.

A fling, Miss Eugénie said. It's just a fling. It's just a fling. It's just a fling.

It's nothing like a fling, it's an earthquake. Whoever survives the aftershock will never be the same.

When Paquin enters the classroom, I'm that close to spring forward, my hand shot up. Come on Paquin, do your best. Look at me, challenge me, interrogate me. Keep my mind busy.

It takes a few minutes for her to set up. I haven't been able to take my eyes off Michael, especially when he did his thing, stretching his long legs and his arms above his head while cracking his neck. François is showing him something. It looks like pictures of his holiday. Poor Michael. No one deserves this.

Pull yourself together, Louis. Michael should be sitting with François. It's all for the best.

Yes.

Because I'm with Lucie. And I'm straight.

"So, Wuthering Heights, yes?" Paquin sits on the edge of her desk and looks around the room. "First impressions?"

Eyes straight and chin up, I dare Mrs Paquin to interrogate me, dare her to add to my misery. The book is fresh in my mind. I know all about it. But guess what. She must feel the confidence emanating from me, because she barely throws me a glance.

Tell me again that she's not some sort of witch.

Lucie is interrogated this time. She puts her hair up with a hairpin before she answers. Her delicate neck is a thing of beauty. More beautiful than anything I've ever seen, probably. The moment she speaks, every head turns to her. Every head but Michael's.

Lucie does well during her interrogation, to no-one's surprise. Paquin then stands up and begins to analyse the book. I keep my head down and spend the hour sketching in the margins of my notes, distracted, worried, eager for the lesson to end, so I can run away and hide in a bathroom stall to recompose myself. I almost make it to the end.

Paquin's voice rises above the ringing bell. "Now, you all know what I'm going to say. You will write an essay about Wuthering Heights and hand it over in a month. Pair up with another person just like last time."

My heart stops. Michael immediately looks over his shoulder at me. I pretend to read my notes, but when I look up again, it's to find him standing over my desk, pulling at the straps of his backpack.

"Do you want to do the essay together?" he says, his face tense.

My heart says YES!

My brain says NO.

My lips go: "Why?"

Michael expected a different reaction, I can see, from the way his brow furrows.

"We did well last time."

We didn't, though. We went from straight guys with girlfriends to running around like headless chickens. I know I did. The essay itself went well, granted.

"No, I…" I swallow a lump. "I'm going to do it with Lucie."

His chest heaves, his lips tighten into a thin line. "I'll do it with François then."

I meet his gaze and hold it. "François? Hm. Excellent choice."

Dear God, I hope none of this is subtext.

16

THE ONE THAT SAYS M&M

"What is this even about?" Tony says, whining.

Two weeks after Paquin gave us the assignment, Tony and I are spread over two tables in the confines of Colette's small library. Turns out Lucie ditched me to do the essay with her Spanish buddy Chloé, and I'm stuck with Tony to write about the most difficult book I've ever read. At least Tony agreed we would get more work done if we weren't at his house, where — almost — every distraction in the world could have tempted us.

I glance up at Tony. "What did you say?"

"What's the book about?"

"I thought you read it."

"And I thought you were smart."

"I'm not. I'm not smart."

I'm definitely, definitely the worst idiot that's ever lived. I know it. Otherwise, I would be doing the essay with Michael, and I wouldn't be so miserable all the time. Miss Eugénie is right. Guess that makes sense since she's probably older than the Titanic. That's one consolation. If I get as old as Eugénie, I'll be a very miserable, but very wise, schmuck.

"Don't I know it." Tony empties a whole bag of gummy bears into his monstrosity of a mouth.

It's difficult to do any work around Tony, but even more difficult today. My head is in shambles after another series of restless nights filled with chaotic dreams. It's not enough that I see Michael every day again. He won't leave my nights alone either.

The next person who utters the word *fling*, I will murder with my bare hands.

Tony chews for a long time then swallows noisily, earning himself a glare from one of the librarians.

"Oh." He slaps his tummy. "Oh fuck. This one won't go down easy. I shouldn't have had that extra big mac for lunch. Should we text Lucie?"

"Why?"

My bad mood is swelling by the second. I wish he'd just shut up, I can't think with all his chatter.

"Because this is boring, Lou, this is shit, and I'm bored, and you look dead inside. So, we could text Lucie and ask her what she's doing."

"She's at Chloé's and they're probably halfway through the essay already."

"Oh, and where are we?"

"You only wrote the title, Tony. And you wrote it wrong too."

He looks down at the copy. "Shit. Sorry."

While Tony scratches off the title Wurstering Highs, humming to himself *Everything is Average Nowadays*, I smile despite myself. No matter how annoying he is, I love him, and I'd do anything for him. And I did.

I did. I know it because I'll never be happy again.

The price to pay for the alternative was too high. Nothing is worse than watching your people leave you behind without a look back. I know I was right to cut any ties with Michael. And even more right NOT to do the essay with him, and his curls, his blue underwear, and his British accent.

Tony elbows me, his nose once again buried in his blackberry. "Lucie's done in about half an hour."

"What? God damn it, Tony, we'll never be done in half an hour."

Tony's brown eyes look at me from behind his phone. "A lot of things can happen in half an hour, you know."

"Tony, don't overestimate yourself. You've spelt the title wrong again."

Tony grimaces as he strokes his tummy, then takes a large swig of Coke and fights down a burp while I stare, horrified.

"If you know it will make you sick, then why do you do it?"

"Rockstars live dangerously, Lou. Or have you forgotten everything I taught you?"

That settles it. I never had what it takes to be a rockstar, then. Or perhaps Tony's a fucking idiot, and I shouldn't listen to a word he's saying.

"Let's focus on the essay, shall we?" I say in a low voice, quickly flicking through Wuthering Heights, a faint headache growing behind my eyelids.

I glance at one of Paquin's question: *"Explain the theme of nature versus culture"* and slam my head against the table.

Tony yawns next to me. "What do you think about the shark?"

"What shark?" I begin turning the pages of the book again, bewildered. "There is no shark. I don't see a fucking shark!"

Tony leans forward so his long face appears in my field of vision. "The Shark, Lou. The bar. For your birthday. Lucie's asking."

Defeated, I slam the book shut and toss it over my shoulder. A yelp of pain follows and Tony starts laughing. I turn around to apologise to whoever I've hit, but my throat grows dry. It's François and Michael, the new BFFs.

Great. That's all I needed.

"Why would you do that?" François shrieks, rubbing his arm.

Michael picks up the book and hands it over to me. Tony's still laughing. François takes one cold look at our messy table, Tony's snacks, our stupid faces, and lets out a judgmental sigh.

"You know you're not supposed to eat in here, don't you?"

Tony stops laughing, but still smiling, puts another handful of gummy bears into his mouth. Michael watches him, a blank look on his face.

"What are you doing in here anyway?" François asks. "I never expected to find you in a library."

"Why is that?" Tony says. "Do you think we're idiots?"

"At least one of you is." His voice is laced with contempt.

"We're doing our essay," I say, annoyed, knowing exactly who this last retort was meant for. I almost add something else but mercifully keep my trap shut.

Michael leans over our table. "You spelt the title wrong."

With a heartfelt groan, I put my head in my hands.

"Let's go," Michael says. "They're trying to work."

Like an obedient puppy, François obeys Michael, and they sit at a table further. But from my position, not only can I see Michael, but from the look he gives me, he can see me too. We lock eyes. A deep sense of frustration rakes through me. I wonder what he feels about all this.

Tony pats my hand. "Don't worry about him, Lou,"

Startling, I tear my eyes away from Michael.

"What?"

Tony puts a hand on my shoulder. "I said don't worry. I know Lucie likes to say that he's hot, but I know she's not going to dump you for him."

Confused, I shake my head manically. "Wh — Why are you telling me this now? And who said he would be interested, anyway?"

"Lou, my man, I don't understand you. Why are you looking at him like he burned your farm and stole your chickens, then?"

Is that what I look like? Taking a deep breath, I rub my face with my hands to pull myself together. Tony's expecting an answer. It will be hard to give him one without lying, or...

"He gets on my nerves, sometimes. He's too... perfect, you know? Pisses me right off."

Tony stares at me a moment, then shrugs and opens another bag of gummy bears.

"I get it. He annoys me too. Plus he's too good looking. I've got enough of you getting all the attention. Imagine being *his* friend."

His words make me laugh. "What, like François?"

"No, not like François, Lou!" Tony gives me the look he reserves for dumb people. "What the hell is wrong with you? Michael won't be a problem for François, he's gay."

"Hang on. You knew that too? That François's gay?"

Tony sighs. "Lou, everyone knows François is gay. He told the whole school a million years ago." He chokes on a gummy bear and hits his chest a couple of times.

"Michael could be gay too, you know, and then—"

"Then they would be together, wouldn't they?"

Tony offers me candy. I refuse, feeling nauseated enough already.

"Why would they be together? Just because two people are gay doesn't mean that they have to be together."

"You're right, but... They're both rich and smart and boring. They make more sense together than, I don't know..." Tony tosses me an odd look. "Like you and him, for example. You have nothing in common."

"I guess you're right." Feeling quite defeated, I open the book again.

"So, the Shark? Lucie can book it for us."

"Sure," I reply, but my appetite for fun, just like for snacks, has vanished forever.

For a few minutes, I attempt, as diligently as I can, to answer Paquin's questions and get a head-start on what promises to be a difficult essay. Oh, how I miss Dorian Gray, his funny dialogue and his lengthy descriptions of gardens and flowers. The truth is, I miss Dorian very much. I wish I could turn time and be with Dorian again.

I can't help myself, can't help throwing furtive looks at François and Michael. They're both working, head bents over the same volume, Michael's curls almost touching the page. He smiles. Looks up.

Sees me.

My cheeks warming up faster than a Chernobyl reactor, I hide my face behind my book. Beside me, Tony is still texting and laughing at whatever Lucie is saying. But of course, he feels me watching him and puts the phone down.

"Lou, you look like shit, are you okay?"

"I agree. We shouldn't have had McDo for lunch."

Tony pushes his bottle of Coke toward me. "Have a drink."

"No, thanks. I think I need to go to the toilet."

Getting up so fast that my chair falls over, I don't bother to put it back, and I storm out, head down and close to a nervous break-down, in the direction of the toilet.

Mercifully, since almost everyone else is in class, I find it empty. I rest my hands on each side of the sink in an attempt to catch my breath.

One day, I'll laugh about it. I'll tell my kids or my grandkids about that time I was obsessed about a boy and made up stories in my mind that I liked him, like I make stories in my head that I'm, like Tony, a proper rockstar.

My own image in the mirror doesn't reflect that of a rockstar. It shows nothing but fear.

That's funny. I'm standing at the exact same spot where I met Michael, all these weeks ago.

On the other side of the room, the door clicks opens, and Michael enters, taller than I'd remembered, almost surreal, even under the neons lights overhead.

He stops where I stood when we met.

"Are you all right?" he asks.

I keep my eyes on my own reflection. "I'm great, thanks."

"You don't look very good."

"Thanks. I'm working on a new look. The *sick* rockstar."

Michael's mouth twists into a grimace. "You'll never be a rock-star, Louis."

I huff at my reflection in the mirror. "Are you trying to insult me or something?"

"No." He shakes his head. "Do you want to know why you're not a rockstar?"

"Sure, why not." I step away from the sink and back toward the wall. "Tell me."

"Rockstars are true to themselves. Even at their worst. But you, you always act like you're afraid of the truth."

I can't help laughing. "Excuse me, I didn't know you were offering free consultations in the toilets, and I'm grateful, but I'm not interested, so…"

Michael moves away from the sink.

"Why are you angry at me exactly? What have I done that was

so wrong? Did I do something to you at Sacha's party? I can't exactly remember, and that's not an excuse, I know, but if I said or did something, I'm sorry, okay?"

I hang my head, unsure what to say. "You haven't done anything, okay? I just…"

He approaches me. "I thought we were friends."

I don't want him to be any closer. His perfume alone is already filling my nostrils and sending sharp shots of electricity through my nerves. I could make a run for it. And then what?

Glancing up, I meet his eyes. "We are friends."

"Really?" Michael scrunches up his face. "Way to treat your friends."

To my horror, someone cracks the door open, and Tony's voice fills the room.

"Lou? Are you in there?"

Terrified at the thought of Tony finding me in here with Michael, I start moving without thinking. Yanking a confused Michael by the arm, I pull us both into the nearest stall.

"Lou? Is that you?"

Putting a finger to my lips, I beg Michael to keep silent while I lock the door to the stall.

"Yeah, I'm here."

Michael watches me, his expression torn between apprehension and amusement.

"Are you okay?"

We can hear the door and Tony's footsteps as he enters the toilets.

"Yes." I gasp when Michael's knee accidentally, or not, bumps against mine. "I just—I'm not feeling well. Can you give me some privacy?"

Tony's voice sounds giddy. "You're sick? Seriously?"

"Yes."

"I guess we'll have to finish our essay later, then! I'll pack our stuff and wait outside. I love you, man, I absolutely love you!"

Tony's footsteps retreat, and the next thing we hear is the door slamming shut. I let out a relieved breath.

Michael seems perfectly fine, crammed together with me in the small stall. He quirks an eyebrow.

"He loves you, apparently."

"Yes, well, I'm very popular."

Michael gives a strained laugh. I don't feel like laughing. I can't look into his eyes. If I look I am lost.

Yet, I do. I look up. I meet his gaze, he meets mine. How long does he think we can hold it?

No one knows, because the next second we're kissing, his back is pressed against the stall door, and my hands, at last, are buried into his glorious curls.

I can almost hear metaphorical walls crashing down around us, but I'm too busy feeling Michael's tongue against mine, too busy slinking down into eternal bliss

I've kissed before, I've been kissed before. On the other hand, I've never been kissed like *this* before. I'm not frozen anymore. The Christmas tree has been set on fire. The whole forest is ablaze. Every part of me feels awake. Every nerve in my body tingles and sings.

I have just made the most important discovery in the history of the universe, and that discovery is Michael.

We break apart, panting, Michael's face redder than usual, his curls a proper mess, his pupils huge, dilated, and I burst out laughing. Not from derision, but from relief.

Michael runs a hand through his hair, breathless. "I thought I'd never get the chance."

I blink slowly while recovering myself, still too amazed at what just happened.

I have to go. No. I want to stay. I want to never leave the stall. But I have to go.

"I have to go."

"Oh," Michael says. He fixes his expression into something much more neutral in less time it takes me to say my next line.

"Sorry."

Fumbling with the lock because of shaky fingers, I shove the door open, fill my lungs with air. Michael remains in the stall, looking uncertain.

My heart swells until it becomes almost painful. I close the distance between us in two strides and bash my lips against his. Michael loses balance and ends up ass first on the toilet seat.

"Sorry, I really must go." I offer him a hand up, which he doesn't take.

His fingers hover above his inflamed lips.

"Michael?" He nods. "I'll, hem… call you, okay?"

His eyes tell me he doesn't believe me, but it's okay. Because this is not over. This is just getting started.

I run out of the toilet, skid across the linoleum around the corner, and flatten myself against the wall to catch my breath.

It was just as I imagined. No. Better. He tasted like summer on the beachside, like Malabars eaten outside authorised hours, like my first ride on a carousel. He might be an angel. No, a god.

Deep breaths. Don't panic. It was only the best kiss of your life.

Tony runs to me when I make it outside, wincing in the sunlight, and hands me my backpack.

"Damn, Lou, you should throw up more often. You look much, much better."

17

IMPROBABLE ODDS

Now I know how victors of battles with improbable odds feel. I'm in a daze, and everything is golden coloured and saturated with flares like in J.J. Abrams movies, and I've got to make myself stop when I catch myself smiling.

Oh my, the kiss. It happened two days ago, and all I can think of is the way Michael's lips felt against mine, and when will we do it again, and if Michael will kiss me again. Or if I will, because as of now, I sure don't know who kissed whom first, all I know is that I'm so rattled, like I've been pulled out of the darkest tomb and into the sunlight.

I am not undead anymore.

I am reborn.

Minor problem is, I haven't heard from Michael since. We see each other in class and pass each other in corridors, but since Wednesday afternoon, when he blew my mind and wrenched me out of my straight convictions, he hasn't made any bold move toward me, like, for instance, push me up against a wall and kiss me senseless, as he did in my dream last night.

Second problem is, I can't tell anyone about this, especially not Lucie, whose sight triggers the bells of guilt within me and make me feel ashamed of what I've done. I've cheated. I'm a cheater. My reason for cheating is beyond physical, I think. It isn't etched in my flesh, but in my essence.

Lucie's not a guy. And I've got to figure out the extent of my love for her. I spent last night sitting awkwardly between her and Tony as we watched a movie whose title, content, and cast I will never remember, worrying whether they could hear the thundering of my heart.

I wake up on Saturday morning hungry for something else than Michael's lips. What I need, what I really need, is somebody to talk to.

This is how I end up, at noon, ringing Miss Eugénie's doorbell, my hands full of shopping bags, one of my father's bottles of Bordeaux stuck under my arm.

Miss Eugénie eyes me suspiciously through the slither of space between the door and the safety chain.

"I'm not buying anything!"

I feel almost offended. "Do I really look like I'm selling cookies?"

She lets me in. Inside her living room, the plum curtains are closed, plunging the room into semi-darkness. I draw them open to bathe the room in sunlight. Eugénie points at her binoculars.

"I was watching this beautiful blue tit. Now I've lost it."

"Who cares about tits, honestly." I drop the shopping bags on her coffee table.

Eugénie turns around. "You don't look miserable today."

My face splits into a wicked grin, and she feigns to step backwards in horror.

"Did you get laid or something?"

My smile turns into a grimace. "I brought you lunch."

She can't resist the prospect of food and hurries forward to peer into the bags.

"And I brought wine." I push the bottle into her hands.

"You should come more often, kid. Sit down."

She goes with the bags into the kitchen, and I hear her contented sigh as she opens them up. Italian food from Amore Mio never fails to please.

"I haven't seen you in a while," I say, dropping my coat into a chair. "Since last time I came. I thought you were dead."

Her head appears in the doorjamb. "You don't have the monopoly on life-threatening crises." The head disappears and reappears instantly: "And you could have rung if you thought I was dead, little shit."

"Perhaps I did, and you're too old to hear me banging on your door like the outstanding citizen that I am."

Flashing her a smirk, I make myself comfortable on her plump sofa. She walks over to me and hands me a corkscrew.

"Shut up and open the wine."

This task requires concentration, and my hands are still shaking from excitement, which Miss Eugénie notices, but she says nothing. She serves the fresh pasta I just bought from the restaurant in elaborate plates and proper silverware, making me feel like an important guest. We clink our glasses.

Miss Eugénie takes a bite of her pasta alla carbonara and makes a delighted face. "Do I want to know why you're so happy? You're gonna tell me anyway, I guess."

About to explode from the need to get it off my chest, I nonetheless take a dignified air and offer that we should eat first. She nods in agreement and puts on a record by Nancy Sinatra.

While we eat in silence, my eye is caught again by the insane number of framed black and white and photographs Eugénie has nailed to the wall. Just like in the corridor leading to this room, the whole side of the sitting room is covered in pictures of young and less young men and women in their best attire, seemingly having all the fun in the world.

"Are these your friends, Miss Eugénie?"

She follows my gaze, and her eyes fill with warmth.

"Friends, relatives, lovers. Now, they're just shadows on my wall. Like ghosts."

Her statement plunges me into silence. She waves her hand.

"Don't listen to me. For once that you're not miserable, I'm not the one who's going to make you. Pass the wine, please."

I top up her glass. I like the way she leans back in her chair.

Each of her movements is fluid, yet almost mechanical, perfected after a lifetime of practice. That's it. I'm getting soft on an old lady.

"Don't you have friends at all anymore?"

Eugénie sighs. "Don't you worry about me. I have more than enough people in my life to keep myself busy. And as of late, I've got my little obsession with blue tits."

"All right…"

But a bullshitter like me knows when he's being bullshitted. That's all I'm sayin'.

"So, young pup," Eugénie says after a generous swig of wine, "tell me all your grievances. As long as I have wine, I can give you proper advice you'll like. Cut me off and I'll be too grown-up for you to take me seriously."

Now that the time has come to speak up, it seems like I've lost all notion of language, and I can only stutter incoherently until she stops me with a finger.

"We get it, you're in love—"

"I'm not in love!" I protest, cheeks burning. "But… There was a kiss."

Eugénie leans forward. "I'm listening."

"The best kiss that has ever happened to me. It was an out of this world experience. Something you cannot possibly understand."

She makes a face. "Probably not, indeed."

"The problem is… it wasn't my girlfriend."

"Well, I could have guessed that myself but never mind."

"Stop interrupting. We kissed in the stall of the boys' toilets two days ago, and I can't think of anything else."

Miss Eugénie's brow furrows. "What kind of romantic notions do you have, to drag young girls into men's bathrooms? Did the world go that mad in the past few years?"

I pinch my mouth shut. I almost gave myself up, almost confessed to the most scandalous part of my secret. Not that I don't want to tell Eugénie. But I'm not ready to let go of my new friend, and finding out one's acquaintance's hardcore bible-thumping homophobic tendencies tends to ruin friendships, as Tony would say.

"My secret crush followed me there, very dangerously, so this is where it happened."

"So, now you know. You can—"

"I don't, that's the problem."

Miss Eugénie takes another large sip of red wine and shakes her head.

"You liked the kiss."

"I loved it more than anything I've ever loved. Except perhaps Kaiser Chiefs."

She puts the glass down, stuck into a fit of coughing. "Kaiser what?" She clutches her chest. "Say, you wouldn't be a little fascist, by any chance?"

"No!" I nearly spit out wine all over her sofa. "Kaizer Chiefs' a band, Miss Eugénie, not a Hitler support group."

"You're very blonde, after all."

"Please stop. I'm trying to tell you about love, and you're ruining everything with Hitler."

She puts up her hands. "I'm so sorry. I promise. No more Hitler."

"Right."

"But—" she adds, and I roll my eyes to the heavens, "I thought you weren't in love."

"I..." Seeing her mischievous beady eyes throws me off again. I sit back and cross my arms over my chest. "I was kissed. I loved it. I wonder if there will be another kiss. I want there to be another kiss. But I can't just throw everything else out of the window after one little kiss."

Miss Eugénie surprises me by remaining silent, her fingers dancing over her lips as she looks out the window.

"One little kiss can change many things, Louis."

"But everything else remains."

She turns to me, her gaze focused once again. "What do you mean?"

"I still don't know if there will be more than one kiss. And if there is, I can't be sure it's the beginning of something serious. Something worth... telling Lucie."

"So you're keeping Lucie in the dark, chained to you, until you figure things out."

"No, that's not how I see it."

"Then you're not seeing clearly." Eugénie looks at me with a mixture of fondness and pity.

"But Lucie can have anyone, she'll be fine."

"But she wants you, apparently."

I say nothing, glance out the window, letting out my frustration in long-drawn breaths. Eugénie pours me a glass of wine.

"You really over-complicate your life, my friend. You're not stuck in the fifties. Grow a pair, go on a date with your crush, find out for yourself. If your... secret crush is not the one, you'll get another, end of the story."

"Do you believe that?"

"I believe you're overworking yourself up and you're in danger of getting really hurt if you keep secrets from everyone." Eugénie takes one look at me and sighs. "You're not in love, but you want to spend all of your time kissing this secret crush, don't you?"

"Yes, I do."

"So, do it. But tell your girlfriend, so she can move on. If she finds out through someone else, she might never forgive you."

Telling Lucie is exactly what I don't want to do. Tell Lucie and I know exactly how she'll react. A few hours later, I'm likely to never see her or Tony ever again. I'm not going to risk it after one kiss, however amazing it was. Eugenie is wise, but she doesn't know all the facts and doesn't know my predicament. She can only advise me after a fashion, using what she knows.

We go on to talk about other things. Miss Eugénie being an admirer of the Brontes, gives me some tips for my essay, and soon it's time for us to part. When she opens the door for me. I hesitate, wringing my hands.

"Look, Miss Eugénie, you're really okay for someone who was born before Plato."

She looks up at the ceiling and pouts, but says nothing.

"What I mean is... you can talk to me too. If you have a life-threatening crisis. I might be young, and maybe stupid, but—"

"You're a good kid." She smiles. "Now fuck off. *Murder She Wrote* is on.

My phone vibrates in my pocket on my way up. I almost take a tumble down the stairs when I read Michael's name. Breathless, I look over my shoulder as though expecting Lucie or Tony to jump me in my own building, and open the message with feverish hands.

MICHAEL:
HEY

Heart thumping madly, I reply:

LOUIS:
HEY

Eugénie's right. The only way to find out if it was more than a kiss is to jump in there and grow a pair. Or grow a pair first and jump in there. Either way. I have to grow a pair.

LOUIS:
DO YOU WANT TO GO SOMEWHERE TOMORROW? I'LL EVEN LET YOU CHOOSE WHERE WE GO AND WHAT WE DO. IF YES, MEET ME AT 2 PM AT CENSIER DAUBENTON.

I wait for his answer on the edge of the top stairs. This way, if he doesn't want me, I can jump off and break my neck, and that will teach him.

My phone vibrates. I hold my breath.

MICHAEL:
YES! AND I WILL CHOOSE WELL.

Michael has texted me an exclamation mark. He must be madly in love with me.

Elated, I stick the phone back into my pocket, a song on my lips.

170

My phone vibrates once more as I turn the key into the lock. See? He can't get enough of me.

One glance at the screen and my stomach drops.

LUCIE:
WHAT ARE WE DOING TOMORROW?

I'm sorry Lucie. You must bear with me a little while longer. My only way out of this situation is to push forward into the darkness and hope to see the light.

Tomorrow, then. Tomorrow I'll know for sure, and then I'll tell Lucie. Perhaps it won't be so dramatic that I've kissed a boy. Perhaps she'll forgive me. Perhaps she won't leave me at all.

The back of my mother's head, blonde just like Lucie, flashes behind my eyelids. She slammed the door without looking back. She forgot to call last Christmas.

18

THE ORIGIN OF TERROR

Another lie later, added to the lists of things I promised Lucie I wouldn't do anymore when we made up, I meet Michael at 2 PM sharp outside my place, and we set off toward the train station.

As we walk slowly along the wall bordering the Jardin des Plantes, Michael slips me the first glance. We exchange a secretive smile. Mine says: I remember and I want to do it again. Let's sneak into the park and make out in a dark corner. His is mysterious and might be suggesting the same. Then, he speaks.

"I hope you'll like what I picked for us."

"Sure will."

My head is already filling with kisses and the sweet tingling in my palms as I bury my hands in his heavenly hair.

But we don't sneak into the gardens, we keep walking, walking. And once we arrive at Gare d'Austerlitz, my excitement has dwindled considerably. We don't have enough time to ride a train together for a mini trip to the countryside, and I doubt that's what he intended for us. My enthusiasm flickers out all the more when we take the direction of the RER C and descend into the depths of the station.

"Are we going into the suburbs?" I ask, horrified.

"No," he says, amused. "No, nothing like that."

As I begin to calculate really quickly which station he intends to stop at, my elation is almost gone, replaced by a familiar sinking feeling and fastening pulse. I think I know where he's taking me.

I should have decided where to go. I should have just told him, let's go there. I wanted to do something nice. I gave him free rein. And what does he do?

He takes me to the Orsay Museum.

Mustering my whole repertoire of facial expressions, I follow Michael outside without dragging my feet and pretend to be just as amazed by the splendour of the museum as he is.

"I know you said rockstars don't go to museums!" Michael says.

Then why, why are you doing this to me?

"But I haven't finished this one yet." His cheeks are pink with excitement. "And I think you'll like it." Interpreting my clipped smile as enthusiasm, he slaps me on the shoulder, his eyes glinting. "And I was dying to take someone with me."

His hand reaches out to my shades, gingerly removes them. "Don't wear them in the museum, please. Or you'll miss out on the details."

I pocket the sunglasses and follow him grudgingly toward the entrance.

"Why didn't you? Take someone, I mean."

"Couldn't think of anyone."

Michael opens the door just as a group of a hundred and fifty tourists leaves the museum, clustered tightly together. He waits patiently for each and every one of them to exit while I bite my nails.

This doesn't make sense. I could think of at least three people he could drag to the museum. Why not take François? After all, taking François would make much, much more sense than taking me. And François would have probably exploded with joy at the prospect. Or just exploded, period. But I wouldn't be so lucky.

"Why not take François?" I ask, trying not to sound too prying.

"I don't know." Michael takes my arm and pulls me inside. "It never occurred to me."

That's even more of a surprise since they're always together. I want to probe for details, but there's no time. Michael is already storming the place with the look of an excited explorer.

This the beginning of a never-ending torture which consists of strolling from one vast high-ceiling room to another, each filled with ancient pictures trapped in gilded frames. The museum being one of the largest in the capital, a part of me fears we'll never get out of this place.

Michael is excited. He wants to show me everything. The prospects of kisses in the park or in a dark corner soon vanish. There's nothing else for me to do than to follow absently, being all smiles not to offend him, while I begin to think he took me in here to test me.

Tony's words from Wednesday ring especially true. Michael and I have nothing in common. Michael is much smarter than me and belongs with a François. I fear he took me there to test the waters of exactly what kind of things we could share together, calculate how dumb I really am.

This is all a test. I'm going to fail, for sure.

What if he gives me a little interrogation on the way out? I even can't remember a single painting we've seen in the last hour.

I begin to sweat and must remove my jacket. This is my punishment for lying to Lucie. Michael will know shortly I'm a profound idiot, will never kiss me or see me again. I can always console myself, after all there was only one kiss, there was no lasting damage...

Michael stops abruptly and I slam headfirst into him.

"Wow," he goes.

Moving aside so I can peek at the object of his awe, I almost swallow my own tongue in shock.

Framed in a golden monstrosity is a small painting of a fanny.

I'm not sure of what I've seen at first, and I sure don't want to stand any closer to it, but Michael approaches in long strides, determined to stand close enough to smell it. I reluctantly follow him, promising myself that should I get another chance, I'll never ask him to pick an activity for a date ever again.

The painting is worse up close. Its depiction, too realistic.

Pornographic. Vulgar. I hate it, I want to leave and never see it again.

"This is *The Origin of the World*!" Michael says, beaming.

"Say what, now?"

"That's what it's called."

I dare to look at it again.

Why do I feel so threatened, almost disgusted, definitely outraged by it? I don't know. But it can't be because of what it is. I've seen one before and I didn't feel like sprinting away from it like my life depended on it. All I know is that I'm repulsed by it, and if I show it, Michael will think I hate women.

"This is powerful," Michael says.

I grunt something back. He studies the thing, eyes narrowed, an expression of great fascination on his face.

Now would be the perfect time to ask him what he feels about it. Not exactly the painting but the fanny. It could tell me volumes.

But how should I phrase this? 'Hey babe, what does this clam inspire in you? Does it make you horny? What I mean is, are you gay or do you just fancy me?'

Christ. Not only would that sound horrible, but I just realised that my terror at this exposed nightmare might say something about my own sexuality. Something I'm not ready to think about yet. Even less talk about it. My personal life is, unlike this horror, very private.

So now I'm looking at this fanny, asking again the same question.

Am I gay? Am I, gay?

The fanny stares back, but doesn't answer.

Michael is looking from the painting to me, like he's expecting me to say something very deep about it.

"What do you think, Louis?"

There it goes. The test. Are you deep or dumb, Louis? Careful. Your answer will determine our future interactions for the next weeks to come. Whether you get kisses or sent back to the back of the class with a big 'F' stamped on your forehead.

"I don't know..." All I see is a monstrous fanny. "This is... bold."

"Yes, very. Extremely controversial at the time, and still is today."

I pretend to look at every aspect of the horrendous display of flesh. "The painter must have really liked this woman."

"Not necessarily."

WRONG. Just like in the game shows on telly. Two more strikes and you're out.

"Women, then?"

"No, not really."

WRONG! One more chance before being shipped off to a gulag for ignorant fools. Must keep a straight face.

"You know," Michael adds, "since it's your thing, I see Courbet as a rockstar myself."

"You do?"

Where is he going with this, and can we talk about it elsewhere, please?

"Yeah. Courbet and other artists. They're seekers of the truth, about others, and themselves."

This is getting too deep for me. It's a painting of a woman's genitals. But to look disgusted would only complicate our conversation.

"I thought they just, you know, paint pretty stuff. Beautiful stuff."

"Not only," Michael says. "I prefer to imagine they valued truth more than beauty."

"Right."

All I see is a big, fat, terrifying fanny, and its title only serves to remind me of my mother. That's all it takes for a spark of anxiety to become a furious blaze. The tips of my fingers are already growing numb.

"You know so many things," I say, focusing on controlling my voice.

"Not really. But my dad's passionate about arts."

Great. Now I feel even worse.

Michael insists on driving me wild. "You don't seem to agree with me."

Shit. How much longer will we have to stare at it and talk as though it wasn't staring us right in the face? Perhaps, if I give him a pseudo-deep answer, he might let me leave.

"I don't know, Michael. I haven't thought that far. I'm not an artist, and I don't know anything about artists. Tony and I only call ourselves rockstars because we want to be different."

Another look at the painting has me heaving a sigh. Michael's brow is furrowing. Did I say too much? Not enough? Was I supposed to stick to the painting?

"Why do you want to be different?"

"Who wants to be boring? No one likes boring people."

Michael doesn't say anything, turns back to the painting. I probably said something I shouldn't have. Focus back on the painting, say something on the painting.

"But… I like the painting. I mean, I like women, you know? Maybe I don't like staring at their parts like that, I don't know. Not that it means I'm gay, of course."

Michael's eyes widen to the size of teacups.

"Wait, sorry, what?"

Fuck, this conversation does not go anywhere where I want it to go. If he had spent more time with his tongue in my mouth, I wouldn't say such stupid things.

"Not that there's anything wrong with being gay! I'm only saying. Gay, not gay, I'm not sure what I really am. I know I don't think I'm like the other ones. You know. Like François."

Michael gives a derisive sort of laughter, as though he's not sure whether to be amused, offended, or purely horrified.

"You do know they come in all shapes and colours, right?" When I don't reply, he adds. "Don't worry. Perhaps the only thing you and gay men have in common is that… you're a man, and you like… one man. If you say you're not gay, I believe you."

Wait, did I say that? I just wanted to show him I wasn't afraid of the horror of a female sex laid bare, now I've convinced him I'm not gay. Which is perfect, really, since the more I look at his face, the louder I'm asking myself if I'll ever get back to being straight.

Damage not done, my ass.

"Come on, let's get out of here."

Gloomily, I walk away from *The Origin of The World* and toward a darker, quieter room. Michael follows in silence.

The conversation is already too much for me. I have the feeling I'm failing whatever test he wants me to pass. It's over, I've made a complete fool of myself, and on top of that, he's going to think I don't want to kiss him anymore.

We go on for a moment, the silence between us no longer pleasant, but charged with unsaid things. Neither of us knows where to start. We have been struggling for a good fifteen minutes when, Michael, his gaze unfocused on the masterpiece he's been staring for the last seven minutes, takes a deep breath.

"All I wanted to show you is that rockstars do go to museums. In fact, they fill them. They painted, sculpted, photographed every masterpiece between these walls. I just wanted to show you there's no shame in being smart."

"You're saying this because you're smart. It's easy for you."

The corners of his mouth turn down. "I don't get you. Don't you like the museum?"

I let out an anxious breath. "It depends. Did you bring me here to make fun of me? Do you think I'm that stupid?"

Michael, livid, almost leans on a pedestal for support, onto which a fragile-looking statue is perched. Miraculously, he refrains from it.

"You think I brought you here because I think you're stupid?"

"Well..."

"No! I don't think you're stupid, Louis." He draws closer, his hands outstretched. "I think you're great. I just wanted to show you nice things because I think you would like them a lot if you'd allow yourself to enjoy them."

I shake my head. "I don't get it."

"I think you're the opposite of dumb, but... you play dumb."

"Oh, right." I can't help but snigger. "No, I am not as smart as you think I am."

"You loved Dorian Gray, but you would lie to Tony if he asked you if you liked it, wouldn't you?"

A moment of consideration confirms his theory. I stare down at my shoes, embarrassed.

"That's... possible."

"I might be a nerd, but I'm not embarrassed by it. I just — I just want to be true to myself. I want to experience real things. Be around real people. Isn't that your philosophy too?"

"Yeah, I guess it is."

I'm feeling quite tired. This date isn't going as well as I thought it would.

"Louis?"

"What."

"You're not just a pretty face, you know."

"I am pretty," I concede, cheeks warming up.

The way Michael nods makes me think he's thought long and hard about the subject.

"Very."

Oh no. Do not get any closer. Or I will be tempted to throw caution to the wind.

But Michael's apparently an expert at sneaking around and deftly nudges me into a corner. A painting on the opposite wall, depicting a man biting another in the neck, feels almost appropriate, but the demon watching over them has me hoping it's not a bad omen.

"I want to kiss you," Michael says. "All the time."

"What. Here? In public?"

"Why not?"

When he gets close enough that we can touch, I hold up a hand.

"People will see."

Michael looks around us. The room is empty at the moment. Temptation grows. So does fear.

He leans in, rests his cheek against mine.

"I don't care," he whispers.

"But I do."

Michael leans away, his expression a mixture of confusion, disappointment.

"But you do."

"I'm sorry."

He smiles. "That's fine."

Michael's face is so close. I feel lucky just to be so close, to study

179

the deep green of his irises, the olive skin and the angular jaw, the softness of his gaze and the way he smiles, like happiness is easy to him.

Before I can stop myself, my fingers are trailing along his cheek, and he doesn't hesitate. His lips brush against mine first, teasing, before he claims them properly.

It's just as it was in the bathroom, with again, the thrill of the secret, which mingled with my terror of being discovered, adds some kind of spice to our kiss. For a moment my feet, despite being planted firmly on the ground, feel so light that I might as well be floating around.

It's too short, however. Michael soon parts from me, leaves me breathless. I never noticed I stepped back, but I'm almost against the wall.

"Well..." I begin.

He has the indecency the lick his lips while straightening up. "That was..."

"That was nice."

He nods. "Nice, indeed."

I really like museums. Museums are the best thing in the world. It's what I think.

"Can I ask you something?" I ask, feeling emboldened.

Michael nods. "Of course."

"Why did you take so long to contact me after we kissed?"

He gives me a bewildered look. "Are you serious?"

"I get it, Paquin was sick, we didn't get to—"

"Louis, you're the one who told me you would call me, remember?"

"Did I?"

Did I really do that? I have no memory of it. I must have been transplanted to another plane by his otherworldly kiss. How can I have no recollection of this?

Michael laughs. "You're so funny, sometimes."

"What? Why?"

He takes my elbow and nudges me to follow him, but doesn't let go of my arm. Electrified by his touch, I say nothing.

"You're the most anxious person I know."

"I'm not anxious."

Michael tilts his head. "Yes, you're the most anxious person I've ever met."

"No, I'm super chill. The *chillest* person ever."

"Actually, that would be me." He gives my elbow a squeeze. "I don't mind, Louis. I just mean you don't have to worry so much about me."

Chill people are people who don't give a damn about anything. His words could be a warning to me, and should have been, but the heat of his touch made me lose all focus, and soon, his warning words are forgotten in favour of brushing our hands together as we walk closely side by side.

I'm too distracted, too far gone, to notice a voice that I should have recognised immediately and from a distance. When we round the corner, our fingers intertwined, we find Sacha standing right in front of us.

I jump back like a startled cat, pulling Michael with me. We backtrack into the previous room and flatten ourselves against the wall, breathing hard.

Did she see us? No, I don't think so. She wasn't exactly looking in our direction. She wasn't, was she?

A quick look around the corner and I catch another glimpse of her. Her face looks confused, as though she may have seen us, but she isn't sure. But again, Sacha always looks like that. She's not exactly the sharpest knife in the box.

She's not alone. With her are four children, all of them likely relatives, and a group of adults. A woman looking just like her affectionately plays with her ponytail while asking her a question. Sacha, all smiles again, answers, and they all set off together toward the next room.

I exhale a long breath, my hand clutching my chest. We need to get out of here, now.

Motioning Michael, a little pale in the face, to follow me through another exit, I do not stop until we are outside, and I slap my sunglasses on the moment I feel the air on my face.

"Do you think she saw us?" I ask Michael, out of breath.

Michael seems a little amused. "So what if she had? It's—"

"Do you think she saw us!"

"No!" He drops his arms to his sides. "I don't know. I'm not sure."

"Fuck." I start pacing on the spot, my pulse racing. "She could call Lucie. She will."

"Calm down. She probably didn't even see us."

I wave my hand frantically toward the station. "Let's keep walking. Please," I add, because he's not moving, "please, can we just keep walking?"

Michael makes a move at last, his hands stuck in his pockets.

"You don't get it," I say darkly. "I lied to Lucie to come here. Sacha and Lucie text all the time."

"I'm sorry you lied," Michael says, but I'm barely listening.

19

THE TEST THAT WENT DOWN IN HISTORY

On Monday morning, everyone shows up for English Lit as usual, and for the first time in my life I'm early, waiting at the front gate, hidden behind my sunglasses and checking my phone repeatedly, three sticks of gum in my mouth, chewing madly, pretending not to wait for Sacha to arrive.

Tony and Lucie stroll in together in a great mood. Her backpack is a little bee, as venomous as it is adorable. From the smile on my girlfriend's face, whatever Sacha thinks she saw, she didn't tell anyone yet. If I can get to her first, find out what she knows, I might be able to make the whole thing go.

Tony sees me and does a double-take. Lucie's jaw drops open.

"Shit Lou, are you early?" Tony starts patting me all over to check for open wounds. "What the fuck!"

"Well, surprise!"

When Sacha arrives, pigtails and pink jumpsuit and all, as bubbly as ever, it takes me every effort not to pounce on her under Tony and Lucie's nose. I let them walk ahead toward the classroom and deliberately hang behind to fall in with Sacha. Unfortunately, she's not alone. François and his long nose are glued to her side, and Yasmine is only a breath behind.

"Hi, Sacha."

"LouLou!" Her face brightens up. "How are you, baby?"

"Peachy." I realise with horror I'm getting used to her silly nickname. "It's, hem… You look nice today."

I wish I hadn't said that. François, glaring, deliberately inserts himself between us, using his large coffee tumbler. I choose to ignore him.

"Thanks," Sacha says. "Oh wait! That reminds me!" She clutches her chest. "Do you know what I saw this weekend?"

My heart stops; the gigantic ball of gum I've been chewing gets stuck to my palate.

"One of your crazy bands was on MTV Pulse!"

Relief submerges me like a tidal wave. I lose balance and have to hold on to François's sleeve to stay on my feet. He squeals in protest — or pain, hard to know — but never mind him.

Sacha hasn't seen us. She hasn't seen us, or she has seen us but never registered it.

"Which one?" I ask, feigning interest.

"I don't know. It was horrible, I changed the channel."

Relief, sweet relief. I was so certain she had seen us. In fact, I thought it impossible that she didn't.

As we approach the classroom, I notice nobody's entering.

"What's going on?"

Tony, followed closely by Lucie, elbows his way past the crowd to join us. Sacha doesn't register the nasty look he throws her, but I do.

"So, I've got good news and bad news."

"Let me guess," François says. "You're the bad news."

Yasmine, without looking up from her phone, gives a dry chuckle. Tony ignores them both.

"The good news is Paquin still has the flu. Or she was arrested for witchcraft. We'll never know. But English Lit is cancelled."

"Oh no," Michael says.

I hadn't noticed he was standing behind me. The sound of his voice, so close to my ear, makes me melt. I'm immediately transported to Saturday and our kiss at the museum. Then I'm reminded of how silent we both were on the way back home.

When the tip of his fingers graze my own, behind everyone's back, I shiver, earning myself a glare from François.

"The bad news," Tony says, enjoying the attention, "is that Racine, on the other end, is fit as a fiddle. The History test is still on."

Everyone starts groaning. I start laughing.

"The what now?"

The groaning dies, and every head turns to me.

"The History test." Lucie's eyes narrow. "You know, the one you said you would stay at home to study."

"Oh, that one."

I had no idea about a test, none so ever. I told Lucie I needed to study, I didn't say anything about History. When did he announce it? On Thursday? I'm usually so attentive these days. But Thursday was the day I didn't take any notes at all, but spent my time gazing dreamily out the window and staring at Michael's back wondering if I'll ever feel the plump cushion of his lips against mine again.

Probably Thursday, then. That explains why Michael said he wouldn't go out yesterday, and told me I should stay home and study, but I didn't. I went to Tony's at his request and we worked on our essay for less than an hour. Then we played Silent Hill Origins in semi-darkness, which provided an excellent cover for my growing anxiety at the thought of Sacha texting Lucie about what she saw.

Now I must find a way to revise the test without anyone knowing, and I've only got two hours to do this.

Meanwhile, the class organises itself to spend time outside in the park and enjoy the beautiful weather. It's decided before I can even chime in. To my horror, it's decided that the Golden Fork and Tony, Lucie, and I hang out together for the first time in history. Two hours of constant contact between Lucie, Sacha, Michael and I, where at any moment Sacha can recall our time at the museum. But if I refuse too vehemently to accompany them, I might make matters worse. So I've got no other choice but to follow them toward the Luxembourg Gardens, my sweaty palms hidden in my pockets.

Logically, I dump my ass near Sacha to keep an eye on her, should she put two and two together. It's a struggle as François also wants to sit next to her, so I have to glare at him to go on the other side.

"What are you doing?" Lucie asks, standing over me.

"I don't know, sitting down?"

"Then I'll sit too."

She sits next to me, Tony next to her, and when Michael arrives with Yasmine, they close our happy little circle. I pull out my phone. 1h40 left before the test. Why do people walk so slowly in groups! Despair will make you attempt the craziest things. That's how I clear my throat and ask:

"Should we study together?"

François snorts into his tumbler, spraying coffee everywhere. Michael uncharacteristically bursts out laughing.

Tony stretches his long arm behind Lucie's back to punch me in the shoulder. "Are you okay?"

"Fine. I just want to study."

Deploying my History book and my notes under people's shocked gaze, I stick it firmly between my knees for support. The goal is to absorb as much information as I can in a very short amount of time. It's not easy, but it's not impossible. That's how I pass every Spanish test, and I can't speak two words of the language.

Four minutes into my challenge, Lucie nudges me in the ribs.

"What's going on?" Her voice is soft and gives me no cause for concern at first.

"Nothing. I told you. I just want to practise before the test."

"Come on. You never do that."

"I've got to keep up my grades if I want to go to London."

My heart races as Sacha launches herself into an explanation of her afternoon at the museum. My eyes meet Michael on the opposite side of our circle. He doesn't seem concerned at all about Sacha's story. The fiend is absently staring at my girlfriend's cleavage. Is it by accident, or is it not? I'm not the only one who notices. Sacha does not miss it either.

"Mikey, you're such a perv'!"

Michael snaps out of it, and seeing us all staring at him, turns a deep shade of red.

Accompanied by an expected batting of her eyelashes, Sacha cocks her head.

"If you want to stare at breasts, stare at mine!"

"Sorry," Michael splutters. "I didn't mean to…"

Lucie glares at Sacha. Yasmine, bored out of her mind, lies on her back to get a semblance of a tan. François remains very still, stealing glances at Michael, who looks like he wants to disappear into the ground.

Lucie seems more amused than angry. "That's fine," she tells Michael. "Don't worry about it."

Tony is definitely leaning on the side of angry. He scoffs loudly enough for Michael to hear and Yasmine to arch a perfect eyebrow at him.

"So, anyway," Sacha tells François, the only one who seems to listen, "My aunt and uncle were going to let me use their flat in Barcelona—"

A discreet sigh of respite passes my lips. She's forgotten all about the museum. I adjust my sunglasses and resume poring over my notes. The test in 1h30 minutes. Twenty minutes to go there, by my calculations on how slow these people are. I've got 1h10 minutes to learn myself some WWII business.

Everybody converses more and less quietly over the next ten minutes. Behind my sunglasses, I see all, but no one can see me. While Sacha is blabbering on, François's forlorn eyes never leave Michael, who like Yasmine, has decided to lay down to stare at the cloudless sky. Once in a while, Yasmine grunts some sort of answer which gets Sacha going again.

Soon, Lucie interrupts my study again, her eyebrows drawn together.

"Why on earth did you follow them here? Have you lost your mind?"

I don't know what she's saying. I didn't organise this. But my answer in the form of a shrug doesn't impress her. She elbows me in the ribs and hisses in my ear.

"I'm talking to you."

I look up from my notes. "I didn't decide to come here. I thought you did."

"Bullshit."

"No, I'm serious. I didn't plan to come here. Why would I?"

Why indeed would I allow Lucie and Sacha to spend the whole morning together when it could cost me everything?

Lucie starts plucking blades of grass off the lawn, a scowl on her face. I plunge back into my notes.

Tanks, so many tanks. So many generals. I'll never remember any of their names. This is so frustrating. I've paid attention in class every time since the beginning of the year, and still, I remember nothing.

Lucie looking over my shoulder certainly doesn't help.

"Has Tony said anything about the Shark, by the way?"

"Yes."

"So?"

"So… sure, let's go there."

Lucie harrumphs and pulls a handful of grass from the ground. Michael is still laying on his back under François' watchful gaze. He looks so quiet. I wish I could just throw my notes over my shoulders, get up, lay down next to him, and tell everyone else to shut the hell up. Immediately, this thought is followed by a sharp pang of guilt at my own selfishness.

Lucie's pulling so much grass out now that I start to worry we're going to get fined for vandalising the Gardens.

"Lucie, stop!" I seize her hand. "What are you doing?"

Her nostrils flaring, she pulls her hand free.

"What am I doing? I'm trying to do something nice for you, and you're completely ignoring me."

Lucie is so beautiful, even when her face is twisted in anger, like right now. My pulse usually quickens just at the sight of her. But is it from love or apprehension? She has always frightened me a little. However, these past weeks, it has begun to get out of control.

"Lucie… I'm just trying to study."

"And?" She grimaced. "I've been trying to organise your birthday party—"

"A birthday party?" Sacha says. "When?"

Lucie holds up her hand to silence Sacha. "—For weeks, and you never seem to give two shits about it." She peers into my face, her eyes blazing. "Tell me once and for all, Lou. What is your fucking problem?"

The tone of her voice has Yasmine sit bolt upright; Michael too rises up on his elbow, his eyes wide; Sacha lets out a scoff of disbelief; François forgets all about Michael and watches Lucie's face, his mouth agape. Tony alone stares sadly between his legs.

What's my problem… I have so many problems.

Voicing them out loud, today, in public, would create such an earthquake that most of us would never recover from. Everyone here, with the exception of hot stuff over there, is constantly getting on my nerves, asking me to like things, say things, be things, I don't think I want to say or do or be anymore. And everyone here is just waiting for me to mess up once so they can justify their own bullshit and leave me without a look back.

"My problem?" Lucie's face whitens at the angry tone of my voice. "My problem is that I told you a million times I didn't want to do anything for my birthday. But no, you wanted to do something. So I agreed to spend the night with you and Tony. Do something small, maybe watch a movie. And now we're booking the basement of a bar and inviting the whole class?"

Lucie stares blankly into my face. "You're never happy. I really don't know why I——"

"Why you what?" I dare her. "Say it."

Everyone is holding their breath. François's jaw is completely slack. Sacha is gripping his arm, her hand over her mouth. Michael has sat upright, but has the decency to avoid staring at us.

Lucie jerks her chin up. "I really don't know why I bother with you."

Tony's expression screams at me not to do anything stupid. It's too late. I've done plenty of stupid lately, and it felt really good too.

"You know what, Lucie, I don't know either."

Lucie gets up, fuming, sending blades of grass everywhere.

"You're such a dick."

She stomps off toward the fountain. Everyone's head turns to her, to me, to her, to me again.

"Dude, you are so fucked," Yasmine says. She pushes up her own sunglasses up her nose and lays right back down.

"What the hell is wrong with you?" Tony crawls toward me, a look of disbelief on his face. "You can't talk to her like that!"

"I can't talk to her like that?" I give a harsh laugh. "I haven't said anything. I'm trying to study for a test, and she won't stop nagging me."

"Please forgive her for giving a shit about you."

"Yes, she cares so much about me." A mad hunch forces me to bite back with added venom. "Why don't you go and console her. Go ahead. Then you can both complain about me."

Tony's eyebrows disappear into his headline. "You are really acting like a dick."

He gets up, wiping dirt off his jeans, and sets off after Lucie.

Sacha looks at me, pouting. "So… everything's looking good between you two."

I murder her with my eyes. "Please, don't start."

"Okay," Yasmine says, getting up. "We don't need this, let's go." She snaps her fingers and François gets up, albeit reluctantly, with a last look at Michael.

"Are you coming?"

Michael hesitates, then shakes his head. François's expression grows darker, but he says nothing. Sacha gets up last and gives my shoulder a gentle squeeze.

"Hang in there, LouLou."

The three of them walk away. I release a long, exhausted breath, then check the time on my phone.

One hour left.

From the corner of my eye, I observe as Michael brushes grass off his elbows. He's the last person I want to fight with today. The only one who doesn't make me feel like throwing inanimate objects around, save my elderly neighbour. What the hell am I becoming?

"That was something…" Michael says.

"Please don't."

"I won't." He ruffles his hair, inadvertently causing my whole body to stand at attention. "I'll even let you study. Because I know you haven't studied for this test. And I feel it was my fault."

"Nope, it wasn't," I say, breathless at the sight of his bouncy curls. "I should have studied yesterday, but I went to Tony's."

"I see."

Now that I'm alone with Michael, studying seems even harder

than when Lucie was annoyingly poking me in the ribs. He doesn't even have to do anything. Just sit here, as he does, his hand instinctively reaching for his neck to rub it, his green eyes glittering in the sunlight.

Fuck it.

"Let's go."

"What?" He blinks. "Where?"

"Let's walk back to Colette. I have less than an hour to study for this test, and I'm not going to make it if I don't have you against a wall by then."

"Right." Michael, blushing, hurries to his feet. "Excellent."

We hurry out of the park. Where are Lucie and Tony? Are they okay or really mad, am I making another huge mistake by leaving them behind?

Michael, strolling in front of me, is humming an air I don't know. It's like he never has a care in the world, and it's as maddening as it is exciting. At this moment, I want him more than I ever did.

Ten minutes later, Michael opens the door to the boy's toilets for me with great flourish, as though we're entering a five-star restaurant. In an instant, we're back into the last stall on the left, clutching each other like drowning men.

My hands grip both sides of his face. His are digging into my hips. Tanks, generals, Lucie's angry face, everything melts away with a swipe of his tongue. His fingers slide under my shirt, graze my bare skin. A needy sound comes out of me, a sound I didn't know I could make. I sink into his body with the crazed hope of disappearing within its warmth. God knows where this will end if he doesn't stop me. He has to stop me. He has to.

He doesn't.

Demonstrating self-control that I would have never believed I had in me, I'm the one who breaks away.

Michael exhales a deep breath, his lips red and puffy. He reaches out to rearrange my hair, and I straighten his shirt, smooth out the fabric of his sleeves.

Someone comes in. Panic seizes me, but Michael, chill as ever, holds a finger to my lips and leans comfortably against the door, as though it's not the first time this ever happens to him. For a minute, we're quiet and still in the stall, save for the hammering of my heart in my chest. When Michael starts picking at his cuticles, and I watch, bewildered, the person leaves, and we're alone again.

I start picking imaginary lint off his shirt, laughing nervously.

"You don't mind, do you?" I ask.

"No, you're doing a better job than I would."

"Not this," I say, letting my arms drop to my sides. "This. Us. Clandestine kisses in public toilets."

Michael shakes his mane of hair and shrugs. "It's not like it's forever, is it?"

"No, I guess not."

"Sooner or later, you're going to have to tell her you're gay."

My throat tightens like a vice. "I'm not..."

"She's going to notice, eventually. Trust me."

He opens the stall and hurries out, all traces of desire gone from his face. Have I made him mad? I approach him cautiously.

"I'm sorry. Everyone's coming at me from every direction today. I was so afraid she would learn it from Sacha, and then everything would have exploded, you know. I want to tell her myself."

Michael walks over to the sink and checks his reflection in the mirror. "Tell her, then."

His laid-back attitude toward my explosive inner-turmoil is making my blood boil today.

"Why do you act like it's so fucking easy? I'm not constantly harassing you by asking if you told your girlfriend, am I?"

Michael stomps back toward me, his jaw clenched, but somebody enters the toilet at the same moment. A kid I don't know strolls inside and toward the urinals, whistling.

"You're right," Michael mutters, heaving his backpack onto his shoulder. "You're absolutely right. I won't bother you with that again."

What? What does he mean, he won't be bothering me again? If he means to stop pestering me, I'm all ears. If he means to stop kissing me, I'm not voting for it.

The sound of pee splashing against urinal walls bounces off the walls. Charming. Whistling guy looks around his shoulder and nods.

"All right, guys?"

Before I can tell him to fuck right off, François storms into the toilets, dishevelled and panting. He clearly ran the whole way from Luxembourg to here, but why? This might be my worst day at Colette's ever.

"Oh hi," he says, pretending very poorly not to expect us in here. "We were wondering where you were."

"We're here," Michael says, reading my pointed look. "I'll be with you in a minute."

After splashing a sorry amount of water on his hands, The Whistler finally leaves, not without a last curious glance at us.

Michael walks over to the good sink and begins to savagely rub his hands under the water jet. François hangs around anyway, hovering awkwardly by the sink.

"So, Lou, funny that I got you here…"

Here we go for the final act. How will François add to my misery today?

"I was just talking to Tony."

"That would be a first."

François's fake laughter echoes off the walls.

"Yeah… That's true. But anyway, Tony just told me you were planning to move to London after the exams?"

My stomach drops. Resentment toward Tony, a combination of fear and anger at Lucie, terror that Michael will interpret my travel plans as an attempt to stalk him… Everything adds up together.

"Is it?" Michael asks, his brow furrowed.

See? He probably thinks he's got a stalker on his hands. I straighten up and spear François with my most venomous glare.

"I've never had any intention of going to London."

Michael's frown deepens. François cocks his head.

"Tony said you were definitely going."

"Tony probably only talked to you for a bet."

François steps back, looking hurt.

"I joked once that I would move to London," I say, "and now he won't shut up about it. He's pulling your leg."

François turns to Michael. "Didn't you say you were moving back to London after the exams?"

193

Michael, imperturbable, turns around and smiles.

"Of course, yes. I'm going back. It's not like there's anything to keep me here."

It seems decades away since I felt like I was melting into the folds of Michael's arms, in the very stall at my back. Now all that is left is an all-consuming dread.

And to top it all, Michael, calling my name, points at the clock on the wall above the door. My mouth falls open. The test is now fifteen minutes away.

"Good luck," Michael says to my horrified face.

20

YOU ARE MY FAVOURITES

"I'm the worst person who's ever lived, and I'll never be happy!"

Moving past Eugénie as she opens the door, I set off straight across the corridor into her sitting room and slink pathetically on her sofa.

"What's going on now?" Eugénie asks, a worried look on her face. "Should I get the gin?"

As tempting as it sounds, I refuse with a shake of the head. "No, no, I need my head clear when you tell me how to fix it."

"How should I know?" She sits on her armchair.

My God. Eugénie's kind of my best friend now. If Tony saw this, he would throw himself out of the window. But if Michael saw this, he would think it cute. But what's the point! I'll never see Michael again after today.

Picking up a cushion from the sofa, I bury my head in it and let out a groan of despair. Eugénie pats me on the knee.

"Come on now, it can't be all that bad."

I explain to her what has happened earlier, making sure to withhold information about anything she's not supposed to know. Everything else goes. How I forgot to study the test to spend time with my secret lover, how Lucie and I fought in front of everyone, how Tony took her defence and left me, and how poorly I treated my sexy mistress and how *she* left with François.

Miss Eugénie's expression betrays a growing incredulity.

"And as a result," I say, sniffling. "I completely failed the test, my father will think I'm slacking again, and he won't let me go to London."

I notice the tissue box on the coffee table and start pulling the sheets out frantically. Eugénie opens her mouth in protest.

"And François!" I go on, my voice cracking, "François, always sticking his unusually large nose into my business! He made me look like I was desperate to go to London, and now... and now... Ouch!"

Eugénie, worried about her tissues, has slapped my hand away from the box. I carry on, unfazed.

"Now Doriane, who already thinks I'm bat-shit crazy, is going to think that I'm planning to move in with him after the exams, like a creepy stalker."

"With him?"

"With her!" I wail, slapping my fists, filled with tissues, on my knees. "Are you even listening?"

"Right," Miss Eugénie throws a longing look at the bottles in her bar. "First things first, next time you have a History exam, come to me, I can help you."

I lift a handful of tissues to my face and blow my nose. "Is that because you're really old and you lived through most of it?"

"You haven't lost your cheek." She sighs. "There's hope for you after all."

I nod sheepishly.

"Now, your Doriane," Eugénie says, a serious look on her face. "Text her immediately. Apologise. She shouldn't bear the brunt of your bad moods. If she wants you to break up with Lucie, it's probably because she wants to be in a relationship with you."

"But..." I hesitate, my bottom lip twitching. "I'm not sure I want to be in a relationship with Doriane."

Someone rings the doorbell, startling me. With an 'oh' of surprise, Miss Eugénie gets up to answer the door. I cannot see from my spot, but a friendly woman's voice comes from the landing. Probably her neighbour.

I take this opportunity to text Michael. What should I say? *I'm sorry about earlier. I wish I wasn't such a blockhead.* Should I add something else, like XOXO or a little emoticon that looks like a bird? Screw it. Miss Eugénie reappears. I stick my phone back into my pocket.

Eugénie drops an envelope of junk mail onto her chest of drawers.

"So," she says, sitting back down. "Why don't you want a relationship with Doriane? You just told me kissing her is the best thing in the world, and in too many details."

"I didn't say I didn't want to. I said I'm not sure."

"Why the hell not?"

"Because!" I put my head in my hands and start pulling at my hair. How can I tell her without betraying myself? "Doriane is… different. Being with her… would make me different too. I'm not sure I want this. You don't understand. A lot of people will talk, then I'll have to tell my family, and that is the last thing I want."

Miss Eugénie's expression turns incredulous. "How different is this Doriane? Does she have four arms or something?"

"No. She's… She's British."

"Terrible handicap indeed! Your life will never be the same."

"Don't make fun of me, help me, please."

She holds up her hands. "Okay, okay, sorry. So that's why you're always blabbing on about London. You were supposed to move there after the exams?"

"Yes. Sort of."

"Really?" She pulls a face. "You never told me anything about that."

"Because!" My voice comes out a whiny and frustrated as I feel. "Because it was never supposed to happen!"

"What are you talking about?"

Should I tell her? We have grown so close over the past weeks. Telling her about London is not like telling her Doriane is a bloke.

I take a second to recompose myself, pushing my messed up hair out of my face.

"The trip to London is just another misunderstanding in the clandestine circus that has become my life. It happened one evening during which Tony and Lucie weren't paying enough attention to me."

"You are such a drama queen."

Huh, watch the phrasing, please, Miss Eugénie. I slip her a warning look.

"I pretended I wanted to move to London. They got really surprised and upset, they begged me not to go, that it was supposed to be the three of us forever. It felt real nice to be wanted so badly. So… I may have been using this excuse to get their attention every time I wanted it." I attempt to ignore Miss Eugénie as she laughs into one fist and bangs the other on the table. "Anyway, it was fun, but then… Tony told his father, who found me a flat, and instead of trying to stop me, he became encouraging, saying I should go… Then, when I realised he was trying to push me into going, the idea of moving away grew on me and became a bit like an escape plan, a way out if things turned to shit."

"Why would things turn to shit?"

Though the idea has been running around in my head for quite some time, I'm still not ready to articulate it.

"I just know that they will. Things always turn to shit. I don't want to be there when they do."

"You want to run away."

I give a faint nod. "I think I did, for a while. But Doriane, you see… she's from London. She probably thinks I'm a crazy stalker."

Eugénie suddenly rises.

"The same Doriane who asked you to break up with Lucie?"

"Well, that's not exactly what she said, but—"

"Stop running in opposite directions!" She puts her hands on her hips. "If she wants you to break up with Lucie, she won't think you're stalking her. Why don't you ask her directly?"

I freeze at her outrageous question. "Excuse me. Are you insane?"

"Kids…" Miss Eugénie shakes her head. "Did you apologise to her, at least?"

"Yes." I lean back into the sofa. "I wrote a text while you were gossiping with your next-door neighbour. Even called myself a blockhead."

She waggles her finger in my face. "You *are* a blockhead. And I wasn't gossiping. I will have you know that I have great relationships with all of my neighbours."

What is that supposed to mean? And I thought I was her favourite. Now what, I have to compete for her affection as well? Starting with the next-door neighbour, apparently. I have to remind myself to stick some glue into her keyhole on my way back up.

Feeling much better now, I propose that we dig out some biscuits. Eugénie, who loves her food, immediately agrees and moves toward the kitchen.

"Are you still bird-watching lately?" I ask, pointing at the window. "I don't see your binoculars."

"I might be ready to move on. Try something else."

"Like what?"

"Well—"

Eugénie's halfway through the kitchen door when we're interrupted by the intercom this time. She ignores my scandalised expression and walks with short quick steps to the machine in the doorway.

To my stupefaction, it's Michael's voice that I hear loud and clear coming through the speaker, speaking in perfect French, but with his undeniable accent.

"Hello, I'm so sorry to bother you, my name's Michael. Is Louis here?"

Immediately, I spring from the sofa, my heart stuck in my throat, and tear across the sitting room toward the doorway. Miss Eugénie turns to me with a little smile.

"Do you know a British lad named Michael?"

"I do." I attempt to sound casual despite the fact that my chest is heaving. "He's probably lost."

Eugénie picks up the handset. "He's here. Second floor on the right." She unlocks the building door with a light touch of her fingertip.

Half-a-minute later and before I can fix the damage to my hair,

Michael enters, a little windswept, panting, really, from climbing up the stairs. He flashes Eugénie an embarrassed smile.

"I'm so sorry to bother you, again, but—" he notices me lurking behind Eugénie "—I have an urgent homework question for Louis."

"I'm sure you do." Eugénie waves at him to come in.

Michael slips me a quizzical look and whispers in English: "Is this your grandmother?"

"No!" I give a snort. "She's my friend."

Michael takes one look around the living room, the carved coffee table, the plum curtains, the record player, the picture frames, the knitted blankets, and his expression grows from incredulous to dumbfounded.

"Wait, do you live here?"

Eugénie chuckles and nudges Michael toward the armchair opposite hers while I resume my seat on the sofa.

"No, I don't," I say, with a pointed look at Eugénie. "I live upstairs. I told you. Eugénie is my friend."

Eugénie nods. "Nice to meet you, Michael. We can proceed in English if you like."

"We can?" I ask, stunned.

Eugénie clicks her tongue. "Boy, you know nothing about me."

That may be an understatement, and already, my mind starts racing with questions. But Michael is sitting a breath away from me, and to see him here, in this place, feels so out of place, like mixing two different universes that have nothing to do together. Like Ironman having tea with Dumbledore, that sort of thing.

"Perfect," Michael says, his cheeks taking on the most delightful colour. My heart is already doubling in size. "I rang all the doors. Half of them didn't have any names on it."

"Some stupid kid used to remove them for fun," Eugénie says, peering at me from the corner of her eye. "People gave up replacing them."

My shoulders lift in perfect innocence. "I have no idea what you're talking about."

"So, Michael," Miss Eugénie says, "since you're so serious about homework that this couldn't be done over the phone, I'll leave you to it for a minute while I get some snacks and open a bottle of Porto a friend just sent me."

She vanishes into her kitchen and closes the door. Instantly Michael turns to me, panic in his voice.

"I'm so sorry, I didn't know which door to ring."

For once, I'm the one surprisingly calm about the situation. Relaxed, even, considering twenty minutes ago I thought he'd never want to see my face again.

"Just pretend you're my friend, and if you're asked, there's a British girl in our class named Doriane."

"What? Why?"

"She's you. I… told her about you, but she thinks you're a girl."

Michael hides his face in his hands. His shoulders quiver. My hand moves to touch his shoulder, worried. Then I notice he's laughing.

"What?"

"Dorian is a man's name, Louis."

"I know a girl named Doriane."

"I bet you she's not British."

For heaven's sake. Let's hope Miss Eugénie didn't notice.

"Why did you come?" I whisper, but it's quite safe. Miss Eugénie is making a hell of a racket in the kitchen. It sounds as though she's ripping the doors of the cupboards off their hinges and throwing their contents around.

"I wanted to tell you I'm sorry, then I saw your message, and I thought I needed to tell you it was all right." Michael seizes my hand, gives it a squeeze that raises the temperature in Eugénie's flat by about a million degrees. "And I have some news."

Michael leans toward me, hopefully with the intent to kiss me, but Miss Eugénie reappears, holding a bottle of Porto and a small bowl filled with pretzels.

"So much for tearing your kitchen apart," I comment, expecting at least a cheese platter.

She silences me with a glare. "Open this while I fetch glasses."

Eugénie leaves us again. Michael pounces forward and smacks his lips against mine. The familiar scent of fresh apples fills my nostrils. I manage to pull his bottom lip between my teeth before he breaks away.

My head swimming, I set out to open the bottle, but I cannot twist the cap. It's stuck.

"Damn, this thing won't open."

Michael watches with an arched brow as I plant the bottle between my legs to get a better grip. Nothing will do.

"This is hopeless," I say, panting.

Michael's laughing face grows suddenly serious; a dark glint flashes in his eyes.

"I could think of worse things."

"What?"

"Than being stuck between your legs."

Struck by a sudden fit of coughing, I wave my hand around, searching for a glass of water. There's none. Michael quickly moves, and with a hard slap on the back, brings me back to my senses.

"What's going on now?" Eugénie comes running out of the kitchen, and gasps at the sight of my red face and streaming eyes.

"Nothing, Madame," Michael says calmly. "Louis's just having a little trouble with the bottle."

"Are you really so helpless?" Miss Eugénie snatches the bottle and hands it over to Michael.

"I'll show you how it's done," Michael whispers, once Eugénie is back into the kitchen.

I jerk my head away. "I'm not even going to bother looking at you."

Once the bottle is open, Eugénie joins us, and we quickly move past superficial introductions toward the topic of music. The three of us having widely different tastes in music, the conversation quickly turns lively. I'm passionate about rock music, even refuses to hear Miss Eugenie's arguments that good rock music died with the seventies. Michael comments that he's never liked anything more than Ravel and Debussy. To which Eugénie retorts that the true soul of music comes from blues, and opens the large doors of her TV stand to reveal an incredible collection of records.

In a second, Michael is on the floor, tearing at his curls in awe.

"Not the hair!" I beg, bolting after him.

Eugénie leans back in her chair, a smile of her face. "Go on, kids. Get them out, play what you like."

Two hours and a full bottle of Porto later, records are scattered everywhere in the sitting room. Billie Holiday's voice rises, mournful, from the record player. Eugénie is teaching me how to do a perfect smoke ring while Michael watches, a tipsy smile on his face.

I'm not a cheerful person. I might never be. But as such, I can recognise my moments of happiness right as they unfold before me.

In that exact moment, I know myself to be happy.

When was I straight? I'm trying to remember what it really feels like to see a girl and want nothing but to settle into her arms and peel her clothes off, layer by layer. Lucie's beauty always mesmerised me. But is the appreciation of her beauty truly desire? I have kissed her so many times, felt the soft touch of her lips in my hair, tasted her cherry-flavoured lipstick, kissed the inside of her arms. But none of these moments compares to the feeling of Michael's tongue against mine, his powerful hands pressing on my hips, his flat chest warm against the palm of my hand.

To say nothing that the only time I slept with a girl, I was so drunk I can't remember it.

Michael looks up, his gaze unfocused. Seeing my face, he smiles, and a deep-seated yearning starts flooding through me.

If I ever slept with Michael, I would want to remember it all, make sure to taste every part of his skin, his tears, his sweat. I crave him like a starved man craves sustenance.

Is this it, then? What will happen to me when he finds out? No one should have this much power over me. No one should have this much power at all.

After her third demonstration, Eugénie doubles up, overcome with a nasty cough. I help her back to the sofa, administrating small taps on her back in a gentler approach to Michael's cure earlier.

"Miss Eugénie, sit down and rest."

Eugénie hushes me but sits all the same. "Louis thinks I'm at death's door."

"Louis worries too much," Michael says softly.

His remark offends me. Only because people who aren't afflicted with a need for control always act like we act like this by choice. The fact is, our need for control is also controlling us. All we can do is accept it as it is, because we're stuck with it.

"I only worry so much because everything always turns sour. Nothing is safe, you can't trust people."

"Fearful people are always right, in the end," Miss Eugenie says with a solemn nod.

"I'm not fearful."

"You do worry a lot," Michael chimes in.

"Not the same."

"They worry about the weather," Eugénie says. "They worry about change. They worry people will leave them. They worry about death. Eventually, it rains, everything changes, everybody leaves, and everybody dies."

"Oh great," I say, clapping, "really nice, Eugenie. Way to bomb a party. You must have been a great pilot during World War II."

Michael snorts into his glass of port and apologises, his chin dripping wine.

"Little shit." Eugénie picks up a rolled-up issue of Le Monde and pretends to swat me like a fly. "All I'm saying is, bad things happen. You won't have control over them. They'll happen anyway. Might as well enjoy the ride, don't you think?"

Michael nods wisely. "I agree, Miss Eugénie."

I lean back on the sofa, scowling. "Don't you gang up against me."

Eugénie laughs. "And you're paranoid too."

She gets up to change the record, but we won't be staying any longer. From the way Michael is staring at me, and the way his gaze is engulfing every relevant part of my body in unquenchable flames, I have suddenly decided we have outstayed our welcome.

I scramble up to my feet, my whole face burning.

"Thank you, Eugénie, for your wise words. God knows you've had time to prepare them." Miss Eugénie slaps the rolled-up Le Monde on top of my head. "But we have to go. Thank you for your hospitality again."

Michael offers to clean up the mess, but Eugénie pushes him toward the exit, claiming he's probably got more important things to do. She follows us into the corridor. Michael takes notice of one of her framed photographs and stops.

"Is that you and Paul Newman?" His eyebrows rise up to his hairline.

She nods. The small black-and-white picture shows a much younger Eugénie standing in a bikini on a beach with some stud. On closer look, I notice he's wearing the shades she let me borrow the other night.

"I told Louis I had better friends than him, once."

Michael looks astonished. "I must come back and ask you about that."

"Come back anytime, my darling." Eugénie, not skipping a beat, leaves a wet kiss on my handsome British nerd's cheek and opens the door. Michael slips out, but I hang back.

"Who's Paul Newman?"

Miss Eugénie shakes her head. "My dear Louis. Don't you know anything?"

"Well, no, that's why I have you."

She gives my wrist a playful slap and shoves me outside before slamming the door in my face, her laughter clearly audible on the other side.

21

SEVEN IN THE AFTERNOON

What now? Michael is gazing up the stairs, like the treasure he has been seeking for all this time is hidden up there, in the depths of my flat. Upon checking my phone, I learn I have a bit of time before my father comes back from work.

I point my set of keys upwards toward my flat. "Do you want to come up?"

His hand rises to rub the back of his neck. "Sure."

We climb up the stairs in silence. Michael is quite possibly still tipsy from the Porto. Me, I'm just trying to remember if I've picked up my dirty underwear from the floor this morning.

"There's not much to see in there," I say, a little nervous as I open the door, half-dreading my underwear to be waiting in the doorway, ready to pounce.

"I'm sure that's not true."

Michael puts his palm on the small of my back. I shiver slightly under his touch.

"Don't be disappointed when you see it."

Michael enters after me and, standing in the doorway, takes a look around the place, the small sitting room on the left, the old TV, my father's pile of aeroplane magazines. The little kitchen on the right and its crooked cupboards. He whistles in admiration at my original hardwood floors, and I catch myself smiling.

"Is your father home?"

I shake my head in answer. "He'll be around soon."

"Show me your room, I want to talk to you."

I lead the way toward my bedroom, nervous. The underwear is right here, by the desk. I kick it under the bed while Michael gazes at the posters of singers and musicians glued to the walls. He smiles at my childish twin bed and its bedspread with little spaceships flying to the moon.

"Cute," he says, sitting on the bed.

Choosing to remain silent, I close the door behind us and roll out my desk chair to sit in front of him. The leather squeals under my weight, startles us. I've never noticed my room to be so maddeningly quiet before.

Michael thankfully finds the silence too much and slaps his knees with the palm of his hands.

"I told you I had news. Good news."

"What is it?"

"My father is visiting this weekend."

How is that so groundbreaking that he felt the need to rush over here to tell me? I had expected at least something sensational, like telling me he's going to stay in Paris forever and live under the covers of my bed.

Michael, as though he heard my dirty thoughts, gets off the bed and starts pacing around the room.

"He's got us tickets for the Opera." The way his eyes glint with excitement sends a delicious chill through my spine. "I'm hoping this means he's going to fix his problem with my mum! She's been out of sorts without him. I can't even imagine him all alone in the London flat. They're supposed to be together, they really are, you would agree if you'd see them!" Michael sits back down, as though ashamed of his own outburst. "You'd agree." I stare at his bottom lip pinched between his teeth. "Anyway, it seemed important to tell you…"

His voice fades away, everything fades away, dissolves into nothingness. Only his face remains, the subtle arch of his brow, the way his long lashes flutter when he blinks, the elegance of his fingers as he brushes away a stray curl.

Oh, Christ.

This is it, isn't it?

Lucie and I are over.

The rest is too frightening to voice out loud at the present.

"… in London after the exams," Michael concludes, bursting my bubble.

"Say what?"

Mercifully, he hasn't noticed I had completely tuned him out. He's picking lint off my bedspread, his cheeks flushed.

"That would be great if we could move back straight after the exams. Universities are better in London. And as much as I love Paris, I miss my home."

Hang on a second. Something happened while I drifted away.

"You're moving back," I say, unsure. "After the exams."

"Yes."

Michael is really leaving after the exams. Not that I'm surprised. He was always British, and his home was always London.

What should I do? I can't exactly get into something serious with him. I can't exactly continue to pretend I'm Lucie's boyfriend either. What do I do?

Three people, I love. Three people will leave me if I move.

I would never ask him to upend his life after just a few stolen kisses in public toilets and one sorry attempt at a date at the museum. I don't even know if he's gay. He's never told me, after all.

Are we for real, or are we just having fun? What's the difference? Fun sounds nice. Fun sounds like something a guy my age would do.

Minor problem here: I don't know how to have fun. Never did. Where's the guide, and how did I fail to read it? I steal a glance toward my laptop on my desk. Perhaps there's a YouTube tutorial about it. I have to check.

"With my father around this weekend," Michael says, "and the whole week after, I won't have time to hang out as we planned."

"That's all right," I say absently, wondering if it would be rude to ask him to step outside for a minute so I can check something on the internet. "I get it."

Michael probably doesn't worry about where this is going, or how to have fun. It's even funny that he likes to be around me. He is everything I pretend to be. Everything I project, he is naturally. Michael is like the cool, smart, laid-back, possibly gay version of what I want to be.

And I'm... well, me.

It's not a good time to consume myself with self-loathing, however. Michael's here, on my bed. Wringing his hands and worrying his poor lip. "I'm sorry I put so much pressure on you, before," he says, his eyes on his lap.

His apology startles me. "Sorry, what?"

Michael looks everywhere around the room but at me. "I have no right to ask you to break up with Lucie. You're right, you're not like me." He pauses. "I get it if you don't want to tell anyone. It's not an easy thing to say."

"It's not anyone's business," I say, unprompted.

"Exactly." He gives a slow, sympathetic nod. "But I don't like that you're lying to Lucie. It makes me feel awful."

"I know. I have to break up with her." Michael's gaze snaps up. "Not that it means that..."

I've got to stay cool, he can't see that I'm sinking, that I don't know how to be fun, that I don't want him to leave.

"No," he says, "of course not."

I can do fun. I can steal moments together until the exams, then I can let him go. That sounds like what a grown-up would do.

My phone rings in my pocket, startling us both. It's Lucie. I turn off the call and put the phone on the desk. A veil of sadness descends on my shoulders.

"Lucie and I were never a good match." My voice comes out choked. "She deserves better. I know I have to set her free. I'll tell her. Very soon. When the moment's right."

And when I do, will I regret it? Is her bee or polar bear back-pack the last thing I'll ever see of her as she walks away from me? Does Michael not care about Abby the way I do about Lucie? He doesn't have a Tony to add to the mix. He clearly doesn't understand me.

"You know, Michael..." I try not to sound bitter. "I feel bad about Abby too."

Michael gives me a surprised look. "Why?"

"I'm not the only one with a girlfriend here."

To my surprise, Michael springs up and kneels between my legs. He couldn't have thought of anything more distracting really.

"Don't worry about Abby," he says. He rests his hands on my knees. "We've been broken up for months. Before I came here."

I don't understand a word he's saying.

"For months? But I saw her——"

He waves my concerns away with a flick of his wrist.

"Yes. She's calling me, a lot. But that doesn't mean we're together. We're friends."

The way he said 'friends' rings false to me. A shifty glint darkens his eyes, giving me pause.

"But Sacha said..."

"You think I would have been able to stay friends with Sacha if I hadn't lied to her? She's been all over me since the day I arrived, and even then, she still tried to get into my pants at her party. The way she was throwing herself at you to make me jealous was unbearable. It drove me crazy."

That's why she thought I was so wonderful lately! Then it wasn't Eugénie's sunglasses. I might be able to borrow them again, drive Michael mad with them.

"Did you tell Sacha that——"

"I never said a word to anyone."

"And you were never into her?"

"No! I'm——" He stops, looking a little frustrated. "I'm really, really not."

I fold my arms over my chest. "Why didn't you simply tell her you weren't interested?"

Michael shifts in his seat. "Yasmine and I really get along. And I do like Sacha too, you know. She's always happy and motivated about everything. And I like François, when he's not angry all the time. You know, the three of them really have an awesome friend-ship. And I want to be their friend too."

I get up from my chair, laughing despite myself. An awesome

friendship? The one you've almost ruined the day you barged into their lives? Poor François, too angry for Michael. If he knew… He gave me more trouble than Sacha ever did. I turn to Michael, a smirk dancing on my lips.

"You know François's in love with you, right?"

Surprisingly, Michael doesn't seem aware of it, even though it's about as plain as getting hit in the face by a bulldozer.

"No, I don't think so."

"He is, I'm telling you. He has been acting like a complete maniac since you moved in, and we used to be friendly, you know."

"Not too friendly, I hope."

"Ha!" I let out an unseemly cackle. "Fat chance."

Michael approaches, pulls me to him. His intoxicating perfume sends my head reeling. His hands travel from my shoulders to my ribs, to my hips, settle there. Despite my layers of clothes, I feel naked, afraid. We kiss, briefly.

"When did you notice that you liked me?" Michael whispers against my cheek.

Unexpected question. Does it matter?

"Why are you asking me this?"

"I want to know."

"Why?"

He sighs, and his breath against my neck sends my heartbeat flying straight to tachycardia levels.

"It makes me happy to know."

"Fine."

I rack my brain trying to find when, exactly, I decided that I wanted to fondle him a little. Memories of his blue underwear, the dimples in his cheeks when I made him laugh, the sweet tyranny of his bouncing curls come rushing by. A strange image keeps coming back. The uncomfortable first time we gazed at each other in the toilet at Colette's.

No. That can't be it. It doesn't make any sense. I wasn't even gay back then.

Or was I?

"I don't know. I don't know yet. It was many things. I'm sure it's the same for you."

"No, I recall."

"You do?" I meet his gaze, surprised.

"I saw you in the mirror with your leather jacket and your sunglasses. You looked like you were pulled out of a magazine, like you'd seen it all and done it all. I'd never seen anyone look so blasé, you know. Damn, you were hot that day."

"Really! That's funny." I hide my embarrassment by laughing nervously.

Didn't I tell you that he thinks I'm cooler than I am? I have deceived him just as I did everyone else.

Michael's hands travel south. Oddly enough, every ounce of blood in my body seems to race in the same direction.

"You're pretty hot now." His plump lips graze my earlobe. My hands fly to his arms for support.

That's it, he's complimenting me because he wants to get in my pants. Classic. And it's going to happen. There's no way I won't let him. I just need to keep my sweating under control.

"Put on some music," Michael says. "And let's dance."

"Dance?" I glance at him in disbelief. "What do you mean?"

His green gaze darkens. "You know what I mean."

My phone sets off again, sending my pens rattling on the surface of my desk. I have no intention of answering. My finger flies to the CD player and presses a few buttons.

"Is this what you wanted?"

"No, this is what I want."

Our lips meet. My mind turns perfectly blank. I can even hear a gentle breeze, instead of the usual thumping of my heart. It's nice, it's lovely in here. Wish I could stay forever.

When I open my eyes, we are lying on my bed. How did we get there? Not that it matters. The song is far from over. Michael is leaving a trail of burning kisses along my jawline, his curls are tickling my nose. My soul heaves a little sigh.

More kisses follow. Along my cheek, my nose, my temples. I am torn between a feeling of bliss and the need to beg him to stop. I do no such thing. My fears, my doubts, my common sense even, anything unrelated to Michael's mouth opening against mine just fades away. I part my own lips when I'm asked to and am rewarded with the caress of his tongue.

Somewhere, far away, in the confines of what used to be my bedroom, but will forever be known as *the place where it happened*, my phone rings again, evil in its shrill. I don't leave my spot, but smother its ugly cries with my breathless sighs as Michael's hands begin to explore my body.

Afterwards, as we lay on our backs atop my small bed, as content as one can feel after the discovery of a new star, my thoughts return to myself as does the hammering in my chest.

Will this ever be enough? I already know the answer, but I won't say it to myself, nor to him.

Michael, his nose nuzzled in the crook of my neck, lets out a sigh and glances up.

"Louis?"

"Hm?"

"Your heart is beating so fast."

"You said it," I lie, "I'm always so anxious."

Eventually, we all must leave the safety of the nest. We were in my room much longer than I planned, because upon opening the door, we come face to face with my father, standing awkwardly in the corridor between the living room and the kitchen, a beer in one hand, a magazine in the other, and a look of total stupor on his face.

"Oh." He scratches the stubble on his jaw. "I didn't... I thought..."

"What?"

He hasn't heard anything. I haven't heard him coming home, so there is no way he heard anything. No way.

"I thought you were with Lucie."

My stomach sinks. He's heard something, hasn't he?

Michaels chortles. "You and everyone else," he says in English.

He's more cunning than I thought him capable of. But I won't let them affect me. Mercifully, all the tension I had in me was released in a most fortunate turn of events not one hour ago.

"Michael is my English Literature friend, Dad."

My father offers an uneasy, possibly frightened smile. I will have to tell Michael not to take it personally. Dad always looks uneasy and is quite possibly always frightened.

"Michael. Nice to meet you." My father's English doesn't allow him to go any further. He switches to French. "Louis told me about you. You really know your classics, apparently."

"I love classics," Michael says, approaching my father. "I've read so many of them."

"Dorian Gray especially," Dad says, moving aside so Michael can access the front door.

"Yes. Dorian is a particular favourite of mine."

My father nods. "That's great." His fingers tighten around his bottle of beer. "Thank you for… helping him."

I have the distinct feeling something's going on here, that they're talking in code or some other esoteric language I can't quite understand. I can only stand a few meters away, my eyebrows so knitted together that my forehead hurts.

"I hope I was able to help him," Michael says, turning to me. "I hope to help him again very soon."

It's code, isn't it? Like the Enigma Machine, right? What's the combination? Oh great, now I can remember my stupid History lesson.

Michael opens the door, and with a last wave goodbye, and a smile in my direction, leaves us.

His — probably warm now — beer still clutched tightly in his hand, my father turns to me.

"Is there anything you want to tell me?"

Blinking fast, I ransack my brain for a subject of conversation I know will allow us to move on.

"Has mum called?"

He shakes his head.

"Ok. Thanks."

His hand moves, but he thinks better of it. I turn on my heel and retreat into my bedroom.

The funny thing is, it could have gotten so much worse.

22

RUNNING AROUND IN CIRCLES

On Thursday morning, the whole class must gather under an irritating drizzle to run laps around the Luxembourg Gardens. I miss volleyball before we have even started.

A cluster of people catches my attention as I arrive late, clutching a stitch to my side. The Golden Fork, Michael, Lars, and others are assembled around Granger, the P.E. teacher, making weird noises.

Forgetting he's been mad at me since Monday morning, I instinctively turn to Tony.

"What's going on?"

Proving once again that the Lord works in mysterious ways, Tony's wearing an outfit straight from the eighties, long skinny legs sticking out of mini shorts, a tennis headband around his head. He looks absolutely ridiculous, and I miss him.

To my surprise, he gets closer, even cracks up a smile.

"Sacha's got the iPhone, and she's showing it around."

I put my hands on my knees to catch my breath.

"Remind me. Do we care about iPhones?"

"No." I catch him slipping me a weird glance. "We don't give a shit."

"Perfect."

Tony draws nearer still. "You know you're gonna have to run mindless laps like a caged rat in about two minutes. Why are you always late?"

I don't have an answer for him. It took me a tad too long to get out of bed because I was reminiscing what happened on top of it just days ago. I also spent extra time grooming myself in the hope of getting Michael's attention. Either of these answers, I decide, as I tie my hair back in a ponytail, couldn't possibly make Tony happy.

Another awed gasp comes from the iPhone group ahead. Lucie isn't far behind, looking tired, unnerved. Her sharp blue eyes are surveying the Golden Fork like they're the envoys of Satan.

"Is she still mad at me?"

"Better leave her alone for a while," Tony says. "She'll come around, you know."

No, she won't. We're over. If I doubted it before Michael slipped his hand under my shirt, I don't doubt it now.

A sharp pang of guilt assails me. A pissed off Lucie might very well break up with me, and then, I wouldn't have to confess a thing. How convenient would that be? Breaking up with Lucie one day, coming to school with Michael at my arm another?

I don't think so. Even I wouldn't stoop so low.

Michael looks up from the group and around, searching for something, someone. I'm hoping it's me. Is it me? He hasn't texted me or talked to me since he left my place on Monday. Perhaps, just like my mother, he has an allergic reaction to my father. Or to me.

Like my mother.

Perhaps he's just trying to give me some space. Or perhaps I was terrible, so bad he's not interested in me anymore. Come on. How hard can it be? Just like a popsicle, right? But I hadn't had a popsicle in a while. Perhaps I really was terrible.

The good thing about being hammered the first and only time I had sex is that I can't recall whether I was good at it any more than I can remember if I actually enjoyed it.

Eventually, even Granger gets enough of Sacha's new phone, and after an enervating blow of his whistle, our teacher sits his ass on a bench and we are off, shivering under the mild droplets, for an hour and a half of running around in circles.

Tony and I are already last, magnificent in our lack of efforts, Tony already coughing up his lungs, muttering about rockstars not being fit for running. Ahead of us, Lucie runs with Chloe, blonde ponytail slashing the air. Michael, not far ahead of her, runs with François. I wonder if Michael paid attention to what I said and will finally notice how obsessed François is with him. Even now he's happily chatting, no doubt elated to run near his precious Brit.

But hear this, François, two nights ago it was I who tasted his c—

"Any plans this weekend?"

Tony's voice sounds a death rattle fifteen minutes into the first lap. If he truly has a wish to join a band, he's gonna have to do it quick, just saying.

"No, I don't think so."

Michael's father arrives tomorrow, cancelling all of my plans to get more kisses, and for a whole week. So much can happen in a week! I'm already worried I wasn't good enough last time, and now what will happen after a whole week apart? Michael might very well lose interest, just at the time I'm getting about as ready as possible to accept the fact that I'm hopelessly head over heels for him.

"You should probably talk to Lucie."

My shoulders slump. "I don't know what to say."

More precisely, I don't know how to say it. I've cheated. I've lied. I've... stood and watched as our relationship turned into something that looked too much like a formal agreement. But what if I could tell her that I care? That I still care so much that I don't want to lose her friendship, and that I never asked for any of this? Could she hear me then? Or will she only hear the gravity of my sins?

What a drag. I'll never get out of this unscathed. I feel like I have to surrender before even going to battle.

"Say you're sorry, for a start," Tony says, clutching his chest. "She really wanted to throw you a nice birthday party."

I'm sure she did. As I'm sure she had a special idea in mind as to who would have burst out of the cake to bury a knife in my back.

I know, I'm being awfully sarcastic for a cheat. But they don't know what I know.

"You know her when she's angry." I swipe a strand of hair off my face. "She's not easy to talk to."

"Like *you're* easy to talk to."

"You've never had to face Angry Lucie."

"Yes, I have." Tony gives an unnerved laugh. "Of course I have. You're not the only one she terrifies at times."

At this moment, as though she heard us, Lucie turns around and throws us a look so hostile I hesitate to bolt in the opposite direction.

"What were you saying, Tony?" I ask, amused. "I should talk to her this weekend?"

"Maybe you should wait a little, you're right."

Michael and François slow down, probably because François looks as destroyed as I feel. Lucie overtakes them, Chloé huffing after her. François sinks to his knees, whining about his laces.

Tony and I soon reach the Medici Fountain and its surrounding trees which allow us to hide and enjoy a well-deserved micro-break. Lucie has had the same idea, but when she sees us hot on her heels, she gives a grunt of frustration and takes off to rejoin the fray. Tony stares after her, looking anguished.

"Just go, Tony." I exhale a breath.

"Really?"

"Sure."

Tony doesn't ask twice and darts after her. Silence envelops me, soothes my burgeoning headache. From here, Granger can't see me. For a moment, everything is peaceful. It's me, the trees, the still water and the statues watching over it.

I don't love Lucy. Why is so hard to let her go? I wish I was braver. Even if I don't have any guarantee that Michael will pick me... I have to let her go. To let her choose... to let her be truly happy.

My selfishness twists my stomachs, and my guilt is like salt being sprinkled on the wound. I guess I'm reaching Guinness record levels of self-loathing these days.

Michael appears on the main path, his handsome face flushed with effort. My dark thoughts like clouds part to let the sun through. François must still be lagging behind, trying to decipher the wonders of shoelace tying.

If I wave at Michael, will he stop? Please let him stop.

I wave. He trots up to me.

"Done running already?"

Linking my arms behind my head, I lay down on one of the benches by the water. If I bare my throat to him like this, perhaps he'll kiss me.

"It should be outlawed to be outside in the rain."

"We wouldn't get much done in Britain. Come on." Michael holds out his hand. "This barely categories as rain."

Trying really hard not to show my disappointment, I accept his hand and pull myself up.

"When does your father arrive?"

"Tomorrow."

Part of me wants to whine. To tell him I can't be a whole week without having him to myself. Another doesn't want to embarrass myself by acting love-struck and pathetic. So I just stand there, doing nothing.

"You look upset."

"Me? No." I shrug. "Lucie's really mad at me."

Michael's expression turns surprised. "Did you break up?"

"No! No. She's just mad at me. About the other day. Now's not a good time to break up, not when she's so mad at me."

"You prefer to wait until she's happy?"

I stare down at my shoes. "Now that you say it like that…"

Was it always so difficult to talk to him, or did this begin when we started kissing and hiding in corners and doing secret stuff in my bed? Was he always so unobtainable?

If I speak up, I'll do more damage. If only I knew of another way to communicate…

Michael is worrying his lip, looking tense. He jerks his thumb toward the main path.

"François's not far behind, I should…"

He turns on his heel. My fear makes way to something else. A mad fever possesses me.

I grab his hand and yank him bodily behind a tree, hidden from view. Then I slam him against the trunk and stand on my toes to steal a kiss.

For a second, fear that he might reject me presses on my chest, until I feel his fingers dig into my flesh, and he nearly plucks me off the ground.

Breathless, Michael spins me around until my own back collides with the tree. His hand reaches into my hair, tilts my head back. My hair slips free of its tie. Our kiss grows messier, hungrier. But the moment our bodies meet, and my hips quiver and buck, he pulls away with a curse.

Someone runs by, the sound of their carefree laughter reaching us. Behind our tree, we stand frozen in alarm and in my part, excitement as the group of girls comes giggling by.

"Damn, Louis." Michael runs his hand through his hair, his eyes wide. "Damn."

Reluctantly, I tear my gaze away from his crotch. "What? Don't you like me anymore?"

Michael's cheeks darken, and he opens his mouth to reply, but instead, horror dawns on his face and he glues his hands to his sides.

I turn around, my pulse racing. Tony and François are stomping toward us.

"There you are," Tony says, looking annoyed. "I was starting to consider you lost to an alien abduction."

"I fixed my laces," François says, starting off toward us. He takes one good look at our faces and stops. "They keep getting loose…" His voice trails off. "It's annoying."

Tony, too, looks from Michael and his red face to me, my messy hair and my glistening cheeks.

"Were you fighting?" he says, lifting a hand to his mouth. "Please tell me you were fighting? I always wanted to be in a fight."

With a bored eye roll, Michael quickly motions François to follow him, and they set off back toward the main path.

Tony urges me to do the same. "You won't be able to hide for another lap. Granger knows you."

We run in silence for a moment. At some point, we pass François on his knees, fixing his laces again. Michael watches us run by, an odd look on his face.

Tony sucks his teeth and nudges me in the rib. "What did he want, seriously?"

"Nothing."

"You weren't really fighting, were you?"

"No. We were just talking."

Tony snorts. "Why could he have to say? He has as much conversation as a toaster. Except the toaster is less boring."

Anger rises within me, fast. But understanding it's sometimes wiser to be silent, I keep running, my eyes focused on the path ahead.

"You're not saying anything," Tony insists, his voice low. "Perhaps he's managed to make you as boring as him after all."

I skid to a halt, the gravel crunching under my foot. "You know what, Tony? Perhaps he did. And would that be so bad? He's nice, at least. You, on the other hand, always have to shit on other people."

Tony stops too, red in the ears. "I have to shit on other people? Are you serious?"

"Yeah, I am, actually." My heart's thumping, and for once, not out of fear. "No one's good enough for you. This one's too stupid and this one's too snobbish and this one's too boring... No one can compare to Your Highness. Have you ever stopped to wonder what people think of you, for instance?"

"I'm wondering now, actually," Tony says, his mouth slack. "Nice to know what you really think, for once."

"What I really think?" I give a crazed laugh. "I think it would be nice, for once, to get along with people, instead of always being the sad, edgy ones."

"That's a bit rich coming from you, don't you think?"

I scoff, annoyed. "What are you saying?"

"You're the one who can't get along with people. You're the selfish one who treats his friends like garbage, who takes what he wants and doesn't give a shit about anyone else."

His outburst, spoken in a voice laced with bitterness, freezes me on the spot. We stare at each other, full of resentment, then Tony advances on me, snarling.

"And you were wondering why François hates you, for example, so much that we can't even go to Sacha's parties together."

Because I know exactly what my quarrel with François is, I start laughing.

"What?" Tony says, smirking. "Who's the one shitting on other people now?"

"You don't get it, do you?"

"No, you don't." His confident demeanour gives me pause. "I asked him, you know. For you. If you hadn't ruined his coming out, we would still be invited to their parties, together. Oh wait. Lucie and I still are. You're the only one left behind."

Tony enjoys watching my expression turn from angry amusement to disbelief, then shock, but soon, he stops laughing.

"Stay with your new friend, by all means. When he's done with you, we both know you'll come running back."

I stand rooted to the spot, too stunned to run. What did he mean, I ruined François's coming out? Of course, as I wonder what I have done, François comes running by, and our eyes lock. His awkward, even frightened expression tells me he has heard everything. When he accelerates in an effort to put as much distance as possible between us, I know it for sure.

It must be true, then. My legs refusing to pick up the pace, I give up running entirely, not even caring when groups of other students overtake me, some of them sniggering at my lack of efforts.

Could Tony be right? Could I be as selfish and awful as he claims me to be? I don't even recall François's coming out, except for that time at Shakespeare and Co. Could it be that I just wasn't paying attention?

It was undoubtedly a very important moment for him, and I can't even remember blowing it. What stupid thing did I do or say? Despite everything, I still believe Tony when he says I did it.

I'm halfway through the last lap when our teacher whistles for the end of class. Seeing me arrive last, and walking, Granger warns me that next time, he'll give me a zero. I acquiesce with a nod, too upset to fight him.

When I turn to pick up my backpack buried among the pile of other belongings, I can feel Tony's angry gaze burning into my back, and my resentment, mingled with shame, intensifies. But then Sacha pops out of nowhere, grabs my hand, and pulls me toward her friends.

"Picture! Let's take a picture!"

"Why?"

I try to wrench myself free. A picture's the last thing I need right now. But Sacha's grip is like a vice.

"I want to test my new phone's camera. Just stand there and stand still!"

That's how I find myself shoved in the middle of the main path between François and Michael. François's flushed from his neck up to his ears. Michael, bless him, looks as though posing for pictures is just another side effect of his general awesomeness.

Sacha calls out to everybody to join us, even dragging a scowling Tony and a pale Lucie toward us. Granger comes to Sacha, a smile on his face.

"Am I to be in the picture too?"

Sacha lets out a tittering laugh. "But then who would take it?"

She thrusts the iPhone into his hands. There is an audible gasp as Granger fumbles with the phone and almost drops it. Tony and I instinctively turn to each other, and just as quickly look away.

Sacha pounces forward to claim the spot on my left, but Michael is faster and reproducing what he did to me earlier, twirls her around, a clipped smile on his face, and places her on his left.

"Impressive," I mutter.

His fresh apple perfume fills my nose as he leans toward me. "Thank you."

On my left, Tony watches us with open hostility. The shot Granger snaps represents us all perfectly. Sacha, laughing, in the middle of our makeshift group of friends; Tony and I shooting glares, my face red with shame at the words we have just exchanged; Michael looking ever so elusive, tall and a little stiff and definitely the prize for us all; and François and Lucie looking thoroughly miserable, the real losers of the game.

Sacha takes one look at the horrid picture, decides she looks amazing, and posts it on Facebook right away.

If I had friends, I would be mortified. But from the look on Tony and Lucie's face, the hostilities are officially open. As for Michael, he might be mine for a clandestine, stolen moment, but in essence, he belongs to England.

I am truly on my own.

23

I CAN'T BELIEVE I'M SAYING THIS

Years ago, long before I met Tony, when I had baby teeth and much shorter hair, wispy and so blond it looked white, as well as two parents, I had a fight with my best friend Thomas about which Ninja Turtle was the best. A really deep issue, as you can see. We didn't speak for two weeks, and I was utterly alone and thought I'd never, never be happy again. Life was over.

Now I'm almost eighteen and much more mature, I can guarantee you I feel just as terrible. And I'm not even one day in. Tony and Lucie haven't said a word to me all day, and we spend our breaks glaring at each other.

Lucie and I are like two generals of enemy armies, circling each other, wondering who will say the first word, draw the first weapon. Lucie's backpack is, ever since our fight, the same surly raccoon.

However, none of us is willing to take the first step, both too aware of the disaster that would ensue. And with Michael still sitting with François in English Literature, I don't even have the comfort of his company.

And there's François. Every time I see him, I'm reminded of Tony's words, and my cheeks start tingling with shame.

On Friday evening, I naturally end up slouched on Eugénie's

sofa, eating pickles out of the jar, watching her smoke one of my joints.

We are waiting for *Don't Forget The Lyrics* to start. It's Eugénie's new thing; she, just like me, has had enough of birds. She's trying to convert me to the joys of prime time karaoke. It's never gonna happen.

"The best thing is to apologise." Eugénie blows out a perfect smoke ring, when I have told her about my fight with Tony. "Grown-ups apologise, or they lose their place in their social circles. That's how it works."

Tony's long face appears behind my eyelids.

"Rockstars don't grow up," I say, followed by a sigh.

Why should I be the only one to apologise? Tony said some pretty nasty things himself. If I should apologise to somebody, then it should be François. But there's not enough Porto in the world to compel me to do that.

Eugénie gives a harsh laugh. "You don't know a thing about rockstars. Sometimes I feel like I'm talking to a kid."

"I am a kid."

"Not anymore. Now's the time to get on with your responsibilities."

She hands me the joint.

"Nah, thanks, I don't feel like smoking." I lift myself up on an elbow. "By the way Eugénie. Who's Paul Newman?"

She points toward the door. "Get out."

But I stay right where I am. *Don't Forget The Lyrics* has just begun.

Tony's the first thing that pops into my mind when I get up the next morning. Well, no, he's actually the second. Michael has his own privileges.

Shortly after we met, Tony took me to his place, showed me his music collection, his poster of Rage Against the Machine, and we lit up our first joint together. Sprawled on the floor of his bedroom, we looked at pictures of rock bands in magazines.

Tony had said: "Wouldn't it be great to be a rockstar?"

"I guess," I said, already high. "It would be pretty cool."

Tony nodded. "They can do anything they want. They're

surrounded by the coolest people. Haven't you noticed? Even the ugly ones have the best-looking girls swarming around them."

"How do you become cool, then?"

"Easy," Tony said, in a tone that suggested he knew what he was talking about. "First, take shit from no-one. And we've got to be bold. We've got to be bold and free and take shit from no one. Oh, and it would probably help to play a cool instrument. I play the bass pretty well."

"I don't know how to play any instrument."

Tony slapped me on the back. "You've got to become your own instrument, man."

The clock has been ticking since the first time Tony and I met. Since he threw that rockstar persona over my shoulders like a blanket, and I followed in his footsteps. Now that time for us to part is drawing near, I'm becoming in serious danger of drowning in sentimentalism.

In the afternoon, sunlight pours into my bedroom and bathes the whole space in golden light. I have never noticed, since I spend most of my time outside with Tony and Lucie. I open the window to let some clean air inside.

It's the beginning of April. My own birthday's right around the corner.

Eighteen years old, not a rockstar, possibly gay.

When did I ever think I had it all figured out? Next time I better keep my mouth shut.

A walk is all I need.

Outside, tourists are flocking in noisy groups, armed with their cameras, their kids hanging on their arms, looking exhausted. Behind my sunglasses and with my earphones on, they are no threat to me.

On a day like this, you start getting ideas about laying down in the grass, going on a mini-trip with your crush, feeding the ducks, and you know, other urges...

Perhaps I should go to Michael's and hire a Mariachi band to sing under his windows, tell him to meet me outside, let's feed the ducks together, perhaps our other urges.

Or I should grow a pair, go to Lucie and say, 'Surprise! Did you know I was into guys?'

My phone rings, making me jump.

Is it Tony? Or Michael? Or even Lucie?

Neither. It's from an unknown number. Like I would ever answer a call from an unknown number. I jam the phone back into my pocket. That's when I notice that, while I was daydreaming, my feet have taken me straight to Tony's flat.

I have to stop in the middle of the street. I want to apologise, I want him to forgive me. But sometimes he, too, acts like a dick, and I hate the way he speaks about Michael…

I decide to take refuge in the first coffee place I see, yes, even the tacky one around the corner with dancing coffee beans painted on the windows. Happy Beans. I'm not making this up.

It's not very busy at this time, perhaps because no one likes to see cute little coffee beans dancing on the window when they're about to be ground to oblivion to become your next caffeine shot.

Damn, I'm becoming awfully bleak when I don't get my dose of Michael in the morning.

I haven't waited more than a minute, my eyes cast down, when my turn comes. I step forward, ready to greet my barista, and my jaw drops.

Before me stands François, wearing an apron and a deep scowl.

I look from François's face to the apron — where coffee beans are dancing too — back to François's face, blinking, not sure I'm actually awake or if this is just another anxiety-induced nightmare.

"What are you doing here?"

"I work here."

"But why?"

François looks really pissed off to see me. But a word of advice. If you don't want your mates to find out what you do, try not to work in a coffee place, in a busy street, in a busy city.

"I want to spend the summer in *Barcelona*." He forces a bit much on the accent and sends spit flying all over the counter.

Wiping a fleck of spit off my cheek, I give him a suspicious look. "I thought you were rich."

"I am, thank you." Talking about his fortune always works. His shoulders relax. He even does a little curtsy. "But my father thinks having a real job won't hurt me, for once."

"For once, right."

I don't know what else to say. He doesn't know either. Eventually he drops his arms to his sides.

"Anyway, what do you want?"

An idea comes to my mind. A crazy idea. Looking around to make sure no one can hear me, and ignoring the woman huffing and puffing impatiently behind me, I lean over the counter and whisper:

"Actually… Can you take your break? I want to talk to you about something."

François's whole face twists, torn between suspicion and oddly, what looks like fear. He steps away from the counter, his arms folded over his chest.

"*Vale*," he says eventually, and thankfully turns around to remove his apron, or he would have seen my smirk.

Two cups of smoking coffee clutched in his fists, François meets me under the awning outside where two narrow tables and sets of chairs are waiting for customers.

"Thanks, man." I pull up a chair.

François sits opposite me. I've never been so close to him in broad delight. His hair colour is like it couldn't decide between ginger and blond, and settled for something in between. It looks vibrant under a fierce sunlight. I've always complained about his freckled face, but up close, they're really not that bad. His eyes, too, are green, a washed-out kind of green, nothing as deep as my Michael, of course. Right now they're staring at me anxiously.

"So. What do you want?" He's struggling to remove the lid of his paper cup.

"I think we should sort our problems. Man to man. I offer that we beat the shit out of each other tonight on the roof of Colette."

He looks up, his eyes popping. "What?"

Sorry, couldn't resist. It's the face he made. It was worth it. But if I want to get to the bottom of this, I'll have to stop trolling.

"I know you heard Tony and I when we were arguing."

He lifts up his chin. "How do you know?"

"You don't know how to lie."

"Oh, and you do?"

"Yep. I do it all the time."

There's a silence while François looks at me while chewing the inside of his cheek. Then he shrugs and starts dunking an impressive amount of sugar into his cup.

"Let's say I heard you fight with Tony. So what?"

I take a swig of scalding coffee. "So is it true? Did I ruin your coming out?"

"I guess so…" He hesitates. "You were drunk, you were loud. You didn't care."

"I'm sorry. I don't remember it."

François scoffs and puts the sugar down. "Of course you don't. I just said you were drunk. Like, really drunk." He changes his mind and adds more sugar into his cup.

Should I tell him he's going to die if he goes on like this, or…

"What happened?" I ask, forcing myself to remain focused.

François puts the sugar down again.

"I said I wanted to tell my friends something important about me. Then I said I was gay, and you stormed out, said you didn't need to hear this."

"I did?"

François nods. "Not many people heard you, but I did. It was a shitty thing to do, you know."

I ransack my brain trying to remember, but I simply cannot.

"When was this?"

"September last year, for Sacha's birthday party."

I shake my head. "No… I'm not sure——"

"The night Yasmine puked on the Persian Rug!"

"Oh, right. Yes, of course."

I don't know what to add, so I watch François pick up a plastic spoon and start twirling it around his mountain of sugar with added coffee. He keeps slipping me looks that he thinks are discreet, but there are only two of us, and he's standing right in front of me, so eventually, I burst.

"What? What?"

"I know about you and Michael, you know."

My heart leaps straight into my throat. I want to lurch forward, grab him by his apron, and shake him for information. But that wouldn't be very nice. Instead, I clear my throat.

"What do you know?"

François looks like he's enjoying himself, at least. "It doesn't take a genius. Though, sometimes, I wonder. No one else seems to have noticed that you're screwing each other behind everybody's back. Even Sacha, who saw you together at the museum, didn't come to the same conclusion. Oh yes, she saw you," he adds, smirking, "and she tells me everything. I'm the one who told her to zip it about it."

I say nothing. But I'm expecting my pale complexion to betray me, and surprise, my cheeks start burning.

"Why?"

"Why what?"

"Why did you ask her not to say anything?"

François takes a deep, affected breath. "Because, Louis, I shouldn't get to decide when or how you come out. You do."

I flinch under his pointed look. "I'm not—"

"What, gay?" He starts laughing again, a little at first, then a little too madly. He stops when he registers the scowl on my face. "Even better. You should tell Michael."

I've done François a lot of wrong. I messed up his coming out announcement and I'm fooling around behind everyone's back with his crush. That's the only reason I don't throttle him right here and now.

"You know what, Louis?" François says, his voice high-pitched. "I never got it. You always act like you're so cool and we're so lame, with your side-kick, your hot girlfriend, now your secret lover everyone's pining for. You treat people who love you like crap. It's like your shit doesn't stink. I always wondered, why is that that no one has ever noticed that you're faking it?"

Excuse me while I take another swig of coffee to wash down the brick I just swallowed.

"So, what's the act?" François says. "Do you pretend to be cool, do you pretend to find us lame? Do you pretend to be straight, or do you pretend to be gay? Do you like treating people like shit? Or do you just pretend that you do? I'm so confused with you at times."

My last sip of coffee sends me into a coughing fit. "You sure spend a lot of time watching me, François. You shouldn't bother, really."

"So." François ignores my attempt to throw him off. "Which is it?" He takes a sip of his diabetes-inducing monster and smiles.

It's a diversion technique, really. I pretend that I fit so people don't look too deeply into myself. It's none of his business.

I can only offer him a dumbfounded half-shrug. François slumps back on his chair, clearly annoyed.

"But all these people are crazy about you, and you just mess around with them."

Hang on. I've got to stop him here.

"What people?"

He scoffs. "You really have no idea the effect you have on people, do you?"

I try not to look too disgusted as he takes another large swig of his drink then decides he's not sweet enough and starts pouring extra sugar in it.

"I seem to piss everyone off. Like you. I pissed you off, didn't I?"

He sighs. "Yes."

"We used to be friendly, remember? Then Michael arrived."

"Yes, Michael arrived."

François seems satisfied with his drink now. He meets my eyes. Here we are, then. Let's get to the bottom of this.

"I'm sorry Michael likes me better than you, if that can console you."

François raises a hand to his chest. "You think I'm mad at you because you're screwing Michael?"

I wish he'd stop saying that. I mean, first, WRONG! Second, none of your business!

"So you don't mind that?"

He doesn't answer.

"Is it because of the coming out thing then?

"No!" François rolls his eyes to the sky. "You don't even remember what happened at New Year's Eve party?"

I shift in my seat. "What did I do this time?"

François's expression turns to one of astonishment. "You convinced me to change the music, remember?"

"Yes. I gave you a joint." The memory gives me pause. "And you didn't hate me then! I clearly remember us talking. You let me change the music."

A proud smile twitches the corner of my lip. François wipes if off with a withering glare.

"So, you don't remember us snogging in the bathroom?"

My body turns limp with shock. A bucket of icy water poured over my head would have had less effect.

"We what?"

François grimaces, like the memory is painful to him. "You came into the toilet when I was in there. You said you were sorry. I said it was okay. You asked if I liked the joint. I said I liked you better. You giggled like a schoolgirl. I kissed you. And you let me."

My throat is suddenly very dry.

"I would have remembered."

"How so? You were extremely drunk again. You drank shot after shot after shot. I have a great theory why, but that's not the point. Look, I have my part of shame; I knew you were drunk, I took advantage. But you kissed me back, you kissed me back so well, and..."

There was a compliment in there. What? He said it.

"And?"

"Then you snort in my face and tell me it's all very well and funny, but you're not gay at all, and you leave me, you spend the rest of the night all over Lucie while Tony is holding the candle. Fair enough, I decided, I kept my mouth shut, berated myself for kissing you when you were so drunk, making you do something you weren't into. But for a straight guy, you really seem into kissing boys. And then arrives Michael."

I know that one. "I stole him from you."

"You what?" François looks even more astounded. "You are so stupid." He shakes his head at my outraged expression. "You didn't steal Michael from me. Michael stole you from me!"

So, apparently earthquakes are not reserved for, as you might have suspected it, Earth, but can also happen within the human body, as demonstrated by the rip I feel upon hearing, well, this.

"I don't hate you, Louis, I fancy you!" François makes a move for my hand but stops himself at the last moment. "You told me you're not gay, but from the moment you met, you two have been circling each other and it's not fair! I was only waiting for you to remember I was there first!"

I lean back from the table to take a moment. This is all way too confusing. His attitude toward me… toward Michael?

"But I thought you loved Michael?!"

François drinks another sip of sugar and tilts his head. "Look, don't get me wrong, I like Michael, he's great. And he's hot, yes, but he's not really my type."

"Not really your type?" I can't help snorting. "I'm pretty certain even an Australian wallaby would find Michael to be his type."

"I prefer blondes," François says, shrugging. "And Sacha called dibs. Our friendship's stronger than this, you know."

"But you were always staring at him."

"I can stare at someone, and it doesn't mean I want to sleep with them! I barely even look at you and—"

"Right! I get it!"

I stare at François's amused expression. I didn't see this coming. I just didn't.

"But you're always so mean to me…"

He shakes his finger in my face. "No. Well, yes, maybe that time at the Shakespeare, when I was trying to make you admit that you were gay, that you remembered kissing me, that I was first. But that didn't work. I didn't plan on you having a real case of amnesia."

"You barred me from Sacha's party."

He grimaces. "That one is true. Sacha wanted Michael for herself. When I saw what was going on between you and him, the looks, I… I figured I would keep you separated."

"It didn't work."

"Well," François says, his fingers tightening around his cup. "When Michael wants something, he gets it, I guess."

Poor François. And I called him goat-like. Oh well.

"François…" I wait until he reluctantly meets my gaze. "I'm really sorry. I'd like us to be friends."

François lets out a dignified sigh. "Don't worry, I know. You and I, it's not going to happen. I've decided to drop it when I realised I was turning into a proper psychopath, that time I chased you into the toilets."

Yeah, I can recall.

"You were trying to separate us again, weren't you?"

"Huh?" He looks at me, surprised. "No, I was panicking! Tony just said you were moving to London. I thought you were moving away together, and I almost confessed I had a crush on you right there. That's when I realised I had to stop."

François glances down at his watch and rises up.

"I must get back to work."

I get up as well, unsure what to do. Should I hug him? Or pat him awkwardly on the shoulder? Should I just leave?

"Thanks, François." I jam my hands in my pockets to be safe. "It feels nice to tell the truth, for once."

François's eyes brighten. "It's funny. You said the exact same thing in the bathroom that time, right before I kissed you."

My hands shoot out of my pockets and fly to act as a shield between him and I.

"Please, don't kiss me."

"Are you sure?"

I nod fervently. "I'm in deep enough shit already."

François laughs. I watch him awkwardly. I can't believe I'm saying this, but… François is kind of nice, really.

My phone rings as I walk away from the coffee place. Unknown caller again. Could it possibly be… It wouldn't be the first time she uses a weird number. I stop a few feet away from an Irish pub and pick up, half-hoping, half-dreading to hear my mother's voice.

"Yes?"

The person on the other side hangs up immediately.

God damn telemarketers probably. A complete waste of time.

Tony would go on a proper rant if he knew. I could… I only have to turn around, walk over to his place, tell him what just happened. If he knew François had a crush on me, he would be so entertained.

But of course, I can't tell him without telling him the rest. I know exactly how he'll react when he finds out I cheated on Lucie.

"Louis?" a voice says behind me.

Surprised to hear my name, I turn around, expecting François to want to profess his undying love. It's not François, however, but Simon, Tony's brother, accompanied by Gretchen, his tall girlfriend.

Simon shakes my hand. "Are you coming to the pub with us?"

"Us?"

Simon points to the pub. "Tony just texted us to join him. He said he's in there with a friend."

A friend? But I'm his friend. Who else could it be?

A feeling of dread descends on my stomach and twists it in knots. When Simon pushes the door open to reveal Tony and Lucie seated closely together, laughing at something on Tony's phone, my anguish turns to bitterness, turns to anger.

"Look who I found!" Simon says, pushing me forward.

Lucie and Tony both look up at the same time. Their smiles vanish when they see me standing behind Simon, my hands balled into fists.

I have no intention of staying here to wait for explanations. I spin around and tear out of the place, my teeth clamping so hard on my lips that I can taste blood.

Tony calls out my name in the middle of the street. I keep moving without a look back.

24

WHAT ELSE DID I MISS?

Mondays suck. Whatever you do, however hard you try to not think about how they're about to sneak up on you, they still happen every week whether you like it or not. For many, it brings the horror of having to get back to a dissatisfying job.

For me, it means having to face Tony and Lucie.

Needless to say, I have a hard time finding the motivation to get out of bed this morning. Tony has sent me a dozen texts, Lucie half of that. All requests to call them back. I have replied to none and kept myself busy the rest of the weekend. As a result, our essay on Wuthering Heights is done. In an interesting twist, I ended up filling the role Michael was once supposed to fill for me: I wrote the essay on my own because my assignment partner is a blockhead.

In the kitchen, my father asks me again what I'd like for my birthday. That's right. I'm still turning eighteen, I'm still crashing headfirst into a wall, and there's nothing I can do to stop it… I don't know yet, I tell my dad, and he doesn't insist.

I have turned and turned the problem in my head, and I can't see another solution. I can't have them all, and I must sacrifice one. I'll talk to Lucie. Today.

My phone rings as I put on my shoes to go to school. The same unknown number again. Cursing under my breath, I stick the phone back into my pocket. It has to be some kind of telemarketer, a poor sod from Bouygues Telecom who wants to know how happy I am with their relentless customer service. Because harassing your clientele is guaranteed to earn yourself popularity points.

Dragging my feet to school, late as usual, without any hope of encountering Michael, I'm all choked up. My conversation with François is still fresh in my head. The New Year's Eve party is getting less and less blurry as well, and as for my decision to get so drunk that I let François kiss me, well, it can all be traced back to that one little moment.

"Rockstars don't let anybody let them down," Tony once said to me.

I laughed in his face when he said that, but I knew more than him about being let down.

"And they should respect their mentor!" Tony added, then pretended to strangle me.

What if your mentor is the one letting you down? Tony is full of lessons but he's as treacherous as most.

"Louis, for heaven's sake!" Some shrill voice calls behind me. "Are you deaf AND blind?"

Whipping around, wondering who could possibly speak to me in this way, I'm surprised to see François, looking impeccable in his Burberry trench. He clutches my arm for support as he catches his breath.

"I was screaming your name!"

"Didn't hear you." I point at my earphones. "I always play music when I'm alone."

"I saw you from the bus," he says, wheezing. "I got off and ran after you."

I look at him, startled. "But why?"

Enlightening conversion around coffee aside, François and I have never been close enough to even walk to the cafeteria together.

He tosses me a look. "You looked miserable."

"You know, I'm starting to believe it's just my face."

I break free when I notice Francois's still clutching my arm with an iron grip.

"I hope you're not thinking we're part of some gay club now, and that we have to stick together or some bullshit."

"How nice of you, Louis." He gives a forced smile. "I forgot how much of a prick you can be. But I forgive you, because at least you're not trying to pretend you're straight anymore."

That weasel. A grunt is all he gets in response.

François tilts his head. "I don't get it. You always act like you want to be different from all of us. Now you get to be different. So, be happy!"

"Shut up, François!" I hiss. His shrill voice is even louder than the traffic and the wailing child in front of us. "Everyone can hear you."

"You are so closeted."

"I'm not."

I am, it's quite clear by now. But he doesn't get to hear that.

"What is it then?"

"It's simple. I don't want to be known for being gay." I grimace at François's surprised look. "Don't look at me like that. You know what I mean. I don't want to be 'the gay guy', I don't want it to define me."

"Why should it define you?" François laughs with good humour. "It won't, silly. It just adds to your awesomeness, doesn't it? Louis, the gay rockstar. Also, Michael is the second best-looking guy in the whole school. You could be the hottest couple at Colette's."

Very aware of the compliment François just threw my way, I answer with a smile, and he seems satisfied with the results.

So now I'm best friends with François? This year is getting weirder and weirder.

We walk through the front gate together, in front of everyone, in front of Tony himself, whose jaw drops to his shoes.

"Just because of the look on his face," François whispers in my ear, "I forgive you for everything."

François turns left to join Sacha, Yasmine, and a very stilted Michael, who clearly hasn't missed my entrance with François. Let him think what he wants. Let him be consumed by jealousy. It will only make our reunion better. I'm already rubbing my hands at the thought.

I wave François goodbye and make my way inside the building. Tony bolts after me, an anxious look on his face.

"Lou, wait!"

I slow down and wait for him. I'm about to break up with Lucie. If there's any chance for me to have Tony by my side in the aftermath, I'm not going to waste it.

"Lou, listen, I'm sorry, okay?" Tony begins, gesticulating. "I said some things, you said some things, and—" he turns to look at the Golden Fork and Michael chatting by the gate. "I'm sorry, I'm really sorry you came to see me and Lucie was there, she didn't want to talk to you, and—"

"That's okay, To—"

He grips me by the shoulders and gives me a healthy shake. "I didn't know what to do! But you don't have to hang out with François, okay? You can stay with me. I didn't mean it when I said I hated you."

"You said you hated me?"

He screws his eyes shut. "Hum…"

His face looks so dumb that I can't help laughing. "You think I replaced you with François after a couple of days?"

"Well…"

"The fact that you consider yourself so easily replaced hardly makes you a rockstar."

Tony watches me through worried eyes, but upon seeing my smile, his whole face relaxes.

"Are we good, then?"

"Sure." We enter the building, Tony bounding by my side. "Where is Lucie? I need to talk to her."

Tony's smile falters. "She's sick."

"What's wrong with her?"

She seemed awfully fine on Saturday, at the pub.

"I don't know," Tony says. "Some kind of flu. She said she won't be coming today."

Is she really sick or just avoiding me? As though he heard my thoughts, Tony adds:

"She was already sick this weekend, you know. She sneezed in

Gretchen's hair. Gretchen freaked out, and we went home after that."

My break-up with Lucie is inevitable, but yet neither of us wants to draw first blood. She doesn't make it easy. Now what? I can't possibly go to her place and confess to cheating on her when she's already feeling down. My friendship with Tony is too wobbly. Any delicate change of the wind could ruin us all.

My phone vibrates in my pocket. Same odd number.

"Who's that?" Tony asks.

"No clue, but they're insistent."

"Give it to me!" Tony attempts to pry the phone off my hands, but I'm able to shove it back into my pocket. "Please, Lou, I'll pretend to be a Jehovah witness, and—"

"No. Let's leave it."

"All right, fine." Tony gives my shoulder an old, familiar squeeze. "So, joint?"

This is the first time in a while that I've got Tony all to myself, for a whole week. Lucie is ill and doesn't make an appearance. Michael is busy with his father, and there isn't a single opportunity all week to steal a kiss beneath the neon lights of the toilets.

Tony does not leave my side for a minute. It feels like old times, how we were when we met two-and-a-half years ago, and every minute had to be spent around each other. Too happy to ruin it all, I'm perhaps reverting too quickly into our old habits. All the while, my secrets are still nagging me, but Lucie really does have the flu and doesn't leave her room.

On Thursday, however, Tony confesses she's afraid to see me, afraid of talking to me. In my cowardice, I say nothing. As long as no one speaks, our friendship still stands.

On Friday, I'm positively shaking with anticipation. Michael's father is leaving tonight. Will he come straight to me? And what if he does? Will I tell him the thoughts that have been simmering around in my head? Will I tell him the truth?

That I want to kiss him in public, hold his hand, plunge my fingers in the glory of his hair, watch the rising sun reflected in the green of his eyes, feel his breath against mine, his heart against mine, his hips against mine, the weight of his love through the soft pressure of his lips…

I'm like the little girls plucking petals off a daisy, playing 'he likes me, he likes me not'. Michael's father is to leave in the afternoon. I might just run over there after class and confess everything, and I'll break up with Lucie. I will, I will.

If Michael loves me back, I'll go straight to Lucie and confess all. But if Michael doesn't care, I get to spend the weekend in bed weeping into my pillow.

In English Lit, we submit our work on Wuthering Heights. Tony thanks me for fixing the essay and falls right back asleep behind his binder.

Expertly waiting until Michael walks over to the front desk, I make sure to drop the paper at the exact same time as him just so our hands can touch.

"What's up?"

I'm all casual, you know, but also hoping he'll notice how blue my eyes are in the warm ray of sunlight hitting the front of Paquin's desk.

He looks at me, eyes so green, curls so soft, and something mad comes over me and I blurt out:

"I broke up with Lucie."

I mean, Lucie and I are over, over, over. It's pretty much official. We're not even talking. It's details, really. But this is how it comes out, because I wanted to see the effect of his face. Lars comes to submit his essay, so we cannot say more. But when Michael returns to his desk, I'm sure I've seen the shadow of a smile dancing on his lips.

It was barely a lie. I'm breaking up with her tonight. It is done.

Michael spends the rest of the lesson lost in thought, his chin resting on his hand. My heart is drumming around my ribcage with no respect for my nerves. I know. I will not settle down until he's in my arms again.

When school is over, I wait home for what seems for hours, ignoring my phone ringing for the hundredth time today, my chewed up nails begging for mercy. Every time this stupid unknown caller uses the line, there is a chance Michael is trying to call me, and he can't reach me, can't tell me he's mine forever. What are we to do if he can't call me!

I'm so worked up that I don't even think of the fact that Michael:

1) hates the phone
2) has never called me, always texted
3) lives five minutes away, on foot

The intercom rings in the doorway. My heart does a cartwheel. It must be Michael. It must be. I tear across the flat and almost knock over my poor dad on his way to the intercom.

"I've got it, Dad."

I wave his reached out hand away. Please, let it be Michael. And it is.

"Can I come up?"

My internal organs liquefy at the sound of his voice. Feeling my father listening in the other room, I hold the headset closer and whisper:

"My father's here."

A silence. "So?"

So, I'm embarrassed, sugar lips, what do you think? Even more so after the weird-ass conversation you two shared the other night. My father has been glancing at me strangely ever since.

"Wait, I'll be right down."

Tearing down the stairs four by four, I almost slip and break my neck. But one look at Michael's face makes it all worthwhile.

"I rang Eugénie first, she told me which door to call." Michael rubs his face and looks agitated, like he hasn't had a good night's sleep in a while.

"Is your father gone?" I ask, barely ashamed to wish his father back to London already.

"No." Michael throws a glance over his shoulder, his heavenly smell filling my nose. "We're going to the station now, we're just waiting for the taxi."

"Oh."

"I thought we could go somewhere to eat when I come back. So we can talk."

Talk? That sounds great. I'm all ready to talk.

"Sure, absolutely, I'll wait here."

Michael's phone beeps. He checks out his messages.

"Taxi's there. I have to go. I'll text you on my way back, we can meet at Rue Mouffetard."

Is he leaving me already, so soon? I stare down at my shoes, disappointed. In a blink of an eye, he closes the distance between us, pushes me into the hallway, grabs my face and slams his lips against mine. Before I can even return the kiss, he's gone.

"Two hours, tops," he says, without looking back.

I slam the door shut and lean against it for a second to recover. The week, the interminable wait, is over.

I'm humming when I get back upstairs into my home and throw myself on top of the bed.

Michael wants me still.

One hour goes by, one hour and a half. I have imagined all kinds of scenarios about our date tonight, and they all end up in ecstasy, the details of which I won't reveal to you.

When my phone rings after one hour and forty-five minutes, I flip it open breathlessly.

"Lou?"

Something's odd.

First, Michael doesn't call me Lou. Second, this voice on the phone is clearly a girl's voice, but not *my* girl's voice.

I sit bolt upright on my bed, a deep frown etched on my face. "Who's this?"

"Hello, Lou," the voice says. "It's Abby. Michael's girlfriend."

25

TRUTH IS SO OVERRATED

Abby's calling. She's on the phone, with me. Speaking, to me. A mounting feeling of horror floods everything inside me, making it hard to focus on what she says.

"I'm sorry, what?"

"Do you speak English?" She sounds irritated.

"Why are you calling me?" I try to control the panic in my voice. "How did you even get my number?"

"Okay, I know it sounds crazy, right?" Abby laughs. "You don't know me, but I kind of know you, through Michael. You know? British? Handsome? Apparently you're fucking him?"

My fist closes around the sheets.

"Rings a bell?" Abby sighs. "Well. I'm his girlfriend."

If all I can say is: "What?" she'll probably believe I'm a little slow, special needs kind of guy. But what else can I say, exactly?

"What?"

"All right." She has determined that I'm slow by now. "I know, it must come as a shock to you, so let me explain."

"How did you get this number?"

Did Michael give it to her?

"Michael told me about you," Abby says. "So I found you on Facebook, because this girl posted a picture of you, yeah? Michael has a type, you see. From the tag on the picture, it wasn't hard to get your phone number. Did you know your Facebook profile is public? I would change that if I were you."

Noted. I promise myself I will remove all traces of myself from the planet and the galaxy, if, and only if, I survive this conversation.

"What do you mean..." My voice sounds all choked up. "... Michael has a type?"

She mutters something that sounds a lot like "French idiot" and heaves another sigh, as though it is particularly exhausting to speak to me.

"You're not the only guy Michael has had fun with, Lou."

"If Michael told you about me, then he told you my name is Louis."

A short silence on the other side of the line. "Your profile says Lou."

"Michael doesn't call me Lou."

There's an odd thumping sound, as though she just slumped into a chair.

"He never bothered to say your name, you know."

"What do you mean?" The muscles in my fingers are starting to go numb.

"All he said was there was a cute boy in his class he was having fun with. I simply knew it was you by looking at the picture. As I said, he has a type. The last one was blond too, like you."

Her words hurt me more than a whole week away from Michael did.

"What do you want?"

"Look, Louis, Lou, whatever. I'm just calling you because Michael's my boyfriend, and he does these things all the time, then he comes back running to me. It's not fair to you, that's all."

"Michael said you broke up months ago."

"He what?" She breathes hard. "Michael and I have been together since we're sixteen."

"Why would he tell me that you broke up, then?"

"To get into your knickers, of course. That's what he does. He gets bored, seduces a boy, has his way with him, then comes back running to me. He's not even gay, you know."

"That doesn't sound like him," I say faintly.

But despite myself, my brain is already scrambling for clues to support her arguments.

"Doesn't it? Have you met his parents? Because I have, and it all makes sense after you've spent a few hours with them."

His parents? What is she talking about?

"What does it have to do with anything?"

"His parents are this artsy 'live your own experiences' shit. The mum's an actress and lives a pretty open life. His dad hosts lectures on Carpe Diem rubbish. They always encourage Michael to have as many experiences as possible."

Michael once quoted Dorian Gray about living one's experiences, didn't he? I thought he was interested in my philosophy, perhaps he was trying to lecture me on his. And his mum... the first time I met her, wasn't she going on about temptation?

My heart sinks. I plunge into the depths of my bed, seeking its comfort.

"Michael's easily bored, okay?" Abby says in a kinder tone. "It's not his fault. He's very smart. I just want to warn you, that's all. He loves to create this chaos around people, and when he's messed around his little prey's life, he moves on to something else."

"I'm not——"

"I know you have a girlfriend too, I saw her on your profile." Abby's voice hardens. "Did you break up with her? Or are you just as bad as he is?"

My eyes start brimming with tears I have no intentions of shedding. Thankfully, Abby can't see me.

"Did he even tell you why he came to Paris?"

"To be with his mother."

"Yeah, right. More likely because he almost destroyed this bloke's life and his parents came after him, wanted to make him pay. Poor lad went mental. He went and made a scene at school, and you know what Michael told him?" She interprets my stunned silence as a green-light. "He said: 'It was fun. You're really cute. But you are nothing to me.' Brutal, isn't it? Poor thing. Broke his heart to pieces."

On my childish bedspread, the tiny rockets have started to blur.

Unable to listen to her anymore, I hang up and hurl my phone across the room, where it bounces against the wall and clatters to the floor. My sheets crumpled in my fist, my stomach heaving with spasms, I bury my head in my pillow, and let out the scream that's been mounting up my throat for days, for weeks, for months, ever since I met his gaze in the reflection of the mirror.

That's why people should never pick up the phone, Tony's voice says in my head.

Not now, Tony. Shut up.

I don't know how long I remain prostrated on the bed, my throat feeling half its size, my legs turned to lead.

Eventually, it occurs to me. My phone is making all sorts of noises, as though everyone I know is trying to get into my head at once. I peel myself off the bed, a bitter taste in my mouth.

Text messages. So many text messages.

Michael, cheerful, wants to meet me at La Crêperie in ten minutes.

Tony says we should meet, no, we have to meet, it's important we meet, tonight.

Lucie writes she's sorry, but she's feeling better now, and we could talk, we should talk.

Laughing hysterically, I return to my pillow and let out another muffled scream.

I try in vain to remember. How did Michael and I come to be together? Did he seduce me, or did I seduce him? Who did what first? The first words, the first looks, the first kiss? Can it all be traced to him? Did he ever show signs of being the psychopath Abby described, or was I too wrapped up in my own fantasy to notice something was off about him?

I wish I could rewind every little moment, see it for what it really was...

He came to my place and turned me inside out, leaving me wanting for more, then ignored me for a day. I had to steal a kiss behind the tree at the Medicis Fountain because he wouldn't talk to me. His father's convenient visit made it so that I couldn't see him for a whole week. I checked my feelings since, told him by mistake that I broke up with Lucie. And now what? He invited me to dinner and says… We need to talk.

I was too love-struck to notice it. He's going to ditch me tonight. He made sure I fell for him. He made sure I abandoned my girlfriend, my best friend, my whole life behind, for him.

He's going to try to burn me tonight.

Seething anger flares up, slow and steady. I want to cancel our plans. God knows I want to. But behind every broken heart is a fierce desire for revenge. This rage I feel is the only reason I don't collapse onto myself right now. I want to confront him. I want to look at him in the eyes and tell him I know what he's trying to do to me.

I can't deal with Tony and Lucie at the moment. I have to send them a text. My plans are all for Michael tonight. My body, my mind, everything is full of poison. I couldn't recognise my friends if I passed them on the street.

I'm a creature of vengeance, moving numbly, typing absently words of apology on my phone, moving to the wardrobe to get my battle clothes. In my mind, there's nothing but my quest for a reckoning. I feel empty, unrecognisable, dangerous. Like a man with nothing to lose.

I leave home, dressed all in black, stick my earphones in my ears, play myself the perfect song. I feel like a soldier on the eve of battle, except my weapon is knowledge. I know what you did, Michael, I know, and I'll burn you before you burn me.

It's not long before I reach La Crêperie, which is just a quick takeaway place nestled between two tourist traps on Mouffetard. The night is warm and tourists are flocking the narrow cobblestone street looking for their next meal.

Michael is waiting at the front door, his hands in his pockets, his bottom lip stuck between his teeth. He sees me approach. The way his handsome face splits into a smile is like a knife being twisted in my gut.

Damn, the hurt, the hurt is too real, because my love for him was real. Damn you for what you did to me.

If only this experience would cure me of falling in love forever.

Perhaps I could run away, leave everything behind, become a monk. Do people still do that?

Michael speaks of things of no consequence. He orders a crêpe, asks me what I want. Incapable of thinking of anything, I order the same thing. His face moves in slow motion. Every little muscle in his jaw, the vein in his temple… I flatter myself to be a good liar, but I've never seen anything like it. He's all charm, all after-shave and silky curls, playing me like a fiddle.

"What did you want to talk about?" My voice sounds far away.

Michael takes our order from the salesman, pushes an aluminium-wrapped crêpe into my hand, unwraps his and takes a bite.

"My parents are getting back together."

Does he want my empathy? Has he ever sought it? His parents are getting back together. Perhaps they never were separated, perhaps it was all a ploy to make me sympathetic to him. But how could he have known my parents were separated? And he certainly didn't know how little I care about that.

"You're not eating?" Michael points at my crêpe, searing hot beneath its packaging.

"You're going back to London, then."

"Yes, during the holidays, first, then…"

He goes on, hungrily taking out chunks of his crêpe, reminding me of Tony. Tony always has a monstrous appetite but not lately. Now, Tony fills my head, fills my heart with painful jolts of guilt and regret. The first signs of a panic attack make their long-awaited appearance: a bitter taste fills the back of my throat, my fingers twitch and freeze and contort painfully. Looking around us, the whole street, usually such a delight for me, looks too bright, feels too hot, too crowded, suffocating. Everyone's smiling face looks like an ugly, mocking sneer.

Everyone knows. Everyone knows.

"Louis? Are you okay?"

Michael puts his hand on my shoulder. I shudder violently, shake him off. I feel like I'm going under. My hand clutches my chest. I see Tony and Lucie's faces everywhere. Laughing, sneering, pointing. I have to bend over to catch my breath. My sunglasses slide off my nose and shatter on the cobblestones.

A sound akin to a moan comes out of my mouth. Michael tries again to help me up. I shove him away.

Two familiar sets of shoes appear in my blurry field of vision. A pair of white and pink Adidas, so loved they're worn out, and a pair of heavy combat boots. I'm not hallucinating anymore... Tony and Lucie are indeed standing over me, in broad daylight, in front of my favourite crêperie.

"I can't believe I was feeling bad about you," Lucie says quietly. Her face is white but determined, cold even.

With difficulty, I straighten myself. "Hey, Lucie."

Tony throws me a disgusted look. "You look like shit." He tosses a similar glare at Michael, standing by my side with his half-eaten crêpe.

I manage a monumental shrug, sure to antagonise them both.

"Let's get out of here," Lucie says, her eyes flashing.

"No, hang on a second." Tony plants both feet in front of me. "When you texted you didn't feel like going out, I believed you, once again, like the stupid guy I am. We felt horrible, with Lucie, about everything that happened lately. We came to your place to fix things."

If I was not losing my mind or wasn't attempting to control a panic attack, I could have been grateful for their attempt. But things don't always happen this way, do they?

"Your dad told us you went out with Michael."

The one time that dad speaks two words to Tony, it's to seal my fate. Maybe I should just abandon pretences and start laughing as maniacally as I feel like right now.

"I thought you might be here." Tony's face is deformed by his contempt. "Your favourite street. Your favourite crêperie. With your new *friend*."

I start chuckling, and before long, I can't stop myself. Michael and Lucie stare in horror. Tony sticks to looking disgusted. Then Michael lightly touches my elbow.

"You said you broke up with her."

Lucie gives a cruel bite of a laugh. "I'm glad to see we're not the only ones you constantly lie to."

Michael drops his arm to his sides, and the crêpe slumps to the ground. I'm that close to clapping. He deserves an Oscar.

"Are you done?" Tony asks, offended by my laughter.

Taking a long shaky breath, I straighten up and wipe my eyes. None of this shit matters anymore. I have lost.

"Yes." I throw my hands up. "Yes, I lied and I went out. So what?"

Lucie jabs a finger in my sternum. "A liar, a cheat, a hypocrite. That's what you are. A fake. I can't believe I was torturing myself with you." She winces. "I have wasted so much time on you!"

"You're nothing like us," Tony adds, putting his hand, intentionally or not, on Lucie's arm. "If you think your new friends are better than us, good for you. We're done." He turns to Michael. "Good luck with him."

Michael's acting skills are slipping. His face is hardening, his jaw clenching.

"That's all right," I say, my own anger palpable in my voice. "Go. I'm not keeping you. You know what? Tell yourselves whatever you want about me. However much you want to help me." I motion them to move along. "And have a great time together."

Lucie's hurt look and Tony's violent flush both confirm what I have known for months, that thing I always refused to admit out loud. They scatter away, my two friends. Scatter so fast, it's as if I'd never known them.

That's it, then. It's done. A great rip tears me in half, leaves me unsteady on my feet. Immediately a wave of grief rises up from the pit of my stomach. I turn to Michael, hoping to finish him off while I still have a bit of anger left in me.

"Anything to add?" I ask, my vision blurry. "Hm?"

Michael stares down at his feet, then at me.

"Why did you say you broke up with her?"

He won't admit it then, will he? I raise my hands to the sky. "Does it look like she and I are in a loving relationship? Did the part about her and Tony escape you? Did you see the look on their faces when they understood that I know? No? Nothing?"

Michael's hurt expression is a masterpiece. I'm that close to bursting into tears.

"You're acting really weird, Louis."

I exhale a long breath. "For the record, I never thought I was better than them. It's actually the opposite."

"I know."

I step away from him. My face is burning, my back feels drenched in sweat.

"What do you know, exactly? You don't know me. And I clearly don't know you. So, I'll help you. Let me know if you understand my English. After all, I'm just some French idiot."

Michael looks completely bewildered. That expression, I believe, is genuine. I do a little bow.

"Thanks, Michael. You wanted to fuck up my life. You did. My real friends are gone, and I've got nothing left. You can leave me alone now. Go home, go back to England. It doesn't matter to me."

Michael stands there, his face frozen. My time's running out. If I stay in the street any longer, I'll collapse into a heap of tears and snot. I won't give him the pleasure.

"Why are you still here? You want to hear me say it? Fine, I'll say it. Thanks for the ride. It was fun. You're really cute. But you are nothing to me."

Upon hearing these words, Michael's eyes have widened to the size of dinner plates. This. This is proof Abby wasn't lying to me. He spoke these words, he remembers them.

"How?" He manages to articulate, his fingers curling. "How did you…"

His disbelief, his shock at my knowledge is twisting his handsome face, pulling at deep-seated strings at my core. Still, in this instant, my heart goes to him.

I just want it to be over now.

"Just go. Please."

Michael turns to leave, walks over a few steps, comes back, his expression so hurt, so vulnerable, that I almost flinch.

"You don't really like me, do you?"

A little taken aback by his audacity, I don't immediately reply.

"No, not really." I say. "Fuck off!"

252

Michael briefly stares into my defiant face, his lips pursed, concedes a nod of surrender.

"Right. I'm leaving then." A quick, nervous pause. "Take care, Louis."

That's probably the best apology I could hope for, coming from a psychotic manipulator like him.

When he's gone, at least, I can feel the pressure on my chest lifting up; my lungs expand, and I can take a real breath for the first time in over an hour. I turn around and slowly make my way home, longing for the darkness of my bedroom, my soft mattress, and the joint I have hidden in my sock drawer for an emergency just like this.

Angry righteousness feels good.

So good.

I'm always going to feel that good, because I was right.

Right?

26

NOW I CAN REALLY FOCUS ON BEING MISERABLE

Spend enough time on your own, and you can convince yourself of anything. Most particularly, that the situation you find yourself in was, of course, inevitable. I should have known, and a part of me knew before any of this began.

It was such a small gesture, and yet, it changed everything.

"You're late, again!" Tony said, but he slaps a beer in my hand.

Lucie pounces, open-mouthed, and swallows half my face in a hungry kiss. "You taste like booze."

"I may have gotten a head start at home."

The party around us is raging. Sacha's place turned into a night-club once more.

It's 2007, for at least another half-hour or so.

I ended the year with a lie, why not start it with another.

Let me rewind a little.

Sacha's New Year's Eve party was in our minds for weeks. It was to be as epic as her birthday party last September, the one during which the cool, collected Yasmine puked amaretto on the Persian Rug. The one where François came out. The time I said I didn't want to listen to him and left the room. You see? That party.

Anyway, there was no way anyone would miss this. And I didn't. I arrived on time, for a party. A decent 21h30 on the clock, carrying in my backpack, two bottles of beer, and one of vodka, courtesy of my father's collection which no-one ever uses. I slipped unnoticed into Sacha's flat, everyone was gathered around in the kitchen doing shots, and that's when my eyes came upon Tony and Lucie, right there, huddled in a corner of the room.

He said something. She laughed. Open mouth, throaty laugh, genuine laugher, so laid-back… I know it's something I could never do. She dipped her mouth into her plastic cup, laughed some more, and a strand of blond hair fell into her pink cocktail. Tony's hand reached toward her face, tucked the strand behind her ear in a delicate, comfortable, and loving sort of way.

The truth came crashing at the speed of an eighteen wheeler truck driven by a formula one pilot on ecstasy. The Truth, with a capital T.

Tony loves Lucie, he always has, he has never not loved Lucie.

And Lucie made a mistake choosing me.

Lucie made a mistake when she chose looks over substance. When she chose the pretty one, who couldn't love her back. And the ugly truth stared me in the face too, but I was too cowardly to comprehend it. Lucie wasn't mine. She wasn't supposed to be with me, but if I let her go, Tony would leave me too, and that, I couldn't live with.

At this point during the party, she might not have known that she loves him, but it was just a matter of time. A part of her must feel it, but to pick her boyfriend's best friend is something of a taboo, and for him too. At first she'll pretend nothing's wrong, she might even attempt to get closer to me… But eventually, eventually they'll both know, and they'll leave me behind, because it's the only sensible thing to do.

Naturally, I panicked.

I climbed down the grand staircase, hid in a janitor's closet between two floors, and drank most of the bottle of vodka. Once more or less recomposed, I pulled myself together, sparkling sunglasses, wicked grin and all, and came back upstairs. I was already known as Ever-Late Lou. No one noticed a thing.

I didn't plan to get so drunk that I would make out with François in the bathroom. But of course, a part of me always knew something was off. Lucie was perfect, and so beautiful, but I wasn't ever really into her, was I?

I thought it normal, I thought I was just embarrassed, ashamed of my secret, that one-night stand with a girl I never saw again. I was drunk. I didn't want to be reminded of it.

The odd churning in my stomach at the sight of boys happened so rarely that I never took it for anything else than my hormones waking up. The first time it happened, I was quite young. It was shortly before my mother left.

The truth is this. I knew. I knew about the cute guys. I knew about not liking Lucie. I knew about keeping them both separated when they clearly were made for each other. I knew and I said nothing, because the truth is overrated, the truth sucks, the truth hurts.

Who wants a hurtful truth when they can have a beautiful lie?

I used Lucie badly. So badly I owe her more than one apology. I lied repeatedly to Tony, time and time again, desperate to fit into his mould, his vision, longing for him to see me as I wanted to be seen. I wanted to be special. So special that he would never leave me.

Anger, hurt, spite. At first, it's sufficient to convince myself it was all for the best; they thought to leave me, but I left them first. That I would be all right, that I don't need them.

But who am I kidding?

My anger quickly turns to grief. My jealousy to longing. And my hatred toward Michael morphs into burning humiliation and unbearable grief in no time.

My real success is to show my face day after day at school for a whole week before we are once again sent home for the holidays.

Each day we drag our sorry asses to school, chin up, defiant glares at the ready, pretending not to see the stares of everyone else around us.

"The band has split up!" Lars said, de facto becoming my new most disliked classmate.

"Who do you think is Yoko Ono?" A retort followed by a burst of laughter.

Yoko Ono — or Michael, for those who are actually following — looking dashing in his dignified mutism, has never looked at me again. Instead, he's given all of his attention to his real friends, Sacha, Yasmine, and François. I can only imagine the lies he told them. My brief truce with François is definitely over. When our eyes meet, his are so full of contempt that I have to look away.

One small mercy is that each of us is keeping their distance. Tony and Lucie are hovering on the edge, as they always did, and Lucie and the Golden Fork's friendship looks forever done with. I guess she took to Tony's philosophies better than I did. Otherwise, why would she feel so much contempt for her former friends? My relationship with Michael, as far as I know, remains a secret for everybody but François.

Lucie was always Tony's true loyalist. I was the fraud.

To find a sign about their happiness, one has to look no further than at Lucie's backpack, a happy kitten from hell whose toothy smile is taunting me about my failures. At least they're not flaunting me with their love, if, as I think, they are already an item.

And through it all, a little voice has risen, and like a broken record, plays a song I'm too familiar with.

I knew, I always knew I would end up alone. Like I knew way before Tony that I wasn't really rockstar material, I was only doing it for his love and attention.

Michael said once that he desired me because I looked pulled from a magazine. It seemed, in the end, I fooled him too. I've got that right at least.

Being alone for the first time in years has its perks, you know. I've had a long time to look in the mirror, make note of what I didn't like, and remove everything I could change.

Out with the Kurt Cobain clothes and the calculated fake

persona that came with it. The baggy clothes, the striped shirts. They end up in a large bin bag. I wake up one morning to see it being driven away. Into the trash. Fitting.

Only my sunglasses remain, the glass on one eye shattered, the last token of my friendship with Tony. My faithful shield for years, concealing my lying eyes from my friends and enemies alike. I was wearing them the first time Michael noticed me. What did he see then? Someone cute to play around with.

I can't complain, we had some good times. Every time I think of it, I must force myself to remember I was nothing but a plaything to him, or I miss him too much and my throat gets constricted with sobs.

I am becoming a person who goes to school, listens, takes notes, hides in corners to smoke cigarettes during breaks and goes home straight after class. Homework done, essays given on time, grades improving so fast my father doesn't know what to think, and once asks me if I'm taking this Adderall thing he heard about on TV.

"Nope."

I'm just friendless and bored. Working is just a way to pass the time, to stop my thoughts from driving me crazy.

And now my escape plan to London doesn't feel so stupid after all, right? And if I carry on like this, I will leave with the full support of my father. I should perhaps go to another city. Wouldn't want to run into Michael and his next victim. Why not Florence? François had a lot to say about it. It has certainly nothing to do with the fact that Italy is filled with dark-haired men with bouncy curls.

At last, after several days of relative hell, haunting the graveyard of my friendships and my two fake lovers, spring holidays are upon us. I can hide in the safety of my flat for the next two weeks.

My father being, well… my father, and unfit for conversation, I naturally turn to Eugénie for a much-needed dose of social interactions. We are getting really good at *Don't Forget The Lyrics*. And I'm getting really good at smoke rings.

But a few days into the holidays, even Miss Eugénie can't take any more of my face. We are trying to watch a documentary, but I'm not really into it. There are lionesses, and there are gazelles. I let you guess what happens next.

"What happened, my boy?"

"Let me guess," I say, not taking my eyes off the stalking lioness, crouched low beneath the tall grass. "I look miserable, don't I?"

She nods sympathetically. "You want to tell me about it?" She pushes the tissue box toward me. She thinks she knows me. But I'm not going to cry.

"Sure, let me sum it up for you real quick." I lift my finger to my chin. "I'm all broke up with Lucie. She and Tony don't speak to me anymore. And Doriane and I are over. That's about it."

The stupid gazelles are drinking from a large pool of water, their gorgeous ears twitching, unaware of the big-ass lioness crouching not twenty meters away.

Eugénie wrings her small hands together. "What happened to Michael? Wasn't he your friend?"

The lioness pounces. It's panic among the gazelles.

"No." My voice has dropped a few octaves. "He wasn't much of a friend after all."

Eugénie gives me a look of surprise. "Really?"

"Really, Miss Eugénie. People are assholes, me included. Michael is just a different kind of asshole, but an asshole all the same."

The lioness has singled one of the gazelles out. It's do or die now. The gazelle is fast, she might get away. Please let her get away.

"I can't believe it," Eugénie says, chewing on the tip of her thumb. "He seemed so nice."

I concede a nod. "I agree. It takes a particular kind of asshole to be so charming and underneath…"

The lioness has caught the gazelle, and they both tumble to the ground in a great mess of paws and hooves. Before I can stop it, stupid tears are rolling off my cheeks.

"Oh, Louis…"

"It's this stupid shit you're watching," I shout, cheeks burning. "Why do people watch stuff like that? We already know life is shit and everybody dies. Why do you have to watch it too?"

Eugénie jumps on the remote and turns off the TV. "It's gone, gone. See?"

It's too late, both for the gazelle and for me. I start bawling in the middle of Eugénie's living room, grateful now for the box of tissues she laid before me.

"Is there anything I can do?" Eugénie attempts a smile. "I'm a million years old, I can do anything."

Our little joke doesn't amuse me so much anymore. Michael the lioness had torn a chunk of my heart, and now I'm food for the vultures too. I blow my nose dramatically in a tissue.

"I'm eighteen tomorrow, Miss Eugénie, and apart from your exquisite company, I'm utterly alone."

"My dear boy, you shouldn't be so miserable on your eighteen's birthday. No one should."

"Don't worry about me, Miss Eugénie." I pat her affectionally on the knee. "I think I was always miserable, and every time I was actually happy was just a bump on the road."

Miss Eugénie looks extremely miffed by my statement. I fear she's going to go into a long tirade about wisdom, stars, and the Church of Scientology. Now's not the time, you see. But Eugénie's not like other people; she refrains from giving me the speech about turning eighteen and not knowing anything about life, but instead says things like:

"You must allow yourself to feel these things. They hurt you now, I know, and they will hurt you more. But you must remember that they will fade away. That's what they are. Feelings. Terrible feelings, but they will disappear eventually. Soon enough, you will smile again. But to heal faster, you must learn to forgive too."

I spring off the sofa, spilling tissues all over the carpet. "There's nothing to forgive, really. I'm not mad at anyone but myself." Eugénie doesn't appear to believe me. "It's true! I'm the idiot! I was always an idiot, and I'm incapable of being loved. See? Nothing to worry about. I just need time to adjust to my new life, that's all. I don't need friends, and I don't need to be loved. I don't need anything at all."

Too upset for another round of karaoke tonight, I storm out of the living room and into the narrow corridor in long strides, wrench open the front door, nearly tearing it off its hinges.

At the last second, I recover enough sense to wave my friend goodbye. "Please don't worry about me, Miss Eugénie. I'll be back tomorrow with your groceries, okay?"

Eugénie, her lips pressed into a thin line, gives a feeble wave. I close the door just as she hangs her head.

27

I DIDN'T SEE YOU THERE

W hy is it that the first time I fall in love, it was not real at all? Will I ever get over it? I wonder. I know I'll never forget him, the way he made me feel when he smiled, when we first kissed, when his fingers dug into my skin, and how I feel right now, like utter shit, because none of it mattered to him.

This morning, my father is late, rustling papers outside the kitchen. He straightens up as I stalk into the kitchen. He's still watching me as I sit at the table with a fresh cup of coffee.

"What?"

"Happy birthday."

Oh, right. It's today. I force a smile. To my surprise, he pulls a chair and sits down and pushes an envelope toward me. I have completely forgotten to tell him what I'd like. Not that I want anything anyway.

It's a credit card. I stare down at it in surprise.

My father scratches his cheek. "I've opened you an account a while ago. Put money on it. I thought now that you're eighteen, you might want to use it. You know… To go to London."

I stare at the credit card, speechless, a gentle wave of gratitude warming my insides.

All these feelings, and no way to express them.

"Did, hem… Did Mum call?"

Habit, a question raised like a shield, an answer I already know. My father looks embarrassed.

"It's a bit early for her. You know."

It is, it's early. Late, for my father, who usually leaves at eight o'clock at the latest, but my mother never calls in the morning, even for my birthday. Truth be told, she didn't call at all last year. She was on holidays on an island and quite forgot about her son back in Paris.

My mother is always on the back of my mind, but I'm not on hers, that's how it works. I never talk about it, especially not to my father. My reluctance to talk has always saved me from hearing the uncomfortable truth.

And look where it got me today. I start laughing despite myself.

"Don't you like it?" My father gives me a worried look.

"I do, I'm sorry," I say. "Thank you, really. I was just thinking of something else."

"Care to share with your old man?"

I look up, surprised. Has he ever been so inquisitive, or is it new? Was I always so determined not to answer, or was there just nothing to say? One thing is certain, I haven't got anything more to lose, do I?

"I know I'm boring," my father adds, echoing Michael's words and sending a chill through my spine. "I was never as extroverted, as flamboyant as your mum. You and her, you were so close when you were a kid." A pause, an awkward slip of a glance. "But I can listen, at least. If—if you want to talk to me."

My fingers curl around my mug. My dear mum. Let's talk about my mum.

"Why did she leave?"

My father's eyes widen. Yeah, I'm going straight to the million-dollar question, no time to waste.

"Are you worried about that now?"

I lift my shoulder in a half-shrug. "I am worried. In general."

That's an understatement.

"She didn't leave because of you, you know," Dad says slowly, as though to make sure I understand him perfectly.

"Didn't she?"

Didn't her attitude change around that time when I was twelve and we went to Biarritz for the holidays? I always wondered what I had done, what changed during that fateful trip. A few months later, she was slamming the door, and she never came back. I thought about it many times. Did she see it, the flush on my face when we went for ice cream and the employee of the shop, a young man, handed me my gelato? She was quiet on the way home. She was quiet a lot in the weeks that followed.

My father leans forward across the table; his hand makes a motion toward me.

"No, of course not." His eyes meet mine. "Remember how close you were when you were younger?"

"But if it wasn't me? Who was it? You, then?"

My mother used to sigh at my father's mild countenance, his compliance, his lack of expression. I'm pretty sure she sighed as she said goodbye to him the morning she left us.

"It was her."

"How?" I pound my hand on the table. "Explain this to me."

Dad runs his hand across his stubble. "She got tired of this life. She wanted something more exciting."

I knew it.

"Because we were boring. We were nothing special."

My father shakes his head. "Because she always wanted more. Always. Something amused her and then it didn't. We would have never been enough. Because the problem was always her. It was never your fault." He lets out a long sigh. "And though I have my faults in this, I don't think it's mine either."

So, that's it?

"She just left us?" I ask, my voice trembling. "And then decided we were only deserving of a postcard, a Christmas card, and birthday wishes whenever she can remember?"

"There was..." My father hesitates, leans back in his chair. "There was another man."

My mouth drops. "What?"

"She fell for another man. Someone younger that she met at

work. He persuaded her to move away with him, to open a store with him. He ended up taking all her money, so she left him too."

She had a lover? My blood rushes to my ears, making my father's voice sound far away.

"Why didn't she say anything to me about it?"

"Because she was embarrassed! She didn't want you to think she was stupid. She always was a pack of nerves. And then her shame grew into this impossible thing. She never calls because we remind her of her shame." My father's gaze falls on me, gentle and, I notice for the first time, wise. "I can't ever let you think that it's because of you. She loved you. She just… loved this guy more. And then she preferred to run. She was never one to face her responsibilities."

Yikes. My mum and I have the worst possible traits in common. There are glaring similarities between her behaviour and mine, but I just turned eighteen. What's her excuse?

I don't want to become like her. I don't want to walk away from my responsibilities and my people and let them think it was all their fault.

This realisation opens up within me.

I must apologise to Tony and Lucie, I must tell them how sorry I am, how selfish, how self-centred on my problems I've been. I must beg for their forgiveness, I must go now.

This all happened silently, but my crazed blinking hasn't escaped my father.

"Why are you so worried about that now? You've never asked me about it."

"Now?" I give a bitter chuckle. "I've always been worried about it. Actually, I worry a lot, about everything. And lately, everything has turned out just like I worried it would."

I couldn't even begin to explain this to my father, even if he asked me.

"I wish you would just tell me things," Dad says. "I know. You're eighteen, you're reckless and young and in need for experiences, flamboyant like your mum. But I'm here for you, always waiting for a sign that you want to talk to me, and when I see you closed up, I don't want to intrude. You always look like you'd prefer to be alone."

I dare to look into my father's eyes. All I can find is deep sympathy.

"And yet I hate being alone. You have no idea the lengths I take to not be alone." Staring down at the credit card, I feel a shiver of self-loathing. "But it's useless. I'm alone now. I've ruined everything between me and Tony and Lucie. My only friend's Miss Eugénie, and she's a million years old."

My father finally finds the courage to reach out and pat my hand.

"There, there. There are worse friends to have than Miss Eugénie. And she's only in her seventies."

The mention of Miss Eugénie is enough to bring a faint smile on my lips. "She said she knew you as a baby, and you were annoying."

My father laughs. "She used to babysit me, but she was too cool even for that. Eugénie travelled around the world, she worked in Hollywood, she dined with movie stars… She's done it all."

Poor Miss Eugénie. I have bullied her with my problems and never even bothered asking her about her life.

"Why did she leave Hollywood for Paris?"

"She got married, I think. Divorced, since." My father gives me a sympathetic smile. "Listen, Lou, you must be kind to Eugénie. She lost someone a few months ago, around Christmas. It was very hard on her."

"But…" I can't believe Eugénie didn't tell me that. "She never told me."

My father tilts his head. "She probably doesn't want to talk about it. She really cares about you. She told me yesterday she worried about you."

With a smile, I think of Eugénie as like the old bat in Cinderella who makes wishes come true. She's kinda cool.

"You know, Dad. And you can call me Louis again."

My father gives me a surprised look. "Are you done with Lou?"

I was always Louis. It's Lou who's done with me. And everyone else is done with Lou.

"Yes, I'm done."

"And…" My father says, trying to sound casual and failing. "Will you tell me why you're so downcast lately?"

"I told you. Tony and Lucie aren't speaking to me anymore. I've ruined it all."

Dad scratches his stubble, tries to work his way around the question he wants to ask. I daresay I know what he has in mind.

"What about your other friend, Michael?"

Bingo.

"What about him?"

Dad tugs at the collar of his shirt. "I don't know, he seemed nice."

He was. He was so nice. He taught me a lesson I'm not likely to forget. The ruins of my defences crumple at my feet. I surrender.

Searching for my father's gaze, I let out a deep breath. "Michael didn't love me like I loved him."

The understanding, the confirmation of his suspicions flashes in my father's eyes. And it's done, without fanfare or drama. Dad smiles, a deep smile that testifies to his relief at being at last trusted with my secret. His finger rises to rub the bridge of his nose.

"I'm sorry to hear that. That boy sure did seem to care about you."

That's a bit rich, Dad. I laugh into my coffee cup.

"Did you get that from your twenty-second conversation about classics? Or whatever that was about…"

"No." My father shakes his head. "I got that from watching him pace outside the door for over an hour last night."

"What?"

Coffee dribbles all over my chin. My father jumps to his feet, hands me a napkin. I repeat:

"What?"

"He was there!" Dad says. "He didn't ring the intercom, he was just pacing. He left eventually."

Why on earth would he do something like that?

"He's not dangerous, is he?" my father asks, furrowing his brow.

"No, I don't think so, but…" But he makes no sense, and he might, just might, be a massive psychopath. "I don't understand him."

In a few words, I explain everything there is to know about my meeting with Michael, our fast-growing friendship, the heaps of curls, how I waved my heterosexuality goodbye, and of course, Michael's unforgivable betrayal.

Without interrupting, my father listens with a cocked eyebrow, only sipping coffee from time to time. He seems to have completely forgotten about work.

I get to the moment I got rid of Michael in front of La Crêperie. My father raises his hand to ask a question.

"How did he react when you confronted him?"

"Shocked, he was very shocked that I knew!" The face he made is burned into my memory. "He asked me how I knew, but I didn't reply."

"Didn't try to explain himself?"

"Well, no, I was in no state to hear his lies."

"But," my father says, holding up his hands, "you thought he liked you before this Abby called."

I think about it. "I did. But it never made sense in the first place. I mean, he's like a Ferrari, and I'm like… I'm like the old car parked outside. The Coccinelle. Cute but useless."

"Listen to yourself." My father scoffs. "You're the only one who ever thought you were useless, you know. To me, you are everything."

Hum… Ok.

Dad taps his knuckle against the surface of the table. "And I think Michael didn't think you were useless either. I bet he liked you very much. I can bet you even Abby didn't think you were useless."

"Why are you saying this?"

"She called to wreak havoc. She was jealous. She wanted to split you up!"

I can appreciate my father being all up in my business and trying to help, but I know better. I was there, after all.

"Michael didn't even try to justify himself. He didn't. He just left."

"Fine." Dad throws up his hands. "I'm not saying he's innocent. I'm just saying when you're mad, you're really not easy to talk to.

The way your blue eyes burn with anger, just like your mother's. It's quite terrifying."

"Michael used me, Dad." My father startles when I use that word. "He used other people before. I was nothing but a thing to pass the time with. Nothing more."

"You'll figure it out, Louis. But be careful what people say to you. Words can be weapons. Sometimes it's better to judge people by their actions, not what they say. Take it from me. Not everybody is equipped with the gift of communication."

Hours after my father has left for work, I'm still pondering his words.

It's true that I was quick to believe Abby's words. I wanted to believe her. She seemed to know about me. How weak, how useless I was. It wouldn't take much for someone to convince me of my worthlessness.

Michael, on the other hand... If he had told me straight to my face that he loved me, would I have believed him?

That's it. Enough with Michael.

I'm not going to spend another day cowering in a corner of my bedroom and wringing my hands like an old lady. I'll get to the bottom of this, sooner or later.

But for once since a long time my priority is with Lucie and Tony. They need to know, they need to get the truth, my truth.

And if our friendship is unsalvageable, so be it. But I must grow up and assume responsibility for my actions. I owe them that, at least.

On my eighteen's birthday, no less, I make the decision to become a better man.

28

HERE'S THE TRUTH, NOTHING BUT THE TRUTH

A pleasant and warm early afternoon brings me to Lucie's doorstep at the end of a quiet courtyard. This is it. The moment of truth. I'm just hoping Lucie won't cut off my head and bury me in the lovely back garden of her townhouse.

My finger hovers over the doorbell. Tony's bike hangs against the wall near the bins. I can't pretend that I'm surprised. It's not exactly a bad thing. I can tell them both at the same time. Rip the bandaid off.

Lucie, in jeans, white T-shirt and loose ponytail, dark circles under the eyes, opens the door and looks at me in surprise.

"What are you doing here?"

Her tone isn't hostile, at least. She throws an anxious look over her shoulder, her fingers gripping the side of the door.

"I came to apologise."

My words force her to look at me again. She doesn't know what to do. Tony is probably in one of the back rooms, she probably wants to avoid a scene.

"Can I come in?"

"I thought you were busy, you know, with the others."

The others? What others? It doesn't matter.

"Please. I won't be long."

After a second of hesitation, she lets me into her home. I recognise the sparkling white tiles on the floor and the aquarelles of wildflowers on the wall. Lucie doesn't invite me to sit, but that's okay. I wouldn't want to see me either if I were her.

She leans against the wall to the kitchen, an anxious look on her face.

"Happy birthday," she says, staring at her feet.

"You remembered."

Her head snaps back up. "Of course I did. I had planned a whole thing, remember?"

The memory of our fight back at the gardens is still too fresh. I better move on to the real conversation. I press my hands hard into my pockets.

"I came to say I was sorry for… For talking to you like that the other day and for lying."

Her expression hardens. "So you were lying, you admit it?"

"I was." I give a shrug of surrender.

She peels herself off the wall and approaches me. "And you admit you were cheating on me?"

Before I can answer that, Tony appears at the end of the corridor, on his tiptoes. His face contorts when he sees me. Anger? No. Surprise, mixed with a bit of fear, and just the right amount of shame. They both fall silent, nervously waiting for my reaction.

"Look," Lucie begins, her eyes welling up.

In an effort of reassurance, I hold up my palms. "No, that's fine. I know about you."

"What do you know, exactly?" Tony approaches cautiously, his face serious.

I can feel their eyes on me, watching me, daring me. My instinct to run away is particularly strong. It was easier to yell at them than tell them I love them. But I stay firmly rooted on the spot.

"I've always known, I guess," I say, my voice calm. "That you loved her."

A deep flush creeps up Tony's neck, while Lucie pretends to be absorbed by a scratch in the wall paint.

"I'm telling you," I repeat, "I'm not mad anymore."

"We didn't do anything," Lucie says. "Nothing happened at first.

We wanted to respect you, and I... I wasn't sure about what I felt. I really thought I wanted to be with you... It's you who didn't seem to want to be with me."

"I'm sorry, Lucie." I hang my head. "I really wanted to like you too. It's just, it never felt natural, you know. It wasn't working. And when I saw how close you were getting together... I don't know. You made such sense together. It freaked me out. I didn't want either of you to leave me. But I made you leave anyway."

Lucie scoffs. "All right. That's what you say. But that's not really a reason to cheat, isn't it?"

A sick feeling of shame swirled around in my stomach. "I didn't plan on cheating. It just happened."

Lucie makes a face. To hear me speak about my infidelity hurts her as much as it hurts me just to think about it. I don't want to cause more pain, but she needs to hear it.

She knows it. She lifts up her chin, her jaw set. "It happened on the night of Sacha's party, then."

"No! I told you I went home the night of the party. It wasn't a lie."

"When, then?" Lucie asks. "When?"

"Why does it matter?"

"Lucie." Tony interrupts, surprising us. "In all fairness, something did happen the night of Sacha's party. Between us." He gestures toward Lucie, then back to himself. "We kissed. We were angry at you, we had been drinking and——"

"I get it." My words come out a little harsh. Despite my wish to make amends, I still didn't want to be reminded of their treachery. "No need for details."

"It was just a kiss. And I felt so bad," Lucie says, tears glittering at the corner of her eyes. "We decided to stop fucking around. We made a decision to talk to you——"

"Hang on." It all makes sense now. "That's why you summoned me the next day. You were so weird that morning."

Tony rakes his hands through his air. "We were ashamed. We never wanted to destroy our friendship."

Lucie folds her arms over her chest, her bottom lip trembling. "I wasn't sure you were cheating then. Actually, I was sure you weren't."

"I wasn't!" I protest, advancing toward her.

She steps back. "But your intentions…"

"Were as clear as yours, apparently."

I get her anger, but no one is exactly innocent here. Lucie knows it. Her cheeks turn pink. Tony walks over to her and puts a hand on her arm.

"We all made mistakes here, right?" We exchange nods. "We didn't want to hurt you, but you started acting so weird—"

Lucie's nostrils start flaring. "And you didn't even care whether people saw you or not!"

Really? And I thought I was being so smart, sneaking in and out of public toilets.

Tony holds out his hands, his expression a mixture of frustration and confusion. "And honestly, ditching us for the Golden Fucking Fork, Lou! What happened to you!"

He'll never live this down, will he?

"I was mad at you for not telling me what I already knew. Isn't that something… The thing is, I was sure to end up like Simon's best friend. From your life from one day to the other, scratched from your life. You, and Lucie, now a couple, and me… well. I could just disappear."

Tony shakes his head, scowling. "That's not a reason to go to the Golden Fork."

"They're not bad, really."

Lucie walks over to her living room, motioning us to follow her. As usual, the place is the definition of sparkling clean and blindingly white, from the frames on the walls to the leather of the sofa and the accent chairs. Tony and I never dared to sit in this room, and judging from the look of anxiety on his face, he is still as reluctant as me.

"Lou, we were afraid too, you know," Lucie says, dropping into one of the chairs. "None of us were planning to ditch you until you started acting completely mental. Then we couldn't even recognise you. You didn't seem to give a damn about us at all."

I hover near the white sofa, not even daring to clutch it for support. I grab the leg of the nearest lamp instead.

"I didn't even want to think of you, knowing where this was going. I just couldn't. Of course, I was ashamed of myself for lying to you, but I was pissed off that you were lying to me too. It all turned into a nightmare."

An uncomfortable silence ensues, none of us willing to look at the others. Since I came here to tell the truth, I decide I'm the best suited to break it.

"Look, I'm not here to beg you to be my friends again. You said it, I'm not like you. I'll never be as carefree as Tony or as fun as you. I can only tell you I really wanted to be like Tony, and I kinda forgot myself on the way." Feeling silly with my hand gripped around the leg of a lamp, I stick my hands into my pockets. "I don't want to get lost again."

"What does it mean?" Lucie glances up, looking hurt. "That's it, then? You found yourself, and we're not good enough for you?"

Why is she acting like I'm the one breaking up with them? I can't believe I have to remind her that I'm the one at fault here.

"Lucie, remember, you're mad at me, I'm not mad at you. I cheated on you."

Anger flashes in her eyes. She grips the armrests on the chair with white claw-like fingers. "Yes, you did. You cheated on me."

"Yes, I did!" I say, my voice shaking. "I lied, I went behind your back, and the worst thing is… I would do it again if I could."

"Dude!" Tony says, looking disgusted.

Another short silence follows. This time, Lucie breaks it.

"I'm not mad that you cheated…" she begins.

"Really?"

"Really?" Tony repeats, his eyebrows arched.

Lucie exhales a long breath. "Okay, fine. I am mad. Mad that you cheated and lied for so long. But I lied to you, and I cheated too."

Tony and I exchange a quick, nervous glance.

"We kissed, okay!" Tony says, his voice cracking from fear. "Nothing else happened until that night when we saw you with Michael. I'm not that sort of guy!"

"I know, Tony."

"I'm not done!" Lucie slams her fists against the armrests. "What really, truly pisses me off, is that you have thrown everything away, and for what?" She stares into my face, a mad glint in her eye. "For Sacha?"

There's a pause. I'm just… It can't be… I haven't heard right.

"Can you repeat? I didn't catch that."

"Sacha!" Lucie says, snarling. "You can admit that you cheated on me, but you can't admit that it was Sacha?"

I stare at her with my mouth hanging open. "Sacha, from class?"

"No, Sacha from Neptune." Lucie slays me with a glare. "Of course, Sacha from class!"

"But what the hell are you talking about? Who gives a shit about Sacha?"

"Damn!" Tony says.

Lucie's thrown off. Her pale eyes dart between Tony and me, full of confusion.

This is insane. Do they both really think that I was sleeping with Sacha?

"I never cheated on you with Sacha, Lucie." I hide my face behind my hands. "I cheated on you with Michael!"

The biggest silence ensues. This time, I can hear a fat bumblebee buzzing on the other side of the window. When I slide my hands off my face, Tony and Lucie are looking at each other in such shock that I'm certain confessing to being the ghost of Napoleon Bonaparte would have had less effect.

To my surprise, Tony recovers first.

"Michael?"

"Yes."

"The British guy?"

"Yes!"

He takes a step back, his eyebrows lost to his hairline. "You banged him?"

My shoulders slump. "No! I… He… and I…" Tony's dumb face grows increasingly stunned. "Yes. Sort of."

275

Never even had the time to get to that point. How tragic my life is, at times.

Tony circles around me, his eyes narrowed, as though he's never taken a good look at me before. Meanwhile, Lucie still looks like a blank sheet of paper.

"But Sacha... the way you rushed to her party in secret, the way she was with you..."

I dispel her concerns with a wave of my hand. "Sacha was only throwing herself at me to make Michael jealous."

Tony's long face pops into my field of vision, startling me.

"So, you're not a Golden Fork, then? You just wanted to bang Michael?"

"Can you please stop saying that word?"

Tony gives a shrug. "It's the curls, isn't it?"

I jump away from him the moment he starts sniffing me.

Lucie slumps limply into her chair. "What you're saying is... You're gay?"

"Are you?" Tony asks, cocking an eyebrow.

Ignoring Tony's idiotic face, I turn to Lucie, my heart in my throat. "Yes."

A world of relief floods my entire self after saying the word.

Yes.

Such a small word. One syllable.

I wish I'd said it sooner, now that it's done.

Lucie's beautiful eyes widen, swimming with tears. "I would have never been good enough for you, then."

Dropping my arms to my side, I draw nearer. "You really can't take it personally."

"I don't..." Her voice trails off, her gaze turns unfocused. "I know it's awful to even think so, but I'm relieved. I'm relieved."

She's... relieved? Relieved of what? I'll never know. Lucie rises from her chair, her hand lifted to her mouth.

"Poor Sacha, I've been so odious toward her. Not even an hour ago, she invited me to join her, Michael, and François at Happy Beans, and I was like, hell no! Who does she think she is! I didn't want to see you both together, so I told her to go fuck herself!"

"I'm sure she'll get over it," I say kindly, knowing full well she'll never get over it.

"Were you always gay?"

I see Tony's still not over the gay thing.

"I don't know, Tony. I had girlfriends, remember?"

"You had one, this one." He points at Lucie.

"Bingo! You were there for all of them."

Tony looks completely deranged, like he's just discovered a secret B-side of Franz Ferdinand.

"What about that time you kissed Sacha when you were twelve!"

I can help but laugh at his dumb face. "You know what? I kissed François too, apparently. At the New Year party. Full disclosure."

Lucie and Tony exchange a look.

"I thought..." Tony says, scratching the top of his head. "I thought I saw something in the toilet, the door wasn't properly closed, you see. But I wasn't sure... and I thought, could be a bet, rockstars kiss dudes all the time." Lucie acquiesces with a nod. "By the way... Very rockstar of you, to bang Michael."

Feeling a sharp stab of pain at the mention of Michael's name, I turn away from my friends.

"He's very handsome. Congratulations," Lucie says, pulling herself together. The initial shock has worn out.

"And a sneaky motherfucker," Tony says. "I noticed he was always around, but I thought he wanted to steal you from me, turn you into a Fork! Not make you his boyfriend."

I say nothing.

"You could have told us," Tony adds, sounding scared. "Why couldn't you tell us? Is it because of my dumb jokes?"

I shake my head. "I thought you'd leave me behind, and for what? It took me months to understand I was seriously interested in Michael and not just losing my mind. And then I didn't want to overreact and make a big deal before making sure Michael was..."

"Was what?"

"Serious about me..." My voice trails off. I suddenly feel like going home and sneaking back under my bedcovers.

Lucie walks over to me and puts her hand on my arm. "And, is he? Serious about you?"

I could tell them. The gay bomb I dropped seemed to have faded into acceptance pretty quickly, so, perhaps I could finally confide in my friends, for the first time in m—

"Oh my god!" Tony slaps a hand on his mouth. "Were you ever in love with me?"

Or, maybe not.

"Come on, tell me!" Tony shoves Lucie aside, his eyes boring into mine. "Like, a little? At least?"

"Sorry." It's hard to apologise while trying not to laugh. "Not really, no."

"Come on, just a bit!"

"I don't want to jump on everything that moves, Tony!"

"Just Michael, then." He moves away, looking miffed. "Well well. Nothing for your best friend Tony. Not even a sniff. Just great."

"Michael's very hot," Lucie says, followed by a sigh of longing.

Tony's expression darkens, for real this time. "We got that, you already said that, like a million times."

Lucie's not paying attention to his shenanigans, however. She's pacing around the living room, a frown on her face.

"Michael told Sacha he has a girlfriend. So, what is he, exactly?"

Gay, bi, or simply a maniac, I do not know at this point.

"I can honestly tell you I don't know what he is. And we're not together, so, there's nothing to talk about."

"Is it because of us?" Tony whips around, alarmed. "Did we cock-block you the other night?"

Lucie tosses him scandalised look that he doesn't register.

"No, not really." This is it. Just get to it, Louis. "Apparently we were never together. I think he was experimenting."

"Aww." Tony makes a scrunched-up face. "That bitch. Did he tell you that?"

"No, his girlfriend did. Well, his ex. She called me. That was a great experience, as you can imagine."

Lucie grabs my wrist and forces my butt down on her pristine armchair.

"What did Michael say, then?"

"Not much. We haven't spoken since that night at La Crêperie.

You know, when I lost my mind with you… well… I also lost my mind with him and he just… left."

Tony's face grows serious. "You yelled at him because some floozie called you on the phone and sprouted some bullshit?"

I nod. "Very convincing bullshit, I'm afraid."

"And he didn't try to defend himself?"

"Nope. Didn't at all. He did look ashamed, for what it's worth. We never even looked at each other since." Forcing a brave smile on my face, I wipe my hands on my jeans. "This is it. My heart's officially broken."

"This is dumb!" Lucie says, her eyes flashing. "Why should your heart be broken? You have to talk to him, ask him to tell you the truth. You can't make a decision based on what his ex said to you. You need his version of the facts." She sinks on her knees in front of me. "You have to go talk to him and make sure! Go, now."

I look at her, dumbfounded. "Why are you so nice to me?"

"For heaven's sake, Louis." She grips me by both arms and gives me a nasty shake. "If I'd known what you were going through, I would have helped you! Right, Tony?"

"Sure…" Tony mumbles absently. "I mean. You were very good at hiding it, though, the whole time you had this little secret…"

Lucie springs up and kicks him in the shins.

"Shut up if you aren't going to help!"

"Right." Tony jumps to the side, looking fully recovered. "What do you want from me?"

"I've got an idea." Her face glowing, Lucie points out outside the window. "Take Tony's bike, ride to Happy Beans right now! Ask him, ask Michael for the truth and see if this chick was lying to you."

Tony slips me a disappointed look. "Why you have listened to some cheap hoe instead of Captain Curls in the first place baffles me."

"She was his girlfriend for years!" I turn toward him, my face hot. "Also, Captain Curls?"

Tony ignores my question and starts nudging me toward the front door. "That's probably why he's gay now, you know."

"You don't even know her."

"Neither do you!" Lucie opens the door.

Tony pushes me outside. "And we don't want to!"

Before she slaps the door into my face, Lucie seizes the front of my shirt and yanks me to her. For a second, I think she's going to kiss me like she always did, open mouthed and a bit scary. But she pulls me into a hug instead.

"Is it wrong of me to be happy you'll never sleep with another woman?"

Probably, I think, but I won't say it out loud, of course.

She sighs. "If I can't have you, then no one can."

Tony waves his hand in her face. "What the hell?"

"Good luck with that," I tell Tony. "And thanks."

Tony approaches, his hand raised, but instead of slapping it on my shoulder, he gently rests it there.

"Take the bike and hurry. Even if showing up on a bike to make a love confession is pretty lame, you know. Not very rock-and-roll for an ending."

I shake my head in disbelief. "Dude, it's your bike, you know. Not mine."

He looks past my shoulder into the horizon, a fake air of wisdom on his face.

"Just... let us know how it goes, hm?"

29

DON'T CALL HIM A SECRET KEEPER

Minutes later, propelled by the favourable winds of hope and their cousin, the breeze of despair, I barge into Happy Beans hopefully looking quite cool—like some dashing Paul Newman if I knew who he was—and expecting, of course, Michael to be seated surrounded by his friends and blushing at my windswept face, but when I kick the door open, I only find François, wiping tables, alone, wearing his stupid apron.

"Damn, Louis!" he shrieks. "Use the handle, please. I am not paying for this door."

I close the distance between us in two hurried strides and grab him by the shoulders. The glint in his eyes tells me he doesn't dislike it.

"Where is Michael?"

François blinks. "Michael? Home, I suppose."

"Lucie told me he was here."

"Oh no, he didn't come." I let go of his shoulders; he looks slightly disappointed. "Everybody was supposed to come here to keep me company. I'm working during the holidays, hello! Yasmine did come. Sacha didn't. Michael was supposed to come, but then he said he wouldn't come if Lucie didn't. Then Sacha said she wouldn't come. Then Yasmine said, Fuck This, I'm leaving, and she left about ten minutes ag—"

I silence François with a hand. "Why did Michael want to talk to Lucie?"

"I'm not supposed to say."

"François!"

My hands slam onto his shoulders again. A flush creeps up to his ears.

"Fine! He wanted to find out if you were still together. Or if there was hope. I told him there was hope because you almost admitted to me you're gay."

"I am gay."

"Right, voilà, wasn't complicated, just a tad too late." François grimaces. "Yasmine said there wasn't any hope, that you're a basket case, and Michael is better off without you, and I don't know why but Michael always listens to Yasmine more than he listens to me, and — oh, Sacha would like to know why Lucie hates her so much? She threatened to stuff her mailbox with one of Rufus' poo, you know."

I let out a groan of despair. "Lucie thought Sacha was my mistress. But it's Michael. I mean, it was."

What a nightmare this all ended up to be! But still. If Michael is hoping there is hope between us, and I'm hoping he's hoping there is hope between us, surely this means there is, actually, hope between us.

"It's funny you should use that word, mistress," François says with a lop-sided grin. "The other day Michael said he doesn't want to be your mistress."

"Oh." So much for hope. My shoulders sag; I slump into the nearest chair. "That's what I got from the phone call."

"Michael called you?" François sits opposite me, his eyes glowing with curiosity. "Yasmine said not to. After his shameful pacing outside your win—"

I put my finger on his lip. "Abby called. Abby called me."

François gasps. "Abby? His EX?"

"The very one."

François looks both thoroughly shocked and exceedingly happy.

So much drama never happens at Colette International. I'm sure he'll have something worthwhile to write into his diary tonight.

"So that's what happened!" He starts gesticulating, making my head spin. "Wait, I need to sit down."

"You're already sitting down."

"Then I need a pick-me-up." He starts fanning himself.

I look around the coffee place, scanning for anything that would qualify as a pick me up for an overly privileged white Parisian. "Do you want weed or something?"

"No!" François throws me an offended look. "I've seen the effects of weed on your brain. I don't want to end up as slow as you."

"Thanks," I say, hurt. "That's really nice."

"Do you have any vodka?" he asks, still fanning himself. "This place doesn't allow the sale of alcohol."

He winces when I shake my head; I wish I had brought Tony with me. Tony would have thought of bringing alcohol, just because dramatic moments are always made better with a bit of alcohol. It's in all the good movies.

"All right, all right," François says, looking slightly recovered. "Let me explain."

"Please."

Took you long enough.

"Abby's crazy, you know. Michael told me. She's really mad at him. You can't trust her."

So, this could be true? She called not to warn me but to lie to me? Could this mean...

"Fine," I say, throwing up my hands, trying hard not to let the spark of hope I'm feeling turn into a brasier. "Why is she mad at him?"

François shakes his head. "Oh, boy, it's really not my story to tell."

I lean forward, my jaw set. "Tell me and I'll never make fun of you ever again."

"Ok," he says, blinking. "Wait. You're making fun of me?"

"No, never." I gently pat his wrist, my cheeks burning. "I don't know why I said that."

François leans back in his chair, squinting suspiciously.

"I'm going to tell you, because I like Michael." He pauses. "And, because he's had such a hard time because of awful people, and I want him to be happy. Especially after…"

"Please, tell me, François," I beg, checking at the old railway clock on the opposite wall. The afternoon is flowing past, and my spark of hope has already grown into a flame. "And fast."

François settles comfortably in his chair. I'm in for quite a ride.

"Michael never had many friends," he begins, his voice serious. "He was always the geek, the ugly duckling of class."

I doubt it, but I'm not about to interrupt François. It would only cost me extra time.

"Then, over the course of a summer, he became all hot and pretty, like, you know," — François gestures at his own head, miming the curls on Michael's head — "and suddenly everybody wanted a piece of him."

I nod wisely. The power of Michael's curls cannot and will not be underestimated in this room.

"Abby was very popular, a real queen bee. She took the new Michael under her wing. Suddenly he had many friends. His life transformed from one day to the other."

Dear Michael, I, of all people, can absolutely relate to that.

"Michael and Abby started dating. Was Abby really interested or did she only want someone pretty? Who knows? But Michael thought he was in love. They stayed together for a long time. Then, this summer, Michael went with her family to Spain."

"What happened with *Michael?*" I ask, worried that François would launch himself into lengthy descriptions of Spanish beaches.

François throws me a warning look.

"I'm getting there, hang on."

I swear, he's relishing watching me hang on to his every word.

"Michael met Abby's older brother, Peter and PAF!" — I startle — "massive crush on him. And Peter too, of course, looked like he really liked Michael, then they got back from the holidays and that's when they started fooling around in secret…"

I listen hard, astonished. I wasn't the first for Michael. I wasn't even the first he was sneaking around with.

"Michael went to Abby's for a party once and Peter was there. He kissed him! And it didn't happen just once. Peter usually found Michael when he was drunk or high and kissed him. Michael was going crazy for this guy, but he understood all the hush-hush around it of course. Being a boy, being Abby's brother and all…"

I swallow a lump. "Then what happened?"

"Oh, what do you think?"

I bang my hand on the table. "I don't fucking know François, that's why I'm asking! What do you think? Honestly!"

François jerks away from me. "You are so moody! Such a bad temper. I don't know why I ever thought I had a crush on you, seriously!"

"I'm sorry, I'm sorry," I say, patting his wrists in an effort to placate him. "Go on, take your time."

"Thank you." François waits for an instant until I look collected enough for his taste and resumes. "Well, Abby caught them, of course, and Michael was relieved. He immediately broke up with Abby, certain Peter would naturally admit his feelings for him. But Peter was all like, *"No no no, I was just experimenting, just having fun, don't know this guy, he's a weirdo, no homo!"* François nods in my direction. "You know what I'm talking about."

Sure… And also: ouch.

"Then Abby, who was legitimately hurt, went all out for this big finale. Classic queen bee. She told everybody at school how Michael seduced her brother when he was drunk and took advantage, etc. So of course, everyone turned against Michael over the course of one weekend, and Michael got really sick and didn't want to leave his home, so his mum told him to just come with her to Paris. And that's how he left everybody behind and followed his mother here."

I'm just now recalling Michael telling me he only packed two suitcases.

"He never said anything like that to me… He said his parents were having problems."

"Oh yeah, they were." François shrugs. "Definitely. But they fixed their problems. Talked it through."

"This is so horrible."

285

My stomach sinks at the thought of what Michael endured. And how I only added to his misery with my attitude.

"I am so horrible…"

And these words… Peter's words to Michael, sound awfully similar to what Abby said Michael had told this other guy. Words I spit back in his face. Words he recognised instantly.

Oh, no, what have I done… I put my head in my hands.

François is too busy inspecting his nails to notice my despair. "So Michael got completely gaslit, as you can see. He wasn't even sure he was gay, you know. He was with Abby for two years, you can imagine they got around to get to know each other, if you know what I mean."

"Please spare me the details."

"Anyway, he convinced himself he overreacted and a new start in a school where no one knew him would be ideal… But then he meets your fat face on the first day."

I slam both hands on the table this time. "Why are you being so hostile!"

François holds my gaze and then some. "You broke my friend's heart!"

A stunned silence settles over us.

"You made him believe you liked him, and you made me believe you liked him, and then you acted all ashamed and secretive like Peter. What do you think? To say nothing of the mess he was when you told him he ruined your life and he was nothing to you."

He's right, I did. I ruined it.

"I thought… I thought he didn't care for me."

"You're a hopeless idiot." François does not give two shits about calling me out today. "That night Michael invited you out? He was planning to ask you to stay with him over the summer, in his home, in London. He was hoping you'd take a chance with him, a boy, even if it was just for the summer."

How could I have been so stupid?

"You're right, François," I say, my voice cracking. "I am an idiot. Who else but an idiot would believe Abby? Why was it so easy for her to persuade me that Michael was lying to me?"

"Hang in there." François's expression softens. "Abby told you the truth, you know, except it was the other way around."

"Damn her!" I've got no qualms hating her for what she's done. "Why would she do something like that?"

François gets up and walks over to the coffee machines. "I may be able to help you with that. A month after Michael moved here, Abby regretted what she'd done. She attempted to mend the fence and get Michael back. She apologised and everything, but it was over, he said he just wanted to be friends. She didn't want to be friends. She insisted and insisted. At some point, he got enough, and he told her he was gay and that he was with someone. How she found you is a mystery." He pauses, his finger hovering over the button on the machine. "Sometimes I think women are different, you know, they have special powers, like—"

"Witches?"

François stares at me, bewildered. "No, not like witches. You're really weird, you know."

"Forget it." I get up and walk over to him. "So in essence, Abby was just trying to fuck things up between us…"

"She was."

As I stare down at the menu over François's shoulder, something occurs to me.

"Abby succeeded where you couldn't. Don't assume I've forgotten what you did."

François pushes a cup of steaming coffee toward me with an apologetic grimace.

"I'm trying to help you now, I hope that will earn me some forgiveness."

I accept the cup of coffee with a grunt.

"And I'm going away to Barcelona," François adds in a small voice. "I'll never bother you two again."

Will Michael and I get back together? Will our ordeal ever ends? The black surface of the coffee reflects my harassed face.

"I have to tell him, François. I have to tell him I love him."

"You better hurry then." François slams a lid on my coffee cup. "Michael said he was going away for a while with his parents."

"What?" My heart skips more than one beat. "Where?"

"Huh, I don't know, Louis, I'm not his personal assistant." François rolls his eyes. "Go to his place and you'll find out."

"And you couldn't tell me any of that before?"

"You didn't ask." He points at the clock behind me. "Now fuck off, please. It's my lunch break."

François walks around the counter, seizes my arm and throws me out of his shop without ceremony. Still, he manages to spare time to throw a contemptuous look at my bike.

"Couldn't get a better ride?"

"You know, François..." I say, putting the helmet on, "you and Tony have more in common than you think."

"Oh, please," François says with a grimace. "Never say that again."

This is how it is, then. Me and Michael. Sharing kisses in broad daylight, sharing a bed, even sharing a flat. Every of one these things could have been mine, if only I had trusted him, and trusted myself enough.

But it's not too late. My heart thumping in my chest, clouds of butterflies swarming in my stomach, I fly toward Michael's place like a crazed lover, avoid two accidents with buses and one with a motorcycle. François has cleared most of my doubts; the sweeping wind does the rest.

Abby was lying, Peter hurt Michael, Michael never hurt a fly, Michael is gay, Michael loves me.

I feel like screaming, crying, punching the air, falling on my knees, all at the same time. But I don't have time for that, despite my French nature. I skid to a halt in front of Michael's building, sweating and panting, and almost run over an old lady the same age as Eugénie — but without the style. A man coming out of the building gives me an odd look. With a strangled word of thanks, I climb the ancient staircase up to Michael's flat, wheezing and clutching a stitch to my side.

An odd sight welcomes me atop the stairs. The front door is ajar, and a large vacuum cleaner is leaning against the wall. Both the soft splashing sound of water and the horrendous music of Celine Dion reaches my delicate ears.

"Michael?" Exhausted from my race across town, I gently push the door open.

Inside the flat, which hasn't changed a bit, a thin woman is going around at the speed of light, dusting with one hand, wiping with another. I walk over to the CD player by the TV and turn down the music. The woman freezes and turns around. We stare at each other, my own face probably just as stunned as hers.

"What are you doing here?" Her eyes narrow suspiciously.

"I'm a friend of Michael's," I say, wincing. "Is he home?"

She shakes her head. "There's no one here. They're gone."

"Gone? Forever gone?"

That's clearly not possible. That wouldn't happen to me. Not today, not ever, especially NOT TODAY.

"How should I know?" The woman shrugs. "I only come here to clean. But I was asked to do a deep cleaning, you see, and it wasn't in my schedule. I was told last minute—"

"Never mind that! Did they say where they were going?"

She gives me a look. "You're very rude."

I'm that close to start bawling like a newborn baby, too exhausted to care. It would really be better for both of us if she answers my questions rapidly.

"I really, really need to speak to… to the family. Please, please can you help me?"

The woman puts her hands on her hips. "Why should I? You barge in here and you turn down my music, you demand answers, I owe you nothing. I was told to clean when it's not even on my shift, but Rachel, my coworker, she called in sick—"

Desperate, I sink into the sofa. The woman lunges at me, seizing my sleeve.

"Stop! You can't do that, I've just rearranged the cushions!" Grunting with the effort, she attempts to pull me off the sofa.

Here we go. My eyes fill up with tears. Bawling's about to start. I press my hands against my face.

"He's gone! He's gone because of me!"

"What's that?" The woman lets go of my jacket. "Well… I'm sure he'll come back, you know."

"You think?" I look up at her face, my eyes streaming.

She makes an embarrassed face. "Not here, no, that's for sure. We only do deep cleaning when we lease the flat to somebody else."

That's it, then. Michael is gone. Gone. All of this because I'm always, always late.

"Come on, my boy…" The woman takes a seat next to me. "What put you in such a state?"

It's hard to speak while my body's being ransacked by sobs. "He left because he thought I didn't love him! But I do, I love him!"

"Christ," the woman mutters. "French people."

"I heard that," I say, sniffing.

She pats me on the back. "There, there. I'm really sorry, but you can't stay here. I'm on a tight schedule, and you're weeping all over the linen."

I'm still sobbing when she kicks me, face glistening with tears, out of Michael's flat. A second later, Celine Dion resumes her powerful wailing.

All hope is lost.

In an act of despair, I try his mobile phone, but it goes straight to voicemail. Admitting defeat, I begin my miserable descent of the stairs.

I hate Paris. I hate it. The most romantic city in the world, my ass. Tony's bike bumps against my shins as I walk my way back home, and I can barely feel it. Tourists flocking to Rue Mouffetard are annoying me. Kids having fun are annoying me. Young couples kissing, their arms intertwined, are annoying me. Pigeons conspiring around a discarded piece of baguette, are annoying m—No, actually, they're fine.

Dear Michael, will I ever see your scrumptious face again?

To make matters worse, and despite some repeated kicks, I cannot open my own front door, and I'm stuck outside, on a beautiful sunny day, the only dark cloud in view being the one over my head.

Little Jérémy and his friends are skateboarding outside. Jérémy comes to my rescue, effortlessly opens the door for me.

He's twelve.

"What's up, Lou?"

"Nothing, Jérémy, nothing," I say, my voice dark. "Only Death comes to us all."

The kid throws me a look that guarantees his parents are gonna knock on my door tonight.

Eugénie is on her way down when I drag myself into the hallway.

"I was looking for you, to wish you a happy birth—" She takes one look at me and hurries down. "My goodness. Who died?"

"Only love, Miss Eugénie."

Sighing, I help her down the last step. There is little else to do for me now but to spend the rest of my life in sighs.

Eugénie doesn't look impressed.

"Young men. All the same."

"Sorry, Eugénie," I say, my voice mournful. "I forgot about your groceries."

"Never mind that." She takes a look at Tony's bike. "Why do you have a bike?"

"Tony gave it to me, it was supposed to be my ride…"

Defeated, I slump against the wall of mailboxes.

"You look terrible, Louis." She takes my wrist. "Will you tell me what happened?"

I stare down at her anxious wrinkly face. Eugénie, my old friend. We can both live as old people haunted by the ghosts of our lost loves from now on.

"You remember Doriane, Miss Eugénie?"

She taps her foot impatiently on the cement tiles. "You're joking, right?"

"Doriane did love me." My eyes immediately fill with bitter tears. "It was a terrible misunderstanding, and now I've lost her forever."

The tragedy of lost love! Miss Eugénie will never understand.

Muttering to herself, Eugénie takes Tony's bike and parks it against the wall. We return upstairs together to her flat where she plops me down on the sofa.

"Do you want some tea?"

Eyes brimming with tears, I hold up a hand. "No. Nothing British, please."

A minute later she slaps a tiny glass of gin on the coffee table and comes to sit next to me.

"Isn't gin British?" I ask, sniffling.

"Drink."

The delicious gin, British or not, does its job. Grateful, I give my old friend's hand a gentle squeeze.

"Doriane's gone."

"Where?"

"I don't know. Home, perhaps." I throw a longing look at the tissue box on the coffee table. "The cleaning lady said they left the flat. She was *extremely* unhelpful."

I explain to her everything that happened, everything except, of course, the real identity of my Doriane.

"I'm so stupid. If I hadn't lost so much time trying to figure out..." I almost give myself away. "Trying to figure out whether she really liked some idiot like me or not..."

Eugénie tilts her head. "Louis... my dear Louis." She chews the inside of her cheek. "I don't want to say anything offensive, kiddo, but it seems to me your girlfriend's a boy, a very handsome English boy, to be exact, or my name isn't Eugénie."

I look at her in disbelief. "How? How did you know?"

She snorts. "You think yourselves so smart, but it was plain as day."

I take a moment to digest this news. You know, if I learn any more things today, I might just burst.

"And... you don't mind?"

"Mind what?"

I give her a pointed look. "Come on."

"The only thing I mind, dear," Miss Eugénie says, "is that it took you so long to figure out what you wanted. That's the real shame. This beautiful boy looked like he was mad about you."

"You know, Eugénie... I didn't think you'd understand."

"Me?" Eugénie gives a harsh laugh. "You don't know me, Louis. I have lived a little. More than a little. I was dancing with people like you at a time where they were risking their necks just for a stolen kiss! But more importantly... Once, a lifetime ago, I was in your position, and just like you, it took me too long to choose."

Her revelation sends me into a coughing fit. "You? Miss Eugénie?"

"Don't look so surprised. I was young and in love too, once."

"With…" I lean in and whisper: "A Doriane?"

"No," she says, in a regular voice. "A James."

I stare into her face, confused.

"What happened?"

"Don't move. I'll show you something."

Miss Eugénie disappears into the back rooms for a short moment. She comes back with the metal box which landed on my head the day we met, the one coming from the cardboard box on top of her wardrobe.

30

THE ART OF TRAIN-CATCHING

Miss Eugénie carefully opens the metal box while I wait with bated breath. Inside the box lay several trinkets and old yellowed photographs. A picture of a twenty-something Eugénie in a bikini catches my attention. I immediately make a move for it, but Eugénie slaps my wrist away.

"James was the risky option," Eugénie says with a sigh, "and my first husband was the safest. I picked wrong, Louis. I picked wrong, and I always regretted it." She shows me a picture of herself in her early twenties, in jeans and a plaid shirt, in the arms of a handsome black man. "When I got divorced, James was long married to someone else."

"Damn, Eugénie. He's almost prettier than me."

She nods. "And smarter too."

"Hey!"

Eugénie gives a small laugh, her eyes glittering.

"How did you two meet?" I ask.

"We worked on a few Hollywood pictures together. Back in the early sixties." She lifts a hand to her mouth. "I wish I'd run away with him every day."

I watch my old friend's face contort from emotions.

"It's not too late, Miss Eugenie, to try to find him." I put my arm around her shoulders. "Old geezer like him, he probably uses Facebook."

Eugénie's laughter escalates, but so do her other emotions. Soon, tears are streaming down her face. This time, I push the tissue box toward her, hoping there's more than one left, after all the outbursts I've had on her sofa.

"Alas," Eugénie says, exhaling a steep breath, "James passed away a few months ago. Now all I have left is a few memories and a lifetime of 'what ifs'. You can do better."

I nod toward the wall where all of her friends are smiling down on her.

"Should we put James on the wall with the others? It doesn't seem right that he should be in a box."

"You're right, my dear. Sometimes you want to keep precious things hidden so you can protect them from any influence, but you just end up boxing them away, letting regrets take over."

She puts the picture down and takes my hand.

"You, my dear, you don't have to spend your life in regret. You should go after him."

"But Michael went back home…"

"So?" I like the wicked glint that flashes in her eyes. "What's stopping you from going to London? It's only a train away. Come to think of it, what's stopping you from going now?"

"Now?" I gaze around the flat in alarm. "I don't even know where he lives!"

Of course, my phone rings at that exact moment. But considering I was friendless not two hours ago, I do not hesitate this time, and I pick up without even taking the time to read out the caller's name.

"Lou!" It's Lucie, shouting loud enough for Eugénie and I to wince away from the speaker.

I figure she's calling about the bike.

"Lucie look, tell Tony sorry about his bike—"

"Fuck Tony's bike!"

"Hey!" Tony says behind her.

Next to me, Miss Eugénie gives a delighted squeal of laughter. I shush her with one finger.

"Louis," Lucie goes on, breathless, "I just talked to Sacha, I wanted to apologise, you know——"

"Get to it, Lucie!" Tony begs.

"Put them on speakerphone," Eugénie says.

I obey her command and switch the call to speaker mode.

"Who was that?" Tony asks.

I never got around to tell Tony about my elderly neighbour who's also my best mate, but now's not the time.

"Never mind, Tony. Speak, Lucie."

"Yes!" Lucie's back. "Sacha said Michael is on his way to London with his mother."

Eugénie and I exchange an animated look.

"Listen, Lou," Lucie says. "It's the 15h30 Eurostar from Gare du Nord."

Eugénie seizes my arm and shakes it brutally, pointing at the clock. It's close to 3h00.

On the other side of the line, there's a commotion. Lucie swears loudly.

"You can make it," Tony says, now in possession of the phone. "But you'll need a better ride than my stupid bike."

I desperately start throwing looks around me, hoping to find a Lamborghini hidden under Eugénie's cushions.

"I'll never make it on time!" I hang my head. "Especially if I take the RER B!"

Eugénie keeps pulling my sleeve.

"What?" I snap, trying to break away.

She waves a set of car keys, a smirk on her face.

"Holy shit! Eugenie, you can drive?"

Eugénie is already putting on her coat. "Only a moron wouldn't know how to drive."

"Tony!" Lurching to my feet, I bellow into the speaker. "I've got my ride!"

Tony whistles. "Fantastic. Meet us at the Shark as soon as you get your man back. I hope you've got some——"

I hang up. Who has time for this?

Eugénie tries her best to climb down the stairs without missing a step and breaking her neck. I buzz the front door open. To my utter shock, my father arrives just as we're exiting. He's inexplicably holding an enormous red balloon that says 'Birthday Boy'.

"You're here!" My father says, beaming. He then sees Eugénie in her black coat and pink slippers. "What's going on?"

"Get out of the way, David." Eugénie pushes past my dad, her set of keys dangling from her fingers. He jumps sideways to let her through. "We must go to Gare Du Nord, now! No time to explain."

I point at the ridiculous balloon.

"How about you? Care to explain?"

My father's face turns an embarrassing shade of pink. "You needed cheering up, and I thought…"

I stare into his mortified face, trying hard not to laugh. "You thought a balloon would do the trick for your eighteen-year-old son?"

"They had nothing else, you know. I was planning to take you somewhere nice."

The sharp bark of an old car horn has us nearly jumping out of our skins.

"Are you done?" Miss Eugénie shouts from the driver seat of her car, which is, naturally, none other than the old Coccinelle I have seen parked out on the street my entire life. "We're a little pressed by time, here!"

"Come on!" I tell my father.

Flipping the passenger seat so that my father and his new helium-filled friend can cram themselves into the back seat, I check my phone for the time, my heart racing.

"Get in!" Eugénie slams the honk again.

I slip into the passenger seat, and we're off!

Well, not really.

Miss Eugénie has trouble getting out of the parking spot. When at last, she squeezes out of her tight spot and slams her fluffy foot on the pedal, the car lurches forward, groaning and sputtering.

"Do you want me to drive?" My father asks nervously, gripping the passenger headrest with both hands.

"Nice try," Eugénie says, smirking. "I have more experience driving than the sum of both of your ages. Now shut up and let me do my thing."

My father and I exchange a look, and as I'm trying to calculate real fast how old Miss Eugénie really is, she blows through a red light.

My father gasps. "Eugénie!"

"I saw that!" I hide my face behind my hands.

"No time!" Eugénie barks, switching gear. "Michael's train leaves in fifteen minutes."

Dad leans in between us. "Will someone please tell me what in the name of Amelia Earhart is going on?"

Now in a shocking twist, I finally got to witness how my father puts his intensive reading to use in real life. This day is probably the strangest day of my life.

"Shut up, David, let me concentrate." Eugénie jerks her head toward me. "Louis. Tell your father what's going on."

I shift around in the old seat to tell my father, or more exactly, the balloon floating in front of his face, about our mad plan to stop Michael from going back home to London where frankly, the food is awful, the weather is shit, and football is way too much of a thing.

"But I thought you wanted to move to London."

My dad punches the balloon away from his face. The thing bounces against my headrest and punches my dad right back in the face.

"That's not the point, Dad!"

We hit a massive bump. My head smacks against the roof of the car. Looking over my shoulder, I see Eugénie drove the car in the middle of the bus lane and several pedestrians are yelling at her.

"Miss Eugénie?" I speak in a small voice. "Do you even know how to drive?"

She slips me a quick glance. "Now's not exactly the right time to ask me, is it?"

My father has never looked more anxious. And each bump in the road sends the balloon up and down and bouncing off his head.

In an awe-aspiring effort that that would have indubitably impressed Tony so much that he would have begged Eugénie to try her luck at GTA, we reach Gare du Nord seven minutes before the departure of the train. Shameless, Eugénie slips into a taxi spot at the last second, earning herself a strong reaction from the taxi driver who was coming in at the same moment.

"Go, go!" Eugénie shoos me out of the car.

"Will you be alright?"

She blows a raspberry. "I'll play old and dumb, trust me, I'll be fine."

My father leans forward, his eyes alive. "Good luck!"

Springing out of the car, I charge into the station, my heart pounding. I haven't been here in years. Slaloming through the harassed crowd, my eyes dart left and right, up and down, anxious to find exactly which platform does the Eurostar leave from.

I can't find it. I can't find anything at all!

I soon stop in the middle of the station, my arms falling limply at my side.

"This way!" a voice shouts.

It's my father, a finger pointed toward the platform one level up, and still holding the infamous balloon. We start to a run, doing our best to dodge irritated travellers, failing at it, getting reprimanded left and right. A woman clutching a large handbag hisses at me. Nothing has ever mattered less to me.

My goal, my Michael is close, I can feel it.

On top of the platform, the way is closed, barred by a security guard in uniform with unusually bushy eyebrows.

"I need to get through!" I try to force my way in, my tone imploring. "Please!"

The guard holds up a hand the size of a frying pan. "You can't, unless you have a Eurostar ticket."

"But it's important! I must get through."

"And I'm telling you, you can't without a ticket."

My father, who was at my heels, stops before him, panting, the balloon tied to his wrist.

"Please! He really needs… to…"

"I'm in love!" I shout out loud in the station, bringing my hands together in an attempt to soften the guy. "And I must talk to my love before the train leaves."

The security quirks an eyebrow. "And I earn minimum wages. I don't have time for this."

With a pathetic sound, I sink to my knees in front of everyone. People start throwing us odd looks, irritating the guard.

"Don't fret, little guy." He jerks his head toward the tracks. "You wouldn't have made it anyway."

"What? What did you say?"

"Look." He's pointing at a train slowly leaving the station, one level below us.

I gasp in horror. "Is that—is that my train?"

"It's the 15h30 to London."

I turn to my father, heartbroken.

"But…"

Dad puts his arm around my shoulders and turns back to the guard, seething.

"When he'll cry about this, I'll remind him it was your fault!"

The security guard shrugs. "Fine by me."

Despair submerges me, draining me of the last of my energy, my spirit.

My fight is over. I've lost.

Michael has gone back to London. My life will never be the same.

My concerned father peels me off the floor, limp and lifeless, and we slowly make our way back to the entrance.

"I'm sorry, Louis." Dad speaks in a muted voice, as though not to set me off. "Perhaps you can give him a call."

"He hates being on the phone!" I heave a sigh. "He was perfect for me."

Aware of the sobs stuck in my throat, my father pulls me closer. We emerge from the station, blinking in the sunlight. The weather, once again, is oblivious to my suffering.

Ahead of us, Eugénie is still sparring with the same taxi driver. He's waving a newspaper in her face. An elbow resting on the roof of her car, Eugénie admires her nails, unfazed.

"At least one of us is having fun."

I slouch against one of the pillars, outside the station, exhausted.

"Oh, no!" My father jumps when Eugénie seizes the taxi driver's newspaper and starts beating him with it. "I better get in there."

Dad pushes the string of the balloon into my fist and runs to the taxi driver's rescue. I look up at the balloon, snarling, angry at its blotted representation of happiness, its happy hopping, its vibrant colours.

The red balloon is just like the people coming in and out the station in great swarms, bustling about their life, all-knowing, but not caring that without Michael, I will never be happy.

And then, the familiar scent of apples. Filling my nose, enveloping me, before I even hear his first words.

"Hey, birthday boy."

My shock, on recognising Michael's voice, is such that I let go of the string. Michael's hand shoots up, but too late. The balloon, still smiling, still ridiculous, takes off under our very eyes.

"Sorry," Michael says with a grimace.

I look at him. I mean, really look at him. I take in everything. His black suitcase, elegant. His Converse, classic red. His blue jeans, a little loose on his hips. The burgundy shade of his T-shirt. The sinuous veins apparent on his wrists and arms, his Adam's apple, which sends a pang of longing into the depths of my groin. At last, his face. The plump bottom lip stuck between the straight white teeth, almost apologetically. The shadow of a crease where his dimples would be. The straight nose, angular cheekbones, furnished eyebrows. Eyes as fine as a lover can imagine when not constrained by limitations of time. Finally, the curls. Dark, glossy, and reminiscent of a flock of lambs.

I blink several times to make sure. But it's him. It's the man I love.

He smiles. Dimples appear, my heart leaps up, the soft fluttering of the butterflies swarming around in my stomach intensifies.

"How?" My brain struggles to reboot itself. "How did you—"

Michael points toward the sky. "I was boarding the train when I saw this balloon, and under the balloon, I saw you, trying to force your way through the gate."

I give a nervous laugh. "Oh, right."

His smile fading, Michael lifts a hand to the back of his neck. "Were you trying to stop me?"

"Yes." One quick glance. "Am I too late?"

Michael shakes his head. "Just in time."

We both glance up to check the balloon's progress, while near the road, my father is in deep negotiations with the taxi driver, while Eugénie makes rude signs behind his back.

"François called me earlier," Michael says. "He told me about Abby. I almost jumped off the train to come to you, to tell you she lied, but... I wasn't really sure how you'd take it, coming from me."

"That's okay, Michael. François told me too. About Abby, and Peter too. He gave me a hard time at first, saying I'd broke your heart."

François the matchmaker. Who would have thought? He might even become my new best friend! I can't wait to tell Tony.

Michael approaches, looking to meet my eyes. I humour him.

"I can't believe you decided to trust Abby so easily. I mean, why?"

I decide to tell the truth and nothing but the truth from now on. With a smile, I dip my head.

"I didn't think you were so into me... you gave me no signs."

Michael lets out a shocked gasp. "No signs? I gave you plenty of signs, you were the one who was lukewarm about everything."

I make a face. "And apparently, you lurked under my windows."

"I did that, yes."

My cheeks start burning. I have to look away.

"I did give you signs," Michael says, pouting in the sunlight. "When I came to your place? And was hammering down the fact that I'd spend the summer alone, etc? Wink, wink?"

"I have no recollection of that. You have to know that I lose track of about half of everything you say every time I look at your face."

As we stand only inches from each other, Michael gazes into my face, an incredulous smile hanging on his lip.

"Are you serious?"

"Very."

"But, the essay?" Ever so studious, his thoughts turn immediately back to school. "Did you even learn anything from when we worked together?"

"Oh, yes," I say, with a solemn nod. "I learned that your curls prefer days with low humidity, and that you only chew on the end of your pencil when you're very close to the answer, but don't have right words for it yet."

Michael leans into my ear. "Valuable skills." He sighs against my cheek, sending my head spinning.

"The most valuable."

My phone rings. Lucie is texting me, asking for news. And apparently, everybody is invited to party at the Shark for my birthday. Including the Golden Fork. Which reminds me of something.

"Michael, did you ever tell Sacha you're gay?"

"Yes," Michael says, waggling his eyebrows. "I had to say something when I turned up to school completely depressed. Don't worry, she doesn't know it's you."

"Apparently I'm having a birthday party tonight with everybody who hated my guts until this morning. So, I'll get to explain."

"Explain…"

"That I'm gay."

"You are gay?" Michael repeats, an uncertain glint in his eye.

"Yes. Gay."

His hands shoot toward the sky. "Finally! Every time I tried to talk to you about sexuality, you acted completely mental, like at the museum."

"What?" I protest, offended. "You were showing me pictures of fannies!"

"Please don't call it that! And you were the one who seemed hellbent on NOT breaking up with Lucie, so I thought you were probably some sort of closeted bisexual—"

I hold up a finger in front of his delicious face. "You were staring at Lucie's boobs in the park! Confess!"

"I… What?" His whole face tenses as he tries to remember. "Was I?"

"Sacha even commented on it, remember? You blushed. I will never forget that blush."

"Oh, that!" Michael's face relaxes. "I might have been staring at Lucie a lot, yes. Wondering what she had that I didn't. Afraid of her… powerful arguments. But, remember what we did that same evening?"

I snort. "Like I would ever forget."

"Did my actions that night really fail to convince you I'm irremediably attracted to men?"

A yell coming from the taxi lane near the road makes me jump. My father has taken hold of the newspaper and is now beating the taxi driver himself while Eugénie makes signs for people to move along.

"Is that your dad?" Michael asks, squinting.

Looking at his face, an overwhelming need to hold him close and never let him go arises.

"I was so afraid I'd never see you again…"

"What?" He points at his ear.

"I said I thought I'd never see you again."

Michael appeased me with a full-on, dimples-all-the-way, laughing smile.

"You know I have to take my exams here, don't you? I was only going to spend the week with my parents. I was coming back."

I shouldn't tell him that none of this occurred to me at the time. Some things are probably better left unsaid.

Michael scans our surroundings for prying eyes and discreetly pulls me to him. He lifts his hand. A little pouch is dangling from his finger.

"Happy birthday, Louis."

Close to giggling, but amazed at my own self-control, I unwrap the strings, wrench the bag open, and hold my breath as I remove a pair of vintage sunglasses.

"I found them a few days ago. They made me think of you. I bought them hoping you'd give me another chance one day."

Michael wanted *me* to give him another chance? This is mental, but I won't say anything. I'll take whatever I can from now on. No questions asked.

"Thank you."

Looking very pleased with himself, Michael pushes them delicately up my nose and steps away to admire the result.

"How do I look?" I ask.

"Good." Michael clears his throat, a violent flush creeping up his neck. "Like a rockstar."

He hesitates an instant then steps closer, blocking the view of

Miss Eugénie and my father slapping their hands together in a high five and waving the defeated taxi driver goodbye with the other.

"Tell me, do rockstars kiss outside train stations?"

"I don't know, and I don't give a damn."

I hook a hand behind his neck and bring our lips together.

31

XOXO

In the dim basement of the Shark, our young bodies flailing, brushing, knocking against each other, boys, and girls, and boys, are swept into a whirlwind of music and whispers, until our identities, our affinities become all but a blur, sweating, screaming, loving, being eighteen, everything's fine, Michael's lips are on my ear, I've never been so high.

High school is almost over. A new stage of my life is about to begin. I might never see my friends again. We were growing apart before we even knew it. It wasn't because of Michael, because of London, because of her, or him, or me. It was perhaps, because it lasted long enough. And it was *good* while it lasted.

I spent so much time being afraid, afraid of losing everything, my relations, and myself, that I have never stopped to admire the present.

I wish you could all see me now.

The moment it hits me, the realisation, Michael's body against mine, Tony pouring champagne over my head, my scream:

WE WILL NEVER BE THIS YOUNG AGAIN!

Have you enjoyed reading this book?

If yes, would you please consider leaving a review?
It is the *most helpful* thing you can do for an indie author like me.
I'm aware that your time is precious, and even a single line can truly
make a difference.
It will help me more than you know.

❤ Thank you for reading, always. ❤

FREE BONUS

If you loved this book, consider joining my **mailing list**, and I'll let you know all about my future releases, promotions, giveaways, etc.

Members will receive a
FREE SHORT STORY about Louis and Michael
and many other bonuses relating to Colette International.

You can find the sign-up form and all kinds of informations about me and my next projects at:

https://www.zeldafrench.com

GETTING IN TOUCH

ZELDA FRENCH LIVES IN LONDON, LIKES CATS, SWEARING, GOOD WINE AND ROCK MUSIC, AND REALLY ENJOYS ANGSTY STORIES WITH HAPPY ENDINGS.

SHE PARTICULARLY EXCELS AT BEING INVISIBLE ON SOCIAL MEDIA.

YOU CAN GET MORE INFORMATION ON
WWW.ZELDAFRENCH.COM
AND WRITE TO HER AT
CONTACT@ZELDAFRENCH.COM

f facebook.com/frenchzelda

🐦 twitter.com/zeldafrench_

📷 instagram.com/zelda_french

g goodreads.com/zeldafrench

BB bookbub.com/authors/zelda-french

NEXT IN THE SERIES

Another year is ending at
Colette International,
and summer promises to be memorable...

You're The One For Me
(Available for purchase on Amazon)

TWO YEARS LATER...

Guarded and studious, sixteen-year-old aspiring actor Zak favours being alone above all else... Except perhaps Alberto, the Italian god from Drama Club, with whom he's secretly in love.

When their drama teacher takes the club to the French countryside to shoot a short film, Zak decides to temporarily hang his introvert hat and joins the party, confident Alberto will be cast as his love interest.

Only... By accident or by mistake, the beloved—and most likely overrated—star football player Eric is chosen to play Alberto's part. But it cannot be! Zak hates everything about Eric. For starters, he's not Alberto. Besides, he's a straight jock, an impossible flirt who takes nothing seriously, and especially not Zak's attempts to keep him at a distance.

If he wants to be seen as the professional actor he always claimed to be, and still get the chance to impress Alberto, Zak must set aside his resentment and put up with Eric and his boisterous ways, at least until filming is over.

But as time goes by, stuck in the middle of nowhere with the most popular boy at school, Zak quickly sees his opinion of Eric shift from *sworn enemy* to *endearing new friend*, and soon his feelings for him threaten to grow into something far more dangerous.

His vulnerable and inexperienced heart only a small kiss away from being shattered, Zak will have to ask himself the right questions and undergo significant changes if he hopes to obtain true love at last.

A story about friendship, self-awareness and
the dangers of appearances, *You're The One for Me*
features characters from *I Want To Kiss You In Public*.